A DAY OF IMMORTALITY

RUSSELL STUART IRWIN

Order this book online at www.trafford.com/08-0352
or email orders@trafford.com

Most Trafford titles are also available at major online book retailers.

Cover Artwork: Russell Stuart Irwin

Cover Design: Dennis Schmelzer

Photography: August Jennewein

Note for Librarians: A cataloguing record for this book is available from Library
and Archives Canada at www.collectionscanada.ca/amicus/index-e.html

Printed in Victoria, BC, Canada.

ISBN: 978-1-4251-4279-7

*We at Trafford believe that it is the responsibility of us all, as both individuals
and corporations, to make choices that are environmentally and socially sound.
You, in turn, are supporting this responsible conduct each time you purchase a
Trafford book, or make use of our publishing services. To find out how you are
helping, please visit www.trafford.com/responsiblepublishing.html*

*Our mission is to efficiently provide the world's finest, most comprehensive
book publishing service, enabling every author to experience success.
To find out how to publish your book, your way, and have it available
worldwide, visit us online at www.trafford.com/10510*

 www.trafford.com

North America & international
toll-free: 1 888 232 4444 (USA & Canada)
phone: 250 383 6864 ♦ fax: 250 383 6804 ♦ email: info@trafford.com

The United Kingdom & Europe
phone: +44 (0)1865 487 395   local rate: 0845 230 9601
facsimile: +44 (0)1865 481 507   mail: info.uk@trafford.com

10 9 8 7 6

Acknowledgments

I am forever indebted to my children, Ryan (and Dana), Ashley, Michael and Jonathan, and granddaughters, Anna, Naomi and Abigail for constant inspiration, encouragement, deep friendship, helpful dialogue and lots of humor; to my circle of "mighty men," August Jennewein, Christian Wenzel, Dan Jones, Dennis Schmelzer, Eric Borcherding, Jim Turner, John Bubenick, Kazumitsu Fujihashi, Kirk Perkowski, Marty Coulter, Paul Prosinski and Ron Cowan for the deep investment of friendship; to my dear Elizabeth, remarkable journey partner, co-treasure hunter and my love; and to my Lord and Savior Jesus Christ, for absolutely everything I find meaningful, including the great wealth listed above.

Thanks to Dave Armstrong for listening to God and preaching the Word of Life!

Humble gratitude to the following very busy professionals for generously *making* time for me and this endeavor—without whom this accomplishment would have been impossible: to August Jennewein for creative input from behind the lens as well as regarding the content; to Dennis Schmelzer for the design work on the cover and enthusiastic support; to Ben Taylor for technical assistance and cover design input; to Ryan Irwin for editing and research assistance; to Dr. Jeff Kloha for editing and scholarly input (right in the middle of your own publishing deadline—wow!); to Herman and Grace Otten for taking in a stranger and giving your time and professional editing input; to Dr. Phil Giessler for technical detailing, scholarly input and encouragement; to Virginia Renkel for editing; to Drs. Rob and Jan Hanson for your interest in and support of all of my creating (and for your review and input); to Dr. Larry Winkers for the tour; to Ted Willis and Dr. Jim Turner for your thoughtful reviews; and to Dr. Tom Riechers for technical input.

A special thanks to the Kramers, Gerald and Diane, John and Nancy, Jeannie Longstreet and Marty and Becky for the generous provisions of places in the country for getting away to write.

Chapter 1
THE NOTE

Rank air leaked into the apartment on the draft coming through the door, cracked open to the back hallway. Mingling with a hazy remnant of the smoke that had filled the air an hour earlier, the resulting odor reached Martin's nostrils. Like dust induces a sneeze, the offense expelled his foul thought.

"No one will even care! No one!"

Martin had been trying to think of someone since attempting to rebuke himself with the words selfish and irresponsible. Names made their brief impressions. But not a single face or voice asserted a convincing protest against his intent. The thought alone nearly compelled a fatal flinch.

"Not one!" he shouted. "Not …." His hoarse voice broke. After catching his breath he whispered, "Who's even gonna notice?"

Trouble had swept upon Martin with a sudden density that left him feeling like a prisoner of his own flesh. He wanted out. Yet, something within him still resisted the dark weight of despair.

Sweat squeezed from between the white knuckles of his fingers, rushed down the steel handle of the pistol and fell in steady drops upon the floor between his naked feet. He trembled. And between the tremors of each labored breath, weeping escaped his attempted restriction. With great effort he moved his hands, redirecting the aim of the long barrel. It was now lying flat against his temple. For the moment, this relieved the possibility of an ending upon anything less than his willful decision.

The tension was concentrated at the corner of the right eye socket, creating a point of searing pain. There, the knuckle of his left forefinger dug in, applying pressure and very slight relief. The revolver was seated in the fleshy cavity beneath his cheekbone. In fighting the pain, he also wrestled against the ultimatum: *Do it, or suffer another day in the miserable shadow of fate's delay.*

The seduction was working its way like a poisoned quill deeper into Martin's heart. He absorbed the appeal of this wooing in his weary spirit as from unknown ministers. Actual words and source were indiscernible. But he heard in their collective persuasion the constant stalking stealth of a single note. It pulsated. Its plucking exploited his feeble will. Its strumming encouraged his despair, disarming this last fragile veil of resistance. Its drone crusaded against him. He desired rest—rest from the wrestling, from battling. He desired relief from the tension. Most of all, he desired refuge from the constant encroachment of the note.

A car knocked over a trash can as it passed in the alley below.

"Morons!"

The exclamation was merely a response of habit. But it seemed to rattle around in the quiet room like the metal can rolling on the pavement outside. Jolted, Martin opened his eyes to the sight of the two guitars mounted above his bed on the dark gray brick of the loft. Beneath the glossy layers of finish on the face of a baby-blue Les Paul was the image of the woman who had moved out while he was away on tour. A purple Fender Telecaster bore yellow airbrushed neon like a signature: Olivia.

From the neck of the Fender a laughing silver skull with red eyes dangled at the end of a thick silver chain. Martin felt mocked as he stared at the sculpted image of death.

He squeezed his eyes shut.

For months he had lifted himself from pits of despondence by recalling his plans and by fondling the hope of his beloved. Now, both were too far removed to fuel any ambition or leap of faith. Leaving him utterly crushed, their combined loss had become the very blow that forced his withdrawal from the battle to thrive. The weeks that followed had been spent in dark brooding and contemplations about how and when.

He had purchased the revolver only days earlier, loaded it and laid it in the open to contrive an arousal of courage, or at least of resolve. Neither had come. And on this day, aided by inhaled and ingested chemicals, and the persuasion of the note, he had come to the uncalculated combustion point of his bitter meditations. Having snatched the gun from its silent, taunting rest on the coffee table, he had stood with the impression of its circular tip between his eyes for nearly an hour.

He did not know what restraint held in balance the near fatal pressure he had been applying to the trigger. Nor did he know by what strength he was able to continue standing upon Jell-O-like legs, except for the terror of the slightest movement at all. But the more dominion the note claimed over his mind, the more Martin sensed that any resistance at all was futile.

Even as these thoughts swirled around in his head, he heard the splashing of a stream into a corner beyond the door, and the pungent smell of urine was added to the stench coming in from the hallway. The cocktail of obnoxious odors made him wince. Tears flowed. The increasing volume of the sound in his head, the pain behind his eye, the white-knuckled tension in his hands and the odor in the air… it all put Martin's senses at an extreme of overload.

"Pigs! I live among a bunch of stinkin' pigs!"

There was the sound of a zipper, then plodding footsteps in the hallway. Martin half-opened his bloodshot, tear-filled eyes, rolled them to his right and quickly shut them again, repulsed. The sight of the filthy orange door added to the sensual calamity.

"Why am I alive *at all?*" he rasped.

"Mans, if you don know, I sho cain't tell yuh," a salivary voice answered with a chuckle from outside the door.

The tension in Martin's body met the impulse of his rage. His right arm swung towards the door and the gun went off, sending splinters from the door jam throughout the room.

"You think that's funny?" he yelled.

The bold, spontaneous action was stimulating. The shock of the noise from the gun and the power in his hand left Martin's eyes opened wide. He had expected the noise. He had feared it more than death itself—the terrifying sound of finality. And there it was, expelled into the air. The startling bang did not disappoint his anticipations.

Nearly as startling, it was again quiet. Only the pounding sound of Martin's heart and the loud accompaniment of a note in his mind could be heard. It was a different note. Staring down at the gun he was mesmerized by the subtle change of pitch in his head. Shifting fingers loosened their grip.

The stillness was broken by the sounds of someone springing to his feet and scurrying up the hallway stairs on all fours. After stumbling and falling upon the landing, the next flight of stairs was ascended just as awkwardly.

As Martin listened, the man yelled, "O-o-o-o-o! Is a crazy man wit a gun dow nare!"

The sound of the voice and the footsteps disappeared into the upstairs hallway. Martin became gripped by dizziness. His mind clouded. His arms were down at his sides. Feeling light, he sensed consciousness slipping away. He looked down and saw a growing crimson puddle coming from beneath a body that lay on the floor. He could not move. He could not breathe. He was spellbound as he stared at the flow of blood next to the body that only seconds before he had thought of as himself.

Seeing a gun lying on the floor nearby, he knew—not like a memory recalls the details of an experience, but clearer, as a foreseeing. He cursed through clenched teeth. Then, as his head drew back his mouth opened.

"Ahaaaaaaaaaah!"

Gasping for air, Martin looked around. A bookshelf in front of the black wall to his right was adorned by twelve crafted skulls of various sizes. He had nicknamed them the apostles. Ceramic, steel, wood, porcelain, wax, their personalities were as diverse as their craftsmanship. But all appeared to be laughing. Even the dragon in the large poster behind them seemed to bear a smile that expelled flames from its mouth and nostrils. Only the screaming, blood-splattered face on the poster beside it opposed the general frivolity.

To the left, a black skull bong sat next to an empty whiskey bottle and a used syringe on the coffee table in front of the couch. And on the couch, a complete, adult-sized skeleton sat with its legs crossed and a Tootsie Pop resting in its lower jaw. Its head was tilted slightly downward and was pointed in Martin's direction. He sensed that Charles, his favorite alter ego, stared at him gloatingly, smirking.

Martin had never seen the apartment so well. The objects it held seemed more consequential to him. Textures and patterns and placements were dearer. He knew their language fluently. They spoke to him in the language of his heart, a language he had denied, or forgotten, or lost at the times that he had been busy making all of these choices. He felt great loss, though all of the items were in their places. Mostly, the dirty studio loft held loneliness, even as he imagined hearing the jeering, snickering, crowing and applause of his various static roommates.

He felt warmth flowing against his feet, and closed his eyes tightly. Several minutes went by before he could again bear to look down. When he did, he was sickened by the sight of his own two feet standing in his own flowing blood. The recognition indicated the duality of his consciousness; yet, he made no connection but a feeling of estrangement from himself.

Looking at the red around his feet, he was astonished by the color. *Life* was the word that came to his mind. Awed by preciousness, he watched the slow movement without resistance to the revelation of glory.

Martin's head felt heavy and drew him downward. Waves of sorrow surged like a rushing tide. Wheezing, he fell to his knees. The torrents came, and he slumped upon the bed before him and wailed as only one liberated from delusion can do. He sobbed unrestrained until there was no more sobbing in him.

"What have I done?" he finally murmured, before more dizziness became sleep.

❧❀❧

As from a dream, Martin's consciousness emerged. He did not know how long he had been there. A multitude of conflicting sensations and thoughts confused him. Feeling with his feet, he discovered nothing unusual about the floor around them.

What happened to the blood and body? he wondered groggily.

It occurred to him that he had been seized by a hallucination as tingling feelings in both of his arms suggested that he was still alive. Compelled to test the hazy feeling of life in his body, Martin attempted to push up from the bed. The effort was unsuccessful. Immediately he understood that both of his arms remained asleep. They had folded beneath him awkwardly when he fell upon the bed and were lacking circulation. Pushing with his forehead, he was able to lift his upper body enough to see the single dark barrel between his hands.

Tears again filled his eyes and softened the image of the cold weapon. The colors in the plaid pattern of his shirt, his hands, and the steel revolver blurred together, washing away the threat. Carefully, Martin removed a finger from the trigger. Movement had restored some feeling to his right arm, allowing it to pull the gun from beneath his body and drop it to the floor. The muscles in his neck relaxed and he again collapsed upon the mattress. His left arm complained that it had been in the same position for too long. But he did not have the strength or will to move.

Kneeling, he thought, *how strange.*

"Help me, God, if you are out there."

Though muffled by the mattress, the expression arrived with clarity and surprise. It had made its way to Martin's voice from a place of which he was completely unaware. He felt embarrassed, foolish, though he alone had heard the words. Yet, it was the renewal of hope that won his attention.

"Dear God … help me," he muttered more boldly.

Using his right arm, Martin pushed up from the bed and looked over his shoulder. He saw the unstained floor. There was nothing back there but pants-legs and the backs of his heels. He recalled the impression of preciousness and glory and turned back toward the bed. Contortions were gone from his face and he was no longer trembling. He noticed the absence of any note; there was only silence. Feeling light-headed, he closed his eyes. His mind went blank and he slumped forward, passed out, his left arm pinched between his body and the bed.

Chapter 2
ENCOUNTERS

— Twenty-two hours earlier in a neighboring county —

Zoltan stared at the tattered manuscript in his hands. He was fighting off the temptation to read it once more. Having read it many times over the recent weeks and months, his hope of a revelation, discovery of hidden instruction, clues, had only increased. And, so far, he had found only *that*, an inspired longing, among the mysteriously biographical details on the pages. Like Zoltan, the document now barely held itself together, for he had not let it out of sight since receiving it.

Invitation, he thought, closing his eyes and shaking his head. "Invitation to what, and how do I get there?" he asked aloud in the usual frustrated tone. Somehow he knew that a simple decision was required to begin. It was this that he had avoided.

What if the invitation is real? What if it's as big as he said? So far just the idea of it has been enough to destroy my career. It's nearly ruined my life. It will if I let it, if I don't stop obsessing over it.

Spontaneously disgusted, Zoltan walked over to a book shelf and tucked the manuscript between two books large enough to hide it. Similar attempts were made numerous times before. But, as if to fool himself into thinking this was a true resolve, he turned and walked back to where he had been standing. By this feeble maneuver he was momentarily free of the pages that haunted him, but not of the memory that haunted him more.

"What is this, some kind a joke?" Zoltan muttered aloud. He was on page forty-seven of the document that he had found lying on his desk upon his four A.M. arrival at the office. Normally he would have just set it aside, an annoying interruption to his calculated activities. But he had left his office after eleven P.M., just a few hours prior to this unsettling discovery.

He noticed an odd smell and glanced around. Nervously reaching into a drawer and grabbing a hand-full of Gummy Bears, he recalled serving his ritual of clearing everything but the phone, his name, and the box of cigars from the top of the desk. His hand swung forward and quickly retracted, leaving three pieces of candy behind. The habit was thoughtless, yet always in threes.

Who could have put this here during the five hours that I was gone, he thought, just as he had when first picking up the manuscript. On the cover, the title, *Magician's Tale,* appeared above a sketch of a wooden doll that reminded him of Pinocchio from his favorite boyhood story. He had begun reading immediately and had not stopped until this very moment. He looked at the cover again, then at the inside of the cover, then the back. No identification of the author. No claim of copyright. Once more he looked down and searched the desk and the floor around it for a misplaced cover letter or hand-written note. There was none.

His eye caught a flash of light from the glass prism on the desk that held the name Zoltan in its center. It seemed to stare at him. Light from sources throughout the office caught edges of crystalline letters and broadcast their sparkling shapes upon his desk, nearby furniture, and the walls and ceiling. This was precisely his intention when designing the small sculpture and the lighting of the office.

ZOLTAN, he thought, as he gazed, entranced. *Why did I leave off Antoniadis? Why not Mr. Antoniadis? Why not Zoltan Antoniadis, President? Why has it never occurred to me before?*

In fact, nothing but Zoltan had ever so much as entered his thoughts as a personal title since the day he had become the president of Universal Syndicate Studios. Zoltan had become – in his mind – a name of dynastic proportions, like that of Pharaoh, Ptolemy and Caesar. Understudies in whom he had taken special interest he looked upon as potential Zoltans.

Consequently, as if by force of his will, the name had taken hold throughout the industry to the extent that many media sources and journalists used it in reference to the company that employed him. In public discourse, Zoltan, or Zoltan Productions had gained a greater recognition than Universal Syndicate. And not once had he corrected it over the many times that mistake was made in his presence. Rather, he had consciously encouraged it in his choice of words for press releases as well as in the interviews he indulged himself in, nearly on a daily basis.

A prominent industry journalist had gone as far as to coin the word "Zoltanic" as a mark of the highest media achievements. Its nearly universal adoption defied the resistance of Universal Syndicate's competitors. And Zoltan never failed to give pause when seeing it in print. His favorite usage of all was the phrase, "Zoltanic proportions."

Antoniadis, he thought distantly, recalling his traditional Greek upbringing and the importance of the family name, a name with which he once identified and which was treasured. But that was long ago. From his signature to the name on all mail addressed to his office and his house, it was now Mr. Zoltan, President Zoltan, or just Zoltan.

A sick feeling had come over him as he stood beside his

desk, just staring. *Why am I thinking about this? Why have I not thought about this sooner?* These were as one question darkening his mood. Zoltan looked around the office suite. Feeling uncomfortable, he looked at the three original M.C. Eschers on his walls and the glass cases that contained the gold, silver and crystal forms of his many awards. The gallery lighting revealed that all were in their places.

The colors and the lighting from the images on three televisions continually changed as they broadcast their various stations. All were muted so that Zoltan could arrive to the gentle sound of his cylindrical, floor to ceiling, saltwater aquarium in the lounge area to his left. Everything appeared to be as he left it a few hours earlier and just as he always left it at night.

Zoltan looked again at the document in his hand, annoyed.

"Some kind a joke?" he asked again, mumbling.

"Not at all."

The voice startled him and he whirled to see who it belonged to. An older man, with slumping posture and the appearance of a homeless person stepped out from behind the aquarium. He walked between two leather wing chairs before sitting in the one to Zoltan's right.

"I do love the little red shrimp on the coral. They're smaller than I remember and not quite as red. But then, I haven't seen them in at least a couple hundred years." He paused, thoughtful. "Great memories." After dragging his sleeve under his nose he wiped his wet eyes and looked up at Zoltan. "I hate it when I get too busy to enjoy some of my favorite things. It's you guys, though … always something."

The two stared at one another.

"So, what makes you think so?" the visitor asked.

"What makes me think what?" Zoltan returned, shaken and forgetting the question he had muttered aloud.

"That it might be a joke."

"Who are you?"

The visitor reached out and grabbed a handful of Gummy Bears from a near by dish. Zoltan frowned and made a mental note to have his secretary clean the dish and replace the remaining gummies. His connection with the chewy candy was between fetish and obsession. Like Bogart and cigarettes, ball players and sunflower seeds, the habit was his signature oral fixation.

"I am a servant," was the delayed answer to Zoltan's question.

"That's wonderful! What is your name?"

"I..."

"And how did you get in here?" Zoltan snapped, interrupting his intruder's attempt to answer. The stranger just stared at him as if this last question stumped him.

"My door was locked. My door is always locked when I'm not here." Zoltan looked toward the door and recalled that he had unlocked it to enter a short time earlier.

"No, of course... I didn't use it," was the stranger's chewy, saliva distorted response.

Zoltan looked around the room. He shuddered. Then he looked down at the document in his hand.

"I suppose you are responsible for this?"

"Yes, I am. You like it?"

"Where'd you get this information?"

"Which part?"

"The details from my personal life that are woven throughout this ridiculous script. No one else... no one but me knows...."

"I'm sorry. I should have interrupted you sooner to clarify. But you were so engrossed. It's not a script. It's an invitation."

"Invitation to what?"

"To your life, your universe, your world. I intended it to communicate the grand proportions of the adventure in a way that you would appreciate. But I can see that I've not done it very well."

"Mr., I've seen a lot of desperate fellas try a lot of crazy stuff to get one of these in front of me. But you're breaking the law here. I suggest you take this and get out of here immediately."

The stranger popped a few more pieces of candy into his mouth. "What law?"

Zoltan flipped through the pages in his hands, ignoring the question.

"And when I find out how you came by some of this information." He paused, grinding his teeth, his face red as he gathered his thoughts. "The incident at the Serapeum… I paid a lot of money to take care of that. If you're trying to … ."

He stopped short, watching his intruder collect the remaining candy from the dish into his fist and then empty it into a pocket of his jacket.

'Watch out for the rabble of this world,' he could hear his father say. *'They delight to see you work hard to fill your pockets as they make plans to empty them into their own.'* Scarcely had a day passed without his recalling these words, recited to him as ancestral wisdom. But never had contempt so convinced him of the truth in them like at that moment.

Zoltan reached for his phone and pushed a button, his usual reflex and one dependent upon his secretary's relay. He stared and then pushed it again several times. He snatched up the receiver and held it to his ear. Hearing no dial tone, he slammed it down.

"You pushed the wrong button," the stranger said in a helpful tone that further annoyed him. "Shouldn't you first press a button for one of the outside lines?"

"OK," Zoltan said, as he tossed the document into the trash can beneath his desk. "Thank you for your submittal. I am sorry, but it's not Zolt… Universal Syndicate material. Try a little bit of believability next time. Now please find your way out by whatever way you came in, or any other for that matter. I have a lot of work to get done."

"Really? What makes today different?"

"What's that?"

"I mean, you haven't gotten anything done for more than a week. What will make the difference today?"

Zoltan stared at the stranger, troubled. He studied him, his tattered clothing, his wiry, disheveled hair and his eyes. His eyes were deep set and severe beneath bent brows, somehow cloudy, as if terribly old and over used, and yet bright and intense. The lines of his face spoke of kindness and generosity. His posture was notably bent, his face was weathered looking, like that of one carved by years of toil in a harsh climate. His mouth was broad, framed by a raggedy looking, multicolored beard capped by a bushy mustache.

These assessments were made in the context of comparison to Zoltan himself, a habit of his nature. And, indeed, the two could not have been more different. Zoltan was one of those rare men who did not need a uniform to appear as an officer in full dress. His dark, wavy hair and dramatic facial features complimented a tall, athletic frame. His posture was so admirably erect that other men subconsciously corrected theirs when standing near him.

"How did you know that?" he finally asked, his voice quiet and dry.

"It's your understudy, Trevor, isn't it? Such a dilemma. I feel for you. So, how 'bout you take your mind off of it for today and ...."

"How do you know all ...." Zoltan was unable to finish the interruption. Once again he just stared at the intruder.

"Come with me, Magician."

"How?" he responded naturally, as though the title was of common use and the invitation was somehow timely. He did not ask for a reason, or a destination. *Mystery bears its own relief of the common tensions*, he discerned with equally natural fluidity.

Then, perhaps through the stranger's unblinking eyes, came the clear, unvocal proposition:

> *Come walk with me for a day. We'll stroll through the sun drenched meadows of timeless mornings, wear the unmeasured wealth coveted by the kings of earth, and explore the shores of heavenly waters upon which the dreams of the sons and daughters of your own offspring may set sail. This GIFT is precious, a day of life in the abundance of now and the radiance of being. It will be a day of liberation from the labors of becoming and the limitations of things finite and imitative.*

It was this silent articulation that captured Zoltan's imagination and cultivated his intrigue. He sensed that it was calculated for validation in his own soul. Such an indulgence, he felt, was nearly irresistible. Unable to take his eyes off the intruder, he was arrested by the power of the unspoken words. Yet, he could not answer, and their silent speaker was on the move. He stood up, walked to the door of the office, opened it and walked away. Zoltan stood alone, without a response.

The clear, bright, resonant blending of the trumpets and the chimes lingered upon the still air of the spacious room. It had been several minutes since they had pierced the silent tension like the alarming breakage of sirens in the night. Startled, Zoltan had been abruptly disconnected from his recollection of the strange encounter from many months past. Now, the throbbing of his heart swelled to a single tremor that held his full attention. And then the tension was gone, the turmoil resolved, the decision made. He glanced back at the bookshelf where he had just hidden the document.

"Yes," he said quietly, but resolutely.

There it was—after all of those wearying weeks and months. He stood still, expecting the often imagined changes, or an evident point of entry. The expectation itself seemed odd and without any context. He felt simultaneously as a victor and one surrendering.

"Yes," he said again, in a more demanding tone. "Yes, I accept!"

For a moment familiar objects seemed increasingly sharp and attractive, as if the focus on a great lens was being adjusted to the dimensions of a new form, calibrated for the reading of a new sensibility. Or, was he trying to convince himself of this to satisfy his anticipation? He was not sure he could recognize the difference.

A feeling of pride accompanied these sensations and compelled a look around the room. This he knew was genuine. Zoltan had always enjoyed surrounding himself with trophies of his success. And presently an indiscernible change made everything around him appear just a bit brighter.

An eight foot Warhol, the gift of an appreciative former employee, hung over his bed. The expense and mastery of its mounting matched that of the art. He enjoyed the reminder of the giver, who had risen to international prominence. She had once shared with him the sheets between the ebony posts that appeared to be part of the art's framing.

Once more seeing the book shelf where he had placed the tattered document, indifference revealed that it had served its purpose. It contained an invitation—one he had just accepted.

His eyes moved to the large, solid copper dish that held in its center a constant visual melody of dancing flames nearly three feet tall. These were enveloped in an elegant stone sculpture that alluded to the shape of a traditional chimney as it rose twenty-five feet and disappeared into the ceiling above. He had always enjoyed the pretense of casual understatement when referring to it as "the fireplace."

In fact, he had practiced in his mind the inflections of the pretense even as the room was being constructed. And he had never tired of its application: "Shall we sit and chat for a moment beside the fireplace?" Or, "Would you enjoy a glass of wine beside the fireplace?" Or, "Let's share a dance in front of the fireplace."

The reflection of the flames danced upon the black marble tiles and copper fixtures around a small pool in the distance, which, in the same fashion, he referred to as "the tub." The pool nested in a cove of windows that gave the appearance of tall crystals.

As his eyes traveled across the room, Zoltan's attention was drawn to the wall of windows nearly fifty feet away. Beyond them a yellow helicopter rested on a helipad that extended out from the multilayer decking and the botanicals of his North Garden. It bore on its side panel a favorite cartoon icon of his company's fame, wrapped in the signature banner that read Universal Syndicate Studios. Beneath it, the name Zoltan dressed the round helipad like a colorful brand.

Zoltan shuddered as a cold chill ran down his back. The stranger had appeared to him only one other time. It was on a frozen evening three months after the first meeting. Returning from his father's funeral, Zoltan fought the biting wind and stood on the edge of a dormant garden staring at a group of children playing in the snow beside the home where he had spent his youth. An oddly familiar child had left the others and run up to him. Reaching out a snow-covered mitten, the child had taken him by the hand.

The door opened on the front of the house and a slouching figure stepped out onto a small porch and called out, "Zoltan!" The child had looked up at him before running off to the animated embrace of the man in the doorway. Holding the child, the man waved, beckoning him to come. It was then that he recognized him as the stranger who had visited him in his office.

If the days following the first encounter were disturbing, those following the second could only be described as dark. Zoltan could not forget the image of the child running to the stranger; it was the only time he had heard him use his proper name, "Zoltan." He found it difficult to eat and became obsessed over his declining self-assurance, his lack of ambition, the meaning of the intruder's advances, and most of all, the title "Magician." It haunted him.

There was no one he could trust with the admission of such unnatural apparitions. So, he resolved to bear the gravitational force of uncertainty alone, as long as he was able.

"OK!" he yelled, after shaking his head dramatically in an attempt to free himself of the recollection. "I said I'm in! I accept your offer."

Disappointment attached itself to the end of each word like an echo. It was the only response. He feared that he had waited too long to answer, that the offer had expired. *Maybe I will just have to wait for him to return,* he thought. *But, for how long?* Feeling he could not face another day in his progressively debilitating condition, he also feared a lengthy wait.

In the months following the encounters, Zoltan had become the focus of concern for everyone around him. An authoritative man of precision and unwavering confidence, his every moment had always been a purposeful stride toward accomplishment and broad influence. All he had to do was mention a desire and instantly everyone jumped to his command. Suddenly, he had begun to question his judgments and ask for time to think things over. He often appeared to be distracted and distant when colleagues requested his opinion or direction.

Still in his forties, rumors began to swirl about "burnout." There was talk of an eminent break down: "We all knew it was coming. We knew he could not keep up that torrid pace. The man never sleeps!" From those who cared for him and others who feared the loss of his formidable talents came the suggestion that he take some time away from work.

Though he craved the relief, each thought of being alone without his work had the weight of a mortal threat. Work was the handle by which he held on to meaning. Yet, as the stranger evidently knew, his work was increasingly unproductive.

Turning to his left, Zoltan looked at the clock on the wall. It was brought back from a recent trip to Germany, a gift. The musicians had all completed their march and stepped back behind an ornate golden gate. Their silver trumpets were at their sides. Miniature maidens were at rest after striking their hammers against silver chimes, some of which continued to vibrate with sound. Two black horses had returned a royal carriage to its place behind the musicians and the grand gate.

How long, Zoltan wondered, staring. When his eyes finally moved again they were drawn to the glass desk below the clock. It was at this desk that he often sat into the morning hours, compelled by his passion for ideas. Commonly he would leave the desk to bathe and return to his office at Universal Syndicate, somehow feeling refreshed after being up all night. Those days now seemed long passed.

On the desk was a computer monitor and keyboard. Next to the keyboard lay a magazine, open as he had left it several weeks prior, the last time he had sat at the desk. Since that time, when he had abruptly stood and walked away in anger, he had unconsciously avoided that side of his room. He gazed at the pristine publication.

Suddenly, his curiosity was stirred by a mysterious phenomenon. He sensed a distance between him and the magazine far greater than the proportions of the room that contained them. Thoughtless, he walked toward the desk. Still staring at the magazine, he reached down to pick it up. As he touched the surface of its pages, he was immediately aware that he could affect no change, even to move a single page.

Zoltan's eyes were wide, and he was holding his breath. Again perusing his room, but as if for the first time, a smile spread across his face. The colors in the room were intensifying. They did not change in hue, or value. They simply appeared more alive. Feeling he was on the verge of a great adventure, the excitement was nearly overwhelming. *I am not insane. It has all been real!* he thought with elation.

"It's all been real! I knew it. I'm not going nuts!" He laughed, just hearing the words from his own mouth and raised his arms as if liberated. "Wow, what a wonderful...," he emoted, attempting a response to an internal novelty. It was as if a million little lovers were inside tantalizing him and touching him sweetly. Tears streamed over his cheeks to find the corners of his mouth and served notice that no apology was to follow.

"Woo, what do you think you're on the verge of here, Mr. Z?" he asked himself aloud.

A person!

The thought hit Zoltan with a shock, as awareness of a presence was unmistakable. Teeth clinched, he whirled around. When he was able to speak, he could only exclaim, "You!"

Chapter 3
SARAPH

*Z*oltan searched the face of his tormenter. There was an intensely eager look in his eyes, like that of a dog at the back door in the morning. *Crazy*, Zoltan thought. *He's crazy.* He recalled his first address: *Magician. Why does he call me "Magician"?* Since he had first heard the name, he had felt both mocked and flattered. His ego enjoyed the title, and he felt well-suited by it. Yet, his distrust of the suitor clouded his interpretation.

Suspicions of malice were building momentum as he peered into the stranger's unyielding eyes. Relieving himself of that gaze, he turned and glanced around the room.

"Something has changed irreversibly."

Joy and elation were replaced with thoughts of great loss. Feeling robbed, he walked to the other side of the room, surveying what he now perceived as things past.

Zoltan recalled a conversation with his understudy, Trevor Langdon, about a virtual set-up. They had mused about the creation of a series of candid dialogues with cultural icons stripped of common means while stretched by uncommon circumstances. They had shared a compelling intrigue with what such a dialogue might reveal. Both had agreed that a broadcast production would be "can't miss" with the ratings. Eerily, he recalled that he had thought of himself as the ideal candidate for such raw and beneficial revelation.

This same recollection had haunted him after his first encounter with the stranger. To Zoltan, it had seemed like the obvious answer to the puzzle of the stranger's entry into his locked office. Yet, even from his earliest impressions of that startling introduction, something about the stranger was convincingly beyond concoction. And to question the authenticity of the second encounter was to tempt the annihilation of his very perception of reality.

Yet, question he had. This and other possibilities had been weighed against one another countless times on the scales of his mind. Even now he turned and searched the room, trying to concentrate on the air around him for any detection of seams. He thought about the changes he had noticed moments earlier in the intensity of the colors around him and the clues these might suggest concerning technology. But as before, as always before, all such analysis was rendered futile. All was checked in his heart by a certainty that the stranger was otherworldly.

Zoltan's emotions began to boil at the sudden conclusion that he had been exploited by one masterfully aware of his weaknesses. *Betrayed,* he thought, *by the hapless compliance of my own arrogance, trapped by my pursuit of grand ambitions.* He silently mused at the irony of it all—that this cosmic mercenary should take him down by the very skills with which he had exploited so many. He turned back and faced the stranger.

"You did this!" he finally stated. "You started this with your 'invitation'."

He stared for a moment before his head slumped down so that his chin nearly rested on his chest. Shaking it back and forth, he sighed bitterly, scoffing at himself in amazement.

Zoltan walked toward the stranger, whose eyes had never left him. He waited, but there came no response. Searching intently, he saw nothing that would serve his wonder. He saw no agreement or disagreement, and no apology.

"You intended this?" he questioned solemnly. The stranger's expression did not change.

Magician was the silent impression on Zoltan's mind, as if someone were calling him by name. The pity with which the unspoken title reached his heart was loud, and he feared that his soul was naked and his thoughts exposed.

"You seduced me with your proposition about 'true power' and 'immortality.' Why?" he asked mildly. There was no response, except for the sudden projection of the stranger's lower jaw, followed by a look of concentration, then several snorting sounds in succession.

Feeling a grave disdain for this intruder, Zoltan again turned and walked slowly toward the center of the room. He recalled the introduction of doubts that stole away the control to which he had been so devoted. Lifting his shirt tail, he put his hands in his pockets while taking slow wandering steps. Then, stopping, he projected his lower lip and gave a nod as if to confirm some unspoken realization.

"So, I have none of my former strengths," he said thoughtfully, analyzing his situation and his opponent. "Stripped of all, is that it?"

Avoiding the gaze that he self-consciously interpreted as judgment, he glanced back over his shoulder. Turning, he continued his thoughtful stroll until a full lap around the vast room brought him back to the stranger.

"I merely prospered by the order of the world," he said calmly, hoping to gain a revealing response. But it was he that was compelled to further the thought.

"It was not an order that was created by me! I was not responsible for it. You know that, of course. Am I to be judged for enjoying the privileges of my placement in the order?" He spoke like an actor under the influence of script and lights.

The stranger reached into a pocket and pulled out a handful of Gummy Bears. After looking at them in his open palm, he popped several into his mouth at once. Unnerved by memory at the sight of the colorful little bears, Zoltan turned away and began another lap around the room.

He was the defenseless servant of his own invested habits. Yet, disguise was a failing currency. Pretense was but a soft shadow in his heart shrinking before authenticity. Every deceptive inclination was like a rumor of foreign pleasures dying upon the sword of a true witness. He remembered his pride, brought to his attention by its conspicuous decline. *Anathema*, he thought unguardedly. *I am anathema*! And indeed, he was a disgrace even to the memory of his former consciousness.

Zoltan stopped and looked around, concentrating. *Light*, he thought. *Light is what continues to change everything around me. Must be some kind of technology.*

Head tilted upward, "Light" he said out loud again. "So it is light that is increasing. Illumination is the new law. I can't help but participate, can I?" Dreamily, slowly shuffling backwards, he momentarily dismissed the plausibility of a technological invention. Turning to face the persistent eyes of his appraiser, his last step brought them toe to toe.

"Not new and not increasing."

Zoltan was captivated by these first words spoken by this mysterious person since the times he had first encountered him. *Back in that life*, he thought, staring. He was short of breath. Anger surged within him as he realized unmistakably that he was not capable of any effective contention or demand.

"So, this is it!" he blurted anyway. "This is how it works! You lure me in. You seduce me out of my rights, my will and my life. And you bring me here where you are able to bully me with your judgment as I stand defenseless, stripped of every valid objection and reasonable challenge."

The stranger reached out to put his hand on Zoltan's shoulder, but Zoltan drew back with a grunt.

"What are you, a ghost? You drop by on the unsuspecting.

You destroy all that I lived for, all that I valued, and all that I had command of, and you bring me here where I am defenseless, without even a capable response. So, go ahead, pronounce your condemnation. What are you waiting for?" he scoffed. "Oh, of course, this is eternity. What's the hurry?"

Three quick snorts, a hard swallow and a vigorous shake of his head left the stranger with a disturbed look on his face.

"My appologies." He cleared his throat. "I was given no authority to condemn, only to 'invite'."

"Invite! Invite? Hah! You call this an 'invitation'? Invitation to what? You destroyed me. You disrobed me, robbed me, humiliated me and made me a mockery in front of all that I valued in the world!" He paused, distracted by the fact that he had intended to say, "everyone I valued." But he had, by some force, spoken truly. *I never really valued anyone else in that world,* his thoughts confirmed nakedly. And he was further agitated by the assumption that this nemesis knew his thoughts.

"A servant?" he questioned, remembering.

The stranger nodded.

"So, is that it? You have no name, no identification but that you're a servant?"

"You may call me 'Saraph.'"

"Saraph? Sounds kind of effeminate," Zoltan said, attempting to revive his former strike first bravado and gain an upper hand. But, looking at Saraph, he felt foolish about the result.

"It's of Greek origin," Saraph said.

"Yeah? Mine too, so what!" Zoltan responded. He thought about the name Saraph. "Yes, of course it is. I should have recognized it. If I recall correctly, it means . . . ." He stopped and stared. *To burn,* he thought, silently finishing his statement.

He turned away and again walked toward the other side of the room. When he reached the fireplace sculpture, he stopped and stood silent for a moment, looking into the flames.

Glancing back at saraph, he asked, "How long did you plot

my demise?" After waiting a bit, he followed with, "Was it difficult?"

Saraph shook his head. "Like a sharp knife put to the skin of rotten fruit."

"I guess I asked for that one," Zoltan said, turning away with a laugh. He walked to the row of windows and stared out.

"Rottenness was learned," he said distantly, hands in his pockets. "And learned of necessity, I might add!"

He turned to look at Saraph. "Why … why me?"

"Wanderer," Saraph called softly in a tone that presumed intimate relationship. "I told you: I was given authority for a single invitation. And, though it was not my original intention, I decided to invite someone who least desired such an invitation, someone who was least likely ever to request the benefit of such an endeavor. I decided to invite someone who believed he had nothing to gain and everything to lose. I turned from my first inclination, and I chose you."

"So, this is a game for you? For amusement you ruined my life and drove me to this decision." He said this missing Saraph's implication of a higher authority from which the invitation originated.

"And the decision was not so difficult after all, was it?"

"Difficult? It was a catastrophe of humiliation!" Zoltan exclaimed, amazed at the suggestion.

"I was referring to the simplicity of it, an act of your will. Standing here in your room, a simple, volitional 'yes' to accept the invitation and activate the … ."

"You minimize the horrors getting there!" Zoltan interrupted.

"Are you sad you have come?"

Zoltan could not answer immediately. He was reluctant to acknowledge the apparent sincerity of the questions. A sense of danger warned that yet another loss might be near.

"No!" he said tersely. "No, I can't say that I am sorry. But, I feel I have lost something dear, that I left something behind, something unfinished, something important. A grand opportunity ended too soon."

"The grand opportunity is before you."

Zoltan walked over to the magazine on the desk. Images of him leaped from its open pages along with the words "decline" and "trouble." Concession moved him toward Saraph. "Are you evil or good?" he asked passively after long consideration. "Tell me plainly."

"You ask a question to which an answer would be a folly. What ability do you have to judge such things? What investment have you made in the wisdom required for such humble appraisal? Right and wrong, good and evil, dark and light, all these you have denounced before your devotion to ambiguity. If I were evil I would likely cloak myself in league with your estrangement from the rule of law and the authority of truth in answer to your shallow query. You would be put at ease with my company. You would feel comforted and affirmed by our agreement and perceive the very "good" you desire for your own deception.

"If I were good I would appear as evil to you, for you are not. Your misery in my presence would dictate your conclusion that I was a malevolent force bent against you. I would, of course, not indulge your demands for a comforting conciliation. For, "good" owes no debt to that born of evil, either to its sensibilities or its insatiable appetite for proof. I would, in fact, insist upon the exposure of your fear and vulnerability. Is this not the very 'evil' which you have sighted as the torment of your mind and the ruination of your life?

"I offered but a single day of true vision, a window through which to look upon infinite beauty, a moment of liberty from the bonds of time and material restriction. I offered the power to transcend the temporal and to take a breath in the fullness of eternal light. Is it this offer that has cost you all? It is, indeed, this generous invitation that you rightly call a terror. Truth and light are a terror to darkness, as I must appear to be evil incarnate to one so depraved as you, my dear Magician."

Saraph's fiery gaze was fixed upon the windows of Zoltan's blank stare, and his calm, compassionate tone seemed to Zoltan an odd fit for the words he spoke.

"Now tell me, Schemer, what answer have you gained? Good ... or evil?"

"How clever of you," Zoltan said. "It is evident at least that you want me to think of you as good, even if I must ignore your name-calling to do it. What is hard to ignore is that you are not a very nice person beneath that friendly tone."

"Nice?" Saraph said, pondering. "Nice is the first law of the effete. The very nature of it is self-centeredness. Pretentious, it has only one use – one's being perceived as nice. Kindness is the currency of the faithful. And it would be unkind of me to mislead you by calling you what you are not in order to secure your good feelings toward me. I am aware that you are conditioned to the rule of nice. I thank you for your acknowledgment that I am not."

Zoltan walked over to the row of tall windows and stopped and stood before one of them, his arms folded.

"As for good," Saraph continued, "there is only one who is good, and you have squandered your birthright as his image bearer. You have invested the good gifts given to you in rebellion, illusion ... falsehood. What conquest of yours do you believe has earned for you the ability to discern between what is good and what is evil? This day may provide you with a better perspective from which to question me or anyone else, if you do not squander it as well."

"So we begin with one thing in common," Zoltan said, as he looked over his shoulder at Saraph. "I am not thought of ... wasn't thought of by many as nice either."

"Mean and not-nice are not kin," Saraph said.

Summoning, he gestured to the far side of the room. Zoltan

turned and looked in that direction. He saw before him a long row of trees beside a meticulously tended lawn and mountains in the distance. Before him also was a step so ominous he felt confronted by a choice that involved leaving everything behind. He began walking as if saying goodbye. The two travelers met and walked side by side. They looked at one another as they walked many paces before Zoltan stopped and looked back. Trees and a sea of green were all he could see.

Chapter 4
THE GIFT

The former impressions were fading into cloudy memories. Zoltan walked beside Saraph in silence along the row of trees that appeared to be marching in line toward the tall, periwinkle mountains in the distance. They both looked around at the extravagant beauty before them. A blanket of clouds softened the sunlight that revealed the landscape.

Saraph finally spoke. "So, help me to understand your view of this gift."

Zoltan was deep in thought. Under the influence of profound impression, he assumed one of two possibilities: Saraph used the words "invitation" and "gift" as references to a life beyond the life he had known, or these were references to a metaphysical translation into a parllel universe. For the moment, previous suspicions of a sophisticated virtual game making sport of him were suspended.

"A deep feeling of regret … something I've never felt before," Zoltan said, answering the question heard in his head, rather than the one that was asked. "I had plans, lots I still wanted to accomplish. It never occurred to me that my time might be cut short." He stopped and looked around. Quiet and thoughtful, he searched the landscape – the field of grass, the endless row of trees, the layers of rolling hills. The shades of green were countless. And there was the wall of mountains beyond them, white-capped as they ascended into the grey canopy above.

"A great sense of destiny may have blinded me. I didn't recognize how fragile my expectations were," Zoltan said distantly.

He looked at Saraph. "This is a beautiful place, isn't it? In a sense, it is where I've worked so hard, so passionately to take myself. Still, I feel nothing but loss. All that I am, or … was … ." He paused for a moment. "It's all lost. All that I looked forward to and invested in was in that world, and all meaningless outside of it."

"And where is *this*?" Saraph asked.

"Oh, I'm sorry," Zoltan said. "Canada … Alberta, northwest of Calgary. One of my grandparent's places originally. My grandfather was certain they were the only Greeks in Canada, or at least this part. He was a hostage, bound by his wife's loyalty to her father's northern inclinations. My great-grandfather was a Norseman. I partly inherited and partly purchased this."

"You own this?"

"Yep. Not the mountains, of course. But I might as well, because there they are. I have a beautiful little stone mansion about two miles from here," Zoltan said, pointing east. "From the top of that third hill in front of us you can see where my property ends. It's pretty obvious. The line of trees ends."

"You planted these?"

"No, of course not," Zoltan said with a laugh. This was all forest. I had a desire for order along here. So, I had it cleared to look like this. Quite an undertaking. It would have been easier to plant them, but would have taken more than my … ." Zoltan stopped and considered the thought that he did not finish: *my lifetime.*

"Magnificent," he said, walking again, and taking a deep breath. He exhaled with some vocal embellishment. "That's what I've wanted to do for so long." He looked at Saraph. "Seems like such a simple thing … exhaling. Sometimes it can be the most difficult. I have been aching to come here for the past year and just get away and breathe this fresh air. It's tempted me, called me day and night. I just didn't think I could afford it."

The two travelers walked on together. As they did, Zoltan asked many questions in his mind, but articulated none of them aloud. He did not want to provide Saraph any presumption of advantage for the mistake of a bad question. Half an hour passed, during which Zoltan frequently grimaced, rolled his eyes or glared over at Saraph in response to his snorting. Finally, Zoltan looked at Saraph and spoke.

"It's gone isn't it? Me—whatever that meant. Mine … it's all gone, like who I was and what I lived for is irrelevant now."

Saraph searched Zoltan's eyes. "You could not be more wrong," he said sternly. "Things that are real, all things of the heart and mind, actions, dreams, behaviors, values, are not so easily undone. And their effects are more far reaching … relevant, than you will want to know."

"The life I've known isn't over?" Zoltan asked, missing Saraph's intended point. "I thought …. It sure feels that way. I mean, it … it felt so final when we walked away, when I looked back and it all was gone." He turned around and walked backward, staring into the landscape over which they had hiked. With a sudden flinch, he turned back around and resumed walking forward beside Saraph.

"Control, that's it. I have no sense of control," Zoltan stated. "I was able to control just about anything." He pointed toward the row of trees. "Turn a company into an empire, or a forest into the fabulous landscaping of my personal yard. It's the thing that made me sure, what I depended on most. And now I have none."

"Again you are far from the fact," Saraph replied. "The gift *is* control, control over more than you can fathom evidently, control as you have never known. This is not the phantom control that is merely in your mind and built upon exploitation of that which is lacking in the minds of others. It was then that you had no control. You were powerless, helpless and lost, though you imagined your control to be ubiquitous. It is, in fact, one of the reasons that I took pity on you and offered you this gift."

Pity! Zoltan thought, as he stopped and stared at Saraph in disbelief. "Pity for me? You and your 'gift' are a hell designed for me, that's what this is!" Anger began twisting his face. "But, what am I being punished for?" he blurted. "Is there jealousy and envy in the heavens just like in that world? Are the gods so insecure that they send out mercenaries like you to destroy the accomplishments and momentum of anyone bold and strong enough to challenge their oppressive hold over the common mind? It's because I distinguished myself, isn't it?" Zoltan had nearly doubled the pace of their strides as he expressed his protest.

"Did my grand pursuits make them nervous? 'Pity!' Do you take me for a fool? You obviously possess the power to play with my life. But don't think I am so naïve as to believe that you looked down upon our terrestrial occupation from some lofty perch and took notice of me out of pity. Hah! Me, from among the billions of sorry creatures and wasted lives among our race? No one could be fool enough to believe that!

"You know of the laudatory reviews and broad praise. You followed my rise to prominence closely no doubt. In fact, I have the most recent . . . ." Zoltan stopped. Looking at Saraph, he recalled the magazine on the desk in his room.

"So, why then did you feel so threatened by my invitation?" Saraph asked. "More significant, why did it appeal to you? Why did it have such power? What was it you were actually eager to escape?"

It was as if the questions were inserted among the pages of the very magazine article that Zoltan's mind was recalling, questions among the many questions of his many recent critics. They walked on in silence for several minutes.

"I may not have accomplished all that I had intended,"

Zoltan finally said, "but with even a cursory glance at our world, an observer with your abilities could not have been unimpressed with my impact. My life had a vast scope of influence. I was by anyone's assessment among the few setting the tempo of advancement and controlling the movements that others saw as fate."

"What is present?" Saraph asked.

"A riddle? That's your response!" Zoltan scoffed, stopping and turning toward Saraph. "That's because you have no response. No worthy response!"

"The gift is a doorway through which you can enter by your will and thereby define what is present."

Zoltan stared at Saraph, trying to comprehend his meaning. Then the two resumed their walk side by side in silence. As Zoltan studied the landscape, only his enjoyment of its beauty and the weight of several pressing thoughts prevented him from addressing Saraph's snorting issue. To his right was the row of trees, beyond which were the countless layers of rolling hills. To his left was the beautiful, lush lawn, spreading out to the distant horizon like an emerald ocean. The pace of their matching strides provided rhythm for Zoltan's thoughts. But what he really desired was their relief, especially from those aroused by Saraph's statement about the gift.

"Why are we here?" Zoltan asked. "I mean … why here?"

"Because you desired to leave. My gesture only assisted your will to engage the gift. Quite simply, you wanted to be here."

They stopped. Zoltan knelt down and ran his hands through the grass. Then he stood and turned, looking in every direction.

"Tell me if you relate to this," he said, closing his eyes. "Of the beauty before me, there is something most beautiful of all. My eyes don't identify it like they do this grass, those trees, the clouds and mountains. But all of them articulate it to me. If I could give it a name…." Zoltan thought for a moment.

"Wide open," he said, turning to look at Saraph. It was the first friendly communication to his escort, and realizing it, he felt uncomfortable.

Saraph nodded. Then he looked down and ran his left hand over his right forearm, raising the sleeve. "What is it you call these … goose bumps?"

"Why can I feel the grass?" Zoltan asked. "Why does it bend to my touch? I could not turn the pages of the magazine. But I could bend the grass to my touch. Why?"

"The gift serves your will. But it will not serve your will to make a change in the world. That is a barrier that is there for your protection … and everyone else's. You did not desire to change the condition of the grass as you did the magazine when you attempted to turn its pages."

"The gift is that attuned to my will?"

"That is precisely the nature of the gift," Saraph answered.

"These aren't so good for hiking," Zoltan said, as they simultaneously bent down to take their shoes off.

"Mine are OK. But I do want to feel my feet in the grass," Saraph replied.

They walked on. Subtle movements in Zoltan's face reflected his reactions to the activities of his mind. Though he was trying hard not to think at all, questions abounded. *What are others saying about me? What will take place in my absence? What will I be able to use this opportunity to influence? What can I lose? A doorway … what does he mean, 'define what is present?' By a simple act of my will?*

"You missed work yesterday," Saraph said suggestively.

Zoltan looked over at him and just stared.

"First time ever?"

Suddenly, Zoltan stopped and whirled around as if seized by an urgency to escape the taunting effect of some thoughts in his mind.

Chapter 5
MARION

Her hair was spread across the pillow and flowed beside her bare shoulder on to the white duvet that was tucked beneath her right arm. Marion opened her eyes and blinked several times. She closed them again beneath a mild frown.

Zoltan stared, his heart racing. He looked at Marion with longing and admiring eyes. Sensing Saraph's observation, he felt embarrassed about their early morning arrival in his secretary's bedroom. They were barefoot, both holding their shoes. Hearing a noise in the bathroom, Zoltan turned to his right. He flinched and his face flushed with shock and anger.

Trevor Langdon, stepped out of the bathroom snugging his tie where his shirt met his neck. "See you in a few hours?"

"Hmmm. Maybe," Marion mumbled.

Zoltan looked at Saraph, his lips tight and his jaw muscles pulsating. His eyes were glassy. But Saraph was unaware. He was bent over retying his shoes. Zoltan glanced at Trevor, the understudy who had become usurper, then at Marion. He turned toward Saraph.

"You filthy little mercenary!"

As Saraph stood up, he met Zoltan's combative glare with comic puzzlement.

"Now you've blown your cover. You think I can't see through

this? Marion would never sleep with Trevor. She despises him. This is all Trevor's little mess-with-Zoltan's-mind game, and you're part of it. How low can you get?"

"How did we get here?" Saraph asked.

Zoltan just stared at him.

"Why did we come? I sure don't care about this. And Trevor? Is Trevor in charge of your will, your mind, and your desires? If I am part of...." Saraph stopped and looked at Marion and then Trevor. Gesturing with his hand, he said, "If these are Trevor's concoctions, how did he get you to cooperate and bring us here?"

The question was well timed and Zoltan looked away to think.

It's him. It's this vile excuse for a ... who-knows-what. Somehow he plants these ideas like suggestions in my mind. This is exactly the kind of virtual punk Trevor would come up with to torment me. He knows that I hate the idea of someone ... something like this vermin having any kind of power, especially over me. He looked at Trevor and thought the thought that had involuntarily come to his mind hundreds of times over the past several months: *What a monster!*

Marion stirred in the bed. Turning to look at her, Zoltan recalled the desire that brought them to her room. He tried, but could not think of a way to put that on Saraph or Trevor.

"Why does this bother you?" Saraph asked, looking down at his hands as he kneaded between his fingers a Gummy Bear he had pulled from his jacket.

"Why does it bother me that...." Zoltan stopped. *He's pretending to be a fool. I'm not letting my guard down just because he looks like one. Look at him!* He shook his head and looked away.

"Certainly you're not resenting her use of the liberty of consent that you cherish."

They looked at one another.

"Perhaps she has a weakness for security," Saraph suggested.

A Day of Immortality

"And perhaps Trevor is just enjoying this particular moment of her weakness. You do appear to be on the way out."

He pulled apart the warm, gooey piece of candy, holding it up in the light coming through a window to their right. "Fascinating," he said. "Do you remember where I got these?"

Saraph moved his eyes wryly from the candy to Zoltan before putting both pieces into his mouth. "This is real," he said. "Not a dream and not a scheme, but an extraordinary gift."

Zoltan looked back and forth between Saraph and Trevor, unsure who he hated most. But it was Marion he could not bear to look at again. Thoughts flooded his mind and mixed with his eagerness to leave her presence. All were equally appealing and troubling. He tried to shut them out, but he wanted desperately to leave.

Chapter 6
WHITE GLOVES

The man sat on the same chair in exactly the same place that he had been the first time that Zoltan saw him. His white-gloved hands were moving back and forth in the dim lighting of the small room between the public lounge on the left of the two visitors and the private club to their right. The base from the loud, pulsating music that motivated the exotic dancers on the stages in the lounge rattled the doors on their hinges. As the man counted money, Zoltan had an angry urge to reach out and snatch it out of his hands.

"Two thousand dollars," he grumbled with a snarl.

Saraph took a mint from the podium in front of the seated man and offered it to Zoltan, who just frowned.

"Hmm, pretty tasty. You come here for these?" Saraph said, after squeezing the mint out of its wrapper and popping it into his mouth.

"You do have a sweet-tooth," Zoltan said, still frowning. "Like a child," he added with disgust.

The door to their left opened and a blast of the loud music accompanied by flashes of colored lights announced the arrival of a club member. As the door closed behind him, a round-ish man stepped before the podium. Sweat beaded on his bald head. The counted money had disappeared, and a white-gloved hand was held open to receive a wad of cash.

Zoltan looked searchingly into the air above him, distracted by a loud tone. He did not remember it from his first visit. Above all the other sounds and all of his frantic thoughts the note rose to claim his attention.

Suddenly, the door to the right opened. Alarmed, Zoltan lunged in front of Saraph, arms raised. His right hand held up a pair of shoes. As he blocked Saraph's view of the doorway and the interior of the private club, he reached with his mind for a safe place.

Chapter 7
THE HALL

As he lowered his arms, Zoltan found himself standing in the poorly lit hallway of an office building staring at the luminescent green of an exit sign, shoes in hand. Just beneath the sign a door was propped open enough to reveal a stairwell. He stood there stunned and partly traumatized by the extreme quiet of the sudden change of environment.

"Choices," he heard, as Saraph's voice came from behind and broke the numbing silence of the dim and stuffy hall.

He turned and found Saraph's smiling face framed by the rectangular darkness of a hallway that appeared to be a near endless corridor of doors. Saraph reached out with his right hand, and his index finger appeared to jab at something in the air. He rose up and smiled goofily. Then he reached out and jabbed with his finger again. Lowering himself to his original position, his eyes widened and he looked childishly pleased. Repeating this behavior several times, Saraph continued grinning.

Finally, Zoltan turned away shaking his head. "I'm not in the mood for your foolishness." He appeared to study the hallway before looking back at Saraph. "Charades?" he questioned in amazement. The temptation to slap saraph was strong and growing.

"OK, I get it," he said. "A kid on an elevator."

Saraph stopped the silly behavior, took a step toward Zoltan

41

and stared up at his rattled companion. "The universe waits!"

Zoltan looked away. The nearest door was just to his left, adorned with brass numbers – 153. Across the hall and down a way were two elevator doors. Directly above each was a horizontal row of numbers. The number 8 was lit above the near door. No number appeared to be lit above the far door.

"Lots of choices. This is what you were looking for … what you wanted, is it not?"

"How could you know what I want?" Zoltan asked defiantly.

"Here we are. You must have willed it."

"Why do you hate me? Why have you taken everything from me and brought me here to amuse yourself with this mockery?"

"I told you. I did not bring us here, you did. The gift is actualized by your will, not mine. I am only your escort."

Zoltan studied Saraph's face for any indication of more information. Finding none, he put his hands on his hips, hung his head and drew a deep breath through his nose. Saraph made a repetitious sound from the back of his nasal passages. In the quiet hall, the ticks of snorting were too much for his companion, who immediately rolled his eyes and turned away.

Zoltan looked back at the distant stairwell. From the instant he had been translated to this new world, he had been without the cool, calculating pathos that he had known as his former self. He was unable to deny the sense of wildness that surged through him, like an unfiltered energy. It struck him as primitive, grotesque and embarrassing. Doubly insulting was the physical reflection of these feelings in the one who had introduced them.

He looked at Saraph and felt disdain turn to loathing and loathing to vicious contempt. He had started with a strong prejudice against him based on appearance. Now, the sight of the bushy mustache and the shaggy, half-grown beard that traveled down his neck and into his shirt made Zoltan angry. He resented having contact at all with such a pitiful person. Then, a glancing thought about the troubles Saraph had caused ignited rage.

"Why!" Zoltan exploded with clenched fists. "What have I done that I deserve this? Why should I be made such a fool in my own eyes?" He turned and dropped his shoes as he lunged toward Saraph. "Why did you do this to me?" he demanded with a snarl, grabbing him by the throat with his right hand, the left gripping the collar of Saraph's jacket. Shaking him violently, Zoltan drove him backward across the hall. "Why!" he hollered. "Who are you? What have I ever done to *you*?"

As Saraph slammed against the wall, Zoltan recoiled abruptly in shock and disbelief of his behavior. He stepped back and they stared at one another. Until that moment Zoltan had not touched Saraph. He had presumed him to be an apparition, an illusion, or some sort of spiritual encounter. Now he had felt Saraph's flesh in his own hand. *This was* the world he had known. Saraph and everything else he was experiencing was actual, real by his usual definition.

Zoltan backed several steps away from Saraph and sat down in the middle of the hallway. Saraph also took a seat and reclined against the wall, seemingly unaffected by Zoltan's attack.

"This is not a curse, Magician, it is a gift. One day to be used as you will. The unflattering view of yourself that you blame me for may be a first fruit of this gift. In the end it may prove to have ushered in a hope of mercy."

Zoltan reached over and grabbed his shoes. Pulling the socks from within them he prepared to put them on. A blade of grass on his left foot caught his attention. He stared. He was trying to comprehend the recent events. *A blade of grass from the foot of the Canadian Rockies*, he thought.

"Didn't you say I couldn't make any changes?" he muttered spitefully.

"Willful change, remember?" Saraph corrected, before making the repetitious snoring sound again.

Still catching his breath, Zoltan looked away. "I asked you a question," he said quietly.

"Why? I already told you in part, but you rejected my answer."

"Pity!" Zoltan recalled aloud, and rolled his eyes.

Saraph leaned forward and reached to remove the cause of a discomfort from the back pocket of his trousers. "Interesting," he said with a shrug. They must put these in all of the clothing they give out." In his hand was a small, green Bible.

"Who are *they*?"

"The people at the shelter. Good folks."

"What shelter?"

Saraph was busy feeling and looking into his other pockets. From a side pocket in his tattered jacket he pulled out a hand full of Gummy Bears. He popped a few in his mouth and replaced the rest. In the pocket on the other side he discovered a crumpled looking cigarette package.

"Hmm, looks like these may have been through the laundry."

"A smoker, huh?" Zoltan asked with disdain. "No wonder you make those disgusting noises. You live on cigarettes and candy." He recalled the sight of Saraph emptying the tray of Gummy Bears at the office into his pocket on their first meeting. "Candy that is months old no less," he muttered thoughtfully. "Same clothes too. He probably hasn't changed since then."

Saraph chuckled. "Oh, no, the cigarettes are not mine."

"Why do you have them?"

"Obviously, they belonged to the fellow who owned these," Saraph said, grasping the lapel of the jacket.

"The clothes?"

Saraph nodded. "Strange ... they said he folded them neatly and set them on the bridge before jumping off."

He put the package back in the pocket and continued his

investigation, which was accompanied by nearly continuous sucking noises from the roof of his mouth. Zoltan stared at him, unable to gather words for a reply in the wake of his utter revulsion.

Saraph's lack of pretension encouraged Zoltan's sense of superiority. His weathered appearance impressed Zoltan as agrarian and uneducated. The borrowed clothing fit him sloppily and appeared worn well beyond what Zoltan considered time for replacement. Their condition and their history conveyed to him dishonor and a lack of self-respect. He wondered how any person could hold low enough standards as to wear such clothing, much less used clothing, still less, those of the deceased.

Even more damning in Zoltan's mind was the posture that bore them. Posture was one of many significant measures Zoltan prided himself on, and by which he judged other men. When Saraph was standing he appeared to be no taller than 5'10". But it looked as if he should be 6'1" or 6'2" if he were to stand straight.

What little awe may have been kindled originally by intrigue had been greatly diminished upon flesh-to-flesh contact. Most significant of all was the adverse effect in Zoltan's mind from Saraph's association with the Bible. Only these first activations of the gift commanded a margin of respect.

Saraph leaned back against the wall, having exhausted his search. He looked at Zoltan and began to make the obnoxious noises again. Suddenly, the sounds became more violent in nature and he hopped up onto his knees and leaned forward on his left hand. The fingers on his right hand pressed against the side of his nose. Between snorts he began to hack. He hacked and hacked.

Zoltan quickly scooted backward on the floor to get out of range of any potential projectiles. A look of shock was on his face. Saraph stopped hacking. Opening his mouth widely, he pushed on the back of its roof with a finger, continuing with a few more sucking sounds.

"I know you're not going to keep doing that the whole time we're together." Zoltan grumbled. "Because I'm about to pop you if you do it again! Pigs make noises like that, not humans – not humans with any decency or self-respect anyway."

"Very compassionate of you, thank you," Saraph said. "I'm choking to death here and you want to punch me." He moved so that his feet were back to their original place in front of him and leaned back against the wall.

"That's not choking," Zoltan said. "What's going on over there?"

"Oh, I just … it's this face. My face is not quite fitting right today. But I think that got it. I think I'm OK. Thanks for asking." He pushed on the side of his nose and made a couple of mild sucking sounds. "Yeah, I think that got it straightened out somehow."

Saraph rested his head back against the wall and let out a vocal sigh. "Much better. I tell ya, I have never had so much trouble with … it's just this one in particular. I don't know. So, where were we?" He leaned his head forward and saw Zoltan looking at him squinting, his mouth open.

"Oh yeah," Saraph said. "I remember. It is true that your life and your activities came to my attention as I observed this generation and the dominions under which it has been shaped. But, it did not happen as you might wish. And you did not make the impression you would presume.

"I saw a man of frail confidence and thin disguise. You were convinced that mastery of human manipulation is a valid authority on which to establish your own supremacy. I turned from my first choice to you because your need was so evident.

"I observed a man blinded by a presumption that all he controlled was all that mattered. I observed a lawless man who considered the affirmations of his contemporaries, his accomplishments, and his accumulated assets more sacred than the counsel of God. By your own admission, you prided yourself on control. I tell you, since the dark day in the Garden, the sons of men have had little to boast in, least of all control. Control was abandoned to disobedience and rebellion on that day."

Zoltan was mesmerized by Saraph's words. The comedy of this articulate, but otherwise crude, homeless looking man lecturing him critically struck him as profound if not surreal. *How can this be happening*? he thought. *Who does he think he is? How low does he think I am that someone like him should assess my condition? Did this slumping worm really just call me 'a man with a frail confidence?' Come on! Can this get any weirder?* And behind all of these thoughts was the distracting reference to the 'first choice.' The only thing more upsetting to Zoltan than second place was the thought that someone else was first.

"Remember our first meeting?" Saraph asked. "You knew then that you were fighting a losing battle. Your dream of control was slipping from you even as you labored to hide your paranoia. Remember the constant craning to see how quickly those encroaching steps of your understudy were closing the gap? And there was the unbridled weight loss, chronic fatigue and uncharacteristic mood swings. Once brought to my attention, you stood out to me among many wanderers as destitute and helpless. I had intended to invite another, but you were the one in need of a severe mercy."

Trevor Langdon, Zoltan thought morbidly, hoping the blood rushing to his face was not evident.

"I can't deny it," he said, shaken.

They sat in long silence. Zoltan began to realize that he was terrified of the gift and any thought that might activate it. He feared allowing any desire to penetrate his conscious thoughts, not knowing what impact it may cause, or what humiliating revelation it may bring.

"Interesting name, 'Zoltan,'" Saraph said, breaking the silence.

"My mother's idea from what I was told."

"What inspired it, do you know?"

"Her compulsion for the grand. Zoltan means 'life.' She saw it as relating to Adam in that way...somehow. Something to do with the Greek symbols Alpha and Omega—you know, the beginning and the end. Adam-A, Zoltan-Z. Adam, the first man, was already taken. So, her son was Zoltan."

"The last Adam? The final man? I'm not quite getting it."

"I think she thought of it more as the quintessential man, final in the sense of Adam perfected. Pretty crazy, but she thinks big like that, and I was her first child, first son. She got a little caught up in the moment."

"A lot to live up to," Saraph concluded.

"Look," Zoltan said. "I don't know what you did when you were here or...if you are from somewhere else... what you do there. But it takes a great deal of passion, and hard work, and sacrifice to fashion a career in this world. Only one in ten million people fashion one that takes them to the very top of their field. I dare say there is nothing more gratifying. And there is nothing more painful than helplessly watching as it is stripped away from you.

"I admit that process was far along when we met. But, to say the least, you did not help matters. In fact, you insured that my ability to fight for what I loved was rendered feeble. If it means anything to you at all, you've caused me a great deal of agony. My only remaining hope is that this gift of yours is...." He paused and looked down at the green book in Saraph's hand, then back into his eyes, "...a good one."

Saraph tossed the small book to Zoltan, who held it in his hands as one braces against contamination. He did not like that it came from a dead man's clothing. He liked less the idea of "Bible." Feeling obligated, he put his thumb on its pages and gave them a perfunctory fan. He then set the book on the floor beside him.

Looking back at Saraph after a lengthy silence he asked,

"You have offered me this gift in order to point out my delusional condition?" He paused and then added, "Seems a bit of a waste."

Saraph looked thoughtful. "This gift and its impartation were entrusted to me," he replied. "What its purpose is, you and I do not yet know. This I do know: In my experience it is without precedent. It is a remarkable opportunity."

"What about you? What is your mission with me?" Zoltan requested.

Saraph looked at him, unresponsive.

"You must have some goal or objective for the outcome of this little project of ours."

"Joy in the service of my God and King bears the reward of its own pleasure. And hope... hope for you, that this 'little project' will be an effective light to your soul."

"'Effective!' Now *that* is a word that I can appreciate. Effective for what? Effective toward winning me to your point of view, making my will bend to yours?"

"Your will was not created for anyone else to bend. It is not in my power to change it, or even to predict its change. My purpose is bound in my joy, the service of my Lord.

What a loser, Zoltan thought as he looked away in frustration. "That does not seem like much of an existence," he said, staring down the hallway. "You don't have anything of your own that you want to accomplish?"

"Yes. His will."

Zoltan turned back and looked at Saraph. "Anything of *your own*!" he repeated with agitation.

"My desire to serve Him *is* my own. That, to me, is fulfillment... home."

"What kind of a life is it where there are no personal advances? What is a home where there are no rooms for personal interests?"

Saraph looked at Zoltan, incredulous. "Rooms? I am not

speaking of a house. I am talking about home … wholeness, contentment. Your self-centeredness is the very essence of homelessness. And its first offspring is the fear that drives your vain pursuits."

"Maybe it is *your* fear of becoming someone and accomplishing something of your own that keeps you 'home'!" Zoltan retorted. He looked around. "Where are we now?"

"We appear to be in some hallway of your choosing."

"You don't know?"

"No, of course not. How could I know? I have never been here before."

"I thought you knew everything."

Saraph chuckled. "You are guessing now, and missing wildly. I am here just as you are. And like you, I can only be here. I travel with you. Of the two of us, you are the one who ought to know where we are." He leaned forward, pointed at the book on the floor and then held out his open hand. "I'll take that if you have no use for it."

Chapter 8
THE MORGUE

Zoltan stood and began to walk down the hall opening doors and peaking into the empty rooms behind them. "So, this is how the gift works, by my will?" As he looked around, a realization accompanied by grief began to inform him. It worried him that a slip of his mind could produce such a result. He could barely recognize the fleeting wish that brought them to this place.

"This is a sad place. More than old, it is dead. It is a morgue of dreams, ideals, promises and the power of will itself." He stopped and looked back at Saraph. "The best I can tell, if my memory serves me, this is the building my father had his offices in when I was a boy. I remember occupying myself for hours exploring one room after another. I wanted to be just like him. Visiting his work world was awe inspiring."

Resuming his examination he said, "I also remember doing my best to avoid being found. My father was a man of many tasks, and he always had one ready for me if I happened to look idle." He poked his head through the open doorway of an office.

"The one task I did enjoy here was completing the Greek writing lessons he gave me. The spoken Greek in our home came from my mother and was fairly constant. My father was a man of few words. So, he taught me to write the language of our family's heritage by sitting me at a desk in one of these offices and placing pages of written text in front of me along side blank pages. I filled the blank pages by copying his perfect, handwritten guides."

"I'm guessing you cheated just a little and got some help from other Greeks that worked for him?"

Zoltan stopped and looked at Saraph as if he had just suggested something silly. "My father would never have hired other Greeks. He didn't like the idea of bossing another Greek around. That would have offended his classical sensibilities about the honor of being Greek. So, hiring them, especially friends, would have compromised his enjoyment of being the boss.

"Even with us, his kids… he never struck a bossy tone. Instructions were brief and conveyed with the compelling expectation that honor was enough to insure they were carried out. 'We do it this way because….' 'We have always been known for this because….' Always 'we' and almost always some implication about hard work and achievement. An amazing man. In his quiet way, always teaching."

"So, what did he have you write?"

Zoltan laughed. "What else: idioms, maxims, quotes by Greek scholars and philosophers, words of wisdom… almost always something to do with work ethic." He stuck his head through another doorway. "But those aren't the ones I've been recalling lately."

"Oh? Tell me one of those."

"Looks like the building, at least this floor, is not in much use anymore. That musty smell is the smell of dormancy." Zoltan looked back at the elevator. The number 8 was still lit above it. He looked at Saraph.

"'If you have a wounded heart, touch it as little as you would an injured eye. There are only two remedies for the suffering soul: hope and patience.'
—Pythagoras."

Leaning into a furnished but otherwise empty office, he flipped a switch on the wall, to which a single light bulb in the ceiling and a desk lamp responded.

"Still, someone must keep the electricity paid for this weak lighting," he muttered.

As he entered the office he called out. "'One must not tie a ship to a single anchor, nor life to a single hope.' - Epectitus."

Suddenly, the dimly lit room prompted a memory and Zoltan flinched. He closed his eyes tightly, but he could not keep the flashing lights from getting past his defenses. He saw the white-gloved man sitting in the chair looking up at him. He leaned against a wall, his struggle not in Saraph's view. He heard car doors slamming and people shouting.

"Have you often wished to come here and escape into these corridors?"

Saraph's voice was a welcomed distraction.

"Always," Zoltan called from the office, his head back against the wall. Feeling a desperate need to get something else into his mind, he quickly stepped back out into the hall to busy himself with further explorations.

"Some of my fondest memories are here," he reported. "Of course, I remember it the way it was—bright, populated, inviting, and busy. Behind every door was enterprise and intrigue. I could go exploring for hours and hours, and then it would be time to go home.

"Yes, intriguing and enterprising people worked here. I learned lots from many of them. I don't remember Dad ever asking what I had been up to all day. It didn't matter I guess. He had always been quite busy, also. 'It's time to go, and time is money!' he would always say whenever it was time to leave. That was my cue to head for the door." Zoltan stood pondering that thought for a moment. "It's the one thing I remember him saying that strikes me as un-Greek-like."

Saraph watched as Zoltan opened a door and stepped into

another office. The hall was quiet and it was five minutes before he reappeared.

"My father lived here and ... ." He paused. "And apparently died here."

"His dreams were not him," Saraph stated.

"That is where you and I are quite different, my friend," Zoltan retorted.

He turned and began walking farther down the hall. "Three things I remember him saying to me. The first he said just about every time he brought me here: 'See this, son? This is the kind of thing you can count on. Do your homework, and then just do the work with all you've got.' The second he stated on the way home after each visit: 'There's nothing that can come between informed determination and success.' And the third he said just once, standing right here in this hall. 'Put it on the calendar, son—thirty years from now you and I will remember that our vast empire started right here.'"

Zoltan was running his right hand along the surface of the wall. "These are always in the back of my mind," he said distantly. He stopped and stared at the wallpaper he remembered from years before.

"We didn't share it, but I think mine did start right here." Turning back to Saraph, he said, "The only thing we actually ever shared after that was a vast distance. I don't know how it happened ... he became a rumor to me. But, I cherished the rumor, and I followed the advice and the example that he gave—'with all you've got.'"

Zoltan stepped into another doorway and leaned against the door frame. "I haven't been here in ... well, over thirty years I'll guess." Turning around, he stood in the doorway and looked down the hall in the opposite direction of where Saraph carried on his own investigation.

"I never wanted to see this. I always wanted to believe he could only be right." Zoltan stepped out into the hall and looked at Saraph. "The distance allowed that."

Saraph pressed his ear against the door of the elevator and listened. "A man is but a man," he said, "until the seed of his will takes root in the fertile soils of offspring. Then he becomes a legacy, a movement, a genetic force, a society, a nation. Words, thoughts, beliefs, decisions, these are more powerful than you know. From one man flows the power to liberate or to enslave generations. From one man's heart flows the raw material for acculturated ideology, pathology and paradigm. 'For by one man sin entered the world and death with it.' Yet, by one man, too, liberty for all who believe."

Zoltan stared at Saraph, perplexed by the seemingly random commentary. He looked into the vacant hallway. As he did he was unable to prevent the thoughts that had frightened him from revisiting his mind. He tried to remain composed even as each renegade thought threatened to become a mechanism of transportation.

"Please, help me to understand the gift."

Saraph paused and stared at Zoltan searchingly. "One day of boundless exploration of your world. One day free of the limitations of natural ... mortal boundaries. You may go where you choose. It is a day as all other earthly days – twenty-four hours. We have used more than three of those already."

"I can go anywhere?"

"Anywhere in this universe."

"Anywhere in time in my world?"

"Yes, but more than that, as you have already experienced. You may go anywhere you will in time or space, as long as there is no law preventing it." Saraph thought for a moment. "For example: Your physical presence cannot overlap. That is, the gift cannot serve a memory of an event that you wish to revisit."

"You mean a past event at which I would be watching me?"

Saraph nodded.

He thought for a moment before adding, "Many of the limits of mortality are suspended, but not all. You will see with true eyes. You will see as you are seen, know as you are known. Nothing false will be your cloak on this day, nor will it prevent your eyes from seeing what is true. We are not held by the physical boundaries to which you have been accustomed."

"And what about my life?"

"This gift does not pertain to that shadow. You have not been granted freedom from harm, but freedom to go and to see. There remain very real dangers that you do not want to tempt. It is my responsibility to protect you from them. I do urge you, however, to heed my counsel at all times. I am your guardian, a servant with long vision for your well-being."

"Anything else?"

"The gift includes a veil, a barrier of protection. Should something cause you great distress, you must not will to leave the protection of the veil, lest you risk losing all."

"You mean my chance to return?"

They looked at one another for a moment.

"More," Saraph said gravely.

"The veil is your responsibility as my guardian, right?" Zoltan asked.

Saraph gave a nod and added, "To the best of my ability."

Zoltan did not find that answer comforting, and it began to trouble him. "You mean I can find myself outside of this veil of your protection by a slip of my will, a simple mistake?" he asked.

"Not a slip, but by an act of your will," Saraph said. "An act of the will is not a mistake."

The more Zoltan thought about this, the more it angered him. "That just seems irresponsible," he complained. "It's dangerous to tempt such a thing. I mean, if you're going to have rules, one that would eliminate that possibility seems obvious."

"It's up to us to abide by what is given."

"So, that is it? That's the gift?"

"I should make one other thing clear. This is a day of seeing only. Nothing can be changed on this day. Its value will not be in doing or accomplishing, but in seeing with true sight." (Saraph said this to convey a reminder, knowing the enormity of Zoltan's ego and his inclination to think that the world was his to change.)

Zoltan was torn. *This experience could be anything,* he thought. *He could be anyone from anywhere, not necessarily someone I can trust. I have served up many a convincing illusion myself. And Trevor? If this guy is connected to that usurper in any way I definitely can't trust anything he suggests.*

But, what if Saraph is trustworthy? What if he can actually get me to amazing places in the real world? No, he coughs and sputters and talks about his face not fitting today. He's not even sane. Why would I trust someone like that, no matter where he came from or who he represents?

Zoltan squinted as he raised his right hand and covered his mouth and held on, afraid to breathe. *Now what? No more accidental arrivals. But how do I decide?* He looked at Saraph, who had gone back to the elevator and put his ear against the door, listening for something. Shaking his head, Zoltan thought, *He just looks too much like some sneaky vermin to be a concocted one. I think he's the real deal. At least for now I have to trust him.*

On the basis of this logic Zoltan began searching his mind for a place of entry, being careful not to will anything prematurely. It was as if he were standing on a precipice preparing to leap. His mind became a jumble of thoughts, all rushing in at once. Ideas, desires and intrigues were competing with obligations, temptations and fears.

Chapter 9
COUNCILS

Saraph's head was flung back and tilted. His upper body was bent to appear as if he were horizontal. He was staring at Zoltan with crazy, wide eyes and a freakish smile on his face. His arms were fully extended out to the sides making random rising and falling movements. The two travelers were standing near the center of the hallway, only thirty feet from where they had been just a moment earlier.

"What is that?" Zoltan snapped.

Saraph's expression and his behavior did not change.

"How did you get to be such a ridiculous person? Stop that, its ugly ... as if you could get any uglier."

Saraph made a gesture with his right hand, which was holding the small green-covered book and nearly smacking Zoltan in the face on some of the upswings.

"You want me to guess. No, I'm not guessing. You better stop grinning like that. You'll pull a muscle and your face really won't fit right."

Looking at Saraph, a troubled expression transformed Zoltan's face. *How does he know me so well?* he thought, certain that only those who frequented his private parties knew of his love for charades.

Saraph just continued his antics and waved with his right hand again.

"OK, OK . . . I get it. You're a skydiver."

Saraph relaxed his face and his arms, and righted himself. "First guess, very good! You're good at this," he gushed.

"What was that about?"

"I was just feeling the wonder. Wow, big-time risk you took."

"Yeah, well, very funny. I'm trying to get the hang of this... learn how to drive this thing, OK? My real desire was to ditch you, but it wouldn't let me."

"Hey, nice effort. Here, let me adjust those training wheels, maybe we can get all the way to the end of the hall next time."

"'Nice?' More like supreme effort! That was a lot of work, both in determination *and* resistance."

Zoltan turned and walked away. The effort to weigh and guard his thoughts simultaneously was consuming and he wanted to think without Saraph staring at him. But Saraph soon caught up with him.

"Will," Zoltan muttered. "I would never have anticipated such a problem over something I thought so ordinary and natural." He looked at Saraph out of the corner of his eye. "What a strange little activation mechanism for your 'gift' invention."

"Not mine," Saraph replied.

"Whosever!"

They were fully facing one another, staring. Zoltan appeared to concentrate as if working out complex calculations, tension constantly moving his lips.

"I have to admit, I had assumed to be in greater control of it. But it seems to know me better than I know it. That is . . . with the aid of the power you've given to it."

"No more than usual," Saraph corrected. "*You've* been given the power."

Zoltan's brows expressed his question.

"To see," Saraph answered.

Zoltan looked down at the little New Testament in his hand. Then his eyes traveled up to meet Saraph's.

"Do you take that seriously?" he asked, as he slowed his walk down the hall.

"Of course I do," Saraph said. "It is true. Is there someone you would suggest I listen to instead of God?"

They stopped and stared at one another.

"Just when I was thinking we might actually get along." Zoltan began walking again. "How disappointing."

"Example," Saraph said. "The Holy One says, 'For this a man shall leave his father and mother and cleave to his wife.' You, I'm sure, would suggest that God's word is a hindrance from what is more, what is better. Thus, here she is disrobed in a photograph, and there she is in a motion picture performing as you wish. Paper and ink… celluloid, pixels, illusions of illusions. You choose bondage, imagining you have gained advancement through your rejection of God's word. So it continues. Should a man listen to Him or you?"

"Me, of course, because there is no *him*. And how could anyone trust a compilation of writings that was controlled by one of the most notoriously corrupt organizations in history?"

"You are speaking of…?"

"The church, of course. Councils of lobbyists, men serving the church and state marriage, Pope and Emperor alliances, war mongers, power brokers, people herders. Isn't that the reality of holy writ?"

"You are making poor use of the gift." Saraph stated.

Zoltan looked at him and shrugged. "I'm getting there," he said.

"We could sit in on any historical council you wish and see for ourselves instead of standing here launching wild speculations."

"Where?"

"You choose."

"I don't know if I care enough to bother with any of those."

"You care only enough to disqualify Scripture on unqualified grounds?"

"I'm as informed as I need to be about this."

"Not if Scripture is truth and knowing the truth has the power to set you free."

"I think I could make better use of this gift of yours."

"Then, please do."

They turned and walked down the hall in the opposite direction in silence.

"Carthage, Hippo, Nicea, Trent," Zoltan said, attempting to demonstrate some knowledge of the subject. "I really care little about the tedium of those proceedings."

"Then wisdom would suggest that you care even less and make no errant indictments."

Zoltan looked down at the small book in Saraph's hand. "Where would you go?" he asked.

"Nowhere on your list," Saraph answered. "Not if you are looking for movements and decisions among men that created the authority of the Scriptures. A bit of mopping up concerning details is what took place at those councils. The Scriptures were already universally embraced by believers long before any of them."

Zoltan was becoming more intrigued by the idea. But it was not the subject that compelled him. It was the exotic nature of visiting an actual historic event that was gaining a grip on his imagination.

"So, where would you go?" he asked again.

"There are a few men meeting in Alexandria. I think their dialogue could shed some light on your assertions."

Zoltan stared at Saraph for a moment, hoping that his astonishment was not evident. He wondered if it was just a coincidence. *How would this guy know such a quirky detail about my personal history? Alexandria? I don't remember saying anything to anyone.* He looked down at the floor, his brows bent. *I know*

I've never said anything to Trevor. He looked back at Saraph.

"'Meeting,'" he repeated with a tone of curiosity. "Aren't we talking about a historical encounter?"

"Yes, a meeting in the late first century AD," Saraph answered.

"Then you mean *met.*"

"Only if you view time as strictly linear and not geometric as I do." Saraph said this hoping intrigue would prove persuasive.

Zoltan frowned when he realized that he was trembling. He then heard words that provided the push he needed.

"The meter reads four hours. You have twenty remaining. If time is money ... ."

They stopped in front of the elevator and Zoltan looked up at the number above the door. He turned and looked at Saraph. With an effort to connect his will to Saraph's suggestion he asked, "Ancient Alexandria in its glory?"

Chapter 10
DEVOTIONS

Zoltan was staring at a square, gift-wrapped package sitting in the middle of a table. His attention had been drawn to it immediately upon their arrival. It was elegantly wrapped in black linen that held intricate stitching bearing characters and symbols that he did not recognize. The material formed a bow atop the wrapping and the ends of the bow flowed off of each side of the package to lie upon the surface of the round table.

The table was made of variant shades of grey and brown tiles. The tiles were laid in a radiant pattern that gave the table top an illusion of depth. The package was oriented in such a way as to appear the center point of the radiating stone work, and the entire presentation seemed a puzzle to Zoltan.

His attention was interrupted by a movement to his right. A man held a teapot and was serving a dark-complected man wearing a long black robe and black dome hat. Though the server was standing, he rose only a modest amount above the height of the other man who was seated at the table. The server had not yet finished directing the hot tea into the tall, thin cup when the seated man leaned forward and settled his nose over the rim.

"Ah!" the server exclaimed, turning down the pot and pulling back in amazement. "Don't do that!" he commanded. "Your nose will get a terrible burn and you'll blame it on me."

"But the aroma of mint tea is wonderful," the robed man said in defense. "And it is strongest when rising from the cup as the tea is poured."

"Yes, yes, of course…No!" the server chided with a stomp of his foot and an animated shake of his head. "This is just your imagination. Please, Solomon, it makes me nervous. Don't do it!"

"The server's name is Jaek," Saraph informed Zoltan. "He's an Alexandrian Greek."

"Best mint tea in Alexandria," Solomon commented, his eyes closed and his bottom lip pressed against the rim of the cup.

Jaek smiled, appeased.

"…that isn't imported from the orient," Solomon added, amending his previous statement. He opened one eye to see Jaek's pleased expression turn to a frown. As he set the small tea pot on a stone pedestal, he turned and walked to the other side of the table and took his seat between two other men.

They spoke to one another in Greek, though each spoke it so differently that they gave the impression of communicating in two different languages. Jaek spoke with a crisp fluidity, the rapid discharge of his words carrying tonal fluctuations that conveyed command and confidence. Solomon had a distinctively slow, gravelly, monotone speech. Though fluent, an evident effort in his delivery betrayed the fact that this was not his native tongue.

Zoltan was delighted to recognize the prevailing language of the home in which he grew up, though he felt he was missing portions of what was being said.

"Archippus, are you sure I can't get you something to eat?" Jaek asked a solidly built man in a brown wool robe and matching hat to his left.

"No, thank you. The water is perfect."

Not seeing a cup of water on the table, Zoltan glanced around and saw that a glass mosaic cup rested on the ground beside each man's chair. *Glass?* he thought. He raised a brow and pursed his lips as if he were watching a movie and had picked out an anachronistic foible. But he decided not to say anything to Saraph.

"Josiah?"

The dark, diminutive man to Jaek's right pulled his hands out from where they had been tucked inside the opposite sleeve on each arm and raised them palm up to indicate his respectful decline of the offer.

"Who are they?" Zoltan asked, looking over at Saraph.

Saraph nodded. "Solomon is a Copt, a native Egyptian of ancient lineage, and a follower of the Christ of God, one of the first." He looked at Zoltan and restated with emphasis, "One of the very first *of Egypt*." They were both quiet for a moment as they watched Solomon enjoy his mint tea.

"Josiah Ben Yadin, an Ethiopian Jew, a rabbi." Saraph said with a hand gesture, continuing to answer Zoltan's question. "Archippus is a transplanted Alexandrian Greek, solitary, of the kind that will come to be known as monks. He makes his trek here from Palestine each year. But he spent the better part of his youth right here in Alexandria."

"Christ followers, too?" Zoltan asked.

Saraph thought for a moment, looking at Josiah, then nodded. "All but Jaek. And all but Jaek are scholars of the Scriptures … professionals, that is. Jaek is the owner of this quaint establishment."

Zoltan was not certain, but he assumed Saraph used the word quaint facetiously. Only twenty feet from the table where the men were seated was a small server's hut that fit the description. But the hut was stationed in the middle of a vast stone patio. He was squinting from the glare of the sun upon the sea of white stone.

The nearest building was more than two hundred feet away. It was an impressive stone structure, white, with multilevel wood decks that cascaded down from both sides and met in the middle very near the patio level. The decks were full of dining patrons enjoying the shade of the many varieties of trees that adorned the architecture. Some appeared to be growing directly out of the decks. A beautifully crafted stone wall connected the building to three smaller buildings and enclosed the patio on all sides. A tall wood fence beyond the stone wall prevented a view of anything but the peaks of a few shining roof tops in the distance.

Suddenly, as if recalling their location, Zoltan began scanning the horizon in every direction, looking like a man who had lost something important. He turned and looked over his left shoulder as far as his neck muscles would allow and then careened to his right. A frown drew his brows together and his movements slowed as he attempted to study every detail beyond the distant wall. He looked at Saraph.

"The Pharos ... it could be seen from anywhere according to all that I've read."

"Not from here," Saraph said flatly.

"But it was over four hundred feet tall."

Zoltan glanced again over both shoulders, then turned his palms upward and shrugged, animating his protest.

"*Is*," Saraph corrected. "We are not on one of your sets missing something important."

"Of course, so where *is* it?"

"Not here, and not as important as what is before you now."

Zoltan looked back at the black clothed object in the middle of the table. Then he surveyed the men around it. Stopping at Jaek, he stared for a moment.

"More important than one of the seven wonders of the ancient world?" he said with a critical chuckle as he nodded toward Jaek.

Jaek looked over his shoulder and wiped his brow and his neck with a cloth. As he turned back toward his friends, a look of distress on his face suggested an objection to the choice of location for their meeting. They were sitting in direct sunlight on a morning that already pushed 90 degrees, and they were thirty feet from the shade of the nearest trees, which were plentiful everywhere but this spot. Zoltan thought the choice evidently strategic, as the nearest people were more than one hundred feet away. No other guests would be migrating to this part of the patio until the cooler evening hours.

Jaek stared at Solomon for a moment. Then he muttered in amazement, "Hot mint tea," as he shook his head and again wiped his brow. His bronze skin was contrasted by the pale yellow vest that lay open beside his taut, rug-like belly and chest. The flowing material of his white pants and the wide red belt around his waste were trimmed in gold. These, too, were calculated, flattering accent to the deep, rich tones of his skin.

Though not obese, Zoltan thought he was the roundest man he had ever seen. From back to front his barrel-like torso was nearly the same dimension as it was from his shoulders to his hips. He was bald, except for a precisely trimmed strip of hair at ear level that traveled from cheek to cheek around his head and flowed into a dense beard on either side of his face. The beard filled in nearly all contours of his face, further pronouncing his round appearance.

Zoltan studied Jaek. Something seemed familiar to him and he instinctively began to take the party's round Greek host more seriously, disregarding his comic appearance and behaviors. He had a regal quality that Zoltan found curious. His mannerisms, his dress, his humor, even his service had the distinct air of privilege. Though the men he served were scholars and he was not, Zoltan sensed that they were his honored guests, and that such honor elevated *their* status.

The voice of Jaek broke a long silence. "You know, for a man of conversation, entertainment and social investment, I must say that these first few hours of the day with you three …." He paused and then pushed out his lips and made a humorous blowing sound. To further communicate his exasperation, he waved a hand through the air.

Josiah and Archippus looked up from the scrolls that were on the table before them. Solomon did not move but to open his eyes ever so slightly. It was evident he was more interested in keeping the bright morning sunlight out than he was in letting anything in to disturb his concentration. His hand-wrapped tea cup was propped up from two elbows spread widely upon the table. The cup remained pressed against his lower lip, his broad nose hovering above it and casting a shadow that consumed its deep circumference.

He must be meditating or praying, Zoltan thought, as he watched subtle expressions continually move like ripples across Solomon's face.

"I mean, I know I complain about this every year," Jaek continued. "And I apologize for that. But this much silence is a shock to someone who doesn't practice every day like you three."

The four men exchanged meaningless glances before each resumed his former state.

"What is the time?" Zoltan asked Saraph.

"Close to nine in the morning," came the distracted answer. "They began gathering just after six."

"No, I mean time of history."

"Oh, I'm sorry," Saraph said, giving his full attention to Zoltan. "I told you, late first century AD, eighty-two, to be exact."

As he said this, Saraph reached inside of his pocket and pulled out a cluster of Gummy Bears, obviously affected by the heat. He held them in his open palm and attempted to pry one apart from the others with his thumb. Zoltan stared at him as if entranced, silently pondering the candy's origin. Saraph popped the freed bear into his mouth.

Looking around, Zoltan tried to comprehend the reality of his journey. He felt exhausted. Noticing that his heart was pounding, he realized it had been doing so since before the conversation in the hallway. Now, it again picked up its beat as awe mixed with disbelief aroused his enchantment for this extravagant privilege.

His palms were sweaty and a shudder charged through his body like a herd of wild animals across an open plain. He pulled his head back, closed his eyes and attempted to impose upon his mind a meaningful recognition of the feeling of ancient in the sun's heat upon his face. Hearing a hawk above him, he opened his eyes to see it gliding across the sky. Its ordinary appearance struck him as surreal. Zoltan looked intently at Saraph and then at each of the four men at the table. The impression made by Saraph's gummies lingered. He felt a sensation of separation connected to something his mind could not grasp.

"So these are prominent scholars of the first century?" he asked Saraph.

"No, not at all."

Zoltan looked surprised and disappointed. "So, why are they here? No, why are *we* here? Who are they?"

"No one in particular." Saraph looked at each man. "Common men at a common café. No one anyone will speak of or remember fifty years after they are gone."

"So, what is their significance? What made you think of them? Why would we cross twenty centuries to observe them?"

"Because I thought it would be fun."

A frown twisted Zoltan's face as he stared at Saraph.

Saraph smiled broadly, rubbed his hands together and clapped twice. "Now *that was* fun. What control I have of the muscles in your face. I might have a hard time controlling myself now that I've discovered it."

Zoltan rubbed the inside of his right cheek with his tongue and turned away from Saraph shaking his head.

"They are quite ordinary men for the most part," Saraph said, "though the three scholars are brighter by far than some of their contemporaries who will be much more celebrated than they. But, together … in this place, the four offer a voice of the times. They are all good thinkers. Jaek, though he is not officially a scholar, is highly educated, and a man of uncommon worldly discernment.

"A few years ago they met each other here, thrown together under unusual circumstances. There was an uprising that cost the lives of twenty-four Jews and saw dozens of others imprisoned. Mostly Christians in both counts. The three scholars were stuck in a room together, awaiting the resolution of the calamity. During those tense days they discussed the time in which they live. They discovered a valued understanding of the world from each other's perspectives."

"They came to this city from different places and just happened to wind up in a room together?" Zoltan asked, incredulous.

Saraph reached in his pocket, pried off another piece of the gummy candy and popped it in his mouth. "I would tell you how these things took place, but you do not believe such nonsense."

"Try me, please."

"The three scholars shared an interest … you might say a compulsion, regarding the preservation of the Scriptures. Compelled, that is, by the turbulent times, and by the collective response of their communities of faith. Were you to ask them how they wound up together, all three would give you the same answer."

"Orders from superiors, I would guess," Zoltan said.

"Kind of. The answer they would each give is 'the hand of the Lord.'"

"In other words, you're telling me they just wound up here, voila, like that," Zoltan said with a snap of his fingers on both hands.

"By different means and influences, they were directed to a

street corner on the other side of that building over there, the smaller one," Saraph said, pointing across the patio. He looked back at the foursome around the table.

"Josiah, Solomon and Archippus had each stood as if frozen with fear and bewilderment. They were overwhelmed in the unfamiliar surroundings as the shouting began and the sounds of panic and terror rushed through the streets and enveloped them."

"The hand of the Lord works with that?" Zoltan asked. "Fear, I mean," he added when Saraph turned and looked at him. As soon as the question had left his lips he realized it was a question for which he desperately wanted an answer.

"With you … your race …," Saraph answered thoughtfully, "almost always. With some, almost exclusively," he added, turning back to the group. "It is the only way some will respond and participate in the relationship beyond academics."

"What happened then?" Zoltan asked. He was keeping a distracted eye on Jaek, who had become so restless that he was making comical gestures and movements. Saraph laughed at Jaek and then continued his story.

"Hearing the noises from inside, Jaek had come rushing out. And seeing their attire, he knew they could become targets. He grabbed two of them, wrestled them inside and threw them into a room. Then he went back for the third, which happened to be Solomon. He proved to be adept at recognizing help, having escaped several similar situations previously. They all had, actually …." he said, trailing off.

"Josiah narrowly escaped Jerusalem with his life by the aid of my warriors just over a decade ago."

Zoltan's face bore an expression of protest, but he did not speak. The story had just taken an unexpected turn. The last detail cast a long shadow that fell upon his present experience and the host who had initiated it. He stared, thoughtless.

"They spent the better part of the following week together

in there," Saraph continued, "waiting for the turmoil to dissipate. They also completed all of the research that they came here to do in a fraction of the time they had respectively anticipated it would take."

"Pressure and fear have their benefits," Zoltan concluded, familiar with both.

"It was Jaek, actually," Saraph reported. "He made all of the contacts for them. He also fed them and waited on them extravagantly. They were all looking for texts." He looked over at Zoltan. "Scrolls, copies of texts they had learned they could find here, in some cases the same copies and sources."

"Why would a restaurant owner be able to aid them with those?" Zoltan asked, unable to make the connection.

They looked at each other.

"His father is Chief Librarian . . . ."

Zoltan was immediately wide-eyed. "The Mousseion!" he exclaimed. "The highest official at the Mousseion?" he emoted, looking back at Jaek. "His father would be the equivalent of Head Curator at the Louvre in our day."

"No, far superior to that I must say," Saraph responded. "The Mousseion is still the cultural and intellectual center of the entire Mediterranean world. It has enjoyed and perfected that status and influence for nearly three hundred years. The Library is grander now than even during the Ptolemy dynasty, when it was built and fed the intellectual wealth of the nations. Librarian? He is at the epicenter of the entire cultural movement, if you will."

"That explains a lot," Zoltan said, looking at Jaek admiringly. "So, this elegant portly fellow no doubt grew up in the company of the greatest authors, intellectuals and scientists in the world, whose accomplishments and influence reach all the way to my generation."

They paused and watched Jaek move around the table refilling everyone's glasses of water.

"And he learned the art of hospitality from watching his father, no doubt, who summons them all to Alexandria," Zoltan said, further displaying his knowledge of Greco-Alexandrian history.

"Was he raised in the palace complex, like royalty?" he asked.

Saraph shrugged. "Let's just say he's never been a stranger there. Scarcely a resource or opportunity exists to which he has been denied accesses his entire life."

Zoltan shook his head in amazement. "So, when these three scholars unwittingly stumbled into his care they inherited the same access by virtue of his generosity: the library, the museum and introduction to the current resident scholars from around the world."

Saraph nodded. "Beyond the Mousseion, other valuable contacts are here, such as the famed Jewish school founded by the great scholar, Philo. And just as important, they took a keen interest in each other's work during those days. Each proved to be a great wealth of information and help to the other. A bond formed under those conditions and they agreed to meet back here on the anniversary every year for as long as they were able. Jaek agreed to always host the meetings and house each of the travelers."

Zoltan looked at Jaek. "He's an unusually generous man. I liked him immediately."

"Actually, it's the only reason he is included in the meetings—that and their gratitude for his rescue. And he is well aware of it. He is the odd man out occupationally. The others would normally have no reason and no inclination to include him."

"Typical elitist snobs," Zoltan said, resisting the inclusion of the word "religious."

"They're scholars," Saraph said, in a tone that communicated amendment but not necessarily disagreement. "Have you ever let nonprofessionals contribute to your productions because of their funding?"

"I get your point," Zoltan answered without hesitation.

"When they are not obsessing over their work, they are each quite generous servants as well. But Jaek is special that way. He is Alexandrian to the core. He truly loves hospitality."

"Everyone's got their thing," Zoltan concluded, pleased that servitude was not his.

They both chuckled, watching Jaek pretend to be taking an animated nap, his three companions remaining motionless and trying to ignore his antics. Jaek never had liked waiting through the devotional hours. Normally he brought some work along to busy himself. But this year he had a surprise for his friends and today was the day he would spring it on them. Like a child, the distraction of his anticipation grew the nearer he came to the moment of delivery.

His sprawled body barely remained in the chair. His belly rose and fell back with each grotesque vocalization of his pretend snores.

"Hey, he sounds like you," Zoltan exclaimed with a laugh. "Maybe he's having troubles with his face today." Watching Jaek, he asked, "How do they arrange the meetings? Or, should I say, how do they communicate with each other between the meetings."

"They don't. They just set out and trust the others will be here."

"That is a lot of commitment... and faith in the commitment of one another."

"Yes it is," Saraph agreed distantly. He was looking across the patio at the smallest of the four buildings, remembering. "This will be Solomon's last year," he said softly, turning to look at the man who was ignoring Jaek's protest and giving himself a refill of mint tea.

"How do you know that? How do you know about them at all?" Zoltan asked.

"I said they weren't famous. I didn't say they weren't important." Saraph paused. "This is the second day of this year's meeting—presentation day. They always spend the first day catching up."

"They …. It all seems a bit obscure," Zoltan said, consciously trying not to imply trivial.

They watched Jaek, as everyone at the table began moving. Jaek had moved first, as he had leaned to his left to look beyond Solomon. Seeing the shadow of a large sun dial reading nine o'clock, he had turned to inform the others, only to discover that somehow they already knew.

"How do you do that?" he said with a tone of resentment.

Josiah smiled at him. "As you noted, practice."

"You and your disciplines," Jaek said, pretending disgust.

"You know, Jaek, you could just save yourself some frustration by skipping the devotional hours and just coming to meet with us at nine," Solomon suggested.

"Yes, yes, you suggest that every year Solomon. But, if you recall, I did that once in the second year, only to arrive and find that you had randomly begun the meeting an hour early that day. Who knows what I missed."

"And we promised never to do that again."

"Yes, of course you did. But you also failed to answer my question concerning the larger matter: Who would serve the three of you properly in my absence during these early hours?"

The three scholars glanced around at one another and exchanged smiles and shrugs.

"No one could do that," Josiah said, expressing the very thoughts of his two peers.

Chapter 11
JAEK'S SURPRISE

Zoltan watched as Archippus and Josiah wrapped their scrolls in fine linen sleeves. Each had stolen glances at the other's wrapping and both had been pleased to note the other's impressed expression. They were placing them in travel bags beside their chairs. Jaek and Solomon had examined the scroll wraps earlier that morning when they were brought out and had admired their elegant beauty. Now, enjoying the friendly competition across the table, Jaek patted his waist, reminding the two men that he wore his own expensive wrap around the investment he considered sacred.

"An adornment of a worldly testament, you might say," he announced cheerily.

Solomon stood up just as his two scholarly friends were rising simultaneously from their house keeping duties beneath the table, and suddenly all three were standing there facing Jaek. The impression of attention took him off guard.

"Whoa! Did I say something wrong?" he asked, rising from his chair.

"Not at all," came the answer from the deep baritone voice of Solomon, his hands clasped behind his back. "No, in fact," he continued, "the Scriptures tell us that we are created in the image of God. So, every man bears in himself a testament to that fact. Your statement was quite correct. Like the holy texts, you are a peculiar revelation of the Creator."

"Fine, Solomon, just jump right in there with the deep stuff," Jaek responded.

Solomon smiled and looked at Archippus and Josiah. Their mannerisms were revealing restrained curiosity about the object in the middle of the table, now that the devotional part of the morning was complete. The next tradition was the presentation of a text of Scripture. Josiah and Archippus thought the shape of the package was strange even if it contained an unusually small scroll. *Perhaps a boxed set of very small scrolls,* they had both been thinking.

They both had also thought it inappropriate of Solomon to place the distracting package there prior to devotions. But Solomon had arrived much earlier than the others to labor over the visual arrangement. He had asked Jaek the previous evening to have one of his servants move this particular table to this specific location. And he was now pleased to recognize the earnest anticipation in his friends, having long been eager for this day himself.

"My brothers," he began, "As it is my turn and honor to present a text, I . . . ."

"Your turn?" Jaek said, feigning surprise. "I thought it was my turn."

He watched as the looks of shock and disorientation were passed between his friends. Not one of them had ever remotely considered that Jaek would expect to be included in the tradition of the annual presenter's text. By their standards it was a serious undertaking, even for seasoned biblical scholars. Thus, when the third turn had belonged to Archippus at the last meeting, each had assumed it was back to Solomon for this year's presentation. Not one of them had even considered a discussion of the matter to be necessary when closing the meeting the previous year.

Jaek was aware of this and had decided at that time to have

a little fun with his friends. He had even practiced the look of offense that his face now bore. But unlike the times he had practiced, he presently found no difficulty holding the convincingly serious expression. Looking from one to the other, he added shoulder movements and hand gestures to the act to convey questions, such as: "Are you kidding? How could you have forgotten me?"

Solomon was especially distressed about the matter, as he took the bulk of the offense upon himself. Yet, he was conflicted, feeling annoyed by the delay of his long awaited moment of unveiling.

"Well, I guess … I don't have to … ." Jaek put his hands on his hips and looked at the ground, pretending to struggle in his search for words and a suitable resolve of the matter. Looking up again and perusing the faces of his friends, he said, "I guess I will just put my presentation away and wait until next year." As he said this he leaned over the table and moved his hands toward the black package at its center.

"No, no," Josiah said, almost in unison with the sound of Archippus saying, "No, please don't!" Neither of them had been there early enough to actually see who had placed the package on the table and had only assumed it to be Solomon. And Solomon looked utterly scrambled.

Stopping and hovering over the package for a few seconds, Jaek finally raised his hands and said, "Just kidding, this wonderful creation evidently belongs to Solomon. I don't do black." He lowered his hands, which he then clasped in front of him as he watched the bewildered looks being exchanged between his three friends. Each began to crack a cautious smile.

"But mine is in the hut!" Jaek exclaimed, as his hands sprang up again. "I'll be right back."

And with that he turned and walked toward the server's hut. Had he seen the silent expressions of confusion being volleyed between his friends as he walked away, Jaek would have lost his composure and fallen to the ground laughing right then.

But it wasn't until he reached the hut that he felt he could let down his act. When he did, the release of tension brought an immediate feeling of silly pleasure for his successful gag. The laughter began as he reached through an open window on the side of the hut and grabbed three rolls of fine woven cloth held in silver sleeves. When his laughter finally disabled him, he leaned against the sill and began to shudder.

Watching this from behind him, the other three men were mortified. Their confusion had turned to alarm, thinking that their offended host had broken down in tears, and they looked back and forth between one another for a sign indicating who was the one designated to go console him. But none of them was eager to handle the awkward situation.

Observing all of this, Zoltan, too, was confused and feeling angry at the three insensitive scholars for offending Jaek. Looking at Saraph for an indication of what was happening, he was shocked to find him chuckling.

Just then, Jaek turned around and, propping himself upon his elbows, leaned back against the window, his belly shaking with his laughter. One by one, Solomon, Josiah and Archippus all realized that it had been a spoof and they'd been had. As they did, each left the table and rushed at Jaek, each in turn wrapping their hands around his neck and shaking him in mock furry.

Zoltan looked at Saraph. "Somehow I can relate."

"Oh, me too," Sarraph quipped, rubbing his neck.

Turning back to the group, they laughed as the four friends hugged one another, leaned upon one another, and pushed each other around as the impulse arose. Finally, as the mayhem died down, Jaek handed each man one of the rolls of cloth and they began to walk back to the table, a tangle of arms and shoulders. Solomon leaned down and kissed the top of Jaek's bald head before returning to his seat, still rumbling with laughter.

"Really men, I am appalled," Jaek said, finally able to speak. "Strangling a man with your bare hands—this is not an appropriate inclination for men of God. And three of you at once. It's not even sporting."

"Indeed," Archippus muttered as he collapsed in his seat.

"You're alive aren't you?" Solomon said. "Be grateful."

"Amen," Josiah added.

When all were back in their seats, one followed the other in letting out a deep sigh.

"I'm exhausted," said Solomon.

"*You* are?" Jaek responded. "You didn't have to hold a straight face amid such morbid company."

"True enough. And I could not have. Very impressive ... demented, but impressive."

"Yes, Jaek, you are full of surprises," Josiah said.

"And they started when you came out of nowhere and threw us into the room in that building over there," Solomon said, with a glance toward the other side of the patio. "That one saved our lives."

Jaek waved his hand. "Yeah, yeah. You can stop mentioning that. It's long past."

Solomon looked at Archippus, who did not appear to be paying attention to any of these interactions.

"You do have a way of bringing us together, my friend," Archippus said. With tear-filled eyes, he peered at Jaek over the top of the opened piece of material in his hands. "This is beautiful. Thank you."

"My pleasure," Jaek answered, suddenly quite serious.

Josiah and Solomon quickly opened the cloth rolls before them to see what Archippus was referring to.

"You actually weren't kidding, were you?" Archippus suggested.

"Oh, not entirely, I guess," Jaek said.

Zoltan leaned down over Solomon's shoulder and looked

closely, unable to contain his curiosity. He shook his head and looked at Saraph. "With all of our technology, our machines ... I've never seen anything so beautiful. How is it possible?"

"You have machines. Why bother?" Saraph answered, as Zoltan looked stunned.

"This must have cost you a small fortune," Josiah exclaimed.

"Powerful. Beautiful and powerful," Solomon said.

They were all running their fingers over the surface of the cloth, holding it in different ways to catch the light. The cloth was made of many different colors that appeared as one. When the light moved upon the different surfaces of the threads it revealed stylized Greek letters that were subtly raised by exquisite stitching. Some of the threads had been coated in precious metals and others carried tiny gem fragments.

"The quality ... I have never seen such fine stitching," Josiah said.

"Well, this is Alexandria, and such things are available if you know where to look. And, you must admit, a standard has been cast. I have to keep up with you three. Please, someone read it," Jaek requested.

They looked at one another and Solomon and Josiah both nodded toward Archippus, whose Alexandrian Greek seemed most appropriate for the reading. Zoltan continued to look over Solomon's shoulder, thrilled to be able to read along.

> I am willing to take the chance of facing great pain and bitter disappointment for the opportunity to do my very best. I know that upon the stage that holds the moment for greatness looms the possibility of failure. I know, too, that there are no guarantees. If I am not afraid to fail, I have a hope of success. Yet, should fear be aroused, what then? I will conquer my fear with courage and free myself to compete with the zeal of a champion.

The text was divided into two sections and Archippus indicated to Josiah that he should read the second one. As he began to read Jaek recited it with him. Zoltan also read aloud.

> It takes courage to admit the champion is inside of me. Sometimes I am afraid to face him, to look him in the eyes. I shrink back, knowing that his standards are high, his expectations daunting and costly. If I acknowledge him, what might he demand of me? And there, too, is the derelict, the threat to all.

Seeing the last line Josiah stopped. He looked across the table at Jaek who had stopped as well and was waiting for him. All four men looked at each other. Slowly, they spoke the last line together. "So I kill him, for love of the champion."

Solomon, Josiah and Archippus each set their cloths on the table, and all sat quietly for a moment. Zoltan's head hung down between his shoulders, his hands on his knees. He appeared to be staring at the stones beneath his feet as he recalled the many Greek quotes he had hand written to mimic his father's perfect Greek penmanship.

"How I wish he could have been here. He would have loved this." He looked up at Saraph. "How did you know?"

Saraph gazed back at him, unresponsive.

"They are from two different stones at the Alexandria Gymnasium," Jaek finally informed his friends.

Of the three scholars, only Archippus had seen the engraved stones that Jaek spoke of. He sat enveloped in a cloud of memories. Zoltan stood up and took his place next to Saraph.

"Alexandria takes great pride in its athletes," Jaek continued. "And its athletes take great pride in being Alexandrians. There are others engraved upon other stones, many actually. But these are my favorites. The second one they call The Athlete's Creed. I find it profound that the only statement of creed in it is the killing of the derelict.

"I know they don't qualify as Scripture," he said. "I recognize the standards we have for your work and the annual presentation at our meeting. But I thought you might enjoy them nonetheless."

All three scholars silently noted and enjoyed Jaek's use of the word "we."

"No, they are not Scripture, but somehow, for me these words crystallize its effect upon me and its impact in my life," Archippus said. "I have often thought that the word I most closely associate with the fellowship of Christ is 'Olympian.' That is how I see my calling. It is the highest calling, the highest standard. It is the most I have to give Him and the very least He deserves – my all. And I am grateful to say that it is the same for all of my brothers and sisters."

As Archippus spoke these words, they bore with them a weight of credibility with each of his friends. Prior to his conversion he had been a dedicated and noted athlete, whose fame and exploits were known to each of them.

"It is true. Yes, it is true, but not just of you," Josiah said soberly. "I must admit, it is true among all of the followers of the Messiah. At least it is true with all that I have come to know. And I must admit that it troubles me. Both of you represent to me every ordinary Christian," Josiah said, looking from Archippus to Solomon.

"Don't you mean the three of us? Of course, you include yourself," Archippus said.

Moving past this interruption, Josiah continued. "And what do I represent but the Jewish scholar. Among our people today, scarcely anyone but the scholar has any zeal for the sacred utterances, the Holy Scriptures."

"If I may be so bold," Archippus said cautiously, "the followers that you speak of, are you not one of them? Those with whom you are acquainted, they are almost entirely Jews, are they not? And that is the case in my experience as well."

"And mine," Solomon agreed.

"The likes of Solomon and me," Archippus continued, "are very much in the minority. Even though, yes, Gentile converts are increasing in some areas. Those you are referring to as 'followers of the Messiah' are born of a Jewish faith at its very core. You speak from a Jewish consciousness of what is predominantly observed and advanced by dedicated Jews. That is especially true here in Alexandria. Perhaps what troubles you lies in a distinction between Jews, a separation you see developing."

"I only know that with the Christians, they...." Josiah paused. "*We* all seem to have the passion of the Essenes for the Scriptures, Jew and Greek alike," he answered. "I can't help but wonder if it will always be this way. I have heard rumors that there are places here in Alexandria, in Rome, even Palestine where Christianity is becoming widely accepted and popular. That has never been good ... for us. Love for our God seems to abide only in a remnant.

"I do wonder...." He looked intently around the table at each man. "When our infant faith is no longer held to the fires of persecution, will its offspring come to take the living word for granted as the common Jews of our day have? And will its devotion fall to the religious leaders and the scholars? Will hundreds of years render a faith of mostly disinterested followers who see the Scriptures as religious tedium? As I watch the movements of our times unfold, I think about this constantly. It is one of the things in the entire world that I am most curious about."

Jaek watched as his three friends picked up the cloths once again. Their lips were moving as each silently reread the creed.

Chapter 12

ALEXANDRIA

"It is hard to get Egypt out of the heart of a people," Josiah said, looking out over Alexandria. "Even after many generations."

He stood beside Archippus atop the highest deck level of the large building that was across the patio from the meeting table. His hands were tucked inside his sleeves. The two men had walked up to this top deck after Solomon had suggested a break to stretch their legs. Zoltan and Saraph had followed behind them and were also taking in the view.

Archippus understood Josiah's use of Israel's history as symbolic of worldly attachments and disloyalty to God. "Are bondage and taxation that compelling?" he asked his friend with a wink that returned a smile.

"I have often thought about Egypt and its wealth ... " Josiah continued, "that we are inclined to bear a love for it and its gods as though they are superior gods. Then, we condescend to worship the true God with a secret motivation of hope that He will bless our ascent to the house of those other gods – the ones we believe to hold out to us the things of this world that our hearts so cherish. How offensive our duplicity must be to Him ... how vile and insulting to the One who is truly worthy of our love and devotion."

They stood quietly for a moment looking down upon the

busy streets of the city's Jewish quarter. Archippus was contemplating the mini sermon.

"I have been guilty of it," he said. "I am always surprised to see it in me, dismayed. A testimony to the gentleness of His correction ... the surprise, that is."

After several minutes of silent watching, Josiah said, "I've heard it reported that Christianity is spreading faster here than anywhere else."

"I have too," Archippus said. He turned and placed his hand on Josiah's shoulder. "It's because of the large population of Jews in this city." They looked at each other. "That's where it started, at least," Archippus added.

He waited for a moment, watching his friend. "You seem conflicted. I have never seen you this way before."

Josiah did not respond, but stood silent, watching a young family pass on a street beneath them. A few moments later he broke the silence.

"Strange ...."

"What's that?"

Josiah looked up at the stout Greek peer whom he had come to trust and admire. He looked back down upon the people moving through the streets.

" ... to call 'popular' what is so marked by persecution and the hate of the world."

They stared, thoughtful.

"You said it yourself," Archippus finally responded. "Only a remnant."

Though he was near enough to listen, Zoltan paid no attention to their conversation. As he watched the activities of the street below, his face was flushed red with emotion from the sensory overload of his Alexandrian experience. His cheeks were still wet from tears. They had begun to flow the instant he had stepped onto the middle deck and saw the distant Pharos emerge from behind the building that had been blocking it from his view. He had stopped and stared, breathless as he gazed upon the grandest lighthouse ever produced by the engineering of man.

Ascending the stairs to the top deck, he had involuntarily wrapped his right arm around Saraph and grasped a handful of his jacket. The sounds of the activities on the streets beyond his view had stimulated his anticipations to a crescendo. And as more of ancient Alexandria was revealed before him with each step of elevation, he had pulled Saraph more tightly against his trembling body.

Saraph had found awe not in the Alexandrian landscape, but in the extravagant joy upon Zoltan's face. His eyes had been fixed on Zoltan's until the two travelers had reached the top deck. It was then that Zoltan had turned, enveloped his escort in both arms and wept. Thus overcome with emotion, he scanned the blurry white and gold beauty before him as his chin pivoted upon the top of Saraph's head.

With his face buried beneath Zoltan's arms, Saraph saw very little. Yet, a sound had inspired him. It did not rise from the streets of Alexandria, but came from the heart he heard pounding within Zoltan's chest. Never before had he been so close to that wonder. And he, too, had wept. Beneath Zoltan's embrace, his silent praise rose for the glorious works of his Creator.

Now the two stood side by side, arm in arm, leaning against a railing, gazing and silent. Atop one of the highest points in Alexandria, and at the highest deck level of the four-story building, Zoltan looked out upon the ancient city. He wiped his eyes again, attempting to correct the fuzziness he assumed lingered because of his tears. Then he realized that the haze was due to the sheer brightness of the city. Everywhere he looked, white marble was accented with gold, silver and copper. And every attempt to focus on a detail was rebutted by sparkling reflections of the sun. The only relief was the cool aqua backdrop of the Mediterranean Sea.

"It's like great pearls strung with gold," he said dreamily to no one.

"What a wonder," Saraph said. "Poeima," he added in Greek.

"Mmm...master works," Zoltan emoted in agreement. "Material poetry."

"Who am I to disobey God?" Saraph followed.

Zoltan immediately turned and looked at Saraph. The thought, *What a strange thing to say*, was conveyed by the look on his face. Unable to make anything of the statement, he turned back to revel in his original amazement.

"What a wonder man is," Saraph said. "What a wonderful God. How I love to stand in awe of Him. How I love to consider even the dimmest glimpse of His majesty."

Zoltan again looked at Saraph, perplexity etched upon his face. *He's referring to man as god?* he thought.

"How glorious, O God, are the manifestations of your splendor upon the earth," Saraph whispered.

"You credit your god with the works of man?" Zoltan asked, aghast, finally understanding Saraph's meaning.

Saraph looked over and met Zoltan's stare. "Man is God's creation, Magician. He is God's idea, to put it in your terms...His invention, if you will. How could I not credit Him?"

They both turned back to their enjoyment of the gilded landscape.

The Hellenic influence that prevailed throughout the architecture resisted an appreciation of the Egyptian context. Yet, the abundance of gold and silver challenged a purely Greek interpretation. *Alexandria is truly a city unto itself*, Zoltan thought, as he struggled to orient himself amid the many extraordinary features clamoring for his attention. His struggle was aided by a trip to Alexandria a few years earlier that revealed a city of very different geographical features and few hints of its ancient splendor.

"Not a single sunset has ever been repeated on any horizon upon the face of the earth since Creation's dawn," Saraph said instructively. "All of the elements, the raw materials, the balancing forces and integrated systems, all supporting one another perfectly, beautifully, dynamically. You could look at this sky with the wonder of one who has never seen the sky before, because you truly have never seen this one. In fact, it has never before been seen." He looked at Zoltan. "By anyone. Today is its first day, just as this is your first and only today."

He looked back at the city. "Into this dynamic wonder God placed man. He gave him, not an invitation, but a charge to manage it, master it, to participate with Him in creation. And look," Saraph said, waving his hand, "integrated dynamic systems, habitation, design and infrastructures supporting all of man's activities. Every wall, every home, every street, every ship, every business and every implement of harvest — all began with an idea.

"I am amazed by the power of ideas, and the capacity to have them. Someone believes in an idea, a preposterous idea like the Pharos. Many people contribute many other ideas to support the first — solutions, inventions. And there it stands. Then, many millions of coordinated ideas and you have this — countless golden roof tops reflecting sky and sun as they dance in the glittering backdrop of the distant sea, reflections of the Creator in the works of His children.

"Yet there are two things that spoil God's enjoyment: the arrogance of man to believe that it is all about him, and the foolishness of man to credit creations of his own hands with lordship."

"How I wish my father could be here with me," Zoltan said disconnectedly. "He would have really…." He paused. "He was the one who would not relent from passing on to me everything he ever read about her, always ignoring my indifference. I brought him here several years ago."

Zoltan gathered his breath before he spoke again.

"It made him sad," he continued, "as if the glorious bride he'd anticipated laying his eyes upon had been revealed as an old lady. She betrayed him. And worse, my disinterest had been validated." He shook his head slowly. "Her splendor had long passed. He never brought her up again and never talked about the trip. One of my few genuine efforts … it just seemed to widen the void between us."

Saraph reached up and grabbed Zoltan's shoulder and gave it a firm squeeze.

"How I wish he could see her," Zoltan whispered.

They again stood in admiring silence.

As if desiring relief from the business of mingling roof tops and streets, and the brightness of sun-bleached white stone, Zoltan's eyes again defaulted to the refuge of the solitary Pharos. It stood alone, like a sentinel keeping watch over the Western and Eastern harbors in the foreground before its base and appearing to split the distant Mediterranean into two parts.

Its massive square base was more than two hundred feet tall, its smooth surface marked only by windows. It was topped with a cornice, upon which numerous tritons posted vigil. Zoltan's gaze ascended the octagonal second tier and the round upper tier before focusing on the brilliant light at the top. He estimated there to be more than three hundred windows based on the two sides that were visible to him. And he was delighted that not a single description among the many reports he had read about the Pharos had been capable of exaggerating its magnificence.

"The world's first sky-scraper. That thing is five hundred feet if it's an inch," he said aloud.

"Not quite, but close," he heard Saraph respond.

"A star by day, I can't imagine how bright that would be at night," Zoltan mumbled to himself. "That's probably just the sun's reflection we're seeing caught by the mirrors. I don't guess they'd have the fire going during the day."

He looked at Saraph. "Dad told me that its light reached thirty-five miles out to sea."

"Reaches," Saraph corrected. "This is not a post card or a page in an encyclopedia or on a web site you're looking at."

"Right. I forgot."

Zoltan looked back to the Pharos.

"More than once he told me that the reach of its light was only outdistanced by that of its fame. Then he would remind me that the root word for 'lighthouse' in French, Italian and Spanish all the way to our day comes from Pharos."

His eyes moved slowly to his left and he saw Pharos Island, anchored like a last rights of land before the endless sea. Feeling like he was beginning to gain some orientation, he realized that the building to which they were attached via the deck faced northwest. It looked directly toward the Eastern Harbor and was positioned catty-corner to the Pharos. He located what he thought must be the upper part of the Heptastadion, the thin strip of land connecting Pharos Island to the heart of Alexandria. But it disappeared immediately behind another enormous building. His mouth fell open.

"That must be the Caesareum. It's definitely newer and more complex in its architecture," he said, pointing to the second tallest building in the city. "Do you know? Is that it?" he asked Saraph without looking away from the building.

Saraph nodded. "Yes it is," he said, enjoying Zoltan's boyish wonder.

Feeling self-conscious, Zoltan looked over and saw Saraph staring at him. His brows dipped, he shook his head, and then turned back to resume his examination of the Caesareum.

As he looked upon the western façade, Zoltan thought the building looked nearly half the height of the Pharos, a worthy sea mark in its own right. Every feature was accented with gold, every surface defined by extraordinary carvings. Rising above the golden cornice of the façade were the tops of colossal columns in a great center colonnade. Other roof planes capping lesser walls and colonnades began nearly halfway down the façade and descended in tiers. Their gleaming gold and waves from the heat of the sun created the illusion of movement and the appearance of great oars in an ancient galley.

At the lower levels these tiers and their roof lines blended into the roof tops of the surrounding buildings of the city and were swept into a sea of stone sculptures, waterfalls, courtyards, gardens, porches, smaller temples and long halls with innumerable marble columns. The overall impression struck Zoltan as intentionally that of a great waterfall. He made several attempts to identify the base of the Caesareum, but each ended in the realization that his search had lead him to an entirely different section of the city and architectural modes of a distinctly different era.

Having a sense of their elevation, he looked further to his left and nearer in the foreground and located the theatre, which shared the high ground with Jaek's building. He followed its descent beside lush green-terraced groves back toward the Sea. As he did, he recognized a race course and the Alexandria gymnasium complex from which Jaek's poetic verses had originated.

"OK, then…." he muttered to himself, squinting and breathing nervously into a loose fist that he held in front of his mouth. Going back to the base of the Caesareum, he followed the shore of the Eastern Harbor northeast.

"The Palace complex should begin somewhere around … ."

His eyes spotted a beautiful building on an island and then the ships in the palace harbor; they widened as his pulse began to race all the more. "There!" he exclaimed as if he were finally beginning to see.

Placing his hands on the railing, he leaned forward and projected his upper body outward as if cutting through the wind like the bowsprit of a great sailing vessel. And indeed, his mind was now gliding over the waves of Alexandrian landscape. He followed the city wall along the coast to a promontory as it emerged from the sea harbor. And there, laid out before him, the palace complex began to distinguish itself from the rest of the buildings. *Wow, just follow the gold and silver, the polished white marble and the brightly colored flags,* he thought.

Subtle architectural variations further distinguished large sections of the complex from one another. He assumed these to be the personal palace additions made by each of the Ptolemies throughout the dynasty. The largest section, and nearest the Sea, he persuaded himself, had been the palace of Ptolemy Soter I. *Either him or the second one, Philadelphus,* he thought. *They were the ones who adopted the original vision of Alexander the Great and took this Greco-Egyptian city to these heights of glory.*

Alexander the Great! he thought, as with a jolt. He looked to his left and began to look for street colonnades. He saw clusters of beautiful pillars here and there, but nothing that satisfied his search before his view was blocked by the building that held his current observation deck. But he saw also that the deck at this level continued across the front of the building and wrapped around to the opposite side.

Zoltan stood up straight and thoughtlessly put his hands into the pockets of his pants. His right hand immediately felt a set of keys and he became distracted, amused by an idea. He stealthily pulled the keys from his pocket and tried to place them on the railing behind an ornamental cap, desiring to leave a mark of his own. When he discovered that he was unable to open his hand, he slid the keys back into his pocket and freely released them. Embarrassed, he glanced back at Saraph and was relieved to find him looking in another direction.

Saraph followed as Zoltan began to walk across the front of the building, his eyes again combing the sprawling palaces with their perfectly sculpted gardens, parks and groves. Suddenly he stopped. He leaned forward and pointed, his mouth open for several seconds before expelling a guttural sound of astonishment. Then a wildish smile transformed his face.

"Do you see them? Three giraffes right over there. And there, look to the right of them, across the mote. There's a lion sunbathing in the grass. There... there are three females under those trees," he said, looking over at Saraph, who was trying to follow the line of Zoltan's extended arm to the location he was indicating.

"I see a zebra," Saraph said, looking intently. "But ...."

"Where?" Zoltan asked.

"Well, do you see that olive grove just below the double line of red flowers along that pathway?"

He leaned over and pointed far to the left of where Zoltan was focused. Zoltan looked at him, annoyed. Then he looked for the zebra.

"I see the grove and the flowers," he said.

"OK, now just to their left, directly below the observatory," Saraph instructed.

"Yes, yes I see it, three or four of them, actually. But where's this observ ...."

Ascending the building immediately beyond the zebras, Zoltan's eyes located a group of towers that spiraled up from the tops of a series of connected roofs. All but one were covered with canopies of brightly colored patterns generously trimmed in gold and silver. The one that was not covered appeared to have the sides of the canopy rolled and tied at the top of the open observation deck. Rising from it was a pedestal that held a machine that Zoltan did not recognize. It pointed skyward.

Noticing a slight movement, he realized that what he had thought to be parts of the arms of the pedestal were two men standing beside the machine. So diminished was their size in the context of the machine and the observation deck that held them that Zoltan immediately recoiled. He looked back at the zebras and then relocated the lions and the giraffes. Then, as he scanned the buildings before him with the adjusted sense of scale, he found his awe refreshed.

He reached out and grabbed a handful of Saraph's jacket where his arm met his shoulder and gently, thoughtlessly rocked him back and forth.

"The birthplace of the modern mind. The voices of antiquity have spoken in truth," he said faintly. "Zoos, parks, gardens, water falls, observatories, and somewhere in there, the laboratories and the libraries. Even what we have assumed to be the embellishment of legend turns out to be understatement. Mousseion and palaces are more seamlessly connected than I had imagined."

He began to notice people everywhere. Wherever streets could be seen between buildings, or walking paths through the trees of the parks and wooded areas, people moved about on foot or in carriages. Carpenters populated the many sites where new building projects were under way. Everywhere he looked he noticed children at play, gardeners and masons at work, and people on every level of every building.

His vision now focused for pedestrian dimensions, Zoltan's attention was drawn also to statues and carvings and other elements of the common architecture. Human size marble, terra cotta and golden jars seemed ubiquitous. He began to identify countless statues of sphinxes, lions, crocodiles, winged scarabs and eagles. *My goodness, the only things outnumbering the people are the statues*, he thought. Busts were plentiful throughout as well, and he assumed them to be representations of the Ptolemies or their officials.

He recognized a statue of Horus with a falcon head, statues of Isis and Osiris, of the bull, Apis, the cat god, Bast. A colossal sculpture of Hercules stood in a courtyard next to a large square building of the Mousseion complex.

"That must be the library," he said aloud.

Just below where he and Saraph stood he found a sphinx with its paws crossed, a statue of Isis nursing Horus and a serpent entwined around a lotus. And everywhere he looked he saw clusters of polished white marble columns from a few feet tall to heights of twenty or thirty feet.

"You paid way more attention to what your father shared with you than either of you may have realized," Saraph said.

Zoltan looked at him. Slowly, a smile transformed his face. He nodded and resumed his exploration.

"Sad, but true," he said, looking out toward the sea. "He really would have enjoyed this. He deserved it. This is what I'd hoped to give him when I brought him here a few years ago ... just a couple thousand years too late."

Zoltan sighed. "'Bear patiently, my heart – for you have suffered heavier things.'"

"Homer?"

"Yep. One of the many. I wonder how many times he had me write that one. You know what's strange?"

"No, what's that?"

"I don't recall either one of us ever reciting one of them aloud. Just on paper." Zoltan shook his head. "'Intimacy is the reciprocal movement of inspiration,' he once had me write for ten solid pages. It was the only one he ever had me write without crediting an author at the end. That, and the fact that those inspiring writing lessons endear him to me to this day, assure me that it was his own.

"Hey, more animals," Zoltan said, pointing. "See those camels lying along that fence line? See, up that hill, west beyond the observatories and back toward the Sea."

"Yes, of course," Saraph affirmed.

"The zoo must be woven all through the city. That's quite a way from the other animals."

Saraph laughed. "No one in Egypt, even Alexandria, would think of a camel as a zoo animal. Those are the palace stables to the right next to the harbor. And look up the hill beyond the fence."

Zoltan laughed. "Horses... of course, the royal stables."

"No, not anymore," Saraph responded.

"What do you mean?"

"Alexandria is no longer royal. This bright torch has been handed off to Rome and begins to flicker. It has some prominence yet to enjoy. But we now stand in the capital of a Roman Province, presently ruled by Domitian."

Zoltan stood and contemplated the historical significance of Saraph's words. Silence prevailed for several minutes. He recalled the city's historical movements, and the scenes in his mind were being reported by the subtle changes of expression upon his face. He looked over at Saraph, who he again found staring back at him.

"Why do you do that?"

"What?"

"Stare at me."

"I am enjoying you."

"Well, I wish you'd stop. It's strange."

"Why do you stare at buildings, which this landscape in your day forgets?"

Zoltan looked out at the buildings, the harbors, the Pharos and the Sea. He noticed more activities – builders on scaffolds, the busy pace of the distant commercial streets beyond the far end of the deck, and ships moving in the harbors. Remembering the disappointment of his earlier visit, he considered Saraph's question.

He looked at Saraph. "Among others, I have a residence atop 900 North Michigan in Chicago overlooking another sea, which some ineptly call a lake. It is the quintessential picture of modern opulence. I have visited the Petronas Towers in Kuala Lumpur, Malaysia, Central Plaza in Hong Kong, and have been an honored guest at Burj Al Arab and Emirates Twin Towers in Dubai on a coast not so far from here."

He looked back upon the city. "Yet, nothing prepared me

for this. It is wonderful. So I stare," he defended.

"And you are a greater wonder than all that you see before you and all that you have mentioned. Life flows within you, and unlike their collective wealth and glory, you are eternal," Saraph answered. "So *I* stare."

They looked at one another extendedly. Zoltan made a modest effort to appreciate the message in Saraph's statement. But he could not fend off his suspicions of a hidden weapon in it. *Why would he suddenly be flattering? He's been unimpressed, even critical of me from the beginning.* He wasn't sure why he thought this, but he was certain it was true.

Remembering his desire to see the colonnades, he turned and continued his interrupted walk along the deck. And as he did, on a distant hill directly before him, the Serapeum emerged from behind the opposite end of the building. Suddenly he stopped, turned and leaned against the railing with his head on his folded arms.

"You OK?" Saraph asked, stopping beside him.

Your first time… unforgettable, but just the beginning. They're expecting you. But then, we've expected you for several weeks based on… well, the information we received from our mutual friend. But hey, finally, huh? You'll be pleased.

He cringed as he saw the pockmarked face of the man to whom the voice belonged and the gloved hand that reached out to take his money, $2,000 in cash. Then he saw the lights and heard the shouting, the car doors slamming, and he felt the arms grabbing him. Again he winced.

"Fine," he answered, as he stood and continued the walk. "I'm fine. I just got a little dizzy there for a moment. It's a lot to take in all at once."

Shortly, he began to see tall marble columns emerge from behind buildings and trees. By the time he reached the end of the deck, he was looking to his left at the Gate of the Sun, the entrance to ancient Alexandria described by many an awe-struck visitor.

As if their striking statement needed embellishment, a spiral wreath adorned each white marble pillar and crowned their tops with golden flowers. And at the base of each was a hand-arranged floral splendor. It was as Zoltan had anticipated. They ran east and west along Canopic street from the Gate of the Sun to the Gate of the Moon and the Western Harbor, and north and south along the street of the Soma from the Eastern Harbor to the harbor of Lake Mareotis. But he was surprised by the width of the two main arteries and by the density of their travelers.

Near their intersection he found what he was looking for: the tomb of Alexander the Great. He leaned forward, his elbows upon the railing, and stared. Then, scanning the city, he tried to take it in as a whole.

But Saraph was impressed only by the fact that Zoltan said nothing about the Serapeum, or the new library that extended from it, the grandest sight in Alexandria. He marveled, and he waited.

"It's hard to fathom that none of this was here." Zoltan's breathing was labored as he spoke.

"None of it was here when? Before Alexander's builders began quarrying limestone, or when you and your father arrived to find not one of those stones atop another and all of these nicknacks and yard monuments cast into the Sea? Which impresses you most?"

"Before Alexander," Zoltan answered, scowling. He stood up and was silent for a moment, distracted by the implications in Saraph's question.

"One man's visit," he said, continuing with his previous thought, "some four hundred years ago ... it changed this landscape along with the course of history. What was he, twenty-something? But what vision and leadership! And what a shame that he never saw it take shape. Has there been a more important city in the entire course of human history?" he asked.

"Yes," Saraph answered matter-of-factly.

Ignoring the answer, Zoltan continued. "Likely from this very hill Alexander and his architect, Dinocrates, stood and conceived the plan, seeing the military, political and economic advantages of a city in this location."

"Or from that one," Saraph said, pointing in the direction of the Serapeum and testing his hunch.

Zoltan again ignored him. "There, to Canopus and the mouth of the Nile," he said, nodding toward the gate of the Sun. "Or out there, on the other side of that immense lake, the canals that also connect to the Nile. Either way, trade with the Near and Far East." He looked to his right. "And out across the Mediterranean, the coastal wealth and all of Europe!"

"And right on the other side of this building," Saraph interjected, "right behind where we came up, there is the Jewish Quarter. Probably forty thousand Jews."

Zoltan chuckled. "I'm going to guess that this was one thing Alexander didn't plan, and that Dinocrate's surveyors were not instructed to lay that area out."

"Still, extremely important historically," Saraph reported, turning back toward the city.

With a smirk on his face, Zoltan watched him. Then he looked out at Pharos Island.

"Isn't that where the seventy rabbis were supposedly held hostage and separately invented the same Greek translation of the Hebrew Scripture ... the infamous Septuagint?"

Saraph was silent for a moment, not wanting to indulge Zoltan's sarcasm. Then, looking out at Pharos Island, he said, "The Septuagint. I'd do battle for its creation all over again if I had to. What a grand accomplishment we fought for. And its value is more evident in these days than in those."

Uneasy, Zoltan stared at Saraph. Then he shook his head and turned to look back at the Mousseion and the observatories.

"My father swore that the three wise men were scientists from the Mousseion, though I could never get any sources out of him. And every Christmas my mom would lean over and whisper 'Alexandria' to us whenever that part of the story came up where the angel sent the couple and their new baby to Egypt."

"And *these* wise men ...." Saraph said, watching Archippus and Josiah walking across the patio below to rejoin the meeting. (Solomon and Jaek were already at the table.) "Look," he said, pointing toward the far end of the patio.

Zoltan was quiet for a moment, staring. He shook his head and turned. "I can just picture Mark Antony and Cleopatra leading the Royal fleet from that harbor to contend with Octavian. "Somewhere right ... ," he said, pointing and waving his right hand across the general direction of the palace harbor. "And somewhere right over there they committed suicide as the wrath of Augustus loomed."

Saraph noticed that Zoltan was stealing nervous glances back in the direction of the Serapeum as he spoke.

Suddenly, Zoltan clasped his hands behind his head. "Wow, think of that. Just over a hundred years ago Octavian was declared Pharaoh right here!" He brought down his arms and folded them tightly in front of him. Both of his hands were grabbing bits of material on the back of his shirt.

"Magician, is something bothering you?" Saraph asked.

"The bookends ... Alexander the Great to Cleopatra and Caesar Augustus," Zoltan said, as he walked over and leaned against the railing that ran along the front of the building. "And in between, right along that same little strip of real estate, the Ptolemies, patrons to the foundations of science developed right there at the Mousseion." He looked at Saraph. "Foundations that support the wonders of my day, even my industry ... my empire."

Zoltan looked back at the tomb complex and recalled the brevity of Alexander the Great's career. Angry, he slammed his hand against the railing and turned his back to Saraph. He walked several steps away, his hands in his pockets, fidgeting.

"Magician, have you ever read the verses in the Scriptures by King Nebuchadnezzar of Babylon, or King Darius of Persia?" Saraph asked.

Zoltan turned around and looked at Saraph. His mood changed, and slowly a smile overtook his face. The question appeared to provide him with a measure of relief in distraction. He walked back to his escort and placed a hand on his shoulder. Suddenly, his head flung back as he laughed heartily. He shook Saraph by the shoulder. Then he studied his eyes.

"I'm sorry," he said, "but you have given me far too much credit. Persian and Babylonian scriptures...?" He chuckled again. "No, I have never read anything like that."

"I may give you less than you think," Saraph responded. "These Scriptural writings are in the Bible."

"A Persian and a Babylonian king wrote things that are in the Bible?"

Saraph nodded. "You may find what King Nebuchadnezzar wrote a bit disconcerting. But I will tell it to you. Concerning the Most High:

His dominion is an eternal dominion;
His kingdom endures from generation to generation.
All the people of the earth
are regarded as nothing.
He does as he pleases
with the powers of heaven
and the peoples of earth.
No one can hold back his hand
or say to Him: 'What have you done?'

"And to the men of all nations, King Darius of Persia wrote this:
For He is the living God
And He endures forever;

His kingdom will not be destroyed,
His dominion will never end."

The frown had returned to Zoltan's face. "What's the point?" he demanded.

"Isn't it obvious?" Saraph stared out at the city for a moment. "You've heard of the Apostle Paul?"

"Something else from the Bible?"

Saraph smiled. "Not yet. But it has been written down."

Zoltan thought about this for a moment. "I'll humor you if you insist."

"A very short time ago," Saraph said, "right across this Sea in the more ancient Greek city of Athens, a city full of idols like this one, Paul addressed a gathering of Greek nobles and philosophers at the Areopagus. His words were recorded by Luke, a physician from Antioch:

> The God who made the world and everything in it is the Lord of heaven and earth and does not live in temples built by hands. And He is not served by human hands, as if He needed anything, because He Himself gives all men life and breath and everything else. From one man He made every nation of men, that they should inhabit the whole earth; and He determined the times set for them and the exact places where they should live. God did this so that men should seek Him and perhaps reach out for Him and find Him, though He is not far from each one of us.

"You see, Magician, the rise and the clamor of great empires and rulers is not as impressive as you are inclined to herald. Nor is their loss as tragic."

Saraph reached up and placed his right hand upon Zoltan's chest and felt his heart beating beneath it.

"It is what happens within the hearts of people toward the living God, people who move within the nations and throughout every generation ... it is this that is truly consequential. This is the opportunity He gives within the kingdoms He establishes. It is the individual who uses this grace for good or evil, to reach out for God or not."

"So that must be the new library ... the daughter, yet even greater than that of the original at the Mousseion," Zoltan said, appearing mesmerized as he looked above Saraph toward the hill in the distance. He had heard little of what Saraph had just spoken to him.

"And they are preparing to extend it further south by the looks of those markers and the excavation being done."

Saraph could see that Zoltan was not looking at the library as he spoke. He was looking beside it to the northwest atop the acropolis of Alexandria. He was looking directly at the temple of Serapis.

"Magician, why does the Serapeum unnerve you so?"

Sweat was running down the sides of Zoltan's face from the soaked hair of his temples. He rolled his eyes toward Saraph and glared. Without speaking, he turned and took several strides before descending the steps to the lower deck levels. As he reached the middle deck he stopped, drawn to watch the activities of a building directly across the street. He looked back at Saraph.

"What does it say?" he asked, referring to a large gilded sign that crowned the building.

"Jaek's Fire."

"Our Jaek?"

"None other."

"Why can't I read it?"

"It is ancient Egyptian written with Greek letters. Jaek uses it to endear himself to the Egyptians and secure their patronage. It offends some of the more traditional Greek sentiments, but they are usually attached to the affluent who are unwilling to do without the treasures inside."

It appeared to Zoltan that all of the commercial activity within his view was spun from that building.

"What is it?"

"It is a glass factory. Jaek applied some of what he learned from hanging around the scientists at the Mousseion to inventing a method for blowing glass. Merchants come from far and wide to do business with him and return to their home lands with his prized colored glasses, vases and other creations. His wealth comes mainly from Europe and the Orient. But Jaek has a special place in his heart for the Egyptians."

Zoltan stared at the sign. Then he looked up at Saraph, who stood several stairs above him. He looked up and down the street. Carriages, three and four wide in spots, paced with the brisk strides of soldiers and businessmen. Women held tightly to the hands of their children, lest they stumble and be trampled in the crowded marble street. Greeks, Egyptians, Jews, Asians, the entourage of a Roman emissary, and that of what he thought to be an Indian delegation now passed before him.

Bright, colored banners, street-side kiosks with the demonstrative chatter of their attending merchants, musicians, leashed animals, as well as a symphony of delectable scents contributed to the festive atmosphere. Zoltan had been oblivious to these while looking outward atop the upper deck. He recalled hearing some of these sounds even as he had climbed the stairs of the decks on the other side of the building. But that side of the building did not offer a view of such a commercial scene, as it faced the residential streets of the city's western region.

"These four buildings appear connected," he said to Saraph inquiringly.

"Actually, there are six. The one in front of you is the factory. But all of these to the end of the block are part of his internationally acclaimed glass and ceramics retail business."

"Jaek's?" Zoltan asked in amazement.

Saraph nodded. "He has a few more in other parts of the city—grocers, banks, a little bit of a shipping operation, some business offices and such. A few of his distributorships are scattered across the Mediterranean... over on the European side, that is. And, of course, he has this," Saraph said, gesturing toward the building to which they were connected.

Zoltan looked down across the patio toward the four men at the table. Three were seated. Jaek appeared to be standing. Zoltan looked back at the sign and a smile spread across his face. He shook his head.

Across the street in the other direction a tall, slender Egyptian woman arrested his attention. She held the hand of her equally beautiful teenage daughter as they stepped inside a doorway. Zoltan automatically looked above the door and saw the Greek letters that read: "Bath House." Immediately the beads of sweat began to reappear on his forehead. He reached out and grabbed hold of the railing with both hands, and bending over, hung his head between his arms and grimaced.

Your first time... unforgettable, but just the beginning.

He shook his head abruptly and lifted it up from beneath his arms, his eyes still closed tightly. Comforted to hear that the sounds around him remained the same, he opened his eyes, though squinting. And rising just above the buildings directly before him, he saw the golden-white splendor of the top of the Serapeum.

He saw the sign again, Bath House. As if juxtaposed over it, he saw in bright red neon – The Serapeum. Then he saw the man again, seated before the dimly lit entry to the back room.

You will be pleased.

The door behind him opened and the flashing lights broadcast their alarming news upon the walls around him. The shouting... and the hands grabbing him. He flinched and desired to run as he had then.

His head dropped back down and he gave it another violent shake. For several seconds the image of the Serapeum atop the hill, his memory of its name in a modern neon banner, the words Bath House, the gloved man, and the nearest memory of the woman and her daughter wrestled for preeminence in his mind. He desperately attempted to distract any response of his will.

Chapter 13
SORCERY

Zoltan heard voices, but they were distant and reverent, *like spectators at a golf tournament,* he thought. Presently, he saw no one, and was at once relieved and disappointed. He had labored to keep the words from entering his mind, knowing that the journey of the gift was as a walk along a slippery ledge. Orgies, lewd, licentious—all such words had often been sprinkled throughout his readings about the Egyptian cultic practices. One of the books he had received from his father stated that the rights of Serapis of Alexandria made even the Romans blush.

His view was consumed by a column directly in front of him that was ten feet in diameter. As he followed it to its full height his view expanded and the columns multiplied.

"Like reaching to the heavens," he said, with his head as far back as it would go. "They have to be a hundred feet tall, at least."

"That's the idea."

Zoltan leveled his head and turned around to look at Saraph.

"What's the idea?"

"To reach to the heavens. That is what columns such as these symbolize to the Egyptians."

Zoltan looked past Saraph at the colonnade that appeared to recede to infinity from where they stood. He looked back up at the ceiling and squinted. Hearing a note that seemed intrinsic to the environment of the temple, he felt that he was inside of a great musical instrument from which it originated.

"I wonder how they got the art work up there?" he said, attempting to distract his mind from the haunting sound.

They stood in the midst of a colonnade made up of three rows. He looked over his left shoulder and saw the great wall of the temple enclosing an outer courtyard that bordered the columns of the first row. Turning back toward the direction he had originally faced, he looked between two columns and saw that a great open space separated these columns from their counterparts on the other side of the temple. Everything looked brand new.

Looking up again, Zoltan took notice of spaces around the perimeter of the ceiling from which light poured in. He looked around. The note seemed to be a perfectly harmonious accompaniment of everything making an impression upon him. He looked at the art work all around him and the light coming in. His mind could not distinguish the note from the general brightness.

"That doesn't even make sense," he said.

"What?"

"How bright it is in here with just . . . ."

Saraph pointed to their right and Zoltan walked between two columns and stepped out into the open space. To his right he saw a great pedestal of polished white marble and immediately began squinting. Several beams of light landed directly upon it and gave it a mysterious illumination. Two flights of long steps ran 90 degrees to each other from his view and led to a flat plane more than twenty feet from the temple floor.

Further to the right Zoltan could see the open doorway at the front of the temple. The top of the opening he estimated at fifty to sixty feet tall by comparison to several people who were entering through it. He looked back at the pedestal and noticed that there were a number of people scattered around it and others that could be seen walking between the columns.

"Is it an altar?" he asked, looking over at Saraph, who simply nodded.

"Wow!" Zoltan said, as he looked to his left. By compulsion he began walking along the row of columns toward the golden doors at the far end. He figured there to be a hundred or more people in the main temple area. As he and Saraph walked side by side, he counted a group of ten columns across the great hall from them. Using these as a measure, he duplicated the section in his mind, placing it over other sections of ten. Suddenly he stopped.

"There must be ... ." He shook his head. "At the very least there are two hundred of these giant columns in here. That means ... ." He paused and looked back down the hall. Realizing that the sparsely scattered people were ten for every column, he turned and looked at Saraph. "There are two thousand people in here right now?" He looked around. "How is that possible, it feels nearly empty?"

Zoltan surveyed the space around him as he slowly turned and they resumed their walk along the colonnade. He realized that there was scarcely anyone who was not carrying out some sort of task or service of the temple. He wondered if everyone that he saw was employed at the temple. He did not speak again until they reached the golden doors, which were the same height as the opening at the other end.

"They looked small from back there," he said, as he admired their carvings.

Zoltan looked over his shoulder as an Egyptian man came up behind them and stood in front of the doors. As they slowly began to open, Zoltan and Saraph passed between them following behind the man.

The inner chamber was closed in on all sides. When they entered it the statue suddenly raised up, appearing to grow by fifty percent of its size. As it did, the Egyptian worshiper hit the floor as if diving from the flight of flaming arrows. Zoltan studied the bearded, fatherly looking, Greek statue with the basket containing gifts of prosperity on its head. A beam of light reflected off of flecks of gold on his robe and made him appear to sparkle. When he settled back to his original height, the beam of light landed upon his lips.

Zoltan looked at Saraph, impressed but not awed.

"Technology," Saraph said. "Special effects."

A smirk was upon Zoltan's face as he shook his head. "The Ptolemies."

"There's some of the application of things discovered at your Mousseion," Saraph said. "Giant doors that open on there own, directed light, a magnetic system in the ceiling controlled by the sorcery of priests … or technicians, depending on how you look at it."

"No wonder the fame and popularity of Serapis spread so rapidly throughout Egypt and the entire Mediterranean world," Zoltan muttered.

"And with it, the power and authority of the Ptolemies," Saraph added.

Zoltan watched as the man stood to his feet, walked up to a shrine next to the statue of Serapis and removed some food that was sitting out. He turned and walked back to the doors. As they opened, Zoltan and Saraph followed him back out into the hall.

"That makes me angry," Zoltan said, as they headed back down the hallowed hall.

"You have no idea," Saraph responded, with a tone grave with implication.

They passed eight of the great columns before Saraph spoke again. "In this day," he said, "the technological sorcery that controls the masses is in temples. In yours, it is in theatres and in electronic broadcast boxes sitting on entertainment shrines and hanging on walls in nearly every home."

Zoltan stopped and turned toward Saraph. "I am not a religion wielder!"

"No, Magician, I never said you were. But false religions are not the only wielders of false authority. The use of deception to manipulate and control, by whatever name and motivation, is destructive to humanity. Your notion of the secular as an inviolable nobility does not, in fact, constitute a right of sorcery beyond condemnation."

Zoltan stared at Saraph for a few seconds before he turned and continued walking toward the front of the temple. "Now that your meaning is clear, you can stop calling me by that offensive name," he said as he looked around. He was attempting to take in as much of the beauty of the architecture as possible. Each column, he thought, was as a giant scroll of symbols and story. The floor was a shiny marble wonder of mosaic artistry.

As they passed a large circle of hieroglyphs inlaid in the floor at the center of the hall, it occurred to Zoltan that he had never slept with an Egyptian woman. The randomness of the thought angered him. He made an abrupt turn back and to his left and walked toward the circle of symbols in the floor. Looking down, his hands in his pockets, he pretended to be intrigued by the mosaic images.

Beneath the cover of his outward actions he saw the mother and daughter walking into the bath house. He abruptly moved to his right and began walking around the circle in the other direction.

... unforgettable ... but just .... He blinked hard twice, the twitch he'd developed attempting to erase the chalk board of his mind in times like these. It never worked.

It's really not what I want. I know that. It's intimacy ... it's intimacy I really crave. Chuck's right, listen to Chuck. Just remember ... I know all this stuff. I know what I'm really about, who I really am, what I'm really made for.

He realized he was walking back to his left. Recognizing the awkwardness of it, he shuffled his feet, stopped and stared as though he had discovered something interesting.

1-800-IF-U-WANT

Zoltan started back to his right.

Stop it! Where did that come from? I haven't called them in more than a week. No, don't even go there. It's all just natural anyway! Why wouldn't I desire all of these things? No! It's not real intimacy! They keep me from…. OK, I'm locked up. Why am I locked? How did I get here?

Pressing a fist to his forehead, he tried to recall the path of his thoughts. *What did Chuck say to do when this happens?* He had paced his way around the circle back to where Saraph had remained standing.

Zoltan's upper body was nearly at a right angle to his legs, which were spread out for balance as he leaned over the top of a silhouette graphic of a bird. He closed his eyes for concentration.

"What was it Chuck said?" he muttered aloud unknowingly.

He heard a noise, and opening his eyes, he turned to see Saraph mimicking his stance and gazing at him with an odd expression from only inches away.

"Who's Chuck?" he asked.

Startled, Zoltan looked back down at the floor.

'Hello, this is Bridget… and Melody' "Oh, no way," he muttered aloud, as he abruptly rose up and stared at the ceiling with his right fist pressed against his mouth and the sound of giggles echoing in his head. *Don't even go there. Just don't even ….*

"Have you studied hieroglyphs, Magician?"

Saraph's voice was a welcomed distraction. But all Zoltan could do was continue staring at the ceiling, speechless.

"I mean, it's not a common understanding that these hieroglyphs on the floor are answered by those directly above them, especially in your day, when the ceilings and most of the floors no longer exist."

Zoltan continued staring for a few seconds and then dropped his gaze to meet Saraph's.

"It's not that complicated really. The puzzles of earth answered in the heavens," he said, exhibiting his penchant for quick thinking.

"Hm … impressive," Saraph said. "You truly are a man of many surprises."

Zoltan looked back down at the floor. *That's it*, he thought. *'There's always an opportunity, something to take hold of and pull yourself out with.' That's what Chuck said. 'But it has to be immediate.'*

Zoltan stood up, looked at Saraph, nodded toward the front entrance and started walking. He tried to think of a worthy place to fix his mind. But consciousness itself felt perilous. He noticed that the white altar at the front was illuminated by beams of light from different directions and different openings than the ones that came through earlier.

Who knows what they do with that thing, he thought as they approached it from the side. He thought of how enormous the entire complex looked from the deck. *Cultic rights that made even the Romans blush,* he recalled. *There must be hundreds of chambers, hidden crypts, chapels and rooms connected with this place. That's probably where all of that goes on.*

His mind quickly became a clutter of imagined scenarios and fantasy destinations. He was relieved to realize he had no ability to actually conceive of such places or activities in the temple complex. Nor did he know if any such things truly took place there. But he knew of places where they did and he felt ambushed by invitations to countless deviant pleasures. *Any destination* … so near, but which one? He felt the shortness of breath and the surge of adrenaline as if he had just rolled up his sleeve and shot it into his vein.

Then the resentment hit him like a cold crashing wave and he became flushed with anger. He looked over at Saraph self-consciously, concerned that his face and ears were showing the heat that he felt. But Saraph was looking straight ahead at the open doorway.

What kind of gift is it if ruined by the giver hawking over it? If I could just get rid of him, then I could really take hold of this thing. I could.... He shook his head. *Why should I fear these things? What could be more natural than these desires?* He clenched his teeth. *Egypt, Rome, Greece, entire nations, billions of people throughout history obsessed with the same thing. There, that alone affirms my rights. That's humanity. That's human! Is there a more evident signature of human nature?*

No, I'm rationalizing. This is not good. He was nearly breathless. *Tangled up in the web again. Help me here, Chuck... What's the antidote? 'There's always an opportunity, something to take hold of....'* Yeah, *something to pull myself out with... some way to get unstuck. 'Find someone to connect with,'* he could hear Chuck saying. He looked over at Saraph again and was filled with contempt.

From the time Zoltan and Saraph had drawn within twenty feet of the front entry, ten minutes had passed without a word between them. Zoltan's mind, too, had been quiet, relieved by the distraction of the scene before them. After passing through the entry way, they had gone down a short flight of stairs and walked to the end of the courtyard to the gate of the outer wall. One-hundred stairs now descended before them past the lower courtyards and into the Alexandrian landscape.

"It's somehow more impressive than our last view," Zoltan said. "I wouldn't have thought it was possible."

"My personal favorite," Saraph answered. "The first city in the world with a population of a million people," he added, seeing more of the city's business from this vantage point.

"And what of all this 'sorcery?'" Zoltan said. He looked at Saraph. "I mean, I thought you objected to all this wielding of technology."

"Technology is subject to the purposes of its wielders," Saraph answered. "That great wonder over there," he said, pointing to the Pharos, "is a credit to the Ptolemies, their engineers, the scientists of the Mousseion and the labor forces that built it. It guides sailors and warns them of the coastal dangers. It welcomes weary travelers. And the elegant proportions of its technology inspire wonder to the ends of the earth and to future generations, like yours."

He scanned the city. "The same can be said of the Gate of the Sun, the Mousseion, and even Jaek's Fire. The intent of these was not deception, exploitation, power and the control of the masses. But, that was precisely the intent behind the Ptolemy's invention of Serapis and the sorcery that supports it."

"I think we are in agreement," Zoltan said, unsure.

They looked at one another.

"Are we?" Saraph asked.

He looked out at the Pharos, then turned and looked at the building behind them. He turned back to look at Zoltan.

"One intent follows the Creation mandate and pleases God, and the other denies His supremacy in its ascent to moral license based on false authority. One is a legitimate invitation from your Creator. One is not. To which have you attached *your heart*, Magician?"

They stared at one another. Zoltan swallowed and then looked away.

"I admit I am familiar with the second. I wish I knew of the first," he said distantly.

He looked until he found the building where they had started. He was surprised by how small it looked in the context of the entire city, barely able to make out the decks against the white stone. He thought about Jaek, the meeting and the black package. He located the top of Jaek's factory by the smoke rising from several stacks in its roofs.

Suddenly, usurping all of this, in his mind's eye he could see an image of the sign—Bath House—and the mother and daughter entering beneath it.

Chapter 14
THINGS

The activities of the busy street were reduced to a soft background blur of noises that traveled around the layered walls of the entry and were absorbed into the dense humidity. These mixed with the sounds of the water and the echoing voices from within the bath house. But all offered little competition for the note and the recurring sounds of shouting and car doors slamming in Zoltan's mind.

The woman that he had noticed from the deck across the street held a stack of linens she had just received from an attendant behind the counter. Zoltan watched as she and her daughter disappeared into the steam and behind the pink and blue tiled partition that blocked the open interior from view. He heard the happy voices of women greeting one another and the ensuing chatter of conversation.

He turned to Saraph with rage etched upon his face.

"What is this? What do I have to do with this ordinary woman and her skinny little daughter?"

"I don't know. But you must have ...."

"I must have what? I must have made a huge mistake agreeing to join you for this journey of your trickeries."

Saraph stood silent, staring at Zoltan.

"Sure, this makes me look pretty silly. Is that the point? Like

I need something in here. Right! Every day I have my pick of pretty things."

"Things? Your daily picks don't appear to be enough to satisfy you." Saraph clapped his hands twice and then rubbed his palms vigorously. "Maybe something more exotic … something Egyptian … something ancient will do."

"Don't kid yourself. This isn't me."

Zoltan whirled and pressed his palms against his temples, the flashing lights appearing to invade the building's entry with colored rays that pierced the steamy bath house.

… unforgettable … but just the beginning.

The shouting again drowned out all other sounds.

"I am aware of the incident, if you'd like to talk … ."

"This is not me! Don't you get it?" Zoltan spun away from Saraph. "Sure, like he doesn't know," he said aloud to himself. "Something, or someone is betraying me, and he's part of it. That is evident. Something concocted by Trevor, I know it."

He looked at the entry to the bath house and saw the light coming from both sides of the wall blocking the inside from the opening onto the street. He strode toward it and quickly found himself back out on the busy street. He felt Saraph's arm brush against his as he, too, stepped from the entryway. Zoltan looked at him.

"Why don't you leave me alone? All this following me, staring at me … enough! I can take it from here OK? Just go … go help somebody in some other place and time. Help someone fight something, escape something, or whatever else you want to add to all your pretend heroics. You didn't really expect me to fall for those silly illusions to your make believe exploits, did you? You and your warriors in Jerusalem … then, back a few pages to fighting for the creation of the Septuagint. Really … what do you take me for?"

He looked across the street and saw the place they had been standing just above where the stairs disappeared behind the tall wooden fence that surrounded Jaek's patio. Like a man reaching a city of refuge just ahead of his pursuers, he thought of Jaek and the meeting.

Chapter 15
COUNCIL OF THE FOUR

Zoltan ran his tongue across parched lips that felt like the surface of wrinkled paper. The trembling breaths of his panting and the dryness of his mouth defied his craving to swallow. Wide-eyed, he looked beside him at Saraph, somehow comforted by his presence. But he gave no reaction. The shock of sanctuary had transformed his consciousness the instant he'd found himself standing again beside the table at the far end of the patio.

Freed of memories and temptations that had plagued him only moments before, he searched his mind, puzzled. He was aware of the elements of fact that had supported them, but could not find any remnant of the power they had possessed, or the fear they had aroused. They were tangibly distant and meaningless. His compulsion of curiosity concerning their absence made him feel that he almost missed them. A longing for resolve filled the void they had left, and he sensed an inclination to go back and find them, if just to follow the flight of their departure and comprehend what had happened to them.

Where are my accusers? he thought, surprised by the question and unable to make any sense of it. Looking around, he tried to consider what it was about the place in which he now stood that could make such a difference. He blinked hard and tried to move on.

"You're getting good at this," he heard Saraph say.

They looked at one another.

"I'm encouraged to see that you must have some interest in these proceedings."

Zoltan stared at him, his eyes conveying the question that his trapped voice could not express.

"You got us back to the meeting just as everyone is returning from the break," Saraph said to clarify, seemingly unfazed by the recent insults.

Zoltan, in fact, had greater interest in the meeting than he was able to consciously acknowledge or manage. Anticipation was lingering over the mystery of the black package. The seed of genealogical intrigue planted by his father was growing into a sense of kinship with Jaek. And he was compelled by the extravagant opportunity to gain insight regarding some gnawing questions he had ignored. All of these conspired to keep his personal identification with the intimate council stimulated.

He looked at the black package in the center of the table. He watched as Jaek and Solomon stood to honor the return of Josiah and Archippus. As the four men took their seats and chatted about their activities during the break, Zoltan found his attention to be divided between the black package and Jaek. He could not help but think of Jaek as a man much like himself.

Finally able to speak, he leaned toward Saraph. "This Jaek must be one of the wealthiest men in this wealthiest of cities."

Saraph did not answer, to agree or disagree.

"I still have the pages of genealogical research he gave me and asked me to read," Zoltan said, his mind still a jumble of thoughts.

Saraph looked at him. "Your father?"

Zoltan nodded. "Of course, I never had time to read them, and quite honestly, wouldn't have read them if I'd had the time. I thought it was just the hobby of an old man. What's that to me? Five-hundred pages no less. As little as we saw one another, and as little he spoke, this subject made up ninety percent of what he had to say to me in those years just before the trip."

Zoltan looked at Saraph until he gained his eye contact.

"He was absolutely certain that our family line could be traced all the way back to this ancient city and some prominent family, even the Mousseion. Convinced my mother, too, and several other family members. Mom still bugs me about getting those pages out and looking at them. I thought he was just trying to get me to start using our family name, maybe include it in press releases here and there, add Antoniadis behind Zoltan on my door and desk at the office."

He watched Jaek as he interacted with the others. "Does he fund their travels?"

Saraph nodded.

"Why?" Zoltan asked. "What is his interest in these writings?"

Saraph shrugged. "*He* doesn't even know. But, you should understand that such an investment is quite insignificant to him financially. It amounts to a minor hobby. What is far more impressive is his dedication to the meetings themselves. This holds the highest priority on his annual calendar. Like the Scriptures the three scholars study, this week every year is sacred to Jaek."

Just as he finished saying this, Jaek stood up to speak. "Men of scroll and discipline," he began, "now that I have had my fun, please allow me to reassure you that I hold each of you in the highest esteem and the work you do with nothing less than reverence. In all of my acquaintances there is no one that is endeared to me on a level with any of the three of you. Your depth of character alone is of greater value than all the wealth of Alexandria and Rome combined. Your professional devotion to integrity and thorough evaluation is ever an inspiration to mine.

"Now, since I was the one who so rudely interrupted Solomon's presentation, it is only right that I redirect all of our attention to him. Solomon . . . ."

Jaek sat down and Solomon nodded. He slowly arranged his robe and prepared to stand even as he measured his words and prepared to speak.

Zoltan began looking around as if distracted. Then he looked at Saraph.

"There are no statues," he said. He glanced around again. "Not a single statue within sight."

"Association has its influence," Saraph said as he nodded toward the group at the table.

Zoltan recalled the question about his accusers as Solomon cleared his throat. He again considered the absence of that note.

"My dear brothers," Solomon said, "I have long considered this moment and have now concluded that many words will not add a single blessing that the contents of the package before us today will not far surpass on its own merits. So, without any help from me but to unwrap what I have traveled far to bring to you . . . ."

He began to rise from his chair to unwrap the package. The abbreviated introduction was the result of the time now shortened for Solomon's presentation and his eagerness to get it in before the morning was gone. He actually had two Scriptures he had intended to use in his introduction. Standing, he leaned forward and reached toward the package.

"Solomon, dear brother and supreme friend among friends, forgive me, please."

Solomon stood up straight and looked to his left, from where the voice of Josiah had just arrested his attention along with everyone else's.

"For what could you possibly need my forgiveness, Josiah?" he asked, poorly masking his annoyance.

Josiah stood to his feet.

"It shames me to interrupt this moment and risk any offense to you, not to mention any harm to the traditions of our meeting. But I came this year with two burdens on my heart, and I have already shared one of them with you. I fear that the other might cause me a distraction to your presentation that will prove costly if I do not first put it before you."

Understanding this to be another significant interruption, Solomon carefully gathered his robe and retook his seat. "Please," he said, "if our studies have taught us anything, it is that the heart of every man is the very thing that the Scriptures are intended to reach. If your heart is burdened, Josiah, please speak. No forgiveness is necessary."

Josiah and Solomon stared at one another for a moment. "Thank you," Josiah said. "I know it is true."

Zoltan looked at Jaek and noticed that he appeared impressed, perhaps as he himself was by Solomon's ease of spirit, and by this selfless love between friends. Perceiving that monumental efforts were required of each year's presenter, Zoltan thought that this demonstration was as powerful in its message as any written authority could possibly be.

"Friends, I have never spoken openly with you about the nature and motivation of my work," Josiah began. "I have preferred to only discuss the details of our textual dialogue. This is partly due to my private nature. But I also regard that I represent more than myself with my attendance here each year.

"In this I have treated you with some suspicion, as an opponent for whom I did not want to allow an advantage – that of knowing me. However, I have come to appreciate that the greatest of the fortunes of our unlikely introduction is not our shared scholarship. It is our friendships. Thus, I have decided that I must risk this disclosure if I am to hope for the help of my friends.

"I left Ethiopia some years ago because of an opportunity to study under the renowned Rabbi Gamaliel II. It was he that commended me for a disciplined nature readily applied to research and its administrative necessities. That is how I came into the service of Rabbi Simeon Ben Nathaniel, a disciple of Rabbi Johanen Ben Zakkai. I understand that you are not likely to be familiar with the celebrity of these great men. But, be assured, they are among the finest scholars of our time.

"My place among them is but the management of a few details of research – this in preparation for an upcoming gathering of seventy-two elders at Yavneh, in the vicinity of Joffa. Rabbi Nathaniel assigned me this task. It is this that originally brought me to Alexandria. Though once a sedentary scholar, my travels have not ceased since that time.

"In those days, if you recall, the primary focus of my research was the Great Synagogue – the one hundred and twenty elders who returned from exile. I had learned of two rabbinic academies in Alexandria that were sources of ancient records dealing extensively with the Great Synagogue.

"Almost immediately upon my arrival in Alexandria events took place ... calamities, the details of which we are all familiar. My plans were greatly altered, as were each of yours. Yet, with the help of our gracious host and his network of contacts, I was able to perform all of the research for which I came to this place."

Josiah stood before the others for a moment, silent and thoughtful. Then he continued.

"Perhaps I should back up a little and explain the motivation of the research. Some years ago a contention arose between two of our most influential rabbinic schools, Shammai and Hillel. The contention is over the *Qoheleth* and *the Song of Songs*, and whether these defile the hands. Probably due to the lofty status of these schools, the contention continues among some of our scholars to this day."

Jaek appeared puzzled as he glanced around to see if any one else looked the same. Getting Josiah's attention, he held his hands up and said, "That's the issue ... holiness, the handling of God-breathed texts making the hands unclean?"

Jaek's tone implied that he found this matter to be a mere triviality, and Josiah did not miss the implication.

"So, why the question of holiness only concerning *The Song* and *Ecclesiastes*?" Jaek wondered aloud, trying to cover his error.

Josiah looked at him. "Yes, that is the very nature of my dilemma."

They stared at one another.

"Most do consider these sacred Scriptures," Josiah said, letting go of the offense. "But that is the point of contention. There are those remnants of the school of Shammai that do not. Rabbis Nathaniel, Zakkai, and Gamaliel II hold the *Qoheleth* and the *Song of Songs* to be holy. Akiba, perhaps our greatest scholar, does also. But they are concerned that this contention will arise at Yavneh. If it does, it threatens to disrupt the meeting at Yavneh and the strategic proceedings that have been in planning for longer than most would guess."

Josiah again stopped to think for a moment. It was evident that his emotions were stirred. Taking time to settle himself, he stood silent.

"Please ... excuse me." He waited.

"The desolation of Jerusalem and the destruction of our Temple, along with the dispersion of the people of Israel far and wide, and the continuing persecution .... This is not a time for a division among our elders. Judaism is a Scripture-based foundation of faith. Now more than ever we need our Scriptures to be the focal point of our identity and unity, not a point of contention.

"That brings me to my humble roll in all of this. It was my job to prepare evidence of authoritative, official pronouncements from the past of the holiness of the two disputed books. Such historical evidence would inform against any disruptive contentions at the meeting of the seventy-two. Quite simply, I have failed."

"Meaning?" Jaek asked.

"Meaning, I have found no evidence for any such authoritative pronouncements. Even the Great Synagogue did not make such rulings. It only interpreted the texts that were already regarded as Scripture. I have not accomplished my assignment and Yavneh is nearly upon us."

"So, what you have found is that the Scriptures were established beyond any historical record? There's no previous office that authored their status as Scripture?" Solomon asked for clarification.

"For the Law and the Prophets that is true. Though I find no record of a ruling body or authority that established them, they were established just as we know them to be *before* the scope of our records. But for the Writings, there remain these two that are in question. I have yet to find any authority on which to base the resolve that is needed."

"Why is it needed?" Jaek asked.

The two men stared at one another as men speaking different languages.

"At this time, when our solidarity as a people is being threatened from all sides, we believe it is important," Josiah said slowly, "that when the elders meet at Yavneh … ."

"Forgive me," Jaek interrupted, "but, that is not what I was asking." He thought for a moment. "I am Alexandrian. I enjoy the identification. I shared words from the stones at the gymnasium with you. No one had to tell me to embrace those ideas. I had only to stop and read them to see myself as in a mirror chiseled in stone.

"Now, my love for those words is based on cultural identity. Surely something holding the status of Scripture should do the same and more in the hearts of believers. Perhaps all that is needed is the faith that such authority is already established.

What resolve could accomplish more than that, if identity is what you are concerned with?"

"Yes," Solomon agreed, "even more so where the Spirit of God penetrates the heart of a people with his word to set them apart for his holy purposes."

After a lengthy pause, Jaek looked around to see if anyone else was preparing to say anything. Seeing no indication, he said, "OK, my friends, another problem solved by the council of the four. Moving on now?" he asked suggestively. He was hoping to create a transition to the mystery of the black package.

"Council of the Four. I like that," Archippus said. "What do you think Solomon?"

Solomon spoke without hesitation. "We never needed a title before . . . ."

Archippus and Jaek looked at one another and shrugged. Archippus cleared his throat.

"Problem solved?" Jaek heard Josiah say. They looked at one another. "You have merely helped to confirm my problem. There is a list, if only in our minds. It is a list of those of the school who are suspected . . . of the movement. And there are signs, patterns that all recognize, like remaining silent when heresies come up that we once boldly denounced. Resurrection, for example," he said, looking to his left at Jaek.

"Three times I have been called before a council. And three times more pressing matters have spared me their questions. I have seen the excommunication of some of my brothers. I am not ready to . . . .

"It is almost too much that I am suspected and that my loyalty is in question. I must now return to Rabbi Nathaniel, the least of my superiors. I must tell him that I have failed in the task for which he has employed me over these many months."

"Failed?" Archippus objected. "You would have failed if in your zeal you had turned up something misleading."

"You have confirmed the work of God that *is*," Solomon added, "instead of the requirement of men that you wished to satisfy."

"But I have nothing to offer on which to anchor *Qoheleth* and the *Song of Songs*. Nothing to show for my employment, though I have labored diligently and with all my heart and whatever skill I possess. You yourselves have observed my passion in research. Yet I have nothing to show."

"Why not?" Jaek asked.

Again, the two men stared at one another blankly.

"You said yourself that you found no official ruling for the Law and the Prophets. You found only the authoritative testimony of antiquity – that observance beyond memory and record. Why would you demand anything less natural for these so called Writings."

"Or less *supernatural*," Archippus amended. "You … I should say we have the anchoring assurance that if it is of God, it will be done. He will anchor it in His time and His way. And it will likely not be by the authority of men. Perhaps you should use all you have gathered about the Scriptures and write a treatise on that for your superiors."

Josiah silently recalled the wisdom of the Gamalian maxim, as it had come to be called in his rabbinic community: *If it is of God, you cannot stop it, and if it is not of God, it will stop itself.*

"From where, after all, do the Scriptures come?" Solomon asked rhetorically.

"From the Holy Spirit of the Living God," Josiah said slowly, savoring the opportunity.

"The Holy Spirit is the uncomfortable answer to so many of our questions and demands for worldly definition," Solomon said, reminding himself most of all.

There was a long silence. They looked around at one another, each feeling that a statement of closure was needed. Yet, no one found that it would come to him. Josiah sat down.

"So, you actually came with three burdens," Archippus said, "the question about the passion for Scripture among the common Christians, your concern about failing in your commission, and the list. You'd have a hard time convincing me that, of the three, the third is not the weightiest for you to bear. The sooner you taste resolve, however difficult, it would seem the better."

Josiah looked back at Archippus, but gave no response.

"I know," Archippus added, "it's easy for me to say. I apologize for that. But I do believe it is the same for all of us—forsaking the world for Christ."

"Thank you," Josiah said. "Thank you all for your understanding and your counsel. It is like anointing oil upon my head. I will weigh these things. Solomon, please, continue in the tradition of the presentation. We are all eager."

"I must say, I, too, am eager to reveal to you my package," Solomon said, as he again stood. "I have longed to share it with you. It is the object of my labors to fulfill the duties of my turn as presenter these months since we last met."

He looked at Jaek. "A turn that I selfishly assumed to be mine, and thus stole from our esteemed host. He rightly pointed this out to all of us in such good humor earlier. In both his presentation of the cloths and his astute contributions to our dialogue, my heart has been quickened to apologize."

He bowed his head to demonstrate his respect. "My apologies to you, my valued friend."

"Mine as well," Archippus added, with an evident tone of contrition.

"And I," Josiah added, removing his hands from inside of his sleeves and holding them out palm up. "Your thoughtful contributions have often aided us in clarity."

Jaek was moved by these affirmations and held his emotions with difficulty. It was the first time that he had felt the inclusion of the others beyond his default roll as host. He had always attended the annual event bearing the unspoken status of outsider. He thought of himself as the worldly one who lacked official scholarship status and who was privileged to just attend. And he was willing to invest financially in that privilege, prizing the education.

"I suggest that in the future our meetings be hosted by a different man each year in his homeland," Solomon declared. "And Jaek will henceforth take his rightful turns with the duties of scholarship. In fact, I believe next year is your official turn as presenter."

Everyone looked at one another with unguarded surprise. "Oh my," Jaek exclaimed. "I will need a good bit of direction if I am to serve the group's traditions. But it will be an honor, one that I will support with the exhaustive industry that each of you have demonstrated in your turns."

Archippus put his hands in the air and the other men looked at him. "As long as everyone agrees to host by the example that Jaek has set for us these five years," he qualified. "I do think it is too much to host and present in the same year. If I may suggest an early amendment to your plan, Solomon: I suggest that one man presents in another man's homeland. I offer my home as our sight next year."

"Here, here!" Solomon followed.

"Agreed," Josiah said, with a smile that weakly masked his concern. He was thinking about the challenges that such an endeavor would pose in either his homeland, or his present community. "As long as my turn to host is last," he finally added with a laugh that was quickly joined by his friends."

"Now brothers, I must say that we have demolished the tradition of presenting on the second day. My presentation will have to wait until tomorrow if it is to receive its due," Solomon informed them.

As levity around the table turned into animated abjections, Solomon reached over and removed the black package from its placement in the center of the table. "I am sorry," he said, "but as you can see, we are nearing the lunch hour. I didn't prepare for a year to rush through this."

"What about this afternoon?" Jaek asked.

"Our tradition is to spend the afternoon hours making use of Alexandria's vast resources for our studies," Solomon answered. "It seems unwise to destroy a second tradition merely because we did so with the first."

He looked at Archippus and then Josiah. "And tonight our host has planned for us another of the extraordinary dining experiences of this fine establishment of his... suffering the peculiarities of each of our diets. I will see you all then."

Solomon bent over and carefully placed the package into the travel case beside his chair. Then, he stood up to face the bent brows on each of the other three men.

"I am as eager as you are. But we will wait until tomorrow."

Zoltan and Saraph looked at one another and Saraph shrugged his shoulders.

"Are you kidding me?" Zoltan protested.

Saraph smiled. "We'll just have to come back tomorrow for another episode of...."

Zoltan shook his head. "No, they will have to come back. We get to fast forward."

Chapter 16
TO THE CORINTHIANS

Solomon was already seated at the table when Josiah approached, returning from the break that followed the morning devotions of day three of the meeting. Josiah's arms were crossed; his hands were inside of his sleeves, each grasping the opposite elbow. Jaek and Archippus walked together not far behind.

Josiah politely bowed, greeting Solomon as he rose to his feet.

"Welcome back," Solomon said.

The greetings multiplied as the other two men arrived at the table. And, as cheery as they all were that morning, the conversation quickly died away. The black, bound package on the table had again stolen everyone's attention. And they all knew that Solomon was willing for no more interruptions. Nor were they, for that matter.

"Solomon's not fooling around today, is he?" Zoltan said to Saraph.

"No, he's definitely not."

Everyone stood at attention around the table without saying a word. Solomon leaned over and pulled two ends of the black ribbon that had bound the package, forming a large, simple bow at its center. As he let go of the two ends, they fell to the sides and two others naturally fell open upon the table at the top and bottom. The longer end fell toward Jaek's orientation.

The result was the scalloped form of a cross laid out upon the table, the square package at its center. And raised upon its black surface was royal violet stitching that formed the Star of David. In its center was a scarlet dot the size of a small coin.

So great was the impression that the four men stood in silence for several minutes. Three of them were staring at the forms on the table before them. Only Solomon looked around to observe the faces of the others.

"Wow," Zoltan said. "That is powerful. A man after my own heart."

"With regard to aesthetics and drama perhaps," Saraph responded. "But he follows the tradition established in previous years. Each has treated the Scriptures with this sacred dignity in his turn. There is an unspoken agreement upon excellence in their presentations."

Jaek quietly pulled out his chair and took his seat while looking up to see the reactions of the others. Then he leaned forward to admire the craftsmanship more closely. Solomon was next to sit down. Archippus remained standing, his left arm resting across the top of his abdomen, his right arm propped upon it and his hand slowly stroking his thick beard.

Josiah's crossed arms seemed to be tucked further into the opposite sleeves than usual. His head was bent downward and his eyes closed. Solomon looked up and watched as he turned and began walking around the table slowly, his head still bowed and his eyes appearing to remain closed. Archippus sat down.

"My brothers, please forgive any offense that the combining of these symbols before us may arouse," Solomon said. He was perplexed by Josiah's response.

He sat quietly for a moment.

"I beg your forbearance," he continued. "It was with trepidation that I proceeded in this manner, understanding the usual dichotomy imposed between these treasured icons of our respective origins of faith.

"But as I studied the Scriptures during recent months in preparation for my journey to be with you here, the Spirit of God would not relent in this impression upon my heart."

Solomon reached down beside his chair and brought up two scrolls, which he laid on the table before him. He thought for a moment. Then he reached for one of the scrolls.

"From the Septuagint," he said, "and the book of Jeremiah." He then began to read, carefully articulating each word of the Greek text before him.

> "The time is coming," declares the Lord, "when I will make a new covenant with the house of Israel and with the house of Judah. It will not be like the old covenant I made with your forefathers when I took them by the hand to lead them out of Egypt, because they broke My covenant, though I was a husband to them," declares the Lord. "This is the covenant I will make with the house of Israel after that time," declares the Lord. "I will put My law in their minds and write it on their hearts. I will be their God, and they will be My people. No longer will a man teach his neighbor, or a man his brother, saying, 'Know the Lord,' because they will all know Me, from the least of them to the greatest," declares the Lord.
>
> "For I will forgive their wickedness and will remember their sins no more."

Solomon closed the scroll as he lowered it. Then, moving slowly, he leaned over to put it in the container beside him. He took great care, using a methodical process in the handling of his scrolls. The others waited patiently. Josiah continued walking around the table.

Zoltan was watching Josiah and noticed tears streaming

down his face. He tapped Saraph on the shoulder and nodded toward the Rabbi. Saraph looked at Zoltan. "He knows by heart this passage and the Scriptures that follow. And he and Archippus were prepared, just as Solomon was, with these same passages before they came here."

"Who told them?"

"The Holy Spirit of God, of course."

Like, he can know something like that, Zoltan thought. *Who does he think he's kidding?*

Solomon picked up the second scroll and opened it. "From the Hebrew text," he said, "and from the book of Ezekiel." Then he began to read:

> I will give you a new heart and put a new spirit in you; I will remove from you your heart of stone and give you a heart of flesh. And I will put My spirit in you and move you to follow My decrees and be careful to keep My laws.

Solomon lowered the scroll.

Knowing that it would be a few minutes before Solomon would emerge from his work at the side of his chair, Jaek stood up and walked to the nearby hut. He poured four glasses of water and brought them to the table on a tray. Then he returned the tray to the hut.

It wasn't until he returned the second time that Solomon was again sitting up in his chair. Three of the glasses had been safely placed on the ground beside each man's chair, one on the table.

"Sorry," Jaek said, looking at Archippus. "I forgot." He quickly took a drink and then set his cup on the ground.

"Brothers," Solomon began, "in the desert of Sinai, not so far from where we sit, only a millennia and a handful of centuries from our day, Moses declared to the people of Israel, 'Behold, the blood of the covenant!' In the passages I have just read to you and in many others that I have not, the Lord made known to us His intention to establish a *new covenant*. And we would all attest to the importance of considering the Scriptures in their covenantal context.

"To think of the Scriptures in any other way ... ." He paused. "As an example: to allow the title 'wedding contract' to suggest only a revered legal form, is to risk honoring a medium of strictly legal communication, while disregarding the spirit of what is communicated. And that is, a binding commitment based upon covenantal love. In this same way, the Scriptures are a documentation of a covenantal relationship.

"We know that even before Sinai our God established His covenant with our father Abraham. We also know that His covenant was established by blood and sacrifice. Thus, we had this precedent upon which to anticipate the advent of the new covenant spoken of by the prophets.

"Now, when Jeremiah and Ezekiel make their declarations of the new covenant, they identify two novelties that distinguish the new covenant from the previous. First, they inform that the new covenant will be written on the human hearts of God's people. Its faithful observance will be compelled *from within* and not managed by external offices and authorities.

"The second novelty is perhaps the greater departure from the former relationship. It is the declaration of *complete forgiveness* of *all sin*."

Solomon looked to his left, momentarily distracted by the sound of Josiah pulling his chair away from the table, finally concluding his prayerful walk. He watched as the rabbi took his seat.

Solomon thought for a moment. Then, he stood. "Dear friends, it is in this context that I present to you this year's scriptural text."

He leaned forward and removed the black covering, revealing a leather-bound book of papyrus pages.

Jaek sat up and leaned forward, his eyes wide.

"An accounting book?" he exclaimed.

"It is a codex."

"I know what it is," Jaek said. "I use them to manage my businesses. All of my administrative details are in these. I didn't know they were used for anything else, let alone something sacred. May I?" he asked, looking at Solomon.

"Of course."

All four of the men were leaning forward, their chests pressed against the table.

"To the Corinthians," Jaek read aloud. As he turned the pages his mouth fell open. "Why a codex?" he asked, looking up at Solomon. "I mean, so common." He looked back down at the book. "It seems strange to move the sacred from the scroll to the medium of the common businessman."

"I'm not certain," Solomon stated. But I have had several Christian writings pass through my hands recently and they have all been on codices. This one is a letter. I have yet to see one on a scroll. Have you?" he asked, looking at Archippus.

"Are we not ahead of ourselves in calling the text on those pages sacred?"

"So, Jaek objects to the physical form and you object to the content? Have you seen it before? Have you read it?"

"I have avoided such writings all together. So, I've not seen them on scroll or in codice form."

"Really? Why?"

"Obviously you have changed your position on this matter as well as forgotten our discussions from the last meeting," Archippus said. His tone indicated his concern about Solomon's judgment.

Solomon sat back and reflected for a moment. "Help my aged memory," he requested humbly.

"There are several reasons," Archippus began. "The crudest is that I have dedicated my life to transcribing the Scriptures.

I will never complete what is before me should I live to be a hundred." He chuckled. "I don't need a new career."

Archippus said this for Solomon's sake, to relieve some of the tension he sensed at the table.

"Most important, however, we have the Scriptures. It goes back to our conversation yesterday. The Scriptures are known. Among all believers, Jew and Christian, they are as they have been for generations, and everyone acknowledges them. There are issues, questions about peripheral texts. But primarily we know them for their God-breathed content.

"They are the Scriptures that our Messiah himself used, meditated upon, quoted and fulfilled. I haven't seen it, but I have heard of a book written by a physician named Luke, a historian. He relates a story about the risen Christ meeting with two unbelieving followers. As I understand it, on that occasion the Lord Jesus opened their eyes by revealing himself to them in all the Scriptures – that is, the Law, the Prophets and the Writings."

Zoltan looked at Saraph and raised his brows, recalling his earlier reference to Luke of Antioc. "Same guy?" he asked.

Saraph nodded. "But a different record."

"If he revealed himself through all of the known Scriptures, what need do we have of others?" Archippus asked in conclusion.

"Wait a second," Zoltan said to Saraph. "So, this guy is a Christian and he doesn't believe in the Christian Bible?"

"You have to remember that it doesn't exist yet. This is all brand new to them. To Archippus, the Jewish Bible *is* the Bible. There is no other. To him, all others are newly introduced, individual writings, not a cohesive body of divinely inspired literature."

Solomon was thinking about the assertions by Archippus.

"What about this gospel of Luke's? I have not seen it either. But I understand it to be about the Lord's life, His actions, and

His teachings. You don't want to know these things?"

"I do, I must admit. But does that make the report of them Scripture? Besides, I have them. The Scriptures proclaim them, they point to Him and identify His character, His ways, details about His life and death and resurrection."

Zoltan was again surprised. "They believed that this early?" He asked Saraph. "I thought that part of the legend didn't begin developing until the third century or so."

Jaek's attention also keyed in on this last point and he made a note to himself to talk with Josiah about this privately. They had had a running dialogue on the matter of resurrection in previous years. He had chosen Josiah because he considered his opinion on this one to be more objective than those of the other two, and thus, more credible. He found the whole notion outrageous. But he was continually amazed to discover that many people believed it.

He looked up to see Josiah looking at him as if he wanted to say something. Archippus and Solomon had also noticed this and appeared to be waiting for Josiah's words.

Josiah dropped his gaze and looked down at the table in front of his arms. He shook his head.

"Resurrection?" Jaek asked.

Josiah tilted his head and nodded subtly. "I asked Gamaliel II after you and I talked last year."

"And?"

"He affirmed what I thought I'd found, which I had related to you. He said it is in the Law, the Prophets, and the Writings."

Jaek just stared at Josiah, unsure what to think of this information. The four men were quiet for more than five minutes.

A breeze moved across the patio and reached the group carrying the scent of the Sea. Zoltan closed his eyes and took in the pleasure.

"We were talking about Luke, the physician's writings,"

Solomon finally said. "Archippus, you were saying something about the Scriptures containing all we need about the Messiah."

"Look," Archippus said, "before the Messiah came to us, faithful men and women looked for the consolation of Israel because of the Scriptures. For fifty years since His ascension into glory, His Church has grown, spread, thrived and matured by studying the Scriptures. They are the elegant mysteries that beckon the treasure hunter and promise the reward of Christ's discovery. They contain the very mystery of Christ, now revealed to us.

"Of course, I am also partial because I came to put my faith in Him through the Scriptures, as you did also. All of the brothers and sisters known between us did so as well. I know of no one who has come to Christ through any other tool or testament.

"From Boaz to Jonah to Shadrach, Meshach and Abednego, we see foreshadows of the Messiah in the Holy Scriptures. He is the eternal King on David's throne, the Good Shepherd of Psalm 23, the Suffering Servant of Isaiah .... He is our Sabbath rest."

"The Sabbath rest?" Josiah asked, reacting with surprise. In rabbinic circles the Sabbath had grown in prominence since the destruction of Jerusalem and the Temple and the great dispersion that followed. It had become a point of ascent regarding Jewish customs and Israel's solidarity.

Archippus looked at Josiah. "Jesus taught that He is Lord of the Sabbath. He told His disciples to come to Him because His burden is light and easy. He is the fulfillment of the Sabbath, our spiritual rest."

"How do you know that He taught that?" Solomon asked.

"It has been told to me by many faithful witnesses, several who heard the words firsthand."

"One hundred years from now, how will someone know?"

"The same way, except for the firsthand witnesses."

"*Dvarim*: 'And these *words* which I am commanding you today shall be upon your heart.' How do you know of Moses' report? You believe God's words reported through Moses because you have the Scriptures. Wouldn't you expect the same for those who would have the very words of our Lord generations from now?"

Archippus frowned.

"Looks like it is written by two men," Jaek interrupted. He began to read aloud, "'Paul, called to be an apostle of Christ Jesus by the will of God, and our brother Sosthenes.' There's a solid Greek name in the mix for you," he said, looking up. "Who are they?"

"I've been told about a man named Saul who was a Pharisee, but he became a preacher of the gospel of Christ Jesus, proclaiming it boldly everywhere," Archippus answered.

"Yes, he is the same one who is now known as Paul," Solomon agreed. "He was an apostle, and established many churches throughout the Roman territories. It may be that Sosthenes was a scribe and ministry partner. I have heard that Paul had trouble with his eyes and did not write on his own."

"Josiah, you know about this ex-Pharisee?" Jaek questioned.

For a moment it was quiet. Josiah's head was hung low near the table, his chin almost resting on his hands. Jaek resumed reading silently.

"The elders do not like anyone to speak of him," Josiah said soberly.

Jaek looked up at Archippus and then Solomon, silently requesting details.

"Among those loyal to Judaism, he is a heretic," Solomon told Jaek.

"That is not the reason," Josiah said. "It is when any of the brothers speak of him as such that they are rebuked. His name was Saul. He was revered greatly among the elders. He was one of our superior scholars, trained by Gamaliel himself. He was the most zealous defender of our God and our faith among all the Jews. So, they consider him…not merely gone, nonexistent. His loss was great—to some personally, like the loss of a brother. True, he also became a great problem…." Josiah paused. "Still yet, a nonexistent one."

"I see" Jaek said. "He switched sides, and now he has come to be a major force for the other team."

None of the scholars appreciated this crude rendering of the situation in sports terms, least of all, Josiah.

Jaek retreated back to his reading as the others sat in silence, contemplating.

"Yes, a great loss," Josiah said quietly.

Jaek looked up and stared at him, understanding that he now spoke literally of the man's death. A look of apology was in his eyes for his glib remark.

"Martyred under Nero I have been told," Solomon added.

Josiah nodded.

"If I may …." Archippus said, not wanting the cloud of sentiment to influence the group's decision. He waited respectfully until he had received an affirming indicator from each of the others.

"It may have great value," he finally stated, resuming the previous discussion. Then he reached over and touched the open pages in front of Jaek. He shook his head. "I'm sorry, but it doesn't comply with the standards of our tradition."

Solomon was thoughtful before responding. "Which are?" he asked.

"Texts that are universally established among the Jews as Spirit-breathed, authoritative Scripture."

"Will you force the distinction between "Jews" that you counseled Josiah not to make yesterday when he spoke of his burden about dedication to the Scriptures? Those from whom

144

I received this *are* Jews. They regard it as Scripture and many copies are being circulated among the brethren, Jews and non-Jews.

"My spirit bears witness with God's Spirit to its origin as well. Isn't that the authoritative process we discussed just yesterday? It is a letter from an attested apostle of Jesus Christ to a church in Corinth. We are far from Corinth, and my community does not share some of the struggles addressed in these pages. Yet our eagerness for this letter, written to others, grips our hearts and those of believers far and wide. I will say that such eagerness preceded its arrival in our hands."

The four men volleyed thoughtful glances around the table. Solomon reached beside his chair for his cup of water.

"One of the concerns that I bring to this meeting," Archippus said solemnly, "is the circulation of these so called 'new' Scriptures."

"Go on," Solomon encouraged.

"The word *new* regarding Scripture has never been used before. Yet, whenever I hear of these, the word new is used. 'New' is a short lived novelty. It won't be long before it settles in as something more profound, a consciousness about Scriptures that renders the new as preferred and implies another word... old. Isn't this dangerously close to a subtle outmoding of the Scriptures that we each hold dear?"

"Precisely why I chose this text and introduced it in the context of the covenantal procession. Allow me, as is our custom, to read a selected portion of the text."

Zoltan tapped Saraph on the shoulder. "Got any other ideas? This is getting over my head."

"Is that even possible?" Saraph asked. "Trust me, you don't want to miss this."

Zoltan was pretty sure he did want to miss it, and the remainder of the discussion as well. But he was less sure that he wanted to risk thinking about any of the tempting destinations he had been working to squeeze from his mind. The peace he had enjoyed since arriving back at the table kept him there. But he had hoped that Saraph would offer another suggestion. The council of the four, he concluded, was the safest place to redirect his thoughts.

Archippus and Josiah had been sitting quietly, weighing Solomon's request. Jaek had been looking from one to the other anticipating a response. "I found something pretty interesting," he finally said. They looked at him and then at Solomon. Then, Josiah and Archippus looked at Jaek and nodded.

Jaek rubbed his fingers of his right hand across the surface of the page in front of him. He held them up and examined the white powder on their tips.

"Your marking?" he asked, looking at Solomon.

"It is," Solomon responded.

"Very interesting reading right there. Do you mind?"

"Please."

Jaek read aloud:

> For Christ did not send me to baptize, but to preach the gospel, not in cleverness of speech, that the cross of Christ should not be made void. For the word of the cross is to those who are perishing foolishness, but to us who are being saved it is the power of God. For it is written,
> "I will destroy the wisdom of the wise,
> And the cleverness of the clever I will set aside."
> Where is the wise man? Where is the scribe? Where is the debater of this age? Has not God made foolish the wisdom of the world? For since in the wisdom of God the world through its wisdom did not come to know God, God was well-pleased through the foolishness of the message preached to save those who believe.
> For indeed Jews ask for signs, and Greeks search

for wisdom; but we preach Christ crucified, to Jews a stumbling block, and to Gentiles foolishness, but to those who are the called, both Jews and Greeks, Christ the power of God and the wisdom of God.

When Jaek had finished reading, he looked across the table at Josiah, who he had heard mumble something quietly.

"What was that?" Jaek asked.

"Isaiah," he said, "he quotes Isaiah."

Jaek looked at Solomon, who was rising to his feet, and then at Archippus. They both just shrugged, deferring to Josiah's judgment, as both considered him the superior scholar among them.

Solomon leaned forward and placed his hands upon the table.

"You see, my friends, it is this very cross of Christ that Paul speaks of that is the fulfillment of a new covenant that God promised through the prophets. It is this supreme covenant to which the first covenant pointed."

He looked across the table at his friend and Christian brother.

"Archippus, if such as this will come to be realized as Scripture, it will harmonize with all Scripture as one message revealing and confirming this covenantal grace of God. That is the nature of all that is and ever will be Scripture. And the spirit of God confirms this through the members of Christ's body, the Church that He inhabits – Jew first, and also Gentiles."

Solomon took his seat as he did everything else, slowly. He held the back of his robe in such a way as to prevent wrinkling. He shuffled his feet and touched the backs of his legs against the chair for ideal positioning before lowering himself. Collectively these movements had the appearance of a formal bow.

"Interesting," Jaek said. "See if I understand this.... So, this

Paul speaks of Christ and His gospel in the same way that I have heard each of you speak of your Holy Scriptures for these past five years.

"What is it the three of you always say? 'Born of God's Spirit and spiritually discerned.' He speaks of Christ as if He is the Scriptures, like he is the Word Himself."

Solomon and Archippus looked at one another with amazement in their eyes.

"What?" Jaek asked. "Did I say something irreverent?"

"No," Archippus answered. "It's widely known throughout our community of faith that the Apostle John's favorite title for the Master is 'The Word.'"

"Like I said, very interesting."

Jaek looked down and turned a page. "Here is another one of the marked sections."

This time he did not wait for permission, he just began to read.

> Yet we do speak wisdom among those who are mature; a wisdom, however, not of this age, nor of the rulers of this age, who are passing away; but we speak God's wisdom in a mystery, the hidden wisdom, which God predestined before the ages to our glory; the wisdom which none of the rulers of this age has understood; for if they had understood it, they would not have crucified the Lord of glory. But just as it is written,
>
> Things which eye has not seen and ear has not heard,
>
> And which have not entered the heart of man,
>
> All that God has prepared for those who love Him.
>
> For to us God revealed them by His Spirit; for the Spirit searches all things, even the depths of God. For who among men knows the thoughts of a man except the spirit of the man, which is in

him? Even so the thoughts of God no one knows except the Spirit of God. Now we have received, not the spirit of the world, but the Spirit who is from God, that we might know the things freely given to us by God.

When he finished reading, he looked up at Josiah. Josiah nodded and said, "Isaiah again." Solomon and Archippus looked at one another and simultaneously raised their brows.

"OK, I think I'm getting the gist of this," Zoltan said to Saraph. "These men, along with this Paul have deluded themselves—all except Jaek, that is. They believe that anyone that does not agree with their definition of Scriptures, or hold their reverence for the content in them is lacking this special quality they call spiritual discernment. How convenient. I'm glad we came. Next…."

But they remained at their place beside the table, as Zoltan did not actually have a "next" in mind. They stared into one another's eyes for several seconds before turning back toward the small council of friends.

"Josiah, you are unusually quiet. I hope I have not offended you terribly," Solomon said.

"Terribly, no. A little, maybe. I am not so fragile. And, of course, we have touched on some of this before. So I am not shocked. And it is I who set the precedent two years ago for using the presentation to put forward a compelling case for my point of view. I should expect, and must allow you to do the same."

He looked around the table, making eye contact with each of his friends. "Aside from that," he said, "God is instructing me. It is wise to remain silent when He is speaking."

Zoltan tapped Saraph on the shoulder once again. "Hey," he said, "I really just stayed around to see what was in the wrapping."

"It's your call," Saraph answered.

Zoltan heard Jaeks voice, and turned to listen.

"The next section you have marked says this:
> Let no man deceive himself. If any man among
> you thinks that he is wise in this age, let him be-
> come foolish that he may become wise. For the
> wisdom of this world is foolishness before God.
> For it is written, He is the one who catches the
> wise in their craftiness."

Hearing Josiah's quiet voice, Jaek stopped and looked up.

"Job," Josiah said. "He quotes here from the book of Job."

"This Josiah guy is good," Zoltan said to Saraph.

"Only a rare few are better," Saraph said.

"And again," Jaek continued reading, "The Lord knows that the thoughts of the wise are futile." He stopped and looked across the table.

Josiah squinted as if thinking hard. Then he relaxed his face and smiled at Jaek. "Just kidding," he said, "of course it is from the Psalms."

"Yes, of course," Jaek said as his head dropped onto the book below and he laughed with amazement.

"Hey, hey!" Solomon exclaimed. "You'll get oil on the papyrus!"

Jaek looked up to apologize, but saw that all three of his friends were laughing. Archippus informed him of the large white smudge on his forehead and he wiped his brow.

"There is another section I have marked," Solomon said to Jaek. "I marked it last night especially for you. You might have to turn a few pages." He leaned over and helped Jaek locate the passage.

"OK, yes, right there, that's it. I thought you would appre-ciate this in respect to your athlete's creed, which you kindly shared with us."

Jaek read aloud once again:
> Do you not know that those who run in a race all

run, but only one receives the prize? Run in such a way that you may win. And everyone who competes in the games exercises self-control in all things. They then do it to receive a perishable wreath, but we an imperishable. Therefore I run in such a way, as not beating the air; but I buffet my body and make it my slave, lest possibly, after I have preached to others, I myself should be disqualified.

When he had finished, Jaek pushed the book toward the middle of the table. Reclining back in his chair, he looked at Solomon. "Thank you," he said with meaning.

Archippus took hold of the book and pulled it toward him. He began turning the pages slowly.

Zoltan tapped Saraph on the shoulder. "This whole history lesson, and . . . ." He was quiet for a moment, looking at Jaek as if saying goodbye. "Something about Jaek reminds me of an old friend of mine."

Chapter 17
ROOM OF A THOUSAND STORIES

I t was a split-level room with a large stone fireplace in the middle of the lower level. The fireplace was open on two sides. Both levels were custom finished in warm maple woodwork with the evident attention of a skilled craftsman.

The upper level was dominated by shelving systems that took up two full walls, breaking only for the door frame on one wall and a small window over a built-in, roll-top desk on the other. The third wall was covered with an array of mounted animals, framed pictures, small, ornamental shelves holding carvings and sculptures, and numerous brackets bearing rifles that all were at least a hundred years old. Mixed throughout this level on shelves, pedestals, small tables and decorative stands were artifacts, mechanical devices and instruments of every vintage and discipline imaginable.

Just before the step down to the lower level was a large structural beam that descended two feet from where it met the ceiling and formed a long horizontal divider. It suggested the later addition of the lower portion of the room. It also gave the impression of an introduction to that half of the room.

Along this strip of upper divide were mounted three items of exceptional crafting. To the far left was an original flintlock rifle from the mid-1700s with a tiger maple stock, daisy patch box, and brass and silver inlay. On the right was a replica of an eleventh century Arabian scimitar. Its handle bore numerous jewels of many different colors held in gold-plated settings. Between the two was a long scroll in a glass tube with two beautifully carved olive wood handles at each end.

The lower level of the room was a half circle made up of one continuous wall of windows. It was a bright and open space with but a few chairs facing outward in front of the windows. The floorspace was dominated by two large bear hides and two enormous antique easels, both nearly ten feet tall. The two held comically small oil paintings and stood adjacent to the fireplace at the foot of the two stairs on both sides of the room. They appeared as hosts, welcoming, drawing visitors down into that section of the room, or as gatekeepers through whom all must pass upon entering. All who came there had one of these two perceptions of the two easels and the paintings. By this display the two small paintings announced their significance, like precious gems mounted in the center of massive gold rings.

The openness created by the windows and the round shape of the lower level presented a purposed contrast to the business of the upper level. Whereas stories abounded within the shelves and upon the tables and stands of the upper level, the construction of the lower level drew one's attention outside the room. There, even more stories waited, though they were not as easily recognized or told.

It was there that Saraph stood looking out from the glass enclosure to the flowers and trees in the foreground, the winding river below. The multicolored beauty of the hills layered the distant landscape like the feather-spread flight of the great hawk that he presently watched gliding to a perch just below his view. The roundness of the room mimicked the formation of the bluff that it rested on. No more than twenty feet from where Saraph was standing was a drop of several hundred feet to the banks of the Missouri River. He stood awed, a child in love. "Epiphany all!" he whispered.

Zoltan was standing with his hands on his knees. He was leaning forward to study the detailing of a scale replica of a sixteenth century English ship. He heard Saraph coming up the steps and looked over his shoulder to see that he now stood behind him. Zoltan turned back and continued to admire the vessel. "'They marked our passage as a race of men, Earth will not see such ships as those again,'" he finally spoke, quoting John Mansfield. "This marked the beginning of the truly great sailing vessels. The Golden Lion, one of the first English galleons. They out-sailed and outfought the formerly invincible Spanish Armada. Christopher Columbus would have loved to have captained one of these. It's just the way I remember it ... the model, that is." He shook his head. "Brilliant!"

Zoltan stood up and looked around. "It's exactly as I remember it."

"There are a lot of '*its*' here. What *it* are you referring to?" Saraph asked.

Zoltan looked back at Saraph and then made a gesture with his hands that encompassed the entire upper level of the room. "This 'room of a thousand stories,' as I have always called it from the day I first came here."

Simultaneously, Zoltan and Saraph turned, hearing footsteps approaching from another room. A short, portly man walked into the room, passed them and sat at the roll-top desk and began writing. Zoltan was taken back.

"Col. Ericson!" he blurted out, as if expecting the man to recognize him with reciprocal enthusiasm.

"He cannot hear you. Remember ... ?"

Zoltan looked at Saraph, walked over and stood by the man and examined him closely. "Old Spice, just like my dad," he announced with a chuckle. "I remember that."

Saraph came and stood beside them, watching over the man's shoulder as he wrote.

"It sure is him!" Zoltan declared. "I could never forget his face. But, I remember him so tall and stout, like a lumberjack. A bald, spectacled lumberjack, but tall and formidable. He *is* a barrel-chested fella. But he can't … he can't be more than five-and-a-half feet tall."

"Disappointed?"

"I guess I was a little guy myself then," Zoltan said, ignoring the question. "Look at that shirt. Perfectly pressed! I even remember the colors in the plaid. Even his blue jeans look straight from the store." He stepped back and looked under the desk. "Yep, white snakeskin cowboy boots! When he gets up I'll show you, he has this fantastic belt buckle. Well, look … look here, you can see the intricacies of the carvings in his leather belt. Wow, just as I remember."

Ericson stood up, set his pen upon the paper and placed them in the center of the desk. As he turned, Zoltan leaned forward to see the belt buckle. It was five inches tall and six or seven wide. In the center of the shiny silver was a sculpted man carrying a cross. He frowned and stood up. *Wow, how could I have forgotten about that?* he thought, and decided not to point it out.

Col Ericson walked to the end of the room on the lower level and stood still with his hands clasped behind his back looking out of the center window. After several minutes he turned and walked briskly from the room.

Saraph followed him to the doorway and looked into the other room.

"He was my hero!" Zoltan said excitedly, as he watched the man leave. "I really can't remember having any others."

"Was?"

Zoltan looked at Saraph strangely. "Well, that was years ago."

"What do you … *did* you find so remarkable about him?"

"I think I was around seven years old when I first met him, first came here. He was the friendliest adult I remember meeting as a kid. And he made me feel important, like *he* was great and *I* was someone to him. I didn't feel like a 'kid' around him. I felt honored. He was a refined, calculating man. You saw him ... pressed, fitted shirt and pants. Those are the same shirt and pants I remember him in, as if it were yesterday." Zoltan looked around. "I mean, look at this room. Neat, clean, everything dusted and polished. Everything is exactly as I remember it."

Stopping beneath the scimitar, Zoltan stared up at the weapon and admired its quality. He dropped his gaze and looked back at Saraph.

"Best of all, he was a great storyteller. There are stories for everything in this room, and he knew every one of them." Zoltan slowly toured the room as he spoke, stopping to examine certain items that caught his eye as he went. "They were exciting stories of danger, heroism, wilderness, treachery, and history, real names attached to all of the exploits. He told me many and made me long for the others." Zoltan again stopped and looked at Saraph. "That longing he stirred in me may be the most powerful elixir I have ever consumed. My appetite for learning has been insatiable from the day I met him."

"This *is* that day," Saraph said.

Zoltan instinctively reached up to lift a rifle from deer antler brackets. Touching it he remembered immediately that he could not affect it in any way. He felt frustrated by the tension of desirable things appearing so near and accessible. "I'd love to hold that one in my hands as I did before. Would it hurt to suspend the ... ?" He stopped short, noting the stern objection on Saraph's face.

"He never said, 'don't touch,'" Zoltan continued. "In fact, whenever he was telling me a story he would pick up the object that brought the story to his mind and hand it to me. I felt the history in my hands as I heard it with my ears. I felt as though I was a part of it, and that brought it to life.

"Most people ... you know, especially adults dealing with kids ... you know how they are. 'Yes, and here behind the glass case – please don't stand too close – is the porcelain doll my great, great aunt brought over on the boat from Germany,'" Zoltan mocked. Then he shook his head. "Not Col. Ericson. These were precious to him, but I was more. I never dropped anything, but the possibility was there in the invitation. Engaging my boyish wonder and impregnating me with a spirit of adventure was greater to him than the value of any of these things.

"Yes, that is special," noted Saraph.

"I remember feeling dangerous holding that rifle as he told me a story about George Drouillard. He was the Frenchman who served as chief shore hunter for Lewis and Clark's Corps of Discovery. It was about the first encounter with a bear on the expedition." Zoltan continued to peruse the artifacts as he spoke, frequently distracted. "It turned out to be the first bear meal for the Corps just after it was nearly the first mortal disaster. True story! He told it to me himself." Zoltan said this, glancing over at Saraph to mark the point. "That's the rifle…," he said, pointing back to where he stood a moment before. "It's just like the one he used for hunting and for trade with the Osage Indians. It is of Quebec make, late eighteenth century vintage."

"Amazing memory, and amazing retention for a seven-year-old," Saraph said admiringly.

"Are you kidding? That man lit a fire in me. I went home and read everything I could get my hands on about Lewis and Clark and the American frontiersmen. I read about the French explorers who preceded them along the Missouri and Mississippi rivers. I even participated in a couple of reenactments in my college years. We've done a couple of documentaries on the Corps of Discovery throughout the years as well."

Zoltan folded his arms and smiled, pleased to stare into the past. "One Halloween I was Drouillard and my neighbor was Belle Oiseau, my Osage wife. My friend, David, was Françoise Labiche, a colorful Frenchman who served as a waterman and interpreter on the Corps of Discovery. Did you know that there were twelve Frenchman on the expedition? Without their skills as watermen and interpreters, and their knowledge of the river ways and the Indian cultures along them, the expedition would have proved impossible."

"This expedition ... was it big? I mean, was it important?"

Zoltan looked at Saraph with shock and incredulity etched in every line upon his contorted face. "Surely you are joking!" he finally begged.

"Nope. It didn't make it to my desk, you might say. I may have been tending some small movements in other plac-es ... galaxies maybe." Saraph said this with a shrug, taking the opportunity to plant a suggestive seed in the soils of won-der-lust. He hoped his companion would soon take hold of the gift and, inspired by these artifacts, make flight for their origins, or greater cosmic adventures. He was intrigued by the title Corps of Discovery and was developing anticipation of a visit. But Zoltan only rolled his eyes and shook his head, purposefully ignoring whatever he sensed might be wrapped inside Saraph's comment. He noted only what he saw as a bit of gamesmanship.

"Yes, too busy, I'm sure, to pay any mind to one of the most pivotal moments in the grand history of this great na-tion," Zoltan chided. "One that has ...." He stopped short and looked over his shoulder to locate Saraph walking toward the windows at the other end of the room. His hands were clasped behind his back. Annoyed by Saraph's apparent disinterest, Zoltan turned back to his investigations. More than a half an hour passed in silence.

Finally he spoke again. "You might be interested in this," he said solemnly. "Col. Ericson is a World War II veteran." Zoltan stopped and looked toward the other end of the room. "That is a famous war in our history, by the way. It did not take place here, but in other parts of the world. A very big affair. He has here a sardine can filled with water. I'll read you this note he has beside it."

Looking down at the note Zoltan paused again. He could not help but take notice that a portion of the paper it was typed on was wet. Compelled, he reached to touch it to confirm what his eyes told him. Then he stood silently caught in the memory of holding the can to his lips as a boy and spilling some of its contents past the corners of his mouth and onto the typed note below.

"I am listening," Saraph said.

Zoltan began reading slowly:

> Batan fell on April 9th, 1942. While some re-treated to Corregidor, others were taken prisoner and began the march toward San Fernando, approximately sixty miles. On the third day of the march we reached the town of Gua Gua in the province of Pam Panga, some eight miles from San Fernando. Numerous old ladies, grandmothers, dared to stand near the procession of POWs. Though the people of Gua Gua were notorious for their kindness, no other adults risked being seen, for the Japanese soldiers bayoneted any who tried to offer help to the American prisoners.

> But they did not bother with the old ladies. They stood there in their long hoopskirts just smoking their cigars and watching. Once in a while one of the prisoners would collapse. If a Japanese soldier was not in view one of the old ladies would come and hide him beneath her hoop skirt and they would care for him, slipping him water and food. It is hard to say how many, but numerous men received aid in this way.

> The children of Gua Gua, too, extended kindness to us. They hid sardine cans filled with water in the grasses along the route of the march. Whenever

guards had passed safely from view they would come out and get the emptied cans and refill them for others later in the long line of soldiers to find and have a drink.

When we reached San Fernando we were loaded on a train, stuffed into boxcars that were without air circulation and provisions for sanitation. Though our destination, Capis Parlac, was roughly twenty miles North of San Fernando, most were left in these conditions for several days. We estimated later that one third of those in each car were lost.

I have often thought back to cigar-toting old ladies in hoopskirts and children hiding sardine cans in tall grasses and the stark contrast of their actions in the context of the inhumane treatment of our captors. Such mercies endure in my soul and refresh my spirit still. The can that accompanies these words was purchased at a local grocer, but is a symbol of such graces, an offering along the reader's journey. May you find refreshment and a reminder.

Col. Thomas H. Ericson

Zoltan again reached out his hand longingly. He touched the surface of the can and felt its solidity, unable to satisfy his desire to take a drink.

"He was never in a hurry. The long, suspense-filled version of each story was never cheated. Never in a hurry the way you see him today," he said distractedly.

"But this is the day... the very day. It is unlikely that you would will another. It is probably just a short time after your visit," Saraph said, implying the law governing overlap.

Once again Zoltan looked at Saraph blankly. Then he turned

to resume his examination of the objects in the room. Next to be studied was a white-handled pistol in its bullet-ornamented holster. Moving to his left, he stood atop the steps to the lower level, where he saw Saraph in front of one of the paintings.

"Strange," Zoltan said.

"What's that?" Saraph asked, turning to look at him.

"I never left this upper level. I never stepped down to where you are."

Saraph looked around. "Why not?"

Zoltan, too, looked around. "I remember being afraid of these two easels. But I remember them more like two large knights."

For a moment, Saraph studied the easels, glancing back and forth between them. "Well, there is quite a bit of ornamental metal plating holding them together. I could see a child perceiving that as armor. Those large, cast iron wheels, the cranks for adjusting the mounts … they're rather warlike in their impression."

"Look at this place," Zoltan said, still at the top of the stairs. "Clean … organized, precisely arranged. He is a man of order just as I remember him."

"I see more than cleanliness and order here," Saraph responded. "I suspect a preparation of some kind. These rooms are empty of all personal items. They contain not a single stray or unpolished object. And this lower level is oddly lacking in furnishings for a living space of one from your culture, especially one who evidently enjoys collecting things."

Zoltan stepped slowly down to the lower level and stood beside Saraph. They stood in silence before the painting for several minutes as Zoltan wrestled with the internal affirmations of Saraph's words.

"Beautiful, isn't it?" he said, attempting to redirect the conversation. "A classic image, native American motif. Beautiful and yet sad."

"Forgive my inability to enjoy it with you," Saraph answered.

"You don't like it?"

"It's a tragic statement of false."

"You have some issues that do get in the way of simple pleasures," Zoltan said with a smirk.

Saraph stretched out his hand and made several gestures back and forth across the painting. "There are at least five different light sources in this work, subtle but distinctly and unmistakably different. I am guessing that the woman and the child were painted separately in a studio, and the horse was painted from photographs ... hmm, sketches maybe. The position of the mother seems unnatural. It does not speak to me of intimacy with her child, but rather, of a manikin-like display of the clothing and ornamentation of these people."

"How odd," Zoltan said, looking more closely. "She does appear manikin-like even in her face. The child looks more like a doll."

"The effort suggests something entrepreneurial," Saraph continued. "This painting trivializes its subjects, using them as props for enterprise. It makes no statement of sadness or loss to me, except in the exploitation of those who experience them still. Very nice colors ... excellent development of geometry, technically strong in many ways." He nodded his head and shrugged. "Yes, some strong skills are represented here. It is the trivial nature of the figurative subject that puts me off."

Saraph looked at Zoltan. "Please do not let my interpretation ruin it for you."

"No ... no, it's no problem. I don't like it either."

They looked at each other and Zoltan laughed out loud when he saw the comically puzzled look on Saraph's face.

"OK, I appreciate your point of view on this one," he said, still enjoying the humor of his effortless shift of opinion. "You know, truly, I think that painting bothered me before you said anything."

"Oh, really?" Saraph said playfully, as he turned and walked across the room to where the other easel stood.

"Hey, you have an advantage. You don't have the handicap of these cultural sensibilities, no connection or allegiance to our sacred things."

"Nor do you ... remember?"

Zoltan did not respond to Saraph's comment. Recalling his proud identity as a notorious iconoclast, he silently conceded the implication of his duplicity. They stood looking at the two paintings.

"No signature on this one," Zoltan said. He stepped back to see Saraph looking closely at the other painting.

"Not on this one either," Saraph announced, before stepping around to the back of the easel. As he did, Zoltan looked at the other painting from a distance. The painting was of a frame within a frame within a frame. Inside of the smallest frame was a depiction of a tiny toy crucifix.

"Oh, here ... " Saraph said, "right here on the back. It looks like the painting was done by Ericson himself. The title of this one is: '*What We Diminish ...*' "

Zoltan quickly went to the back of the painting of the mother and child. He stood and looked at Saraph. "Title of this one is: ' ... *We Destroy.*'"

"Hmm ... I was wrong, Saraph said. I take back my criticism." He walked to the back of the room and stood in front of a window. "As you pointed out, he's not a sloppy man. Understanding now that he is the artist and judging by the titles, the things I cited are clearly part of his intended statement."

Zoltan arrived next to Saraph and they stood before the glass panes looking out to the deep woods behind the house. Finally, Zoltan looked at Saraph and asked, "What do you object to concerning my memories of Col. Ericson?"

"Nothing," Saraph said distantly. It was quiet for a moment. "I like him. I like that he took the time to enjoy a child, to indulge a child with stories and invitations to the big, wild, wondrous adventure of living and exploring. I like what you remember about him valuing you more than these things. There is deep wisdom in his invitation to the reader of the note beside the can of water. Yes, there is much to like about this schemer. I am impressed that he could be so generous toward you on a day such as this … a day of trouble and loss."

"Trouble? What kind of trouble?" Zoltan asked, setting aside his objection to Saraph's judgment of Ericson as a schemer.

"Did you look at the form he signed his name to, or the note that he wrote and attached to the form?"

"No, I didn't. I was mesmerized by the sight of him."

"It appeared to be a contract with someone to auction all of these items. There is also a realtor's information flyer for this house on the desk. It would seem that he is in over his head for the moment."

Zoltan rushed to the desk and stood beside it reading the flyer. His eyes looked pained, as if he had a sense of personal responsibility.

"How do you know from these things that he is in trouble? Anyone can put a house on the market for many reasons. And maybe he just wants to sell all of these things to get his investment back out of them. Maybe he is simply moving to a place where he will not be able to display them."

"That, for sure, is the case. Did you read the note? It requested that all questions concerning the home and its contents be directed to his attorney, and that all harassing phone calls cease immediately. He apparently left all of these artifacts unpacked and in their places by some order or request. It states that he is no longer employed by the university and could not be reached there."

Zoltan was again at Saraph's side. "I wonder why he was run out of the university."

They stood in silence for several minutes.

"What was your father's occupation?" Saraph asked.

"Why. What does that have to do with anything?"

"Just curious. Just wondering why you would be here on this day … on this occasion. I'm guessing you were here with your father. It may be even more impressive that the Colonel would treat you so generously, you being the son of the man that … ."

"This is unbelievable!" Zoltan interrupted. He whirled around and walked away several steps before coming right back.

"Saraph, I have millions, you know that. Whatever trouble he is in, I can easily cover it. I'll buy this house and all of these things in it for double their value and give them back to him. I owe this man. If it weren't for him I would never have realized my dreams. I caught his contagious love for stories. What millions I have made are because of him."

"You forget that … ."

"I know, I know, the veil. Please, you can help. You must have servants of your own, someone you could send to work it out. You can use your powers, your influence to get the money from one of my accounts into his."

"No, you do not understand," Saraph said compassionately. "This is the very day that you met him, the very day that you remember so well. He looks the same because he is the same, the exact same. As I told you, you could wish for no other. It is all you know of him, all your memory can serve and all your heart can reach for. We are visiting what took place long ago when you were a boy. It cannot be changed. What help you could give would come far too late to relieve the troubles of this day."

Zoltan looked mystified and frustrated. "That is not possible," he said. "I came here many times. How can you talk like I had only one encounter with Col. Ericson?"

"I have only the information before me here and what you have recalled to me. It is not likely that he lived here after this day, or that these items were here long, certainly not exactly as they are now, and as you saw them through younger eyes. As you have attested, he was in the same clothes, and all details about him are precisely as you remember them. It is just as unlikely that a man of his refinement would visit the same items of his wardrobe enough to be identified by them."

Zoltan looked as though he were the one facing troubled times. He put his left hand on Saraph's shoulder, pinched the bridge of his nose between the fingers of his right hand, and bowed his head. He sighed as if in great pain recalling the freshly spilt water on the note beside the sardine can. Several minutes passed before he looked up at Saraph as one confiding unspoken fear in a trusted advisor.

All of the evidences that Saraph had listed were before him and logically led to the exact conclusion that he had just articulated. Yet, he agonized over the thought of surrendering his long-cherished memories to the reality confronting him.

"How…?" he appealed, looking at Saraph and shaking his head.

"Why are you heartbroken, Magician?"

The question pierced Zoltan's soul and the tears he had been fending off now flowed down his cheeks.

"What happened to him?" he asked, wiping his eyes.

"I don't know, I.…"

"I know, I keep forgetting, you are only my escort, you only know by observation."

"He seems a resourceful fellow, and one of deep character," Saraph said. "I imagine he will, or he did land on his feet, better off for his painful education."

"I hope so," Zoltan said, staring out the window.

"You need not diminish the significance of the impact that he had on your life because of this adjustment in your perspective. He never was more than a man. And you are fortunate that he never was less. There lie the grand proportions of the paradox that is humanity. I would consider it a plus that one encounter had the power of many."

"It's not just that," Zoltan said, "or the disappointment. It's the many other pieces of my identity that come into question. Things like this, which I have never doubted, and which I built my life around … it's disturbing."

Saraph took a step back from Zoltan and began posing like the subject of a Greek statue. Zoltan looked at him and frowned. Then he rolled his eyes. Soon the comical appearance of the bent old man in the raggedy clothing attempting the poses of mighty men transformed Zoltan's somber look into a smile. Finally he began to laugh at Saraph's antics.

"You are such a complete goofball."

Saraph stopped posing, took a few steps forward and reached up to place a hand on his companion's shoulder. Looking Zoltan in the eyes, he said, "Humility is not a tragedy, Antoniadis, off-spring of Adam."

Chapter 18
JOHNNY

Saraph waved his open hand across the surface of the windows before them. "What do you see out there?"

Zoltan did not want to look. He stared numbly without regard for an awaited response. But the horizon seduced him with the silent movement of billowy, slate-gray clouds tumbling like boulders connected by a fluid yellow mortar, moving beyond the sea of oaks, elms, cedars and pines. They traveled to unseen landscapes, to an eminent disappearance. He found himself wondering about the sunny places that those clouds might soon cover with their thunderous tumult, and the changes that they would impose upon a world of plans made for clear blue skies.

Suddenly, a great flash of lightning broke upon the landscape and owned, with the aid of violent thunder, a dramatic and sudden claim upon Zoltan's thoughts. He watched as strong winds began to move the foreground foliage, bending the towering limbs and bringing a fury of activity to the formerly serene valleys, ridges and rolling hills.

Awakened, yet with reluctance in his voice, Zoltan spoke one word: "Stories."

"What kinds of stories?" Saraph asked.

Zoltan shrugged.

"What are you afraid of?"

"What makes you think I'm afraid of something?"

"The gift is slipping away as you stand here clinging to this one memory as if blocking out all others. Do you intend to stretch this visitation to the end of the day?"

"This was important to me, the most important encounter of my youth."

"The universe awaits you in any and every direction, and you wish only to use this opportunity to relive an experience of your own childhood? What haunts you that you should have such fear of your will, of stepping out any farther than this last safe place of your recollection? What kind of stories?" Saraph persisted.

Zoltan looked at Saraph with resentment for his presumption of insight, and even more for his own evident transparency. Then he looked back out at the stormy scene beyond the glass panes before him.

He was trying not to think about Trevor Langdon, but his mind was working outside of his control. Pieces of a puzzle seemed to be coming into place, and a cloudy suspicion was creeping from his unconscious thoughts and gaining his conscious attention. *Trevor knows that I despise riffraff, religious people and Bible thumpers. He knows I'm a sucker for adventure. He's heard me talk of Ericson, my boyhood hero . . . .*

He tried to push the thoughts aside, but they persisted. *This Saraph guy is smooth. This deconstruction of my inspirations . . . .* He tried to close his eyes and squeeze out the thoughts only to recall the loss of confidence and self-control following the two original encounters with Saraph. With all of his might he tried to block out these thoughts and answer Saraph's question.

"Stories of adventure and exploration," he said dreamily. "Stories of tragedy and hope, treachery and heroism, loss and victory. I see stories of quietness and serenity beneath the canopies of tall trees along the winding paths of those who walk in solitude and listen to the voices of wind and river, the songs of sky and branch. I see stories of legacies long and deep, treasured and preserved, of sacred turf and honored earth.

"I see stories of violence and strife, love and forgiveness, stories of fractured youth and the timeless wisdoms of sage and silence. I hear the peaceful recitations of ancient verse broken by the rushing steps of troops and warriors announcing the advancing pillage of acquisition and ambition. I see stories of word and honor being replaced by contract and deed. Stories of man!" he concluded, as he looked back at Saraph.

"I so enjoy your passion, insightfulness and creativity," Saraph said with meaning. "But I ask again, what kind of stories?"

"I don't understand."

"There are two kinds of stories. Stories made of words and stories that come from The Word. Which do you see when you look out there?"

"From the word?"

"Yes, stories that are true and of infinite scope and eternal proportions."

"Do you mean true as opposed to false?"

"Of course there is that, but I am speaking of big stories as opposed to small stories."

"True or false!" Zoltan stated with a tone that underscored his disdain for cliché. "Does it matter?"

"It matters that you know one from the other."

"Why? What difference does it make? If a person were to believe a story to be true and that belief empowered or inspired him, gave him hope and direction, would you shatter those for a petty concern about true or false? We live in a world where all is illusory at best!"

"Hope in what is false is delusion and folly. And there is a word that describes the followers of directions that are untrue," Saraph said as he looked at Zoltan sternly. "Lost."

"You are rendering things a bit narrow I would say."

"As would I."

Zoltan and Saraph turned toward one another and stood silent for a moment. Zoltan frowned, and then said, "There are stories that are not true by your definition, yet they are thrilling, captivating and inspiring. Good art I call them."

"You do not have my definition. It was you that gave the terms true and false. I speak of origins. I speak of true as you would speak of a plumb line or a level as true."

"I get it, already! And I still say that there are stories that are untrue that are exciting, even brilliant. And there are stories that are true that do not so much as warrant a telling: Johnny went to the store and bought a bit of candy. He took it home and sat down and ate it all by himself. It may be true but, really...."

Zoltan demonstrated a mock yawn. "Bo-o-o-o-r-r-ing!" He was feeling in his element, as if he were in a creative conference hashing out the philosophical problems in the development of a new production.

"That, as you know, is not a story of either kind, but an incident within a story," Saraph replied. "True is bigger than a single act, or a succession of acts. It is bigger even than Johnny, for Johnny does not exist in a vacuum."

"OK, take two:" Zoltan announced. "Johnny watched a story of a big adventure on TV, and his favorite hero ate a certain kind of candy every day because his body turned the candy into energy that gave him special powers to help him fight the bad guys. This inspired Johnny to go out and fight the bad guys in his own world. Now, that is how a story that is not true can spice up one that is. And who cares that the story is not real? It made Johnny's life better."

"Neither is true by my definition. But let's...."

"Oh, for goodness sake, who cares?" Zoltan exclaimed in exasperation.

"Sure, for your sake, let's pretend. Let's say that Johnny is a real boy from the one true story. Who cares? Nobody! Nobody in Johnny's world cares, because they do not exist. You mentioned no one else, no other real person in Johnny's world. He watches his hero on TV alone, he walks to the store alone and comes home and eats his candy alone, because … well, he *is* alone. In his lonely world he attaches his own identity to that of a make-believe hero because there are no true heroes for him to follow in his real world. He does not have the benefit of a Col. Ericson, as you did. That is, there's no one bigger than himself. Therefore, there is no one to tell him that his own adventure is greater, his own story grander than that of his pretend hero.

"So, Johnny goes to the store every day, following his heroes example, and every day he sits alone and eats more and more candy hoping to become big and strong. And because no one cares, there is no one to teach Johnny the truth about the candy, and he becomes a fat and miserable little boy. One day in his misery, inspired by his hero, he decides to go out and find a battle to fight. Because no one cares, there is no one to teach him about real badness in real bad guys, nor how to approach a real battle. So, Johnny finds the neighborhood bully and gives him a good shove. Quickly the bully, who is not a fat little candy-eating pretender, squashes Johnny like a slow bug on hard ground."

Zoltan's mouth was dry, and he looked stunned. *Trevor is trying to deconstruct the power of my thinking and my creativity, that's it. That's why he's concocted this guy. That's how he thinks he can get me out of his way. It's worked only too well so far. Not anymore.*

He flipped through the details of Saraph's telling like one looking through a directory for an address or a number. He was distracted by something. Several points of contention were springing forward to be loaded onto his tongue, but he could not speak. The unidentified distraction made him angry. But he could not remember at which point his feelings were aroused.

"You see, Magician, manipulation of programming to raise ratings and induce candy sales may be smart business, but it is small story, and not without consequence in the true telling. We do not yet have the story of Johnny, only a few of his activities. But we now have implications of the big story he lives in. We have a hint of his part in that story, and of larger movements by which he is profoundly affected."

Zoltan could hardly hear Saraph's words over the distraction in his mind. There was something he wanted. He turned and walked to the other side of the room. Stopping, he turned back to Saraph and looked at him with eyes that labored under brows bent by fear. Even the confusion he sensed due to the trust he had begun to develop toward Saraph added to his suspicion that the "gift" was a web of Trevor's weaving. He was willing for the moment to concede the loss of his former prowess. But now he feared that his mind and sanity were also in danger.

With every thought he was becoming more convinced that Saraph was a servant of his diabolical enemy and former understudy, and that he must escape his presence and the sinister craft of his questions and words. He knew what it was that bothered him and what it was that he wanted. Hints of his desire to go to the studio and see what Trevor was up to forced their way through the clutter in his mind. He attempted to block them.

"There is a sovereign author of the one true story."

"No!" Zoltan shouted abruptly, holding up both of his hands. "No, don't say anything. Not a word. Don't speak. I don't want to know. I already know that whatever it is, it is pure nonsense."

He had already tried to silently request exotic destinations merely to distract the keen attention of the gift. But he could not get it to respond to his insincere commissions; and he did not know how to trick himself into sincere desires for anything but a peek in on Trevor.

Saraph turned back toward the windows and looked out at the stormy weather. "That author is the one you hate. Did you imagine that He should be embarrassed about being God for your benefit? Should He douse His eternal flame maybe, cower in submission to your self-determined supremacy? Yours are stories made of words. He is *The Word*. He does not invoke truth as a concept or an intrigue as you do for measured effect in a script. He is Truth. And I will not pretend He is less to avoid offending your sensibilities."

Zoltan pressed both hands to the sides of his head. He did not want to be in Saraph's presence, but he wanted quiet even less. He wanted to hide somewhere away from his thoughts and the ideas that were coming into his mind. He felt panicked as though he were on a slippery ledge. One wrong mental maneuver and a thought becomes volition, and then ....

Chapter 19
TREVOR

"Oaks, good to see you this morning!"

Michael Oaks looked up and saw Trevor Langdon's hand extended toward him. Immediately, he rose from his chair. Shaking Trevor's hand, he said, "Yes, an excellent morning." Then he gestured toward his computer station and his personal coffee pot. "Welcome to my kitchen. Please, have a seat and join me for a cup of coffee."

Trevor looked at the empty chair near the one from which Oaks had risen. He appeared unsettled by the invitation that threatened to require more of him than he had expected when he initiated the greeting.

"Uh, sure . . . a cup of coffee sounds nice."

Zoltan was having difficulty breathing. He was recovering from the shock of arrival directly in the presence of Trevor Langdon at Universal Syndicate Studios. "Michael Oaks," he said in a whisper.

Oaks grabbed a cup bearing several ink markings that efficiently exacted a representation of Albert Einstein. He picked up the small pot of coffee.

"We've butted heads from the day I hired him," Zoltan explained to Saraph. "I disliked him even when he interviewed." He paused, still catching his breath. "But I did not want anyone else to have the advantage of his formidable skill set, so I hired him."

"A half a cup … plenty, thanks," Trevor said, interrupting Oaks' hospitality. "I'm sorry, my time is a bit cramped this morning." He took the cup from Oaks even as he attempted to recover the control over his morning that had been compromised by his unusually gregarious demeanor.

Oaks and Langdon were the same height, both slender, stylish, though unpretentious in their dress. Both had a crop of brown wavy hair that was streaked with gray, loosely parted on the left and receding. Each had blue-gray eyes, but Trevor's were adorned with sleek frameless glasses and Oak's with dark bushy brows. Both were clean shaven and, but for Oaks' brows, neither had any distinguishing facial features. They could easily be mistaken for brothers.

Trevor looked at Oaks, thoughtful before speaking. "Say, if you don't mind my asking, rumor has it that you and The Man are quite good friends. Any truth to that?"

"Peter? Yes, I think so."

"Really! Very few people can say that."

"Oh, I don't know."

"Get together often?"

"Hmm, dinner once in a while, lunch maybe once a week or so. But we talk on a daily basis."

"So, you have opportunities to give input about this place?"

"Oh, yes, plenty of them. But I never do. We generally avoid shop talk when we're together."

"They're talking about P. Salmone II," Zoltan informed Saraph. "This is all his creation." He paused and looked around. "More so than any of us care to admit."

"Look, I do wish I had more time," Trevor said, "especially since we have never really had a chance to talk. But I have an important meeting in a short hour from now. I still have a few preparations to make."

"Of course, I understand," Oaks replied, nodding toward the empty chair.

Trevor took the seat uneasily. "Einstein. One of my favorites," he said. Turning the cup he read aloud from the side opposite the drawing: "'The significant problems we face cannot be solved at the same level of thinking we were at when we created them.'"

He looked at Oaks, who had finished perfecting the flavor of his cup of coffee, taken his seat and turned to face him. "Albert was an interesting fellow."

Oaks nodded.

"Speaking of the meeting, it's actually the reason for my dropping by unannounced. I'd like to invite you to attend."

Trevor was as surprised as Oaks by this invitation, which was far from what he intended prior to these words leaving his tongue. It was P. Salmone II who had suggested that Oaks be invited, and thus, prompted this unusual visit. But Trevor was against the idea. He had waited until this last moment, hoping a schedule conflict would preclude Oak's attendance.

"What is the nature of the meeting?" Oaks asked.

"Well, just a couple of announcements ... unveiling a few new ideas that could represent a shift in direction," Trevor answered casually.

"My! Directional shifts do not just pop up in companies of this size. I have several tight deadlines, as you might guess." Oaks thought for a few seconds. "But I think I will have to pry myself away for such an intriguing opportunity."

Trevor looked blankly at Oaks, who was a man notoriously disciplined and task-driven. His unexpected acceptance of the invitation was as unsettling as Trevor's own misplay in extending it.

Zoltan was looking around, evidently distracted. Suddenly, he blinked hard and his tightened lips displayed a voiceless curse. "Is there something wrong?" Saraph asked.

"There's a sound," Zoltan said, fighting with the impact of a disturbing memory. "Similar to something I heard in the hall at the club where the man with the white . . . ." He paused to recall where he had heard the note and where he had not. He looked at Saraph with suspicion in his eyes.

"In Alexandria, too . . . it's nothing, I'm sure."

Trevor was reaching for a recovery from his own awkward moment. "Oaks, you know, I have always thought we have a great deal in common."

"Well, we do spend two-thirds of our time in the same place. That alone is quite a bit of 'common,'" Oaks conceded.

"No, besides that. I mean, the whole Christianity thing, for example. Philosophically, we share a point of perspective, wouldn't you say?"

Oaks looked at the top of his coffee cup thoughtfully as he ran the index finger of his right hand around its rim. "No," he said, looking up at Trevor. "No, I wouldn't."

Trevor was instantly transformed. "Good coffee," he said, adding a signature smile. He was known to use it like expressive punctuation. Everyone in the company responded differently to the emotional manipulation intended by the projected warmth of that smile. To Oaks, the calculating mannerism was a boyish drama worthy only of disregard.

"Where would you say we depart from one another?" Trevor asked.

"The 'Christianity thing,' as you called it. I don't know what that is. It's a bit vague."

Trevor smiled again. "Yes, and your narrowness is legendary, my friend . . . and unfortunate. I hope we can go beyond that, as meaningful dialogue among creatives requires. I don't expect to reduce my vocabulary for a shriveled definition, if you know what I mean."

"I do."

"You know . . . ." Trevor paused to look thoughtful. "Our

industry – and especially this studio, I'll proudly qualify – holds a great tradition of parabolic content. Who was it that I read recently?" He paused again. "Can't remember. Anyway, a devoutly religious evangelical sort as I recall. He was asking why secular film producers make the best Christian movies."

Trevor took a sip of coffee. Looking at Oaks, he smiled almost imperceptibly and said, "I think he gets it. Don't you?"

"What is it he gets?" Oaks asked.

"The universal power of story, myth and legend for connection. 'Touch Stones,' I believe he called them."

"Interesting."

"How so?"

"Oh, these terms: 'Christianity thing,' 'evangelical,' 'religious,' 'parabolic,' 'Christian movies.' They're collectively obscure, meaningless."

"Really? I think of them as rather specific."

"Well, by contrast, consider Jesus of Nazareth, the One that is marginally implied in all of these. His earthly ministry can be summed up in *three* words."

Trevor sat forward in his chair, noticeably interested in the boldness of Oaks' statement. "Wait, let me guess," he said excitedly. Tilting his head, he closed his eyes and placed his elbows upon shifting knees. He looked down at the coffee cup that was tilted between his hands so he could see the quote on its side.

"OK, think differently," he said before looking up at Oaks and smiling. "I really like this. You surprised me with this one." He shook his head. "But just three words." Shaking his head again he stared at the floor. "Wow, nothing comes to mind," he muttered quietly.

Oaks was enjoying the moment as well, as he sat back in his chair and sipped his coffee. He had not intended to introduce a contest or a riddle. The idea had come to him quite effortlessly. Now he too was attentive to the boldness of it. He contemplated this as he waited for Trevor.

"OK, I give. What are they?" Trevor asked, expectancy in his eyes as he looked up at Oaks.

Oaks leaned forward, placed his elbows on his knees and looked into Trevor's eyes. "'It is time.'" After waiting several seconds, he sat back in his chair again.

Trevor, too, sat back. He looked at Oaks, puzzled as if stuck.

"You see, the word Christian actually means something, not just anything. It does not mean pious, religious, evangelical, spiritual, or ... ." Oaks hesitated, evidently looking for a word. " ... awakened," he finally said, finishing his thought. "All perfectly useful words, but we already have them. No, Christian simply means Christ-follower. Anything short of that faithful devotion is not worthy of the title.

"And what are we to follow him in?" Trevor asked.

"According to the Scriptures, Jesus came here in the fullness of time. 'It is time' were the first words He spoke to begin His earthly ministry, according to Mark's gospel. It was an announcement of His revelation. And it was an invitation. It was followed by these words: 'The kingdom of God is here. Repent and believe the good news.' His purpose in every moment was to humbly carry out the will of His Father. Anyone who is truly His follower is committed to the same."

Oaks took a sip of coffee and leaned forward to set the cup on his desk beside the coffee pot. Then he leaned back in his chair.

"Before Jesus breathed His last upon the cross He said, 'It is finished.' He had completed the work of redemption for you and me, for whom He had come." Oaks held out his open left hand like a bookend, then did the same with his right. "'It is time .... It is finished.' From beginning to end, obedience to the Father's will. Anyone who is truly His follower is committed to the same," he reiterated.

Trevor smiled. "I knew I should have taken the time to visit with you sooner. It was Zoltan who prejudiced me against you. No desire to get in the middle of those battles, if you know what I mean."

"I really like Zoltan. And I have great respect for him," Oaks said matter-of-factly.

"Really! How surprising. He hates you."

Oaks shrugged. "It's OK. We didn't have a deal or anything."

Trevor looked at his cup contemplating this last bit of dialogue as if it bore more weight than all that was spoken before it. He finished off his coffee and stood up, handing the cup to Oaks.

"Jesus is the one most famous for teaching in parables, is he not?"

Oaks was thoughtful. "You know," he said, "forgive me, but again, the word parable invites a broad application. Parables are like poems. They are a part of every culture, every fraternal order, and every family. So, to speak of Jesus' parables is something quite specific. He used parables in the context of His ministry, along with signs and wonders and His teachings concerning His Kingdom. That was their specific purpose. They conveyed truth about Him and His Kingdom—the Kingdom of God. So, they supported His teachings and did not contain violations of those teachings in their content. Can you think of one that did?"

"No, I cannot," Trevor conceded. He thought for a moment, smiled gently, and said, "But I can think of many such violations historically and currently by those who identify themselves as 'Christians.'"

"By which definition?" Oaks asked.

"Good point." Trevor smiled and dipped his brows. "Still, our representation ought to reflect the reality, rather than the ideal."

"Our representation of the one side of that reality is rather abundant and constant, wouldn't you say?" Oaks answered. "But where is our acknowledgement of true followers? Can you think of one recently? The totality of our work is a denial of their existence."

Oaks waited for a moment for Trevor to respond before continuing.

"You mentioned history. Dionysius wrote of the response of the Christians to a plague that engulfed the city of Alexandria in A.D. 260. He reported that they were fearless in their aid of the sick, and said that they served as followers of Christ, many bearing the sickness themselves, some even dying."

Zoltan and Saraph looked at one another, both thinking of their recent visit.

"Wait a second," Trevor protested. "Christians are not the only ones in history, or now, to care for others in that way. Have you ever watched the documentary on Rome that we produced a few years back? I'm sure you've met John Ray, our history guru. It was some of his most brilliant work. I watched it three times just last week. Fascinating! One of the quotes that got my attention was that of the Roman Emperor Julian. He said something about atheism being advanced through loving service to strangers."

"The point you make, Trevor, bears a measure of truth," Oaks said. "I have worked along side many who were not Christians and witnessed their devoted humanitarian service. But your example is not a good one. Not for your intended use, anyway. In fact, it was uncharacteristically sloppy of John to use the quote in the way he did. Julian was a pagan Emperor. He believed in worshiping many gods. It was because the Christians refused to do so that he referred to them as *atheists*. His statement, like that of Dionysius, was about Christians. If I remember correctly, he went on to say that, 'the godless Galileans care not only for their own poor but for ours as well, while those who belong to us look in vain for the help that we should render them.'

"And still today, when a disaster hits, Christ's Church is the first on the scene to bring aid and the last to leave. Throughout the world there are hospitals built and staffed by Christians in places where no local resources could ever provide such care. Orphanages, homeless shelters, food pantries, schools, teams of medical volunteers, all built and served by Christ-followers motivated only by service to their Lord, not a penny made by any of them. And there are countless other examples I could cite. But they all have one thing in common. Our stories are sterilized of their report. Our representations of the human condition betray our deceptive secular bias.

"The fact is, our productions across the board portray true Christ-followers as odd, misguided cultural relics at best, and as psychotic lunatics at worst. Seems to me we've bought into the bullying lies that to depart from the advancement of a purely secular illusion would risk our secure place in the market, and our careers. Or, is it we that create and perpetuate those lies for the sake of our morally bankrupt liberty of art?"

Trevor placed a hand upon Oaks' shoulder. "I can see why you found it difficult to get along with Zoltan. You live at opposite ideological poles." He chuckled. "You and I will do better for sure."

"I know I raised his dander a bit, but I have a great deal of respect for Zoltan," Oaks reminded Trevor, who continued smiling as he turned to leave.

"It was good chatting with you, my friend." After walking only a few steps, Trevor turned to look back.

"Likewise," Oaks responded.

"But, you know, you must watch that cynicism stuff. It cramps creativity." Shifting as if to leave, he stopped himself, a mild look of puzzlement etched on his brow. "Tell me, why do you work here? I mean ... you know, with your objections and all."

"A measure of influence," Oaks answered without hesitation.

Trevor laughed out loud and walked back to Oaks, grabbed him by both shoulders and gave him a friendly shake. "See, I told you we have some things in common." Giving Oaks one more shake he added, "But I am sure the measure I seek is greater than your modest intent."

"Oh, I don't know," Oaks jested with a suggestive wink.

Trevor again laughed. "But really," he said, "I can't help but wonder why you stay in this field if you think media is such trash."

"Our media," Oaks corrected, "not all. There are a lot of movie houses, media producers, and broadcast studios that are creating great stuff with powerful, wholesome, and integral content. But we are not among them."

"Then why don't you go to one of those. That would make more sense for you wouldn't it?"

"No it wouldn't. This is where God has placed me. And, really, I don't quite understand it either. But until He shows me otherwise, this is where I will stay."

"You do always seem pretty happy about it. So, I guess if it works for you ... hey, we're glad to have your talents on our team."

"I am, and thank you."

"One more question, please, then I'll leave you alone and ... oh my goodness!" Trevor said, glancing at his watch. "I really have to get going."

"Your question?"

"Oh, yes." He pointed to a piece of paper taped to a shelf above Oaks' computer screen. It bore a typed verse of Scripture:

> Behold I am coming soon! My reward is with Me,
> And I will give to everyone according to what he
> has done. I am the Alpha and Omega, the First
> and the Last, the Beginning and the End. Blessed
> are those who wash their robes, that they may have
> the right to the tree of life and may go through

the gates into the city. Outside are the dogs, those who practice magic arts, the sexually immoral, the murderers, the idolaters and everyone who loves and practices lying.

Revelation 22:12-15

"Pretty severe stuff. What if you are wrong?"

"I'm not concerned with *my* rightness," Oaks replied. "So I'll rephrase your question if I may: What if the One who is faithful and true, the One who gave these words of warning is wrong?" He thought for a moment. "A hypothetical of those proportions is difficult for me to seriously evaluate."

"OK," Trevor said with a shrug. "Just asking." He tilted his head back and looked at Oaks through the bottom part of his glasses as if he were measuring him. "You know, I really am not a very religious guy. That's probably the biggest difference between us. But we all get to the same place one way or the other. Look around this place. You see all of this activity, all the zeal and passion?"

He pointed to a group of people gathered in a small area critiquing some story boards and working out the details of a script together. The particular group happened to be made up of all men. "Look at them. That's 'church,' my friend. What man wants to sit around and be talked at? Men want a place to be active, vital and significant. That right there is beautiful. See how engaged they are? It's 7:45 in the morning! Try to make that happen on a Sunday at your local steeple-people-palace."

Oaks did not respond. He agreed with Trevor theoretically, but also knew too well the reality of the contentions and vicious, ego-motivated strife that was seldom absent from groups such as the one Trevor pointed out. But he considered Trevor's definition of 'church' as unifying activity and work, and silently acknowledged that it was very close to that of his own.

"Connection," Trevor said with emphasis. "Isn't that what

we all want? When it is all said and done, there is really no difference between any of the great religions or the important philosophical movements. All of the basic ideas and principles are essentially the same."

To Oaks, Trevor appeared to speak in slow motion. As he attempted to be especially persuasive, he spoke with such physically exaggerated pronouncement of his words that it appeared as if his teeth were not the right fit for his mouth. With every inflection of his dogma, his lips pushed forward and pulled back dramatically. Oaks resisted turning away, as others often did, thinking that the impression was rather overbearing.

"You do your best to put yourself in the position to do your best," Trevor continued. "That is all any of us can really do. And if we do that we will find our way and make the most of our lives and make the world a better place, don't you think? Maybe that's a bit radical, I don't know."

"Oh, it sounds anything but radical to me," Oaks responded. "It actually sounds like the conventional wisdom that dominates mainstream dialogue. Have you studied these things, these religions and philosophies, to come to such conviction?"

"Quite a bit. But it's really rather self-evident."

"I see," Oaks replied. He thought for a moment. "Just curious ... you speak of Zoltan in the past tense. Something up?"

Trevor's expression changed. For a few long seconds they stared at one another. "Everything will be cleared up in the meeting," Trevor said, as he turned and walked away.

"Zoltan is gone for one week and there is a meeting to clear things up? Perhaps a bit of this 'doing your best to put yourself in a position to do your best'?" Oaks mused to himself aloud, watching Trevor poke his head in another office to greet someone.

"Exactly what I was thinking," Zoltan muttered as he set out after his successor. "Treacherous little opportunist! I suspected all along that I was creating a monster."

Suddenly, Zoltan stopped. "'Gone for one week?' I haven't even been gone for one day!"

He stood still and looked at Saraph.

"What did you desire?" Saraph asked. "Was it to merely see what Trevor was up to, or to see him at the point of his true revelation?"

Zoltan stared and then walked to a nearby workstation to search for an indication of the current date. Finding one, he turned and looked at Saraph.

"So, I'm missing for the next...." He paused. "... the past week? Now, does that seem like bad timing to you? Seems terribly inconvenient to me. I'll have to see if I can fix that when your little 'gift' experiment is through."

Zoltan tilted his head. Appearing puzzled, he looked around the room. Then he looked toward the ceiling. *Odd that I never heard that before today,* he thought. *But it seems to be almost everywhere.* He began walking.

"So, Trevor is making his move," Saraph observed aloud, following behind Zoltan.

"Like you didn't already know!" Zoltan snapped. "Whoever you are, you can stop acting."

Chapter 20
MINTING

As Trevor walked briskly through the lobby, Zoltan and Saraph followed closely behind. "You OK?" Saraph asked as they stepped on to the elevator. Trevor pushed the button for the sixth floor. Zoltan looked at Saraph and then turned away. The elevator came to a stop and the doors opened. They followed Trevor across an inlayed marble logo, down a broad hallway and through glass doors.

"Your floor, if I remember correctly," Saraph said.

"You ruined my life," Zoltan said, barely able to voice the words. "I used to love coming here. I loved arriving early in the morning and had to pry myself away at night. I spent many a weekend here. Passion drove me. I can see that those days are gone, no matter what the actual nature of this little experiment of yours is, or its outcome. This rage justifies the need for the veil you said is between me and this world. I am unstable, to put it mildly, in fact, dangerous."

Zoltan tried not to look at anyone as they followed Trevor, not knowing who was involved with him in these intrigues. As they passed through workstations on each side, Saraph noted the universal presence of two posted messages: *Give Them What They Want*, and *Take Them Further*. Zoltan thought they were heading directly for his office until Trevor made a turn to his left and stepped through a short hallway and into another room. Seeing several people who were gathered together around a computer monitor, he joined them. The lively discussion centered on the textual contents on the screen.

"Tell me about the work that goes on here," Saraph stated with a tone of authority.

Zoltan recognized it immediately and reacted with folded arms and a look of mock defiance. The expression abruptly transformed into exasperation and pain. Brows bent, Zoltan looked upward as he turned away. Then he cocked his head strangely to one side, powerless to mask the throes of anxiety. The note and a bombardment of visions had again seized his attention.

"First time?" The white glove reached toward him and the seated man looked at him with piercing eyes. "...you will be pleased.... "

Turning back to the group, Zoltan shoved Saraph out of the way and set his attention on the screen. A back-lit photograph nearly six feet tall dressed the wall beyond the huddled group. It displayed a spectacular image of multiple fireballs bursting from exploding buildings and converging like thunderheads to consume a great modern cityscape. In the billowing darkness of the cloud-engulfed streets were the lighted words, *Give Them What They Want.* Similarly compelling images bearing one of the two mottos were scattered throughout the sprawling, cavernous room.

"Your idea?" Saraph asked.

Zoltan was bent down looking over the shoulder of one of the viewers before the oversize screen. He was studying its contents. Grudgingly he acknowledged the interruption. Looking back over his shoulder, he saw Saraph nod toward the poster.

"Yes, of course."

Turning back to the screen, he heard one of the viewers say, "As usual, Zoltan was right. Look at the results of the second statistical study from the top, just after the subject break:

'Cumulative Retention.'"

"The guy is brilliant," exclaimed a young lady seated directly before the screen and surrounded by the group of assessors. Saraph watched as Zoltan turned his gaze from the screen to the source of his praise, momentarily mesmerized by the eclipse within this constellation of his self obsessions.

"A brilliant sociologist!" Trevor quipped. "But a bit misplaced in the ever changing world of mass media."

Zoltan stood up straight, slid both hands into the pockets of his pants and glared at the understudy whom he had trained for the past five years. He looked upon Trevor as if he were a complete enigma.

"His career and our steady rise suggest accomplishment in both areas," came a rebuttal.

"Scroll back a page or two," Trevor said, ignoring the comment.

"Personal Retention ... Cultural Retention ... Topical Data ...."

The information on the screen began to race by in a blur.

"No, it should be under 'Cultural Affinity,' or, no ... maybe 'Affection Status.'"

"'Affection Study'?"

"Affection Status, Study, whatever."

"That's back the other way. We hadn't gotten there yet." The movement on the screen stopped and the woman got up from her chair. Grabbing a cup and walking away from the group, she said, "I'm going for coffee. Look at whatever you want. If you need me I'll be back at my desk."

"Meeting's at 10:00. You won't want to miss it," Trevor murmured.

The woman stopped and turned around. "I thought it was just for heads of dep ...."

"Oh, that's right," Trevor interrupted. "I'm sorry. I ... forgot for a moment ...."

The woman stood and stared as Trevor pretended to study the screen. His right elbow was postured on his left forearm as it lay across his abdomen. His chin was mounted upon his right hand, his index finger resting along the side of his nose. He looked toward the woman out of the corners of his eyes, and then punctuated the silent communication with a flick of his eyebrows. She turned and walked away.

"That makes me sick." Zoltan said in a whisper, stung by the interaction. "I knew I shouldn't have listened to him. She was among three department heads I let him convince me to remove from my leadership team just...." He paused. "Just over a week ago. I never would have done it had I not been so compromised by your imposition." He glared back at Saraph.

"What does it mean?" Saraph asked, nodding back to the poster, unmoved by Zoltan's regret.

"It's our service motto," Zoltan replied without taking his eyes off Saraph. "It is a statement of duty."

"Explain it to me."

"We are known for leading edge media production. We produce media, but we are really a service conglomerate. These...." He paused, moving his head in a circular motion to indicate the backlit posters throughout the room. "They are reminders of our service obligation, the motivation that keeps us in front. We call this 'The Raking Room.' And this is my handpicked research team. What you see here are layers of analytical teams, anthropologists, sociologists, art historians, philosophers, you name it. Humanities majors have never been put to such excellent use. And, of course, there are the statisticians and the actuaries also. Math is a big part of our research and evaluations, a very scientific process."

"Print that out for me."

Zoltan turned to look over his shoulder, hearing Trevor's demand. He turned back to Saraph.

"We serve a global audience that consists of several genera-

tions and countless subcultures within the larger cultural movements officially acknowledged by sociologists. Effective media
serves a target audience. To do that we must know the level of
media sophistication to which each receptive region has evolved.
'Raking' refers to the gathering of leaves falling from the cultural trees. Where have they been? Where have they come from?
What are the operative mythic systems, their symbols and currently relevant positions of their changing values? What have
they discarded? What do they crave? What do they need?"

"Need?"

"Yes. Frankly, there are many elements of the past to which,
unfortunately, entire segments of society refuse to stop clinging.
These dictate sensibilities that we have found we cannot ignore.
In fact, regrettably, they demand our productive participation
in order to appease their loyal social elements – at least enough
to prevent their disruption of the overall progress. Thankfully,
these have proven to be shallower elements of the social con-
struct and do not require more than, well, rather shallow ac-
commodations. We sprinkle them throughout the otherwise
normal programming schedules and progressive direction."

"Progress toward?"

"That ought to be obvious to a cosmic traveler such as you.
Progress, of course, toward the ultimate evolutionary equilibrium, the balance that beckons our common nature to its
universal awareness, fullness, self-regulation and authentic celebration. That is why our service is so powerful and so essential. We are dedicated to the universal logic. And we educate
likewise. We inform even as we discover and serve the collective
consciousness of the universal soul of humanity. This is what
the raking tells us – what we learn about *us* as we study the
data."

"Sounds rigorous," Saraph suggested after walking over to
the group gathered around the computer. He stood next to
Trevor and observed him closely.

"What about a fellow like this? What does your data say about such a person – or does the individual escape your data?" He turned and looked at Zoltan. "How do you feel about your 'monster' taking over the next phase of…?" He paused and looked back at Trevor. "… of the future of this *progress?*"

"Cute! Your smug enjoyment of my replacement speaks volumes of your character. Maybe you should answer that question yourself since you are the one responsible for his premature appointment. Or, is he the one responsible for you and your 'gift'."

Saraph turned back to Zoltan. They stared.

"Maybe he represents a bigger problem for your media driven utopia," Saraph suggested. "Certainly your data has revealed collections of renegades."

"Not really. Oh, there are some more difficult elements that do tend to be, for lack of a better term, unimpressionable. But these are relatively small and proportionally insignificant. They are not radical individualists like him. Quite the opposite. They're radical remnants of the past, so to speak. We have tried to include them, but their blinding ideologies block progress. We decided to give up concerning ourselves with them long ago. We acknowledge them only for the necessary deconstruction of their social influence. It is not difficult, as it turns out. Just a little stirring is required."

Zoltan and Saraph again stared at one another.

"Stirring?"

"Yes, stirring of the intrinsic cultural eagerness to dissociate with them. They tend to make everyone uncomfortable."

"Intrinsic to who?"

"To the broader, more natural social elements."

"'Natural social elements,'" Saraph repeated. "Another way of saying 'normal people?'"

"If you wish," Zoltan answered with a shrug.

"I don't. But I am interested in how you go about accomplishing the deconstruction."

"I call it 'seeding.' It's just a name, of course, but it is a common practice throughout our more progressive cultural institutions, and particularly our industry. In our case, we simply seed our productions with their unfavorable representations. For example: We have perfected the creation of character isolations that portray their grotesquely extreme and pathetically distorted social and intellectual condition. The sheer contrast to the norm of society speaks for itself."

Zoltan leaned over the right shoulder of a man kneeling beside the chair of the analyst now controlling the screen.

"Let me see if I can find you a good example. Yes, look here, second paragraph from the top." He looked at Saraph wide-eyed, evidently pleased with himself. "This is exciting. This is exactly what I created this research software to do. Several months ago I suggested that we isolate this particular sect of religious fanatics. We've made inconspicuous, but highly calculated efforts to attach definitively unattractive and unacceptable social stigmas to them by subtle methods of association. Of course, all based upon our knowledge of them and our statistical findings, mind you." He looked back at the screen. "Look at this, this is hot off the press – first time I've seen it. Our study shows an eight percent decline in those claiming to be associated with that group since the beginning of our initiative. That's impressive."

Zoltan stopped. His brows sagged into a glare. Shaking his head, he attempted to free himself of the repetitive plucking of the *note* and the layered drone that supported it.

"Stop it!" he rasped, reaching out and shaking Saraph by the arm.

Saraph leaned close to Zoltan. He spoke evenly and solemnly as if to someone beyond the eyes he looked into, someone possessing a hope, someone within reach.

"I can assume there are no instances in which your character assassinations and comic portrayals are unjust? Your views and your data, I mean, are wholly integral. Your values are worthy arbiters for declaring the necessary deconstruction of things past, things sacred? This group, for example, do you know anything about them."

"Everything."

"I mean, really know?"

"Everything!"

"Do you know their history? Do you know that they are all of unsound mind and social condition, that none has character worthy of honor rather than shame for its association? Do you know what impact they have had in the world? Do you have any idea what impact they have had on real progress ... progress that laid a foundation for your enjoyment of this technological playground, including the right to use it for their humiliation and extermination if you choose?"

"Does it matter?" Zoltan asked, almost on top of Saraph's last word. He was regaining his past bravado, inspired by the familiarity of his professional environs. "Don't you get it? There is an order at work, a progress toward balance, equilibrium and unity."

"And you know about unity? Do you know its cost? You speak of progress toward unity in a universe whose foundations are of the holy, an origin for which you lack consciousness. So you fill the void of comprehension with every vain boast. You are like a child who has impressed himself with the discovery that he can block out the sun with his penny when he holds it close enough to his eye.

"So impressed is he that he becomes convinced that his penny is actually greater than the sun. Yet, even as his arm grows weary and his concentration falters, he does not notice the rays of the sun wrapping around his penny and burning his eye. And, blinded in one eye, he does not stop to consider the evidence that his actions have clearly demonstrated. But he continues with his other eye until he is utterly blind and happy for the solitary darkness of his imagined dominion over the sun."

Saraph and Zoltan simultaneously stood up straight. Saraph walked around to the other side of the workstation and stood beside the large backlit image and began to study it. "How many subtle, calculated associations hide among these illusions of photography and pyrotechnics?"

"None. It was a project for in-house promotion and inspiration."

"The others?" Saraph asked, gesturing around the room.

"Same."

"My friend, your experiments are out of control. In fact, it is they that control you. You have become the slave of your own manipulations. You see as you intended others to see. Look closely at the people at the bottom here, the ones below and around your slogan, running from the calamity. Look at these people in the foreground buildings. All ordinary, nondistinct looking folks.

"Look here at the mattress advertisement on the side of this building. Note the beautiful, airbrushed woman lying on the mattress untouched by the explosive forces of destruction. An interesting photo illusion within the photo illusion. Look over there at your '*Give Them What They Want*' promotional beach scene. Eight physically beautiful people by your standards, the standards that you seem to think worthy of progress toward eventual universal equilibrium and balance. All eight of them appear to be less than thirty years of age, athletic, well tanned, endowed with nearly the exact same broad, white, toothy smiles and fine facial features, and all mostly naked.

"Now, as an outside observer, though not necessarily objective, I would have to conclude that the worldview that drives your quest for ultimate unity is one where common folks are fodder for the consuming exploits of your pyrotechnicians. And people favored by the image of beauty stamped upon the shiny pennies of your mintage are privileged to be sleeping peacefully on fine mattresses or running around naked with each other on sunny beaches. Would you say that this is representative of the data that your raking has produced?"

Zoltan was distracted. Trevor had just announced that he was leaving to go make final preparations for the meeting. Zoltan's interest in the meeting was great and its reference had diverted his attention from Saraph's words. As Trevor made his way around the others and started walking away, Zoltan began to follow, looking back apologetically at Saraph.

Watching Zoltan follow after his successor, Saraph waited.

He spoke quietly, solemnly, to no one. "'Here is the verdict: Light has come into the world, but men loved darkness instead of light because their deeds were evil.'"

He stood and watched the small group of researchers as they stared at the computer screen before them as if it were a crystal ball or an altar of divination. Their eyes were wide for the enchantment of discovery. Saraph listened to the banter between them, noting the delight in their voices. "By all means, give them what they want," he said, as he began to follow after Zoltan.

Chapter 21
P. SALMONE II

S araph spotted Zoltan and Trevor nearly thirty feet away. Trevor had stopped to speak with someone and he could tell by Zoltan's posture that the conversation was a revealing one. As he walked toward them he looked around at the sea of workstations. Departments were delineated by color changes and architectural variations and peculiarities, like micro townships, while all maintained a coordinated appearance.

Everywhere he looked he saw enthusiastic devotion, a community of creative zeal. He noted numerous huddled groups echoing the energy of the group he had just left. As he reached Zoltan's side Trevor had concluded his conversation, and Zoltan was turning to match his quick pace and his every turn as he traveled through the metropolitan interior studio complex.

They came to the desk of Zoltan's secretary, Marion, and Trevor stopped to take a mint from a jar. She continued to look at the sheet of paper next to the monitor on her desk, her fingers attacking the keys on the keyboard with obvious aggression. Zoltan saw tears brimming in her eyes and was comforted to recognize her loyalty.

"I can find you another position if this is too uncomfortable for you," Trevor offered.

"Thank you … please," Marion answered without changing her focus or the pace of her typing. Trevor left her and walked into the office.

"See, I told you." Zoltan said, looking over his shoulder at Saraph. He stayed by the desk and watched Marion work for several minutes. He looked at the monitor thinking it might reveal something of the circumstances, but found her to be typing the same sentence over and over: "If I make it througg the next five minutes i will be ok and mo one will have to get hurt or se me completely out of control."

"I didn't think you could type a real paper that fast," Zoltan said quietly, a slight smile coming to his face. He looked at Saraph.

"I wonder what happened between them," Saraph said. "Only a week."

Zoltan frowned and shook his head. "You're unbelievable."

The brief distraction was broken by the sound of a familiar voice and the words, "Give me just a minute." It came from inside the office, and Zoltan turned to see one of the two large mahogany doors standing open. He stepped through nervously, aware that he was comforted by Saraph's presence. P. Salmone II, the company's majority owner and son of the company founder, was seated at the desk with his head down as he concentrated on something he was writing.

Zoltan looked around the office suite sickened by its emptiness. The box of cigars on the desk was all that remained of his personal items. There was a stack of labeled boxes in a corner behind the desk.

Salmone completed his work and sat up. "So, are we ready?"

"More than ready," Trevor responded, his words partly muffled by one of Zoltan's premium cigars. He had stuffed it into his left cheek prior to sitting down in the leather wing chair. Holding a newspaper open, he did not look up from its contents. On the floor beside the chair lay a stack of papers containing some content from the reports he had been looking at moments earlier.

"How 'bout you put that down and remove the cigar so we can take care of a few final matters."

It was ten seconds before Trevor moved. Closing the paper, he stood up and walked to the desk. After turning the paper to accommodate Salmone's viewing, he set it in front of him and pointed to the headline of an article along the side margin. "Read that yet?" he asked, reaching for the lighter Zoltan kept in his cigar box. Then he lit the cigar and sat back down.

"I read it."

"You want it front page? We could make it front page if you'd like," Trevor said, misunderstanding Salmone's flat response.

Salmone's answer was voiceless and expressionless. He set the paper in the trash can underneath the desk. Trevor took a deep drag on the cigar. He put his head back and shot a stream of smoke straight up above him.

"Zoltan was concerned that … ," Salmone started.

"Zoltan is a worrier, and he's gone!" Trevor interrupted. "And you are no longer dealing with Zoltan. One last explanation: These are just sparks. The sparks go off in a million little dialogues until they spread on their own like wild fires in the wind. Where the ideas, the rumors got started is untraceable. The created illusion of their universality makes them convincing and invisible, and thus, supports our greater efforts."

"Trevor, you are zealous, ambitious and thorough, if not maniacally clever. But it is presuming a lot to think that you understand our greater efforts. This seeding is not among them. It is a gross misuse of our arts and influence."

Trevor chuckled and began to cough. He removed the cigar from his mouth. "I like that. 'Maniacally clever' … no one ever called me that before." Adopting a compliment from the statement, he looked away thoughtfully. "Odd, really, someone should have before now."

The two men stared at one another.

"Zoltan led me to believe you were behind the seeding all the way," Trevor said.

"His determination muted my objections."

"Really? What about the research? They kind of go together. Did he mislead me about your support there too?"

Salmone nodded. "Again, he ignored my objections because he had no interest in understanding my values and vision for this company—an attitude that you sport as well. That is why I am coming back to take command."

Trevor took the cigar out of his mouth and held it between his thumb and index finger as he stared at Salmone, unprepared for this news.

"I allowed Zoltan's use of the research because it now serves my own intent," Salmone qualified.

Trevor leaned over and put the cigar out in the ashtray that was built into the top of the cigar box. The cigar stayed in the tray as he sat up straight on the edge of the chair.

"And what is that?"

"Mirrors."

"Mirrors?" Trevor mimicked.

"Just hold 'em up and let everyone see for himself. Mirrors are the best preachers. They just reflect the evidence and let it speak for itself. Valuable items, mirrors, unless the viewer is blind, of course."

Trevor was unsettled by a suspicion that there was something in these words intended for him that he was not identifying.

"That was not our original intent," Salmone continued, appearing distant and thoughtful. "Surely not that of my father," he said, referring to the one who had started the company many years ago. "No, his was a much grander vision rarely recalled anymore."

"Like the things we've been working on are not grand?" Trevor retorted, annoyed by the implication of a diminished significance. "You think the things we'll be unveiling in a little while – revolutionary advancements – are smaller than your pa-pa's ideas way back when?"

"You are a knowledgeable fella, Trevor. Have you ever stud-ied the environment of our conference room ... the technology behind it?"

Because he had, Trevor remained silent.

"You are also a talented guy."

"Thank you, but ... ."

"However, your mentality is that of a pimp, a drug dealer, a street-level supplier, an exploiter and opportunist."

"Again ... thank you. But I think my view ought to be stated as well. I'll give it to you if you're interested?"

Salmone nodded.

"I think of media as candy for the mind. That people like candy or that they like certain types of candy is not my exper-tise, nor is it my responsibility. My passion is simply to make the best candy on the planet. If Zoltan taught me anything, he taught me *that*, while *he* was off inventing new ways to find out what kinds of candy the masses are fondest of.

"Like you, I don't care for all this research stuff. The only use I have for his elaborate research models is the aid they give in the creation of world class recipes, treats that people actually desire and enjoy. Whether someone becomes a candy addict is his own responsibility. I do not concern myself with that phenomenon, either to create it or to exploit it. In that sense, your assessment of me is quite wrong. I make candy because I like candy myself. I also like seeing others enjoy it, and I like supplying it for their enjoyment."

Distracted by the power of suggestion Saraph walked over to the tray of candy, which he had emptied of Gummy Bears months earlier. With a look of disappointment, he returned to stand beside Zoltan.

"More mints. What's with the mint thing?" he said. "I'm glad I filled my pockets with the chewy little bears while I had the chance. I really like these." He held one up and looked at it before popping it into his mouth.

As if reminded by Trevor's comments, Salmone had stopped to write something else on the paper before him. Finishing, he looked up and began to speak.

"That is not our view. We are . . . ."

"Pretenders!" Trevor interrupted, regaining his fearlessness of any adverse effect upon his position.

Salmone and Trevor again stared at one another. Reaching into his pocket, Salmone pulled out a penny and tossed it onto Trevor's lap. "Hold it up and look at it real closely."

Trevor just stared at him, agitated by the conversation that seemed to be designed to spoil his grand moment. What made him most tense was his growing suspicion that Salmone was aware of the unapproved liberties he had taken with the demo for the unveiling.

"Humor me for a minute," Salmone said.

Trevor picked up the penny and looked at it.

"Closer."

Trevor held up the penny and studied it.

"Closer."

Observing this, Zoltan looked over at Saraph with animated amazement for the coincidence. Saraph shrugged, indicating his own amazement at the similarity between Salmone's choice of analogies and the one he had just used moments earlier.

Trevor looked at Salmone, resentful of the expectation that he participate in the silly demonstration. Then he grudgingly closed his left eye as he held the penny only inches from his right eye.

"Closer," Salmone prodded and watched the penny move to within a quarter of an inch or so of Trevor's eye. "What do you see?"

"A blurry copper Abe."

"Nothing else?"

"Nada!" Trevor quipped, taking down the penny and tossing it onto the desk in front of Salmone.

"That is all we are doing here—producing blurry little likenesses. Not likenesses of Abe, of course, but of our viewers themselves. Little self-reflections for our audience to consider. Mirrors we call media—shiny, pretty little dramatic reflections of their most common maladies, fondest self-fantasies, intrigues and obsessions. We show them the collective condition of their character and confront them with their most abundant mortal fears. That is, after all, what they find so enthralling and we so profitable.

"And who are *they*, but the people right outside those doors, huddled around computers on every floor of this complex. They are writing, designing, planning and scripting every form of malicious intent, diabolical plot, slanderous betrayal, and murderous descent of blood lust and vulgarity.

"Zoltan's elaborate research schemes are superfluous. You want to know what's in the heart of man? Build a studio and fill it with the most sophisticated production equipment and advanced technologies on the planet. Invite the most talented creators to make use of it. Give them the opportunity to create whatever they wish and support them with limitless funds and you will find out what flavors of mind candy the heart of man rejoices in day and night. We judge ourselves with the exactness of mirrors and daily broadcast our verdict to all corners of the earth.

"Read our scripts, watch our productions. Turn on that TV over there. From the daytime soaps to the rush hour thriller, we never rest of our appetite for treachery, guile and mutual contempt. The masses find representation right here by people just like you and your colleagues, more so than by any senators or congressional appointments on Capital Hill. Right here in this place built by my father!"

Salmone's face was a shade darker than when he began speaking, his eyes wet, the veins in his neck swollen. Saraph looked at Zoltan, who was moved with emotion, and he received a quick look of disapproval for the invasion.

"Just making sure you're listening."

"Trying to," Zoltan replied.

"As I told you earlier," Saraph said softly, "*I* am not your judge."

Zoltan stared at Saraph for a moment. Then he fixed his eyes back on Salmone.

"But we do generate billions of these," Salmone said after a lengthy pause. He held up the coin as he sat back in his chair. "And what are these, but the means for educating ourselves and equipping ourselves for the making of more impressive little likenesses. Yet, in my view, though not our original intent, reflectivity has turned out to be the redeeming quality of this institution." He thought for a moment. "If people will open their eyes, that is."

"I do appreciate the pennies our mind candies bring in," Trevor said lightly, speaking only to detract attention from the awkwardness he felt at that moment. "I guess I am a pure mercenary. That other use of pennies was Zoltan's vice. And it proved to be one that he could not afford. I have no desire to rule the world, only the candy market."

Trevor had reached his tolerance capacity for this contentious version of the one he had previously viewed merely as one of the gatekeepers to production funding. Zoltan had taught him to placate the man. Trevor had always resented the practice, regarding it as an unfortunate but necessary indignity. His respect for Salmone had diminished in recent months in direct proportion to a swelling perception of his own importance. He thought about those with whom he had positioned himself on this the day of his long anticipated unveiling. He felt invincible.

Trevor glanced at his watch and stood up. "Eight twenty-five, I have a meeting to get to. I'm glad we had this little chat."

"About Zoltan ... " Salmone said, "Let me handle the announcement."

"Gladly," Trevor agreed. "What was it you called me ... talented? C'mon, let's not pretend! Gimme a little credit, why don't you! A strong adjective, at least, is in order."

He turned and walked out of the office and Zoltan turned to follow him.

Chapter 22
THE ANNOUNCEMENT

The tension in the room was palpable. Trevor was uncharacteristically generous with his affections in welcoming each attendee. It made them individually and collectively uncomfortable. As he walked around the room, he distributed a handout that displayed on customized covers the name of each department head integrated into the company logo. He made it a point of giving all a pat of the shoulder, a handshake, or a wink, and to make eye contact with every one of his colleagues.

For most it did not accomplish his desired effect. Several found it unnerving since he had never in all their interactions with him made such friendly overtures. In everyone it aroused suspicion and intrigue. The room was busy with exchanged glances and silent expressions of "*What's up,*" or "*Uh oh! I don't like the feel of this.*"

Salmone was taking mental notes of the chilly climate and Trevor's command of his troops. He sat directly across the fourteen-foot mahogany table from Monarch Charon, the only other board member in attendance. Keenly aware of the impact of his own presence at the meeting, Salmone made no attempt to provide any nerve settling, reassuring gestures.

Zoltan and Saraph stood near the back of the room at one end of a lighted, twenty-foot long wall sculpture of gently cascading water. The impact of the sculpture was larger than its coverage of three-fourths of the room's length and height on one wall, and greater than its conveyance of extreme expense. The adjacent wall was a softly-filtered, slate gray mirrored surface bearing an inlayed circuitry of nearly imperceptible small, moving lights. Alone, it would appear as deep waters or distant space. But the delicate, filtered reflection of the water sculpture upon it and within it gave the appearance of flowing cosmic energies emanating from living depths. Reflections from both walls on the polished glassy surface of the table encouraged a feeling of organic inclusion of all who were seated around it.

Standing in this room nearly moved Zoltan to tears. *I had forgotten…* he thought. *I have taken this beauty for granted.* Introduction to the conference room universally invoked awe. Everyone who sat within its jewel-like atmosphere had a specific seating preference, and, like a natural equilibrium, no preference had ever conflicted with another.

Some liked to sit across from the water sculpture with their backs to the mirrored wall, and others preferred to sit on the other side of the table and face the reflective surface from some particular position relative to the sculpture. Others preferred seats at either end of the room for a greater sense of the length of the room and the relationship between the two walls. Individual perception of the room dictated these decisions, and no one ever made them consciously. On the occasion of this meeting the only seat remaining open was the seat at the end of the table near the doors.

It was known by the popular name, The Chair. Zoltan stared at it mournfully. The Chair was a sacred institution and no one had ever sat in it without appointment by P. Salmone II. Such appointment was a legendary honor by Salmone's design and even he had never violated it. Zoltan had enjoyed that honor for the past eleven years. He had not considered its loss until that very moment, and he strained to control his emotions as it occurred to him that his privilege had passed.

Ironically, Trevor, too, was distracted by The Chair at that very moment. The thought had occurred to him that he would soon be enjoying the honored status acknowledged even beyond this corporate community. *They might even be using this meeting to make my appointment official,* he thought. His heart began to pound. *Maybe just a few minutes from now ... .* Then, in a fleeting moment of regret, he recalled the way he had spoken to Salmone just a short time earlier. *'I wonder what he meant by 'coming back to take command,'* Trevor pondered.

Meanwhile, Michael Oaks was standing very near Zoltan, looking for an open seat at the table. He was keenly aware of the scrutiny he was drawing from the others in the room, who were all department heads, though mostly of recent installment. He was feeling very much the outsider.

"Please, take your seat, Mr. Oaks."

The sudden invocation of the voice of P. Salmone II brought an immediate end to the silent communications of unrest inspired by Trevor Langdon's behaviors. All eyes scanned the room, all faces bore the evident confusion in each person's reaction to the invitation, as Salmone's left hand was extended directly toward The Chair as he spoke.

Trevor stood up involuntarily and stared at Salmone, only realizing the awkwardness of his actions after seeing the amused look in the overseer's eyes. All other eyes in the room were on him. He attempted to appear natural as he sat back down in his seat. Oaks' body language was apologetic as he moved toward The Chair.

Zoltan, however, was the one most effected by the command. He looked at Saraph and then at Salmone, then looked around the room. He was doubtless now in his conclusion that all of this—Saraph, the gift, the meeting, this casual displacement from the place of honor and all that he had experienced over the past months which led to these—was a charade born of a conspiracy to ruin him. Seeing no one taking notice of him, he snapped.

"All right, I've had enough of this!" he shouted. "What's going on with you two? What is this devilry you have conspired to concoct? You think I don't recognize your trademark mind games going on here, Peter? Enough is enough! What's going on, and what is this embodiment of your wizardry supposed to accomplish?"

He was looking at Salmone, pointing at Saraph and realizing that no one in the room was responding to his outburst. Everyone but Salmone and Charon continued to look back and forth between Trevor, Oaks, and one another. All bewildered. Salmone sat like an expressionless stone statue in the midst of a flock of startled pigeons. Zoltan looked over at Saraph, who alone was observing him.

"First things first," Trevor announced in a voice that masterfully disguised his alarm and conveyed an authoritative tone. "I'd like to introduce two of the members of our board of directors who are with us today and whom most of you have not met. Seated to my right is Ms. Monarch Charon." He paused a moment for acknowledgment, but the room remained morgue like except for a few mild nods in the direction of Ms. Charon.

"And this I am sure you know is Mr. P. Salmone II, who has an announcement he'd like to make concerning Zoltan."

Zoltan did not take his eyes off Saraph until he heard his name. After glancing over at Trevor he looked back at Saraph slightly embarrassed and greatly distressed. Saraph gestured to the spot next to him that Zoltan had vacated with his attempted confrontation. He accepted the invitation apprehensively, stepping back and taking his place next to Saraph.

"Zoltan is no longer with our company. For now, Trevor Langdon will conduct this meeting," Salmone stated flatly.

Zoltan ground his teeth.

Trevor looked at Salmone with an expression that said, *That's it? For that, you wanted me to let you handle the announcement?* As he looked around and saw stunned faces staring back, he felt vilified.

"Now, we understand that many of you held Zoltan in high esteem as we have as well. He was an admirably talented leader and creative initiator, and...." Trevor paused for effect and looked around the room. " ... to some, a good friend."

He was trying to ignore the distracting replay in his mind of Salmone's words. *What did he mean, 'for now?'* Trevor thought. As his eyes roved around the room he caught a glimpse of Monarch Charon, who had turned her torso in order to face him. He restrained himself from flinching backward in reaction to the heat he felt coming from her fiery gaze. He looked over at Salmone and was equally assaulted by his frozen stare.

"So, we know that adjustments take time," he continued, trying not to look at either again, "and we appreciate and respect your sensibilities at this time of change. Yet, we all have the benefit of some very exciting and demanding projects to occupy our minds as well. A couple of those are the focus of the rest of our time together today. Before we move on, does anyone have any questions concerning this announcement, or any concerns you might have about its effect upon your own status or that of your department?"

"Yes, uh, I...," someone began before being cut off by Salmone's voice.

"Look, Monarch and I thank you for allowing us to crash your meeting for a few minutes, but we now have a matter to which we must attend. We trust you all will progress toward a more productive continuation of the meeting now that this part has *concluded!*" After he had put added emphasis upon his final word, he nodded at his colleague across the table. They rose together and walked out of the room.

Zoltan leaned over toward Saraph, his heart pounding

harder than it had at the point of his outburst. "I was wondering when he was going to reveal his more lordly colors. Trevor is toast."

"Pardon me for just a moment," Trevor said, standing to follow after the two overseers. He opened the door and Zoltan slipped out behind him leaving Saraph in the room.

"What was the point of...," Trevor began in a demanding tone before Charon met him nose to nose.

"You were on a very short leash, Mr. Langdon. It just became shorter."

Shocked, Trevor took a step back to look over at Salmone.

"I thought we had an agreement," Salmone stated sternly.

"An agreement?"

"That I would handle the announcement. Your short memory will prove to be your fatal flaw."

"What kind of announcement was that?"

"A precisely calculated one. Zoltan is a prominent figure in the industry, as well as publicly. We owe your assembly of selected puppets no apologies. Offering them only encourages a license to shared opinions and speculations whose ripple effects will spread further than you know. They likely will propagate a demand for apologies and explanations beyond this quaint institution. It will also cost more than you can account for in oozing melancholy and distracted service. *Our* diminished authority is not in *their* best interest."

"Look, maybe your threats worked with Zoltan, but I just don't get intimidated that easily. I have bigger things on my mind than ...."

"Than your pretense to consideration of everyone's feelings?" Monarch Charon turned and looked around. "This was a nice situation for a young man like yourself, wouldn't you say? What a shame."

"What do you mean *was*?" Trevor asked.

"You have a great deal of talent, passion, ingenuity, and drive, and have displayed an admirable visionary quality. Yet, I have this against you. You are not humble and have not turned from the ways of your predecessor, who despised our values and authority and used the position that we graciously chose him for to advance his own agendas. Those included the calculated misleading of the people he was chosen to serve. We hate the broadcast shrines. You seek to increase their prevalence and power."

"You know, I can just … ."

"Just take your expertise elsewhere? You will find, as did your predecessor that credibility is not easy to restore. At any rate," she said, reaching out and pinching Trevor's cheek, "I do not think you will find it difficult to get over yourself."

Salmone and Charon turned and walked away, leaving Trevor standing outside the conference room. He shook his head in disgust and muttered, "Whatever that was about!" Turning, he opened the door and reentered the room with Zoltan on his heals.

"Anything interesting?" Saraph asked, as Zoltan took his place beside him once again.

"Very," Zoltan answered. "How about here?"

Saraph projected his lower lip and nodded. "No one has yet said a word. I find *that* very interesting too."

"That's because these people have never attended a meeting together before," Zoltan informed him. "Trevor has shaken up the entire leadership structure. Only two of these present were heads of their departments a week ago. I wonder what he's up to."

"Evidently something that requires minimal resistance," Saraph offered.

As he sat down, Trevor began to redirect the attention of his audience. Trying not to mention anything that would lead to any reference of Zoltan, he took control of the unavoidable subject of transition with a broad use of indulgence. One by one, he strategically selected each of those present and informed them of their elevated significance in the company, as well as their increased responsibilities. Promises of appropriate monetary compensations were implied frequently.

This was the only part of the proceedings he had not rehearsed, and much of what he said was spun spontaneously for his immediate concern. He was pleased by how easily the subject of Zoltan and the residual effects from his interactions with Salmone and Charon went away. They were quickly dissolved by his steady stirring of concocted elements into this soupy spell of flattery, caprice and bribery.

A natural dialogue ensued as the focus of the meeting shifted to project-specific details. Zoltan was distracted and heard little of these interactions. He was thinking about the conversation he'd listened to outside the conference room.

Having observed Salmone from the perspective that Saraph's gift provided, Zoltan was humbled and pained. It was clear to him that Salmone was the real genius behind the company. To some, the company's rise from a second tier media source to an industry leader appeared as a nearly overnight phenomenon. But Zoltan knew that it was rooted in years of meticulously cultivated institutional culture and shrewd industrial positioning on the part of Salmone.

For the first time, Zoltan perceived Salmone's selection of him as generous. And he could pinpoint in his mind the day Salmone had canceled that selection. It had been more than a year earlier when he had detached himself with defiant finality from Salmone's leadership. He had displayed much the same arrogance they had just observed in Trevor.

It pained Zoltan to think that Trevor had so little respect for Salmone, and that he was greatly responsible. Trevor had his own agenda and had only attached himself to Salmone's vision in order to serve his own. Zoltan felt ashamed that both he and Trevor had treated Salmone like a shackle to rid themselves of—just some old nuisance.

I should have known. He thought. He looked at the water sculpture behind him and then at its reflection in the adjacent wall. He glanced at the table, The Chair, the luminescent ceiling tiles, the other chairs and the people in them. For a moment he stared at the far wall that included a seamlessly integrated projection system that defied recognition when not in use. He looked at the marble floor. *All part of Salmone's vision,* he thought, dumbfounded by the absence of any prior detection of the obvious fact.

Zoltan was preoccupied with these thoughts as the meeting continued before him. His mind was as the eyes of a jockey viewing every detail in the action of the final stretch in slow motion. *I thought of him as the lucky old fool and me as the brilliant wizard who brought him his fortunes. I had no regard for his vision or purpose. But it was him all along,* he thought, amazed.

He looked at Saraph, wanting to make his confession to someone.

"Salmone was the one who invited me to think that way."

"What was that?" Saraph said, distracted from his concentration on the dialogue taking place before him.

"It was reckless of him, don't you think? I mean, to invite me to be so important, or to allow me to think I was. I only came to despise him as someone far smaller than me. I remember thinking it was my duty to keep this old guy from interfering in any significant way with all I had to accomplish. I resented his insistence about 'our purpose and values.' I thought of them only as his limiting old line attachments."

He looked at the group before him and realized that not one individual in it had ever been a person to him. All represented only their respective involvements in his projects. They had been like switches on a control board before which he sat and carried out his visionary navigations—human resources in the strictest sense.

Zoltan looked around and pondered the power of *the gift*.

Saraph, on the other hand, had been keenly interested in every detail of the meeting. The tedious nature of these interactions was informing him of the types of media projects that were being developed, as well as the character of the people developing them.

Zoltan's attention shifted to Trevor, and he noted with more than a little envy how masterfully his understudy applied the skills he'd helped him to develop. He knew that Trevor was not interested in the least in these trivial discussions. Yet, every mention of the advertised unveilings was cleverly deflected or subtly deferred to effect an increased suspense. *They are near the peak of anticipation*, Zoltan thought. *I would say that now's the time.*

Suddenly, as though cued by Zoltan's thoughts, Trevor made a few quick statements to wrap up the current discussions and called for a ten minute break. Everyone began shuffling and organizing papers before them, closing books and leaving the room. A few people stood to their feet only to continue a previous discussion as others did so while walking out together. A few people remained seated, looking thoughtful and serious, as though something had not set well with them.

Zoltan and Saraph followed Trevor out of the conference room to where he ran into Michael Oaks.

"Michael, I know you have a lot going on, so you are welcome to excuse yourself," he said encouragingly.

"Well, what is next on the agenda, if you don't mind my asking?" Oaks responded. "It's all been pretty interesting so far."

"Oh, a bit about the new direction I mentioned to you earlier, a new project... some new technologies. I think I might lay a bit of a foundation based upon my own views of the state of the industry."

"My goodness, that alone sounds worth sticking around for."

"Well, thank you. Your choice," Trevor said, as he began to move past Oaks. Then he stopped and added: "Michael, please try and keep an open mind. Positive influence is always appreciated."

Trevor heard Gwen Thomas call his name and turned to see her approaching.

"Excuse me Gwen," he said anxiously, "but I am heading to the men's room. So, unless you want to follow me in there, you will have to wait."

"Ok, I will talk to you later," Thomas replied, somewhat put off. She, too, walked away leaving Zoltan and Saraph standing alone.

So, if Saraph is not part of a Trevor scheme, who is he and where did he come from? Zoltan thought. He looked at his travel companion and said, "This ought to be interesting."

"What's that?" Saraph asked.

"The next phase of the meeting."

"Yes, sounds interesting."

"More for you than me, of course. I've yet to hear Trevor say anything he didn't hear and learn from me first. But, we'll see."

The instant the words left his mouth Zoltan regretted speaking them. *My ridiculous ego,* he thought with agitation. Salmone's demand that any issue pertaining to Zoltan be put to rest had provided him with the perfect cover. *Now I've gone and reattached my authorship through Trevor,* he scolded himself. He was especially concerned about how Trevor's own slant on things might now be attributed to him.

"You know," he finally said, breaking the silence, "I must tell you, this Trevor has some very ... well, experimentally aggressive approaches to things."

Saraph looked at Zoltan blankly, and they stood staring at one another.

"Just thought a mild warning might be appreciated," Zoltan said.

"Thank you," Saraph responded.

Feeling foolish, Zoltan decided to just let it go. He followed several people back into the conference room to wait for the others to return and the meeting to resume.

As Saraph came to stand beside him, he leaned toward him and said, "Did I understand you correctly in saying that you have yet to hear Trev.…"

"Yes, yes," Zoltan interrupted, not wanting to hear the rest of his statement repeated back to him. He rolled his eyes and looked away. *Great*, he thought, *now I'll be sweating bullets with every word that comes out of Trevor's mouth.*

The two stood silently side by side for the next five minutes as they watched for Trevor's return. They observed the others as they all took their seats sooner than the ten minutes that Trevor had allotted. Zoltan fought off his desire for retreat as several destinations came to his mind.

Chapter 23
MEMORY

As they waited for Trevor, Saraph looked at Zoltan and gave him a nudge. Nodding toward the table he asked, "Who are these quiet ones, and why don't they ever speak?"

Zoltan pointed toward a slim and especially refined looking man. "That's John Ray," he said. "He is one of the most knowledgeable men I have ever met. He heads our documentary department. That is Stuart McCauley," he said, pointing at a stocky man with thick, sandy-colored hair. An equally thick mustache hung unevenly in curls several inches below his jaw line and looked like a badly frayed rope at the ends. "Human Resources Manager," Zoltan informed Saraph. "And that is Erin Bankroft. She is . . . ."

"Wait, wait," Saraph said, holding up his hand and interrupting Zoltan. "I am not going to remember all of that. I was just curious about their silence. There's them and, what, two or three others who have not said a word."

"I told you, this is an odd gathering," Zoltan answered. "I don't think I have ever seen fifty percent of this group together in one place before. And there are some icy relationships here. Several of these never speak up because they did in the past and did not like the aggressive style with which some of the others became contentious. John Ray, for example, has told me that he finds the style of interaction that goes on in these meetings to be barbaric. They are very accomplished professionals, every one of them, with some very big egos and unyielding opinions."

Zoltan looked over the group. Saraph's question evoked his sentiments. "Some get this far winning the battles, others by staying clear of them and outlasting their peers," he said distantly.

Trevor walked into the room exactly ten minutes from his announcement of the break. "Ladies and gentlemen, thank you for your prompt return. We have a lot to cover and, unfortunately, an insufficient amount of time to do it in. First, a brief lesson on memory."

The introduction Trevor had been preparing for weeks had begun. Those rehearsals had not included any anticipation of Zoltan's sudden disappearance, Salmone's abrupt departure from the meeting, or Oaks' presence in it. Nor had they included the distraction of his occupation of The Chair. Yet, Trevor felt the room was his and his alone.

Zoltan wondered how Trevor had planned to approach the meeting with him there. He recalled Trevor answering, "Just trust me," every time he had brought it up over the previous weeks. He also wondered about all that had happened to clear the way for Trevor's moment.

"For a few of you," Trevor began, "some of what I am about to say will be painfully elementary." He glanced around the room. "And for others, you will recognize your own contributions among these ideas. So, bear with me where this may be redundant. I can assure you that you will all find it interesting, at the very least, in the end."

Saraph looked up at Zoltan, but Zoltan did not acknowledge the communication.

"This thing we call memory . . . " Trevor continued. "This thing we so lightly call memory is actually quite profound and . . . well, the proper professional word I think would be elegant. The human machine is the most elegant on earth. I walk around—have all of my life—with this sense of something bigger. So do you. It fills in the gaps. Fullness, I think that is a fair definition," he said thoughtfully. "A fullness of life, if you will. Though I cannot explain it, I am unmistakably aware of it."

"Sounds like imagination to me," blurted Patrick Bruce, the youngest person at the table. He wore heavy-rimmed, black glasses, a badly wrinkled T-shirt, and thick, messy hair.

"Now there's your real magician," Zoltan said to Saraph. "Does he look like a multimillionaire to you? The kid is responsible for more than thirty patents. It's been an annual challenge to keep him with us. He swears that he only stays because he wants to buy the company some day so he can own his own patents. Patrick Bruce, our serial inventor. At twenty-six he's the head of the visual effects department."

"No, definitely not," Trevor rebutted after a thoughtful pause, distracted by Bruce's suggestion. "The two are quite easily distinguished from one another. My imagination is consciously activated. I have a handle on it. It comes from me, is generated by me. This memory thing...."

Trevor stopped and looked at Bruce as if revisiting the distraction, and then looked throughout the room. "Let me first say this. This is not discussion time." He smiled. "This is instruction and introduction time. Please do not interrupt. I will tell you when it is time to...."

"Really?" Bruce spoke excitedly with a laugh as his eyes darted around the room and his head appeared to follow with jerky movements as if on a leash. He hopped forward in his seat and put his elbows on the table and leaned on them. Gesturing with his hand toward Trevor, he said, "Go!" And after a few more quick glances back and forth around the table he gushed, "This is exciting!"

Trevor gave him an extended stare intended to convey his

lack of amusement, though nearly everyone else was straining to contain theirs.

"Go!" Bruce repeated enthusiastically, with another quick wisp of his hand.

"As I was saying," Trevor continued, "this memory thing is bigger than my imagination. It comes from deeper inside and further outside than I am capable of identifying. It is something I am part of but it does not come from me. It is beyond me. It is paradoxical, at once memory and longing." He stopped and looked down thoughtfully. Then, looking back up at his audience he said, "It is like rumors of more in every direction. I am in the midst of it."

"Oh, wow!" Bruce emoted as he put his head on the table and rotated it back and forth. He looked up to meet Trevor's stern gaze. "Oh, hey," he said, holding a hand up in front of him, "I'm not interrupting. I'm just *with* you. I mean, I get it, totally!" He gave Trevor a thumbs-up to continue, and then sat back in his chair looking like he might soon explode.

Trevor shook his head. "I have done extensive reading on this—anything I can find that attempts to address it. Guesses, speculations, theories; they are abundant. Some are spiritual in nature, some religious, metaphysical, scientific, you name it. Some find its explanation in incarnations, reincarnations, literal memories of past lives. Others attribute it to spirit phenomena, communications with the dead, and who knows what all.

"None of these work for me. I think of it more as Potential, with a capital P, like a fundamental element."

Zoltan leaned over and whispered to Saraph, "Here it comes."

Trevor paused and looked around the room. Gaining the desired effect, he said, "You might think of it as evolution's voice reminding us of where we've been and beckoning us to where we might go ... if we listen well."

Zoltan leaned toward Saraph again and said, "Next, the DNA elimination."

"Of course, some of you, if you are astute, want to suggest DNA."

"Here, here," Patrick Bruce said with a quick raise of his hand.

Zoltan looked at Saraph out of the corner of his eye to catch an indication of impression. But Saraph showed no reaction.

"And, if I'm going to suggest evolution's voice," Trevor said, ignoring Bruce, "then DNA is partly the answer, of course. All the information – the record of the past is there. And that in itself would likely supply suggestions of what is ahead based upon patterns of the past. Thus, memory and longing. But still, I think this memory, this enveloping, subconscious presumption is beyond that ... more profound than just the accumulation of physiology's data."

Zoltan leaned over toward Saraph and began to speak. "Here comes ... ." He stopped short seeing Saraph's stare facing him.

"That's annoying," Saraph said before turning back toward Trevor.

Zoltan straightened up and shrugged.

Trevor looked around the room and enjoyed the affirmation of attentiveness in everyone's faces.

"Let me give you an example," he offered. "The thing we think of as sight is almost entirely made up of memory. I walked into this room and sat down in this chair and looked straight ahead in your direction. But when I entered, my brain scanned the room and stored the information. As I look at you now I only actually see a narrow field of vision. My memory fills in the rest, every detail of this room and its contents.

"Think of that!" he said excitedly, looking around the room and making a point to make eye contact with each person at the table. "As I sit here and look at each one of you, my experience is actually much fuller than that. I am completely aware of everything behind me, even the context in which this room is in this building. And not just physically, but I'm aware of its significance to the activities of this company. And there are the layers of each of our relationships within it and outside of it. Think of those dimensions, all with their visual qualifications.

"Now add to that the experience of sound. It gets even bigger. Everything we think of . . . ." Trevor paused to think. "Even as I speak my ears are reporting the molecular subtleties of a peculiarity that my mind understands as the space beneath this table. I didn't have to measure it, look at it, or consciously think about. But it is there . . . a constant awareness of everything around me.

"And, as big as memory is in physical sight and hearing, consider the sound of a single word and its meaning, its power within your consciousness and our collective consciousness. Let's take the word 'grace' . . . not just a combination of letters, but the idea of it in your mind. It comes to us from the Greek word *charis*—especially favored, and before that *chairo*—rejoice. So, at some point, logically, it did not exist. Right? Are you with me?"

Trevor looked around the room massaging his set-up. Zoltan looked at Saraph and rolled his eyes.

"He got all of this from me. He's not Greek. And I can assure you Trevor cares nothing about grace."

"Do you?" Saraph asked, staring back at Zoltan.

"Now here's the kicker," Trevor continued. "Try and imagine its absence from your vocabulary . . . no, even deeper, from your consciousness. Go ahead, I can tell you it's impossible. Now imagine the complete destruction of this building we are sitting in, or this entire complex of buildings for that matter. Its not difficult at all is it? Imagine the grandest building or city you have ever seen being completely obliterated from the planet, from existence. Easy, right?" Trevor knocked on the table with his knuckles.

"'Solid?' 'Real?' I'll tell you what's real: I can easily conceive of the elimination of anything in this world that I recognize in physical terms. But one word contributes to my consciousness and its meaning cannot be removed."

"Powerful stuff, wouldn't you say?" Zoltan asked Saraph, gloating. "Of course, he got the entire example from me. And, frankly, he's botching it up badly."

"Did you teach him the words of Jesus of Nazareth as well?" Saraph returned. "'Heaven and earth will pass away, but my words will never pass away.' Even more powerful wouldn't you say? And well supported by his ... uh, *your* point."

Zoltan turned his attention back to the meeting.

"You beginning to get the size of this?" Trevor asked. "On many such levels I am quite aware of our physical, industrial, financial and global positioning as we sit in this meeting. We tend to think of the subconscious as empty, or in the negative – non-conscious. It is actually quite active and full. In fact, the greater part of life's fullness at any given moment comes from memory ... by my definition, that is."

"*Your* definition," Zoltan scoffed, shaking his head. "You don't have a definition. That's because you're nothing without me and all my ideas."

"And the particular part of memory that I am addressing now – that connection to the bigger – is filling in, way beyond just the things around us. It is instructive of something incomprehensible on the conscious level, a great infinite fullness. In a very real sense, my friends, at any given moment what any of us experience is predominantly virtual, that is, memory projected." He stopped and looked around.

"The human mind has the astounding capability of performing dynamic mapping of any and every environmental detail of the individual's experience, interpreting from the individual perspective, and adding this to the vast memory resources of all that is known of the personal experience by the person. I gave you sight and sound, and abstract thought connected to them as examples. The same is true of each of our senses, including the senses for which we do not yet have definitions.

"We carry with us memory catalogues of everything our senses have ever conveyed to our brains. Everything I am hearing right now has meaning in a fluid context of comparison to everything else I have ever heard, seen, experienced."

"And, yes," he said, looking at Bruce, "when I use the word mapping, I mean it in a very similar way that you use anatomical mapping for motion capture. It just happens at light speed."

As Trevor perused the faces before him, he perceived a collective tension between excited anticipation and departure. He deftly took this as his cue for transition.

"You are probably wondering what this has to do with our work and the rumors you have heard of some changes in direction." He leaned back in his chair and assumed a casual pose as he enjoyed the affirming nods and comments that rewarded his instincts. Only Oaks and John Ray offered no reaction to his question.

Trevor smiled. "Our industry is at a point of crisis." He paused, again took account of each face, and then punctuated the drama with another smile.

"Our workplace is polluted with two prominent mandates: *Give Them What They Want* and *Take Them Further*. It is time for us to . . . ." He appeared to search the ceiling as he muttered, "What word should I use?" Then he looked down and set his gaze directly on Michael Oaks and said, "Repent." A gentle smile turned up the corners of his mouth and lifted his eyebrows slightly. "Yes, I believe that is it. "Repent." Wouldn't you agree, Michael?"

Oaks gave no response.

"Ours is the industry of more, louder, faster, bigger. Bigger explosions, deeper melodrama, angrier faces, tighter fists, edgier vulgarities, sweatier love scenes, gorier murders, spookier demons and scarier villains."

"Gosh, it makes me proud to hear you talk that way," said John Belk, a highly respected virtual environments engineer. He pretended to wipe a tear from his eye.

"Yeah. In other words, we're awesome!" Bruce added.

"We're sick is what we are," another voice added. Zoltan looked around, trying to identify who had spoken.

Trevor held up his hands to stem the tide of response. "I'm almost there. Give me just a few more minutes of your attention."

He sat up in his chair, leaned forward, propped his elbows upon the table and folded his hands.

"Look," he continued, "most, if not all of you know that my adoptive use of the word soul is the one that suggests an expressive source. Soulful music, poetry, dance, etc… And of course, I reject the definition relating to some personal eternal occupancy. Thus, you know that I endorse the fabulous – the indulgence of the full range of sensual human passions. Some will call it immorality, hedonism, or licentiousness. I see it quite beautifully as an invitation to a deep bountiful well of expressive innocence. It is not this that I suggest we repent of."

John Belk wiped a hand across his brow and exhaled dramatically. "Thank goodness. You had me nervous for a moment there."

Bruce laughed.

"Still…," Trevor said, again raising his hands for order as several others made similar comments. "Still, we have run amuck. We have destroyed the beauty of it, forgotten the sweetness of the soul and trampled upon its graces in our revelry. *It is time*," he said, looking at Oaks. Once again Trevor reclined and appeared thoughtfully relaxed. "It is time … for the reinvention of subtlety. The shocking has run its course."

"I don't think so," Bruce said, unable to contain his objection. "Stop by my little playground after the meeting and I'll show you some new shock content that will singe your eyebrows."

"The tether proved to be surprisingly long," Trevor stated firmly. He was shaking his head as he looked at Patrick Bruce. "But we are at its end. Any further in that direction and the whackos will have us all rounded up and shut down."

He looked at Oaks and offered an apologetic gesture.

"Hey, it's OK," Oaks replied. "It's a good day to be a whacko."

"It is indeed," John Ray announced.

Everyone in the room turned and looked at him. Trevor was especially surprised by Ray's comment.

"Let's continue," he said, not wanting the diversion to go any further. "Back to memory…We have the power to re-invent subtlety. Note that I did not say reintroduce subtlety. I said *reinvent*. Scientists tell us that our genetic definition makes up only three percent of our DNA – that's ninety-seven percent unwritten definition. That's a lot of human recourse potential."

Patrick Bruce grabbed a pen and pretended to be taking notes. "Hmm, potential, is that with a capital p or not?"

"What do you think of that?" Zoltan asked Saraph.

"Complete nonsense, of course," Saraph answered. "It's all there. You simply do not yet have the ability to interpret the subtleties. It's much like this thing he's calling *memory*. 'Generational memory' is like Trevor's…*your* example of the word grace. It does not go away so easily. It's all there, all in use, nothing wasted. You'll discover it some day."

Saraph looked at Trevor. "Ironic that a man who puts himself in charge of a reinvention of 'subtlety' does so only because true subtlety is the very thing he cannot fathom. If he even considered it, a warning might break through. As it stands, these activities are not comforting."

Trevor sat forward in his chair and put his elbows on the table. "I have spent my entire career focused on synthesized presentations – audio visual, optical mechanical, virtual biological, holographic. I have merged 3D technology with medicine to create virtual environments to aid world renowned neurosurgeons in their healing arts. I have had a hand in creating holographic technologies for military avionics to aid the training of the world's best pilots. And I have developed marine navigation systems to assist some of the world's most renowned explorers. Always pressing for the greater realm… greater application.

"The one thing I have never been able to translate into technology – to synthesize, mimic, control or fabricate technologically is the transcendent dimension, the core of which, I believe, is memory. I only know one thing: it cannot be accessed or defined or experienced by any of our five senses, though it may be predominantly made up of their cumulative input.

"So, I return to synthesis… but not of technology. Memory is the key to Potential, and 'soul' the portal that suggests its invitation to a new dance. Our industry has exploited and pushed the current human senses as far as they can go. The car is bouncing at the intersection and distortion has eclipsed the sound that created it. The point we are at is commonly called 'no-return.' We must invent new senses if we are to reinvent subtlety. And we have the power to do that."

Everyone in the room but Oaks, Zoltan and Saraph were stunned. They looked around at one another not knowing what to make of what they had just heard. It was not what any of them had been expecting Trevor's speech to be leading toward. Trevor sat back in his chair watching the awkward reactions and waiting for someone to vocalize a response. None came.

Zoltan looked over at Saraph and said, "You know, his education was not in communications or media. He brought a masters in microbiology into this field. One of the most religiously zealous devotees that I have ever known… of anything!"

"Of course," Saraph said. "Worldly wisdom is concocted by your intellectual elite and is trickled down through the educational institutions, finding its way into the cultural mainstream through your arts and finally to the status of cultural convention. It is under such influence that nearly every support anchored in the foundations of your society has rotted. The house you live in is termite infested."

Saraph looked at Trevor for a moment. "It is rare to see each of the stages of that process so actively demonstrated in one person."

Zoltan was thinking about Saraph as he watched Trevor talk. He silently humored himself for the concern that Saraph, and the thing he called "*the gift*," was somehow part of Trevor's conspiracy to take him down. The idea had faded to the status of unlikely, as it had several times before. Sensing that he was being watched, he looked at Saraph, who appeared to be looking at Zoltan's ear.

"What are you staring at?"

"Your ear."

"Why?"

"Oh, I'm sorry. Does it bother you?"

"Yes, it does... no, no it doesn't bother me. I don't really care."

Zoltan went back to watching the meeting. Saraph continued staring at his ear. After a few minutes of periodically itching his ear and generally being bothered, Zoltan looked at Saraph again.

"What are you doing?" he demanded.

"I was just thinking."

"You're thinking about my ear? What... is it dirty?"

"No, I don't think so," Saraph said, raising up and leaning back to look.

"Stop it! What are you thinking about?" Zoltan demanded.

Saraph shrugged. "I don't know... I was just thinking through what Trevor has presented here so far. The ear is quite a wonder, as you know. There was Creation ... the world, the universe. The ear was made for its appreciation. Noise technology inverts that. Sound engineers start with the ear and create sound to be applied *to it*—artificial stimulation. Kind of a manipulation of the ear-brain design. Trevor is taking that a step further and inverting it again. He wants to reinvent the sense altogether for the sound he wants to manipulate it with. Very interesting."

"Very interesting? That's your response, 'very interesting'?" Zoltan asked, amazed.

"You're right, it probably doesn't qualify as 'very interesting,' just interesting," Saraph answered. He kept staring at Zoltan's ear. "I was trying to calculate the impact. It's hard to predict, but, if he is successful, it will go way beyond the ear. It's the brain I'm thinking about, a rearrangement of sound processing. We're way beyond technology here. I hope he's doing the math thoroughly."

Saraph turned back to the meeting, leaving Zoltan staring at *his* ear. After a short time he looked back at Zoltan. "You have anything to do with this?" he asked.

They locked gazes for a moment and turned back to the meeting.

"We are developing a few new technologies, of which I will demonstrate crude and simplistic versions to you today…" Trevor paused to scan the room. "…in just a few minutes from now."

Leaning forward in his chair, Trevor again placed his elbows on the table before him and folded his hands. "This technology has the ability to scan an environment, such as this room, collect data points and map every detail nearly as quickly as the human mind, especially every human detail. It can then project sensual impressions that touch, or should I say *arouse*, all of the senses. This arousal is actual and far more convincing…."

He thought for a moment. "More convincing than any 3D experience has ever been, for example. Technology by such definition was always crude at best, identified by limitations.

"By doing so, *we* will be able to manipulate the environment and the elements within it, creating a new environment into which we can introduce subtleties of sensation never before experienced – a new language of senses, you might say. It might be helpful to envision it as virtual acupuncture. We will soon be the masters of memory.

"We are running out of ways to stimulate our human viewers, to give them what they want, to take them further. We must now stimulate evolution through introducing our viewers to new environments that will require adaptation's invention of new senses.

"Our push for more, louder, faster has led us back here … to subtlety, nuance, sanctuary. It is, I believe, what we were craving all along. This is a very exciting time. I hope you can appreciate it. This is where evolution meets revolution, where creator and created merge in the dynamism of collaborative creation. For the first time, *humans* can chart the course of human destiny."

Trevor sat back once again and watched as from afar, like a schoolmaster observing children on the newly installed playground. But the children were not playing. Most everyone at the table appeared rather pensive, even morose.

"Questions, comments … ," Trevor invited. Putting his hands behind his head, he smiled as he reclined, gloating.

"Com'on Patrick, this is your moment. This is discussion time."

Patrick Bruce looked at Trevor and grinned and shook his head. "Awesome … I think," he finally said. "No, definitely, definitely amazing. It's just taking me a minute to sort it out. You got a bit deeper than I was expecting there. You should warn us before you do that."

"Still with me?" Trevor asked with a smile.

"Oh yeah, absolutely. It's like, I work in the machine, if you get my meaning. I create wild stuff inside of the technology. Sounds like you are using the technology to create the wild stuff outside of it and get us into it."

The two looked around at everyone else and realized that the others were nearly all looking at Oaks.

"Michael," Trevor invited warmly.

Oaks did not respond immediately. He appeared to be thoughtful if not reluctant.

"If your purpose for a restoration of subtlety," he finally began, "was a return to simplicity and calm, it would be refreshing. But you're ambition is for a new, larger dialogue for *you* to dominate and manipulate. Pardon my suspicion that your dubious motivation is to conduct whatever amuses you and whatever your sponsors will endorse as long as it sells their products ... at any cost."

"Oaks," John Belk blurted angrily, "why is it always a surprise to you that this is a business. Get over it! Please, no more commentaries on the obvious."

"You know, we can do without that kind of attitude, John," Trevor said.

He stared at Belk with an annoyed look on his face. He had expected a negative appraisal from Oaks. It was Belk's unwitting affirmation of Oaks' statement that he did not appreciate.

Trevor looked back at Oaks. "Everyone has a right to an opinion. That's why I opened it to discussion. Please, Michael, continue."

"There was a king named Agrippa," Oaks obliged, cautiously. "He is famous for being nearly convinced of the truth. Much of what you have said here strikes me as of a similar nature. Close, but ultimately so very far off the mark ... dangerously far."

Trevor smiled and nodded, indicating that Oaks was true to a form he had anticipated.

"As far as potential," Oaks continued, "there is a great deal of potential for tragedy here. And one of the greatest tragedies is that all of your brilliance, skill and ingenuity are misplaced simply because you refuse to acknowledge the true origin and nature of 'soul' and the reality of the spiritual realm.

"You are right, Trevor, to say that we are all aware of it. It is the context in which we live. It is real, it is universal and it is undeniable. And it is the one thing that you will, as you noted, never be able to control or fabricate. It is the fact that you cannot control it that drives you and frustrates you. And it is this, too, that demands that you pretend to deny its immutable reality. Someone is bigger than you, Trevor," he said, pausing. Compassion was in his gaze. "Big enough that His sovereignty sustains the 'bigger' that you call *memory*."

"Thank you, Michael," Trevor said, maintaining his demeanor. "Anyone else?"

"I have one question for you, Trevor."

"Sure, John, what is it?" Trevor turned to look at John Ray. "Who is '*we*?'"

Saraph and Zoltan looked at one another. Saraph flicked his brows. Then he rose up onto his toes as a smile began to spread across his face. Lowering himself, the smile became a look of exuberance. Rising up again, he reached high above his head with his hands.

"Easy," Zoltan said with a tone of annoyance. "A fan participating in the wave at a ball game."

Saraph shook his head to indicate that the guess was incorrect. Zoltan frowned. "I'm really not in the mood for your silliness anyway."

Saraph began to jerk himself back and forth. He leaned far to his right before straightening and rising up tall, again flinging his hands above his head.

Zoltan looked disgusted. "A kid on a roller coaster," he said, turning away from Saraph.

Saraph stopped. "One you wouldn't want to get on, because its engineers have a low regard for you and have been careless with their math."

Chapter 24
ON THE WIND

Surveying the room, Trevor's eyes moved slowly. The corners of his mouth were turned slightly upward. His head was tilted awkwardly toward his right shoulder. But for his eyes, he was as still as death. And all other eyes in the room were fixed on his. Everyone seemed suspended with him in anticipation of a next word. But a second became five when The Chair had caught his attention and exploited his hesitation between thoughts. And five seconds of pause seemed like ten minutes of melodrama in the context of the inflated introduction. Forcing himself to refocus, Trevor looked down at the table.

Unstuck, he said, "The first thing ... ." He looked up at his audience. "The first thing we will unveil for your privileged viewing is a project that is ideally suited for the kinds of developments to which I have eluded. But before we can do that, I'd like to introduce you to someone." Turning toward the door, Trevor said, "Linda, please send in Mr. Baxter."

The door opened and in stepped a white-haired man of average height and slender build, wearing an orange turtleneck sweater beneath a royal blue blazer. For Trevor, this simple activity took place as through a lens of preoccupation. A sense of conquest had worked its way through his clouded memory of the earlier interaction with Salmone and Charon. He was beginning to feel emboldened enough to assert his self-appointed authority as company chief. A vague memory challenged his perception and sent a shiver down his spine. But he found it easily ignored.

"Friends, this is Mr. Ernie Baxter. He is the Vice President of Research and Development for Collins and Boren, which, as you know, has recently broken into the top one hundred of the Fortune Five Hundred." All present applauded graciously, impressed by the revelation of the visitor and his status. But the applause quickly fizzled to an awkward end.

"Mr. Baxter is going to tell you a little bit about the unique, might I say unprecedented, relationship developing between Universal Syndicate and Collins and Boren," Trevor announced distractedly. "Then he will unveil a special demonstration of our collaborative efforts. Ernie," he said, nodding toward his guest.

"Thank you, Trevor," Baxter said, as chipper as a schoolboy at his birthday party. "And thank you all for this opportunity to be a part of this meeting and the ushering in of a new era, not just a new era for Universal Syndicate and Collins and Boren, but a new era for the media industry, and thus, for the world.

"If I may be so bold, what I am about to introduce will very shortly become the most widely viewed series in the history of television. Before the pilot airs, critics will be using the word 'phenomenon' universally when speaking of this production. It will make fading memories of all cultural boundaries. It will make *demigods* of CEOs, *White Houses* of corporate headquarters, and *parliaments* of conference rooms like this one."

Trevor rapped on the table with his knuckles three times. As everyone turned and looked at him, he leaned forward and said, "It is called Monopoly Complex!" He did this by compulsion for dramatic effect, oblivious to his offence to Baxter for the interruption.

The Monopoly Complex was a direct result of Zoltan's design and calculations based upon his research studies. On paper it was a success that could only be measured by his own previous standards. But he knew it to be something much more significant. Even Trevor experienced a fleeting sense of awe at his own treachery for invoking the title of Zoltan's creation as if it were one of his own. Yet, he could not resist the feeling of entitlement.

Zoltan was shaking his head. *So, this is why you are so bold, my anemic protégé.* "There is no spotlight capable of casting you as a worthy shadow of mine with or without Collins and Boren and the pirating of all of my best work," he muttered aloud.

"You don't get it, do you?" Saraph asked.

The expression on Zoltan's face changed.

"Let me say this, before going any further … " Baxter began again, moving past his annoyance with Trevor. "It is no secret that the great success you have enjoyed at Universal Syndicate is due largely to the extraordinary efforts you invest in sociological research. The resulting understanding you have of your audiences, which appears to be ever increasing, speaks for itself.

"Now, for those of you who pride yourselves on your creative productions, please do not misunderstand me. Your media magic came first and will always be the signature of your celebrity as a company. Yet, you must admit, your studio excellence was widely acclaimed long before your rise to the top of the industry. That assent began, in my opinion, when you became the premier developers of sociological research software in the world."

At this last statement everyone at the table was compelled to clap, though, not all were fully appreciative of the praise. Zoltan, however, felt proud and vindicated by the statement, so much so that he spontaneously reached over and gave Saraph's shoulder a good squeeze. They looked at each other, and Zoltan bobbed his head, indicating his personal acceptance of the high praise.

"Your vanity is a thin bravado," Saraph said. "Both you and Trevor, however accomplished, and for however long, have failed equally in the service of your Master." He looked over at Trevor with pity in his eyes and then back at Zoltan. "Your boast and your judgment are hollow."

During the applause, Baxter made a point of making eye contact with every person at the table. "Of course, there is a reason that I mention this in the context of our present introduction," he continued. "In fact, there is a very important reason that I don't want you to miss." He again paused.

"It is the combined use of superior research and superior media stratification that has resulted in superior productions. Market strategies that capitalize on them have seated you comfortably at the top." He leaned forward, placed his elbows on the table, clasped his hands together and pointed both index fingers toward his audience. "The same phenomenon is at work among businesses throughout the world at this moment."

Looking around at his captive audience, Baxter noticed the flat effect in the faces before him. He quickly realized that the point he made seemed perfectly obvious, and thus, anticlimactic.

"Let me explain," he said, attempting to recover his momentum. He leaned back and rested his arms upon those on his chair. "Several months ago . . . ." Baxter stopped and looked at Trevor. "I guess it might be a year by now. At any rate, Trevor noticed some patterns while studying some of the research findings in your Corporate Initiatives project." Michael Oaks immediately looked at Trevor with an expression of scorn, and his extended stare made his disapproval clear to all.

Zoltan looked at Saraph and shook his head. "'Noticed' because they were completely detailed in my notes," he said. He wondered how long Trevor had been putting these things in place.

"Now, Trevor and I have worked together extensively in the past. We have known each other for quite a few years," Baxter added, as a calculated buffer against any objections. "So, he shared this information with me . . . as a trusted confidant, of course." He watched the silent reaction of Oaks and the others, waiting for the anticipated objection. But none came. He did not realize that no one besides Oaks had any awareness of the project he spoke of on which to base an objection.

Relieved, Baxter continued. "We studied the findings meticulously day and night."

"What we discovered was an unmistakable pattern of corporate mergers..." Trevor interjected, pausing for effect. "Globally," he added as if expecting everyone to comprehend the significance immediately. But, in fact, no one did, with the exception of Oaks. Yet, all began to stir. Several people sat up straighter in their chairs. Others leaned forward or back in theirs. Trevor looked around and noted the activity. Only Oaks remained still.

"What it means," Baxter followed, "is that something very big is happening... something predictable, something observable, and something with implications for every person on this planet." He looked around the table. "Are you following me?" he asked, surveying faces that conveyed blank amazement.

Other than Oaks, no one yet comprehended his meaning. Yet, each assumed the others understood what was being said. And no one was willing to be the only one to ask the question that revealed their bewilderment.

"Let me assure you," Baxter said, having difficulty containing his enthusiasm, "we are the only ones...."

"That is a foolish assumption," Oaks said, interrupting.

"What's that?" Baxter asked.

"How did you come by such precious information?"

"Well, as I told you, Trevor...."

"Pirated. Isn't that the word you are looking for?"

Baxter stared at Oaks. Answerless, he turned his gaze to Trevor.

"Michael," Trevor began with a smile, "I really think that this would be a good time for you to temper your severe outlook on things."

"Perhaps you're right," Oaks responded stoically. "Your own opinions will best inform us." Then, looking at Baxter, he asked, "What is it about a pirate that inspires trust in you? Or, what," he asked, turning back to Trevor, "about a man who uses stolen information leads you to conclude that it is safe with him?"

No one at the table but Trevor, Baxter and Oaks understood the gravity of these interactions, but all were instinctively riveted on the dialogue.

"Truth is … " Oaks continued, "you have already lost your advantage by your own participation. You are now in a race to air the first episode."

Baxter and Trevor looked at one another. Trevor put his hands together and pressed his index fingers against his lips thoughtfully.

"If the information is as valuable as you have stated," Oaks said, looking at Baxter, "and I believe it is … ." He looked back at Trevor. "Who among those you employed to analyze it can you trust to be more trustworthy than yourselves and resist pirating it elsewhere?" He looked back and forth between the two men. "It is on the wind, gentlemen. Likely, every major player in the industry presently owns a copy of the files. The research Zoltan and I have done of late suggests as much."

Saraph heard Zoltan groan and looked to see him walk several steps away, turn and rest his forehead against the wall. The only sound in the room was the running water of the fountain sculpture. "My god, he's right," he muttered.

"Treachery reigns," Zoltan heard Oaks say, as if in the background of his own troubled thoughts. "Where every man's advantage is the law, who can rest? But please, do continue your presentation."

"Yes … please … ."

The voice was that of Gwen Thomas, the new head of sports marketing, who was sitting directly to the left of Trevor.

240

"I mean, this is suspenseful and all, but can someone let the rest of us in on the plot, so to speak."

Trevor, expressionless, unclasped his hands and gestured toward Baxter.

"Okay, where was I?" Baxter asked.

"Go back to the global merger patterns in the research studies. That's where I got lost." Thomas looked around the table and saw strains of agreement that affirmed her suggestion. Then she added, "And the bit about 'implications for every person on the planet.' That was pretty intriguing also."

"OK," Baxter began, "let's start there. But, let me ask *you* something. What are the events that galvanize cultures, those that social groups rally around?"

"Sports, competition," said Thomas. "World championships, like the Olympics, the World Cup, the Tour De France."

"Exactly! What else?" Baxter pressed.

"Wars," said Chris Troutman, Vice President of Production Engineering.

"Of course," Baxter responded enthusiastically. "Local conflicts and those on the other side of the world that are big enough to imply a threat to our way of life, right? Those are two of the three biggies I was thinking of."

"Politics," said Ralph Tillman, Universal Syndicate's new CFO. "Elections, uprisings, takeovers, revolutions, power shifts."

"Bingo," Baxter said, turning to face Tillman, who was sitting to his right.

"Bingo is on the list?" Bruce questioned with an animated look on his face. "I wouldn't a thought that. I was thinking video games maybe. But I wouldn't uv guessed bingo." He looked at Stuart McCauley and saw that he enjoyed the comment. "Everyone's got their thing, I guess, but, man, there's some big-time stuff in this world that I don't even know about," he added with a shrug.

"I wouldn't u guessed it either," McCauley said through

his chuckles.

"You guys are good," Baxter said, ignoring Bruce and McCauley. "And that last one is exactly the heart of the matter—'power shifts.' Who's making their move to the top? Is it our guy, our team, our representative, our party, our troops ... is it us? Isn't this the riveting concern that has people gathering around their TV screens and computer monitors throughout the world? Now, imagine you bring them all together in one package."

"Haven't terrorists already beaten us to this one?" Troutman asked.

"Really," Thomas followed. "Checked out the security at the Olympics lately? Politics, sports and war right there—national rivalries, bomb threats and scoreboards."

"And we thought someone out there actually cared about the toss of a javelin," quipped a portly, yellow-haired woman with a smoker's rasp in her voice.

"Meredith Train," Zoltan said, leaning over to inform Saraph. "Archives ... she runs the media library with the exacting standards of a neural surgeon."

"We're getting a bit off track here," Trevor said, annoyed. "The 'one package,' as Mr. Baxter called it...." He raised his voice for effect, perusing the room to command everyone's attention. "As I told you already, the package is called the Monopoly Complex."

Trevor was leaning back in his chair, which he had moved several feet from the table in order to sit with one leg crossed over the other. He watched the scene before him as one looks upon a painting from an appropriate distance. Monarch Charon had assessed him correctly. He cared little for anyone at the table, reserving all emotional investment for his technological obsessions. Like Zoltan, he valued people only for their utility as production resources or for audience response to his impressive work.

At the moment he was feeling gratified by the impression

that the simple two word title was making upon his current audience. The room was quiet and everyone appeared to be frozen in place as they contemplated its meaning.

"What we have found," Baxter continued, "is that there are exactly twenty-six teams in what we are calling The Big League."

"You mean the world?" Oaks asked suggestively.

"Precisely," Baxter answered. "And we call them teams for lack of any more fitting descriptive term. They are not companies but conglomerates. Yet, conglomerates is such a cumbersome title and does not convey the dynamic complexities of these vast organic entities ... these complexes."

"So, why don't you call this Monopoly Complexes," asked John Belk.

"Who cares about the title," Train snapped, irritated by the lingering gaps in the information. "What are the teams ... who are they, and what are they doing?"

"The title refers not to individual teams, but to the prize," Trevor stated coolly, looking at Belk. Everyone in the room stared at him expecting more. Knowing that, Trevor just continued looking at Belk with a subtle smile on his face. Then he looked at Train and saw the agitation in her body language. His smile broadened as he reveled in the calculated effects of the intentional delay.

"It has taken us six months to identify the teams ... that there are twenty-six observable, traceable participants. This, in my opinion, was due to the deliberately deceptive merger schemes they all employ, partly to hide from each other and partly to hide from the national and international watchdogs."

"The prize?" Tillman asked.

"Yes, the prize, we believe, will be the one complex—the last team standing," Baxter announced. "We think—and it is early yet—but we think that the strongest teams will eventually swallow up other teams in mega-mergers, or team mergers, until the one rules them all. Thus the name: Monopoly Complex."

Mouths hung open throughout the room. Several people began to rub burning eyes that had been held wide-open for too long. A few were astonished at the cavalier nature with which Trevor and his guest were reporting activities with such profound implications.

"We do not have evidence of that yet," Trevor stated, pretending a fatherly, stabilizing measure of consolation. He paused for a moment. "But there is plenty to suggest that the positioning activities we are identifying will lead to that. The twenty-six are definitive. We have given each of them names. We observe them on a daily basis."

"Isn't this illegal?" Train asked, becoming uncomfortable with the whole discussion. She looked around the table. "You know, monopolies and all. There are international laws against this sort of thing."

"We're talking about international capital complexes with more natural and manufactured resources than all but a few nations. They are each monetarily more powerful and influential than any government on earth. What laws do you suggest should govern them, and who do you suggest should enforce them?" Trevor responded.

"Wow, this is the first time I have ever been made to feel like the stuff I do is boring," Bruce said.

"Pardon me," Baxter interrupted, "but I think we are losing sight of the beauty of this thing." He looked around and saw a mixture of reactions. In some of the faces he saw eager anticipation for more information. Others looked morbidly serious. "Look, I don't deny the gravity of this," he said excitedly, "but I'm not hearing any of the right questions."

"Like, what do the complexes look like? What are the merger patterns telling us? Who are the star players on the teams?" Oaks suggested.

"Exactly," Baxter responded. "Those are good ones for

starters."

"Or, perhaps more importantly," Oaks continued, "for our purposes here, which team are we on, and is this meeting suggestive of a strategic merger between Collins and Boren and Universal Syndicate?"

Trevor uncrossed his legs, pulled his chair up to the table, upon which he placed his elbows as he stared at the fiddling thumbs on his clasped hands. "Michael," he said with forced pleasantness, the redness in his face betraying a waning of his self-control.

"Exactly it!" Baxter blurted, attempting to salvage some of the enjoyment of the announcement. "I mean, exactly it. Not just the exact questions we should be asking, but the questions everyone in the whole world will be asking very soon. You've put your finger right on it, Mr. Oaks. And it is exactly the reason everyone—and I do mean *everyone*—will be watching the day Monopoly Complex airs for the first time and every time it airs thereafter.

"We're talking about ratings that will take Universal Syndicate from the uncontested media giant in this country to the uncontested world heavyweight champion. Collins and Boren and Universal Syndicate...? Great idea! I'm glad you suggested it, Mr. Oaks. We'll have to look into that immediately." Baxter looked around the room when he heard the laughter in which he was suddenly and unexpectedly enveloped. Relieved by the change of mood in the room, he paused and enjoyed his success.

Encouraged, Baxter continued. "That is exactly the kind of activity we are witnessing and the type of competitive movement that Monopoly Complex will be following, examining, telecasting with live play-by-play coverage, expert analysis, and celebrity commentary."

Baxter was so genuinely enthused that his passion and animation were converting much of his audience. Though a few faces still conveyed serious concerns, most seated around the table began to smile as their faces animated agreeably amazed reactions. Nearly everyone was stirring and beginning to vocalize emotions in terms like, "This is unbelievable," or "Oh, my god, this is huger than huge!" Only Oaks, John Gray and Trevor remained expressionless.

"Everyone will be asking the very questions Mr. Oaks has suggested. 'What team am I on? What is my team doing today?' You think people are compulsive now about checking their stock reports, following their ball team's statistics and watching election returns? I'm telling you, this show might just put major league sports out of business."

Baxter stood up from his chair, put his hands on the table and leaned forward. "It will eliminate all disconnect between the viewer and the viewed phenomenon. Everyone will get it! Everyone will see himself in the context of the team. Everyone will understand the significance of a merger. Everyone will get it because we will tell them.

"We will provide on-site analysis of the strategic importance of the acquisition of an oil company, a health care network, an educational institution, a banking system, and, yes, a media powerhouse. We have developed a point system for different types of mergers. No one, my friends, will be ambivalent about Monopoly Complex. The most important merger has already begun, the merger of individual and team identity and destiny."

Baxter sat down in his chair and relaxed for a moment. He and Trevor observed the stunned faces in the silent room. Only Saraph noticed the absence of the sound of running water. He looked behind him at the static sculpture on the wall and he pointed it out to Zoltan. But Zoltan seemed only to be annoyed by the interruption of his concentration on the meeting.

Leaning forward in his chair, Baxter once again began strumming his fingers on the table energetically. "Trevor mentioned when he introduced me that Collins and Boren is in the top one hundred on the Fortune Five Hundred list. Fortune Five Hundred offers no indication of any knowledge of the complexes. We belong to number sixteen among the twenty-six. Our team, that is, which the complex identifies by another name, is number sixteen. We dropped three spaces last month.

"While it is true that the twenty-six have remained stable since we first identified them. We anticipate team mergers will eventually take place. Such moves would profoundly change the field and shake the global marketplace. Merger of twenty-five and twenty-six, for example, would presently produce a new number one. More importantly, it would reduce the field by one."

"The time is perfect," Trevor announced. "The time is now. We will shift the majority of our resources and attention to this project immediately." He paused to allow for emotional reactions and objections. But there were none. The room had become morgue-like except for the sounds of his and Baxter's voices as they continued their tag-team communication.

"The priority is to launch while the twenty-six are intact," Baxter stated, using a commanding tone for the first time. "Starting with a stable, identifiable field of competitors is essential to the credibility and success of any competitive endeavor.

"There is another," Michael Oaks said looking around the room. "Another priority, that is."

Trevor Langdon immediately became restless. Oaks' "on the wind" comment had been bothering him since it met his ears, and it had made him irritable and impatient with the meeting he had long anticipated.

"There are two fields for you to be concerned with," Oaks offered. "The field of the twenty-six and the field of as many of the twenty-six as have this information and are currently scrambling to be first to launch the debut of Monopoly Complex, or whatever they may call it."

Baxter looked at Trevor, then back at Oaks. Both he and Trevor were disquieted by their mutual suspicions stirred by

Oaks' words.

"Oh, wow," emoted David Carlow, a red-headed, skinny South African, who was clearly enthralled with the proceedings. "This is getting more like one of our prime-timers by the minute."

"Pure genius, that one," Zoltan said to Saraph. "Head of Audio Creations. Amazing the power a guy like this has to manipulate perception."

Ralph Tillman groaned. "Except that we're in it as we produce it," he said. "It's about us … all of us."

"The individual casualties of the big plot movement may get a little close to home in this one. Might get a little spooky handlin' at times," Carlow said gravely.

Ernie Baxter and Trevor Langdon were paying no attention to any of these comments. The silent communications between the two of them and Oaks indicated that they were managing the distraction of Oaks' assertions.

"Do you doubt it?" Oaks questioned, also ignoring the others.

The three men continued to exchange glances that made uncomfortable waiting for the others around the table. Baxter and Langdon were beginning to see that what they had announced as something "very big" was quite a bit bigger.

"The advantages of being the one among the twenty-six in control of the media source that controls the attention and perception of the world concerning this little intrigue of yours ought to be fairly obvious," Oaks said, breaking the silence. "It may be, in fact, that others are already finished with their introductory meetings."

Chapter 25
A SILENT TEMPER

The blue and yellow form of the formula one race car sped around the turn and headed straight toward them. The gears shifted and the engine responded as the car accelerated. In an instant it was there and gone. The sound was deafening, the bombardment of their senses as blurry as the speedy movement. Ralph Tillman, in one of the seats closest to the screen, felt as though he had been run over. For an instant, he consciously struggled to convince his senses otherwise. Tingly feelings in his eyes and on his face had made him flinch and squint as if track debris had flown up and hit him. He, along with several others, reached up to tidy hair that they imagined to have been messed up by the wind coming off the car as it passed.

They were watching the car from the side now as it maneuvered through serpentine turns at the other side of the track. Their view was close up and traveling along the side of the car as it raced along. The details in the glassy surface of the car tempted Patrick Bruce to reach out and run his fingers along the smooth-sculpted contours. He heard the sounds of engines racing along the track behind him. He felt disoriented, fooled by a powerful illusion of reality. He again heard the engine wind as the flashing reflections on the blue surface picked up speed. He saw in those reflections that he was passing an orange, green and white car to the inside as the car downshifted and swept into a turn.

Fluidly, the reflection of the other car moved on and left them all looking at an orange and green logo beside the furious spinning black of the rear tire. Meredith Train felt a warm wind rushing past and she was certain she could smell the hot rubber. The logo grew larger until it forced the tire from view and stood alone before the mesmerized audience. The sound was so convincing that nearly all were compelled to cover their ears. But it softened just to the point of being bearable as the logo began to recede in the midst of a field of darker blue on a dull unreflective surface.

Suddenly, Gwen Thomas realized that the roar in her ears was no longer that of an engine but of a crowd. As the logo continued to diminish, more of its surroundings were revealed. Quickly, she was delighted to recognize the familiar confines of Dodger Stadium. She was at field level and nearly breathless.

A blurry, black band flashed by several times as more of the stadium, the field and the players on it came into view. The once prominent logo was now a distant brand on the right field wall. The black band passed again, then again and again. Then it stopped. A flash of white nearly collided with another sweep of the black band, and they heard a loud pop as a pitcher for the San Francisco Giants came into view. Chris Troutman flinched when he heard the umpire yell something indiscernible. Everyone realized at once that they were watching a ball game from just over the catcher's shoulder.

Zoltan was mesmerized. He noticed that his eyes were watering. "Absolutely seamless transitions," he softly muttered, shocked and pained with disbelief. *Stunning, perfect*, he thought, feeling consumed with jealous amazement.

The view again began to move. As more of the catcher came into view, it traveled down the left side of his crouched form until it focused in on a logo on the back of his shoe. Zoltan's head jerked backward involuntarily as the scene was replaced with complete whiteness and the sounds of the stadium seemed to be sucked out of his ears through a great tunnel until they were completely gone and the logo reappeared before him.

The image before him expanded and the logo was but an element within a larger symbol. Just then a woman stepped in front of it. She appeared to be standing behind the counter of a reception area. The large company seal was on the wall behind her. She raised three publications from behind the counter and placed them upon it. Two were daily papers, the third was a magazine. She appeared to sit down and then disappeared behind the counter. Steam was rising from just beyond the other side of the counter and Zoltan imagined his enjoyment of the smell of fresh-brewed coffee.

A few seconds later footsteps could be heard and the woman's head popped up from behind the counter. Zoltan felt a tension due to her nearness and his desire for her. His heart rate picked up noticeably. She smiled, placed her hand upon the publications and nodded her head. Then the entire view was blocked by the back of a man in a black pinstriped suit. He turned to his left as he picked up the publications and walked away from the counter. As he did, the large title, *Fortune,* could be identified on the magazine.

The man came to a door and the woman stood and said, "Excuse me, Mr. Fujimura, I forgot this one." As she waved a copy of the *Wall Street Journal,* Ralph Tillman was certain he felt a breeze on his face. Zoltan was perplexed by an odd sensation of familiarity with the building and the activities within it. The woman walked toward the doorway where the man had already stepped into his office. She waited there and then a hand could be seen reaching for the paper. As she gave it to him his other hand was extended toward her. She looked over her shoulder and glanced nervously around before placing her hand in his and stepping into his office. The door closed.

Zoltan realized that his palms were perspiring and he was short of breath. He could still feel the tenderness of touch in his left hand. He looked around the room and saw that the other men, too, were looking at their left hands wonderingly. He then noticed that each woman was doing the same with her right hand. All appeared distressed.

He looked at Saraph. "Why can I feel … ?"

"I told you that you could not affect anything you come in contact with. I didn't say that nothing could affect you," Saraph reminded him.

The wood grain on the door filled Zoltan's view. He again took his eyes off the screen and glanced around the room to see others doing the same. Silent communications of amazement were being exchanged. He looked back at the screen and saw that the color of the grain on the door had changed.

The door opened and several people could be seen sitting around a conference table. Through the glass walls beyond them Zoltan recognized the Canadian coast where modern containerships were coming in from the sea, loaded with cargo. Rising prominently in the foreground to the right, a stately Basilica displayed its proud Romanesque architecture. The scene was blocked momentarily by a person with a tray of drinks who was stepping into the room.

When the figure moved away several new individuals could be seen. The table had changed and the scene outside the windows was no longer dominated by a coast but by a modern auto manufacturing plant. A long freight train burdened with steel chassis made its way toward the sprawling facilities. To his left Zoltan saw a distant commercial airliner come into view. It descended toward a runway that was hidden somewhere in the midst of the busy urban skyline. He was amazed by the range of dynamics that his ears were reporting related to the images on the screen.

The view was moving closer to a person sitting at the table

until it zoomed in over his shoulder and became filled by the screen on the laptop before him. Playing on the screen was a scene from the movie *It's a Wonderful Life*, which suddenly stopped, leaving a larger-than-life image of Jimmy Stewart as George Bailey for all to look at. The image faded as the overhead lights came back on.

Trevor gave everyone a few minutes to collect their thoughts as all assembled glanced around at one another. Several people looked poised to speak, but no one did.

"My friends, the images you have just seen were very specifically chosen. We went to great efforts to make sure that absolutely every element, every person, every logo, every product and every clip you have just watched is verifiably a part of the Monopoly Complex. No actors were used, no scenes created. Everything but what you see on the screen now was an authentic, real world capture."

As Zoltan observed and listened, he felt sick. He was stung by how much better the production was than anything he had ever seen or, more importantly, produced. *The industry has passed me by, and it happened right under my nose*, he thought. *It happened on my own distracted watch. It happened using some of my own initiatives.*

Saraph looked at Zoltan. "We can leave at any time. Remember, it's up to you. I don't need any of this. It's rather unimpressive, really. Wonders await … ."

The room was progressively becoming busy with a clutter of questions, exclamations, voiceless communications and expressions of disbelief.

"How on earth did … ?" John Belk began before being cut off by Trevor.

"Wait, wait, wait … just a minute and we'll get to all of your questions. First of all, did anyone notice anything intriguing?"

Meredith Train laughed heartily. "You've got to be kidding. After what you just showed us, you want to know if we noticed anything 'intriguing'?"

"Meredith, c'mon, something in particular."

"Patrick did," Gwen Thomas offered.

Trevor looked at Patrick Bruce. "What was it, Master Bruce?" Trevor asked.

"Oh, yeah, the girl ... woman, whatever, the one who went into the office with her boss. It looked to me like she was also in the second office vignette ... the one with, what was that ... Sao Paulo, Brazil in the background?"

"Yes it was, and yes, you are right. Same person, corporate espionage at its best! You think that our viewers won't be interested in that?"

"This will redefine ratings," Baxter added. "There simply is no competition. I defy you to name any programming that this won't completely shut down."

"Another team's version of this?" Oaks questioned suggestively.

"He's stuck on this, isn't he?" Baxter said, looking to Trevor, who just laughed and shook his head. "You're a bit of a negative minded fella," Baxter said, looking back at Oaks.

"As far as 'memory' goes," Oaks said, "the subtleties were impressive. But at the other end, our transition away from extreme is less than was reported earlier. But I must commend you on the absence of murders."

"Murders?" Baxter questioned.

"What?" Bruce chided with a burst of laughter.

"Yes, murders. Getting back to Trevor's question about things we found intriguing: There were no corpses, no blood-spattered walls, no gruesome homicide scenes or morgue shots. That's intriguing. After all the energy that this and other studios like it have put into creating our number one national obsession, you're not going to capitalize on it here? You're not going to serve the craving you created? You can be sure your competition will not leave that out," Oaks stated wryly.

Trevor stood to his feet, shifted his lower jaw to one side and stared at Oaks for a moment.

"Oaks, you need to lighten up," Patrick Bruce said with a laugh, amused by these interactions. "Just admit it, this is unbelievable stuff."

"Actually, these are important challenges," Trevor finally said. "Thank you, Michael, we will keep your suggestions in mind. I can think of one in particular we may start working on soon," he said with a smile, before sitting back down.

"I would think there are some legal difficulties dealing with the murder thing in . . . you know, reality programming," Bruce said.

"Yeah, but that's what will make it so edgy. And you know there's some of that going on with so much at stake in these mergers you're talking about. I agree with Michael, it's gotta be in there," Carlow said, completely missing the point of Oaks' comments.

"Hold it, hold it," Chris Troutman protested, "Let's not get lost in the whole murder, no murder thing. I wanna know about these shots of real situations. How'd you get this stuff? I mean, I can't imagine these teams are cooperating with our interest in footage of their secret activities."

"Forget that! I want to know about this technology," John Belk said, with his usual intensity. "Unbelievable! What is this? Where'd this neo-3D illusion come from? And these . . . these touchy feelies. Obviously, this is what you were talking about earlier, Trevor, with all that business about memory. I can see what you were saying about this being the ideal platform for introducing it all. But what is . . . where is it coming from? What is producing it? What exactly is happening?"

"I'm not sure I'm comfortable with it," Erin Bankroft said shyly.

"I'm not sure anyone will be," Belk countered. "At least, initially."

"Yeah, I agree. You've gotta wonder if the public's ready for this," Stuart McCauley chimed in. "I mean, it's cool stuff—very cool. But... ." He stopped and ran his hands through his hair, rubbed his arms and shuttered before adding, "Yikes!"

Having anticipated this response, Trevor allowed a few minutes for the flurry of comments and animated expressions to play out around the table.

Zoltan took the opportunity to lean over and inform Saraph that much of the technology was 'barrowed' from a favorite brain-child of his, Universal Syndicate's Medical Media Division. "Much of it came from Oaks' work with synthetic training environments for delicate surgical applications," he added with a tone of admission.

"Ok everybody, reel it back in here," Trevor finally said, raising his voice and clapping a few times. "Ernie, you want to give it a shot?"

"Love to," Baxter answered. Then he sat looking at his hands for a moment, trying to figure out his approach. When he looked up, he looked directly at Oaks. "First," he began, "I must acknowledge the brilliant work of Mr. Oaks, who designed and directed the development of the new system. If you have any questions, I'm sure Mr. Oaks will answer them at another time."

He was attempting nervously to get on to the next point without giving Oaks a chance to speak. But he appeared to be stuck. His original chipper demeanor was fading, and he was beginning to look uncomfortable. He looked back down at his hands, which were forming a rigid box shape by the fingers of each hand meeting their counterparts of the other at the tips.

As he observed these interactions, Zoltan found it inexplicable that Trevor had invited Oaks to attend this meeting. *How did that happen?* he pondered. *How did someone as calculating as Trevor make such a careless mistake?* But he was frustrated to make no progress toward an explanation. Trevor was silently mulling over the same thing at that very moment.

"I think, too," Baxter continued, "that we also must commend Mr. Oaks on his software achievement that made the camera work possible."

"Software?" Patrick Bruce interrupted. "I don't care about software. I'm interested in the ability to see a mosquito on the right field wall at Dodger Stadium with a lens that sits on the catcher's shoulder watching the action, then pans the catcher from . . . ." He looked puzzled for a second. "What?" he said, shaking his head vigorously. "That camera had to be behind the back stop! What?" he said again, looking around the table. "What kind of camera does that?"

"That's not really that impressive," Chris Troutman stated authoritatively. "That technology has been moving forward in generational leaps on nearly a monthly basis for the past several years. Someone in the world is introducing a remarkable new camera development in the latest issue of every publication in our trade."

"One that only we have," Baxter answered, ignoring Troutman's comments. "One that has wide-angle and extreme telephoto capacity—extreme meaning, one of a kind."

"How do you get a camera like that in those places?"

"It's quite small actually. It was developed by a company we own that specializes in security surveillance systems. Its forerunners were developed with the ability to capture an image clarity enabling its user to read the print on a dollar bill in a cash register a few feet away, and also count the eyelashes on a person walking in a door one hundred feet away. As the technology continued to advance, it caught our attention and we gave it some new direction. The one we mounted outside of Fujimura's office in Chicago looks like a motion detector to anyone who might notice it."

"That's how you followed the secretary from her desk to the office?"

"One angle capturing a large area," Baxter answered.

"That's where the software comes in," Oaks added. "Software that ... like the projection technology, was designed under the direction of my boss, Mr. Zoltan Antoniadis, and faithfully created for this company and its purposes alone!"

"And employed for this collaborative effort with Trevor's permission, in Zoltan's absence," Baxter retorted.

"Zoltan has been gone one week, Mr. Baxter. This work wasn't done in a week, now was it?"

"We're anticipating, optimistically, that these, our software and their camera issues will soon be irrelevant," Trevor stated suggestively, attempting to divert attention from the mention of Zoltan.

"You've talked to the board?" Gwen Thomas asked.

"I will. They were invited to this meeting. Most did not show, and those who did were not interested enough to stay."

"A bit of a cart-before-the-horse approach, it seems to me, Trevor," Meredith Train said soberly.

"It will be a mute point when they see what the potential is."

"Wow, more potential. Now that's gotta be a capital 'P'er!" Bruce quipped. Everyone turned and looked at him. Raising his hands, he said, "Hey, all these different kinds of potential, it's hard to keep track."

"I think this one is capitalized, italicized and in bold type, Patrick," John Belk answered with a laugh.

"Trevor," Ralph Tillman interjected, "are we to understand that you have been working for two companies?"

Trevor's expression conveyed that he took this comment as a betrayal of a trusted confidant. "For one ... with another," he stated carefully.

"And which is it that you've been working *for*, if I may be so bold?" Tillman questioned with less caution.

The interaction between Trevor and Ralph Tillman momentarily shut down all conversation. The room was quiet and the two men stared at each other extendedly.

Zoltan's eyes were on Oaks. He was trying to remember why he had despised him so much. Saraph tapped Zoltan on the shoulder and pointed again to the sculpture on the wall. This time Zoltan took serious note of Saraph's revelation. Not only was the water stopped but the lights were no longer on. Zoltan looked across the room at the changes in the lighted wall. He looked back at Saraph and shook his head, wondering. Saraph shrugged.

"Whoa, whoa, whoa," Patrick Bruce emoted abruptly. "I just thought of something. Who made this promo?"

"That's what I was getting at a while ago," Chris Troutman declared.

"Me too," said John Belk. "Remember?" he asked, looking at Bruce and nodding his head as if he were tipping a hat.

Bruce looked back and forth between the two men and then hung his head while giving it an animated shake. "No I don't," he said. "I must have missed that while my mind was being blown." He looked up at Trevor. "I mean, I'm sorry to distract us from such important details, and I would like to talk with you more about these wonderful inventions of yours later, Michael, but, what gives here? I'm sitting here looking around this table, and I'm intimately acquainted with what everyone has been over-their-heads busy with for at least the last two years."

He looked back at Oaks again. "Everyone but you, that is. You're a bit of an enigma, with your banker's hours and all." Looking at Trevor, he said, "But it sure doesn't sound like he's in on this with you guys. So, who produced this slick stuff?"

It was the very question that Trevor Langdon and Ernie Baxter did not want to hear, but knew would come. They purposely avoided looking at each other in order to prevent the appearance of clumsiness. Instead, Trevor looked directly at Bruce and smiled, then began to speak slowly and carefully.

"Some of you . . . ." He paused and thought for a moment. "Some of you are more loyal to this company than others, to the board, that is. So, let me caution you to hear me out. The board, and Peter Salmone especially, are definitely of traditional roots." He smiled condescendingly. "That's not all bad, I'll admit."

Pausing again, Trevor gestured toward Baxter. "We saw an urgency and took some necessary actions. There was no one on our side who was available to take this on. Collins and Boren own a small but significant production house in Europe."

"Trevor," Baxter interrupted. "It's best we deal directly with the intent."

"The two companies need each other," Trevor stated flatly. "And we will be a powerful force together. The board members tend to be a bit arrogant in their adherence to the old ways, frankly. I thought they needed to know that, while a merger would be preferable, this can be done without Universal Syndicate. This promo piece demonstrates that. In other words, we can move on without U.S. if that is necessary."

"In other words," Oaks mimicked, "you thought you could walk into this meeting and strong arm Salmone and the other board members into compliance with your merger scheme. And, if it doesn't work, you're prepared to walk away with pirated technologies to use for your interests."

Every eye in the room was fixed on Oaks, while he was looking between Trevor and Baxter.

"For the best interest of our industry, the best interest of millions of viewers who are screaming for more, more than just hyper definition 2-D media, more than dramas that are interesting but . . . yes, 'th th th th that's all, folks,'" Baxter declared. "Interesting but detached from the real world they live in. Interesting but, ultimately irrelevant."

"What they are screaming for is relief," Oaks countered.

"That is not what the research shows. All the research, especially that of the studies coming from your own company, speaks loudly of a growing disinterest in the norms of this industry. People are getting restless. They are clamoring for something more or something else."

"Silence, too, has a temper," Oaks responded, leaning forward against the table.

"And what is that supposed to mean?" Trevor asked, also leaning forward. "Sounds a bit like a threat."

"To borrow from Winston Churchill," Oaks said, "'The further back you can see, the further ahead you can see.' Past civilizations that chose the path we're on found ruin at its end. Look at the Roman Empire. You don't see similarities in its blood lust, sex obsession and, 'clamoring for more' entertainment excesses and that of our culture? Change is coming. Whether by the natural results of our dashing recklessly toward moral oblivion or by the shocking advent of a revolution that intercepts our course, yes, change is coming. It will not be served by any reinvention of senses or counterfeit posturing about aesthetic subtlety. It is a silent movement that you may not recognize in your studies, though, more likely one you have ignored. Either way, I do not believe the path you are on is leading to the lofty places you have imagined."

"And thank you, Mr. Oaks, for your ever grim opinions," John Belk snipped.

"We are not in need of borrowing from others at the moment," Trevor said, "or wandering around in the past as you so compulsively tend to do. We are moving forward … generally speaking, and with this meeting, if you don't mind. Jimmy has waited long," he added, looking up at the image on the screen.

Chapter 26
A SHADOW OF DOUBT

George Bailey finished lighting a cigarette and cast the match aside. Taking a thoughtful drag on the cigarette, he heard a train's whistle in the distance and looked up longingly. Reaching into the pocket of his suit jacket, he pulled out three foreign travel brochures. Pained, he cast aside the brochures and the dreams connected to them as he had the burnt match.

Coming through the door and down the front steps of the house in the background, his mother approached from behind him. He turned and, as she reached him, he gave her a kiss. She patted him on the lapel and they began to talk.

"Man, I haven't seen *It's a Wonderful Life* in years," John Belk exclaimed.

"The classic of classics," followed Meredith Train.

"I never really got it," Patrick Bruce responded, glancing around the room, frowning and shaking his head of thick, disheveled hair.

"Just watch," Trevor said, annoyed by the chatter and concerned that it might overlap something important in his demonstration.

They continued watching until several people began looking back at Trevor, glancing at one another and expressing through shrugs and other gestures their curiosity concerning

262

the seemingly random viewing.

"Nice," Belk said, turning to look over his shoulder at Trevor. "Nice selection. Meredith's right, a classic for sure."

"Yeah, and this is one of my favorite parts coming up. Very powerful," Chris Troutman added with meaning.

Patrick Bruce looked around the room rolling his eyes, animating his disbelief. "This is reminding me that we are past my lunchtime. I'm hungry. Did anyone order in anything? I'd like to suggest some fried iguanodon!"

"This really is one of the best parts," Gwen Thomas said with a shush, looking at Bruce. "Watch," she added, pointing at the screen. "Jimmy is brilliant."

"Quiet already," Trevor ordered. When Bruce turned around and gave him a puzzled frown, Trevor flicked his right hand toward him.

George Bailey walked beside a white picket fence with a stick in his hand outside of the home of his high school intrigue, Mary Hatch, who had come home from college. Mary opened a window behind Bailey. "What'a yu doing, picketing?" she called out to him.

Zoltan looked at Saraph. "This is where Trevor expects to become the Great Trevor Langdon ... watch," he said, nodding toward Trevor.

Trevor reached over and tapped Gwen Thomas on the shoulder, then motioned to her to move her chair closer to his. She did so apprehensively. Trevor began pointing at the monitor as he leaned over and whispered to her. She looked at him oddly and watched the monitor for a moment, then looked back at Trevor suspiciously. He nodded.

Thomas hesitated, then reached out and touched the screen just as Mary came into the picture again, sitting at one end of a couch and George at the other. Immediately the image on the small monitor took on the appearance of Gwen Thomas. She gasped aloud and switched her gaze to the large screen.

Covering her mouth with both of her hands, she slumped back in her chair utterly in shock. Simultaneously, everyone around the table but Oaks, Ray, Tillman and Meredith Train erupted with cheers and expressions of surprise and amazement.

The initial reactions died away quickly as all became silently enthralled with the reality of seeing their cohort replacing Donna Reed in the part of Mary Hatch alongside Jimmy Stewart in one of the most beloved movies ever produced. Zoltan and Saraph looked at one another.

"Media cloning," Zoltan said. "He's obsessed with it. He's so obsessed that he is blind to any shortfalls. No, actually, he's aware of them. We've talked about them. He's done some limited user tests that have produced some disturbing results. He really just doesn't care."

Hearing a ring, they both looked back at the screen. Gwen Thomas was mesmerized as she watched her own portrayal of Mary Hatch, who began talking into a phone standing next to George Bailey. Their mutual high school friend, Sam Wainwright, was calling from his business in New York as another woman fawned over him from behind. Mary, whom he referred to as "my girl," looked conflicted about the call and Bailey standing next to her.

Thomas' face mimicked the tension in Mary Hatch's on the screen before her. She was absolutely still, her eyes were wide and her mouth remained covered by one of her hands. The longer the scene went on, the more amazed she became. The voice was hers, the inflections hers, the subtleties of facial expressions hers.

"It's like a girlhood fantasy come true," she finally said, barely able to speak. She was mildly relieved to see Bailey momentarily leave the screen. Then Mary Hatch called Bailey to the phone, and they were soon sharing the one receiver. Thomas' heart was pounding, and she became nervous as the intimacy between George and Mary increased. The couple drew closer and closer to one another. Suddenly, the image of Jimmy Stewart playing

George Bailey changed to that of Trevor Langdon. Mortified, Thomas looked over to see Trevor grinning and pulling his hand back from the monitor.

She looked back at the big screen and was again unable to speak. Normally, the room would be filled with colorful humor, whistles and cheers as before, but everyone was so amazed by the scene before them and the fluidity of the transformations that they, too, were dumbstruck. For Thomas, it was one of the strangest experiences she had ever encountered. She was stunned and unable to move.

"So, that's your girlhood fantasy?" Bruce finally asked, introducing some spell breaking levity. "I wouldn't have guessed to be honest, but ... hey ... ."

Hearing snickers around her provided just the amount of thaw that Thomas needed to free her frozen mind. As the intimate tension grew between the couple on the screen, she reached over and slapped Trevor on the shoulder.

"Stop it!" she yelled. "Turn it off."

Trevor just sat back in his chair smiling as she leaned toward the monitor. Extending her hand, she nervously tried to decide what to do.

"Tre-e-e-e-vor ... !" Thomas yelled.

As George Bailey appeared to be mesmerized by the scent of Mary's hair, Thomas reacted thoughtlessly and touched the image of Trevor in a misguided attempt to get rid of him. Immediately hearing animated reactions around the table, she looked up at the big screen. To her horror she saw two swooning images of herself connected by an antique phone.

"Oh, now that's interesting," she heard Patrick Bruce say, followed by the odd noises of failed attempts to withhold laughter.

Mary, the Gwen Thomas on the left, was nervously distracted as her counterpart portraying Bailey on the right spoke into the phone with agitation in her voice. When she stopped speaking she lowered the phone and, turning slightly toward Mary, the tip of Bailey's nose caressed the hair at the top of her forehead.

The real Thomas turned around and punched Trevor in his chest. "Do something about this right now, you moron!" she demanded.

Trevor, tearful from laughter, leaned toward the monitor and looked at Oaks. Oaks stared back, not amused by the suggestive look he saw in Trevor's eyes.

"You don't actually have to have a fingerprint," Trevor said. "Not if…." He paused as he picked up a pen and began writing on a pad that lay on the table before the monitor. "Not if you have the person on file, that is."

As he finished writing, the image of Oaks replaced that of Thomas on the right side of the screen.

"Another of your girlish fantasies?" John Belk asked playfully.

Thomas was again stunned. Her face became flushed in a deep red, like that of an embarrassed school girl. As the phone dropped to the floor, the couple on the screen exploded with passion. Thomas looked at Trevor pleadingly, having no idea what to do.

Oaks did not share the difficulty. He stood up and took a step toward the keyboard. Trevor quickly put up his hand to indicate that he was taking care of the matter. Seconds later the scene changed completely. The image of George Bailey's Uncle Billy replaced the couple on the screen. He stood contemplating something very serious when Trevor paused the clip. Everyone turned to look at him as Oaks again took his seat. Thomas collapsed back in her chair.

Five minutes of chatter passed before Trevor spoke.

"So … your thoughts?"

"Terrifying," Thomas said, still out of breath and inspiring more laughter from her associates.

"Astounding," Troutman answered. "Of course we all knew

you were obsessed with doing something like this. But, wow ... I just had no idea it was this far along in development. Did you guys?" he asked, looking around the room.

"Not at all," Belk answered.

"No way, I had no idea," declared David Carlow, as nearly everyone else just shook their heads to convey their unawareness.

Trevor was feeling invincible. He looked at Oaks and said, "Okay Michael, let us have it. I am genuinely curious ... ."

Oaks looked around the room. Fleetingly, he recalled fragments of discussions and articles concerning the development of these technologies. Giddy projections for their popular use with films and gaming media contained reports of reckless content. These informed him of Trevor's true intentions, which were hidden beneath the modest dress of *It's a Wonderful Life* for this demonstration.

He knew of other media companies unveiling developments designed to drive humanity toward further extremes from authentic humanness. Bombarded by these recollections, Oaks saw them not as separate details of thought, but as layers of exposed calamity.

A thought came. It was clearer than a natural thought. It was conveyed. Many eyes gazed at him as he tried to ignore the report running through his mind like a news bulletin across a TV screen. Scared, he trembled. Not desiring estrangement, he did not want to speak. But, finally, Oaks simply reported what was reported to him.

"A gentle breeze blows across the face of a trembling stone," he began slowly. "And no one notices the bulge in the wall. The tall ears of a hare twitch nervously as they point to the walls' great height. The hare stomps its feet, and of course, no one hears. He dashes away to find refuge. Dogs bark. But dogs always bark ... don't they?

"All have become comfortable with the common sight of

the swirling shadows in their midst cast from the flight of the vultures high above. So, their daily circling attends no warning. In the quietness of the afternoon the breeze moves to the other side of the wall. It whispers to the failing stones in the bulge near the foundation. And foreigners stop their daily chores to wonder about the great cloud rising from the distant horizon."

Tears flowed from the corners of Michael Oaks' eyes and streamed down his cheeks. He did not move, either to wipe them away or to lower his gaze.

"OK, I get it," Patrick Bruce announced. "You're just weird!" He chuckled and looked around at the others, shaking his head and attempting to induce agreement. But around the table the others exchanged puzzled, uncomfortable glances. Meredith Train was busy writing. She stopped and thought for a moment, staring down at the pad of paper before her. Then she looked up at Oaks.

"This has got to go into a script somewhere. You don't mind, do you? My goodness, that was powerful."

"Melodramatic and utterly random, I would call it!" John Belk blurted. "I mean, you really outdid yourself with that one, Oaks."

Baxter put his face in his hands and shook his head. Then, raising his head, he looked at Oaks, and through a broad smile he exclaimed, "You are unbelievable!" He shook his head again, glanced over at Trevor and then back at Oaks. "You know, you're very interesting, maybe even somewhat compelling, but... com'on, man, really...."

"Look at Meredith," Bruce said, laughing. "You're not still waiting for the rest of your quote, are you?"

"Excuse me, Michael," Train said with evident sensitivity. "Could you tell me the part that came just after the vultures again?"

Oaks looked back at her blankly. She began looking around

the room feeling terribly awkward, her pen poised over the paper and her stylish bifocals hanging onto the end of her nose.

Oaks turned toward Trevor. "It's not the technology that you are obsessed with," he stated, dryness in his voice. "It is illusion and . . . ."

"No kidding?" Belk interrupted. "You just figured that out on your own, did you?"

"*I* thought it was perfectly obvious," Baxter added. "Tell me something that is not illusion that commands the kind of money we can get for the work that is done here."

"Illusion and perversion," Oaks said, finishing his statement. "And for that you actively advance and promote the moral decline of our society. Your gluttonous appetites fuel your competitive interests. You consciously, willfully advance the vulgarization of our culture for ratings in a field driven by advertising dollars and advertisers who feed upon people consumed by want. Drama . . . yeah, drama junkies looking to you for a fix, a trivialization of their desires, an exploitation of another weakness discovered by your ever searching studies."

Chris Troutman leaned forward. "Wait a second," he said. "What's immoral? It's technology!"

"Technology that we have demonstrated a penchant for using to occupy the minds of our viewers with everything vile and corrupt. Don't you get it? We are worse than whores," Oaks continued. "At least whores sell only their own bodies. You will gladly sell the bodies, minds and souls of your children and their children for your fame as technological wizard, media mogul and marketing genius . . . for a place on a team in a game that, as you are proudly convinced, holds implications for the destiny of everyone on the planet."

"OK, you're an idiot," Bruce responded, amazed at what he'd just heard.

"What are *you* doing here?" Troutman asked.

"Yeah, Oaks, I haven't heard you complaining about the nice

salary you enjoy because of your contributions to our whoring!" David Carlow added.

"I am wondering what kind of a person calls someone an idiot," John Ray said in a quiet tone that got everyone's attention. Though, less than half of those in attendance were certain of what he said.

"Why *are* you here, Michael, if you feel this way about what we do?" Gwen Thomas asked.

"I think I can answer that," Trevor replied. "A measure of influence, isn't that right, Michael?"

"From what I can gather, Michael's contributions, as you call them, David, are being used for things he did not intend them for and was not employed to participate in. I don't think any of us would be too happy about that," Ralph Tillman suggested.

"So what?" Bruce challenged. "That happens all the time. Get over it!" He looked at Oaks. "I really liked you before this meeting. But this holier than thou stuff is ... like I said, idiotic. I knew you were religious and all, but it never mattered to me. But now I see you're a freak, and I really don't want you influencing my ...."

John Belk let out a boisterous laugh. Startled, nearly everyone turned to look at him.

"Patrick, just shut up!" Tillman interrupted, ignoring Belk's outburst.

"No, I won't," Bruce snapped. "I'm sorry, but I didn't come here for this. I think this new stuff is phenomenal, and I'm not going to be preached out of my enthusiasm for something really exciting." He looked at Trevor. "I'm unapologetically an incurable techie, and I'd just like to get to the nuts and bolts of this stuff as soon as possible."

John Belk was still snickering. "Did Patrick Bruce just call someone else a freak? Man, you gotta be off the charts ...."

The room became quiet and Bruce looked over at Oaks. "To answer your question, Michael: No, I don't get it. I don't get the whore thing at all. I think this is the most revolutionary stuff to hit the media world since the invention of television. That's all… that's how I see it. And to answer yours, John, a punk like me… and without apology to either of you, thanks!"

"And did anyone question it when television came onto the scene?" Ray asked, solemn. "Of course not, it was American ingenuity, American technology, progress… it must be good. All the stories—grandparents recalling the family's first TV set. But did anyone question the wisdom of introducing it into their home?"

"You can bet that millions of wives question it now on every Sunday afternoon and on every Thanksgiving Day."

"Typical—pick on sports," Gwen Thomas objected. "What about every day, when most of those poor, homebound house-wives spend their hours watching soaps?"

"Either way," Ray answered. "Many wonder, as the alco-holic wonders, and the drug addict wonders, and the inmate wonders… 'how will I ever get my life back—all the hours, the days, the years wasted—how will I ever get free?' And here we sit, like drug lords plotting our next advance, scheming new advantages of potency for the control of our minions. I agree with Oaks," he concluded. "God help us if we fail to question *this* stuff."

Patrick Bruce was staring at John Ray with his mouth open. "Are you guys Amish, or just ridiculous?" he asked.

"How about anti-American," Baxter followed disdainfully.

Oaks placed his right elbow on the arm of his chair and reclined. He looked over at Ray and then at Baxter. "I love America. That is precisely why I object to reckless activities that advance her demise."

"But technology is neither good nor evil," Train said.

"Exactly right," Oaks replied. "That is why it ought always to be questioned in light of those two possibilities, rather than granting it automatic passage as good simply because it is progressive, impressive or American made."

Saraph tapped Zoltan on the shoulder and pointed at Trevor, who appeared to be nervously looking around the room. Zoltan thought several other people also seemed to be quite distracted. It was then that they both noticed that the wall across the room was dimming. They watched as it faded until it was no longer illuminated at all. The entire room, in fact, had the dull gray appearance of a utility room. The only lighting was provided by the ceiling lights directly above the table, which were quite a bit brighter than they had originally been.

Trevor sat back in his chair and looked around at everyone else. Oaks sat up in his chair and watched Tillman as he got up and walked around the table to examine the wall on the other side of the room. Everyone in the room was struck dumb as each reacted to the room's transformation. The only remaining dynamic element was the image of Uncle Billy suspended on the big screen.

Unknowingly, everyone was experiencing the same disillusionment. When the wall was lit and reflective, they had felt like a significant force in an important meeting in a strategic location. Now, everyone felt like individual peons in a small gray room.

"Strange," said Trevor. "I was thinking that there might have been a power issue. But the overhead lights and the projection system are still working."

"Not as strange as this," Tillman said. "This just looks to be a painted gray wall from up close. Have you ever seen this wall unlit?" he asked as he continued his inspection.

"No," several people answered at once.

"Where did *that* technology come from?" Tillman asked. "What is it?"

The room was filled with glances and puzzled expressions.

"Were any of you guys here when it was built?" Belk asked.

"I was just wondering the same thing," Train said.

Everyone else just shook their heads.

"You think this facility is his only creation?" Oaks asked, referring to Salmone. "He could have had this designed and built in any number of other facilities throughout the world."

"How do you know that?" Belk asked, annoyed.

"He said so."

"Oh, he told you that personally?"

"He told everyone that was listening."

"I have come in here for personal retreat many times, including the wee hours," Thomas reported. "With Zoltan's permission," she added. "It has always...." She paused. "Well, it has always been glorious. I agree with Meredith. It's seems odd that I never wondered..." She looked over at the wall, and then at the unlit, waterless sculpture on the adjacent wall. "...until now."

"Okay, everyone," Trevor said with his attention demanding tone. Thomas' reference to Zoltan's authority was unsettling in the context of all that was going on. He was trying to ignore the thought that his momentum and his feeling of invincibility were lost as he attempted to get everyone to refocus.

"Ralph, have a seat, bud."

Ralph Tillman turned around abruptly and looked at Trevor. He knew him well enough to know that "bud" was a reference that Trevor usually defaulted to when someone had fallen outside of his favor. Noticing that he continued to stand there, Trevor peered at him over the top of his glasses. This, too, Tillman recognized as unfavorable.

"Let's start wrapping this up," Trevor said impatiently. "I am certain there is a simple explanation for the outage," he continued, though he was quite uncertain at the moment.

In fact, he was terribly upset and everyone in the room could feel it and had begun to look forward to the end of the meeting. Trevor waited, collecting his thoughts.

Zoltan looked at Saraph. "It is painful to be in this life-

273

less room," he said. "I feel like I'm at a wake observing a close friend in a casket. I've seen enough. I'm ready to leave."

"Any non-philosophical questions or thoughts concerning the clips we just showed?" Trevor asked.

John Belk, who normally just blurted out what came to his mind, raised his hand like a schoolboy.

"Put your hand down, John," Trevor snipped, annoyed at the flagging of his mood swing.

"Well, can you give us a rundown on the cupid business – you know, getting Jimmy and Gwen together after all these years?"

"Yes, briefly," Trevor answered. "The key to this *marvelous advancement*," he said with authority, no longer leaving room for any but his own evaluation, "is a little platform like this." He held up a thin device made of hinged aluminum panels. "This, my friends, is a scanner. And what it scans is ... ."

He looked at Gwen Thomas and, peering over the top of his glasses, motioned with his index finger for her to come to him. As she leaned toward him he examined the shoulder of her sweater. Finding what he was looking for, he reached over and picked up a stray hair and held it up for the others to see. Holding the hair in one hand and the scanner in the other he said, "Actually, I like your terminology, John. I think, from now on we will call this the Cupid Project, because bringing these two together, we can work magic."

"DNA?" Troutman asked.

"None other," Trevor answered.

"All right, I get the DNA scanning, that's been coming for a long time," Bruce said. "But how do you get her information or identity into that movie?"

"The same," Baxter said.

Everyone looked at Baxter as Bruce said, "Please explain."

"We developed that scanner at one of our European facilities for identification in a dynamic touch screen environment of another sort. We've been working on it for a number of years.

274

Another company has been working on a software package capable of watching a film, so to speak, and creating a DNA output. We can work with nearly every kind of media. DNA in this case stands for Definitive Numerical Analysis. We bought that company six months ago for its software developments. They enable us to numerically define every detail of nearly any type of media product, old and new."

"Actually, *we* bought that company six months ago," Oaks corrected.

"Yes, absolutely, I apologize," Baxter replied quickly and awkwardly.

"We developed a third component to bring them together," Trevor said, stepping in to reestablish his control, though he was becoming increasingly disquieted by Oaks' ascending bravado. "It's rather a simple thing called an Aspect Assimilator."

"Thank you," Oaks said. "Simple, but patented and owned by Universal Syndicate."

"Of course, bud, relax," Trevor retorted, tilting his head and smiling as he looked at Oaks over the top of his glasses. Oaks sat back in his seat and the two men stared at one another.

Patrick Bruce slumped on the table and vigorously shook his head, as if mystified by these interactions.

"Look ... ," Stuart McCauley said in a sober tone. "Here's what I'm getting out of this. Pretty soon people won't even know what dimension of the media layering they're in."

"Yeah, like what's real and what's not?" Bruce said, popping up and eager for a cue to move on.

The room was quiet. Bruce looked around at the others, who were all staring at him. "What?" he said, in protest of the uncomfortable attention. "It's cool stuff. Let's get to it, I say."

"I agree, it's great ... wow, amazing technology," Chris Troutman responded. "I just want to know why we were all left out of the loop, not to mention the creation of these things. This would be a much better meeting if we were introducing our own creations."

Bruce leaned forward and looked down the table at Troutman. "Where have you been?" he asked with a laugh. "Even I get *that*." He shook his head and laughed again. "Business, man, business ... take-over, merger, get it?"

Saraph leaned over toward Zoltan while continuing to watch Trevor. "So, it seems to me that Salmone knew what these two were up to before he hired this Trevor fella. There is some reason he wanted to be the one in control of creating these things. But putting them in their hands ... that part I'm not clear on. How do you see it?"

When he did not hear a response he looked up at Zoltan and saw tears streaming down his face. Saraph just stood beside him and waited.

"Salmone appoints who he will for what he will," Zoltan said, finally answering Saraph's question. "We think it's about us and he just laughs that goodhearted laugh of his all the while."

"Winds of change," Saraph said. "He knows something is coming. That much is certain."

Zoltan snickered. "I think he appointed Trevor because of his overzealous, blinding ambition. He and Baxter are bunglers. If Oaks is right, when change ...." He paused. "If a revolution comes, they will be isolated, culturally exiled among the insignificant fringe element, and they will have carried away their precious toys with them to pollute only what remains of their intoxicated subscribers.

"And my appointment?" Zoltan said morbidly. "It's over." He looked at Saraph. "It's either over, or there's a cruel, cruel, sinister magic at work here just playing with my mind. Which would you say it is?"

Saraph had no answer for his tragic question.

Observing Oaks in The Chair, Zoltan recalled his ascension throughout the meeting to a prominence worthy of The Chair. Then he recalled his own tenure in the place of honor. *It was all so perfect. It was all designed ideally for my opportunity to thrive and to sustain my privilege in this place. It was an environment engineered so precisely for me, for the success I enjoyed. And I thought it was all me. Now it's gone and I will never see anything like it again.*

He looked back at Trevor, noticing that he had stood to his feet and was looking around the room with that signature smile on his face. But in that moment it was merely a pitiable spectacle. He had wanted desperately to resist smiling, just this once. But force of habit prevailed.

"Well," Trevor said, looking at Baxter, "It looks as if it is time for us to leave. We have failed in some respects, but gained access to some valuable tools, we pirates." With this resolve, Trevor was feeling relieved of a great tension.

"I would like to leave you all with one last clip that I think you will enjoy." He reached over and started the scene from *It's a Wonderful Life.* Uncle Billy came alive before them. Then Trevor picked up the writing tool and soon the character on the screen looked like Zoltan. Uncle Billy looked frightened and confused, having lost a large sum of money. Everyone realized immediately that it was a satire on Zoltan's recent stumbling and bungling.

Bruce, who thought very highly of Zoltan, found the humor hysterical and was the first to begin laughing. Belk and Baxter, too, laughed out loud and Trevor chuckled quietly, pleased with their response. All the others present appeared to find it in poor taste and began turning away from the screen and looking at Trevor to communicate their disapproval.

Suddenly, seeing Trevor's eyes widen with surprise, they all turned back to find the image of P. Salmone II in the center of the screen and appearing to look directly at Trevor.

"Trevor," he said, in his usual gregarious tone, "I thought you might attempt to take a swipe at Zoltan in his absence. So, I decided to take a shot and load myself in. Hey, maybe the two of us should start a media highjackers' club. By the way, thanks for being predictable. I don't know what I would have done if you had not stayed true to character. I guess you just would have missed me. What a shame that would have been."

Patrick Bruce's mouth was open in amazement. He slumped with his head in his arms upon the table and began to rumble with laughter. Then he sat back up and continued to laugh as he watched Salmone. "Oh, wow," he said, "this is the best entertainment I've seen in a long time. You guys should have sold tickets."

Trevor got Baxter's attention and was annoyed to see him smiling from ear to ear when he turned around. Then he nodded toward the door. He did not want to stay and be the object of Salmone's fun any longer. As he turned to leave he saw the door open, and a man walked in holding some documents. He set them on the table next to Trevor.

"Please, don't leave without your things," he heard Salmone say. "You'll find that our attorneys have done a thorough job transferring all rights to the technologies you so covet over to your name. I would not have you leave us as a thief. There's no dignity in that, now is there?"

Suddenly everyone was startled by a loud burst of laughter from Patrick Bruce. "Oh, wow," he said as he howled, "No dignity in being a thief...." Hearing himself repeat it, he laughed all the more. "Wow ... I never knew this guy was such a comedian."

Trevor picked up the documents and looked up at the screen to find it empty. He looked at Oaks. Then he raised the documents in Oaks' direction and shrugged his shoulders communicating a silent question.

"I trust him," Oaks said plainly. "But you might want to note that there are thirty-two teams, not twenty-six. I don't know where you got that number, but it would be a shame to cripple your show from the outset. I see no evidence, by the way, that any of the participants are aware of their participation. The movements follow more organic patterns than that."

A shadow of a doubt entered Trevor's mind. It occurred to him that he might be walking away with less than he was walking away from. Had he invested the slightest reciprocity in Salmone's goodwill, he may have summoned the courage to request a pardon, inquire of other choices, seek a counsel. Instead, he looked down at the documents clutched between his fingers. He looked up at Baxter, who gave him an eager nod, and he turned and walked out the door. Baxter was close behind.

A business of exchanged glances ensued around the table. Finally, Patrick Bruce shook his head and said, "I just don't get it." Then he sprang to his feet and dashed out the door calling for Trevor to wait for him.

Zoltan appeared to be on the verge of sickness as he looked at Saraph. "It's over," he said. "If there was something I could have gained from this 'gift' of yours... no... there's nothing to come back to now." He slumped forward, his hands on his knees, his head hung down between his arms. As he did, the taunting memories and temptations distracted by the studio activities returned with a vengeance.

Saraph observed him for a moment.

"Waiting is a sweetness on my side of the intimacy between me and my Lord," he said gently. "Often I have waited long, believing, anticipating a savory revelation of His goodness—waited when all appeared wrong, lost. Often, too, it is not my accomplishments but my trust that pleases Him most. Perhaps it is so with Salmone."

Zoltan rose up and looked at Saraph with bent brows and tightened lips. "Do you think I need you to remind me that Oaks is the better man?"

Saraph returned Zoltan's glare with a puzzled look. "I was in no way referring to Oaks," he said. "I was identifying a possibility for...."

"Don't you see?" Zoltan snapped. "It's over! I've blown it, ruined everything just as Trevor has. We are in the same standing with Salmone, on the other side of his favor from Oaks."

"But, mercifully, as you said yourself, it's not about you," Saraph stated pleasantly.

The casual tone of this reminder caused Zoltan's mouth to fall open. He again leaned forward, put his hands on his knees and hung his head. "There is no hope here," he said. "I could never bring myself to ask ... to hope for ... ." He was silent for a moment. And with a shake of his head, appeared to change his thought. "... to be just some pawn of his. What is that?" His voice cracked, his lower jaw was trembling. "Nothing! That's what it is, nothing!"

"Now, that is the first really stupid thing I have heard you say," Saraph announced. He looked around the silent room at the stunned faces and thoughtfully added, "The first thing that makes me wonder if you are right." He sighed and closed his eyes, as if his mind needed a rest.

Chapter 27
IN THE DARK

When Saraph opened his eyes, darkness greeted him and the sounds of Zoltan's groaning seemed much louder, though they quickly subsided. An unfamiliar smell caused Saraph to frown. It had become nearly silent, but for a distant sound of running water. Something rested upon Saraph's left shoulder. *A strand of film. Interesting,* he thought, taking hold of it and feeling a clip that was attached to its end. Reaching out, he discovered a wall, then a doorframe. He hung his head and sighed.

Startled by the sound of Saraph's sigh, Zoltan grimaced. The moment he smelled the processing chemicals, he had opened his eyes to the stark shock of darkness. His sweaty palms were pressed against the sides of his head in an attempt to push down the drone of the *note*. There was something else he wanted to hear, and the distraction frustrated him. But he discovered that the note was inseparable from his consciousness and the taunting thoughts leaking through the cracks of his feeble defense. His heart was pounding as he attempted to listen.

Saraph stood silently amazed, contemplating the dilemma. '*Why do you boast of evil, you mighty man?*' he recited silently. The verse was from a psalm that had been impressed upon him from the very beginning of his encounters with Zoltan. '*Why do you boast all day long, you who are a disgrace in the eyes of God?*'

His eyes were again closed. As much as he was able in the dark, Saraph examined his environment as he continued his recitation. The room was small enough that he could feel a wall in each direction in which he stretched out his hands.

'Here now is the man who did not make God his stronghold but trusted in his great wealth and grew strong by destroying others.'

"What could have driven you here that is greater than the shame of being in here while the universe awaits?" Saraph questioned annoyed. Reaching out, he felt for the doorknob. "I wonder what is . . . ."

"Stop!" Zoltan demanded. "Don't open it!" It was quiet for a moment. "There's someone in there."

"Someone in where?"

"The main darkroom. This is just the light-tight room where I processed my negatives. The main area for processing prints is through that door. I think it's my brother. I always knew he . . . ."

"Where is it?" Saraph interrupted. "I mean, where are we?"

"Shush!" Zoltan snapped, realizing that the running water had stopped.

They heard a chuckle just beyond the door and Zoltan's heart pounded more violently.

"Oh, wow! Sweetie, you are unbelievable!"

Hearing his father's voice, Zoltan was immediately breathless.

"But it's still kind of lifeless. How does that kid get his pictures to turn out so dramatic?"

"Magician, what could cause you to desire . . . ?"

Saraph was stopped by the shock of Zoltan's hand colliding with his shoulder in the dark.

Zoltan's focus on his father's darkroom activities provided a measure of relief from the threats of random desires and his fear of the gift. But the note did not relent. He strained against its distraction to identify each stage of the development process taking place in the other room.

"D76," he announced.

"Oh, really?" Saraph responded with a tone of disinterest.

"Developer. To this day my favorite smell in the whole world."

Five minutes passed.

"Stop bath," Zoltan announced. "He's working on a new test strip."

"How can you tell?"

"I heard him tear the paper a little bit ago. You don't tear the paper for a final image."

"Ok, that seems obvious enough," Saraph said through the sound of a yawn.

"Even without the tearing, I could tell by the way he adjusted the enlarger. I remember it like it was yesterday," Zoltan gushed. "Its squeak going up is distinctly different from that of it going down."

"Even better ... today ... right now," Saraph said.

"Yeah right, of course," Zoltan answered, considering the reminder.

This must be during my high school.... He searched his memory. Must be, because the divorce was right after my senior year. The move was that summer. Continuing to think and listen, every once in a while Zoltan announced another detail of the process. But when he heard his father muttering, all thoughts stopped.

"OK, that's a little better ... I think I'll go with that one, it's got the best contrast ... I wish her smile wasn't so forced ... every one of them, the little snob ... I need to find someone else. She's costing me too much money to put up with this."

Saraph felt helpless. For thirty minutes he stood there, thoughtful, powerless as Zoltan was fixated on the sounds from the other room. A door opened and closed. Zoltan's father was gone. The only sound he left behind was that of the occasional drop of water dripping from the faucet. And, for Zoltan, the darkroom quickly became a cell of concentration, thick with the very thoughts and images he had wanted to escape.

"About six inches behind you and directly above your head you will find a string," he said. "You might want to give it a pull."

When Saraph followed the instructions a soft red light filled the room. He turned and looked up at the light, intrigued.

"It's called a safe light."

"Safe light?" Saraph repeated. "Interesting."

"Not really. Common sense. Saves ruining your film."

It was quiet for several minutes, as they stood face to face, cast in red hues.

"Based on your smug indifference, I don't guess it would interest you to know why this is such an important place to me."

"That interests me a great deal."

"I grew up in here. This is where I became a creator. This is ...."

"Excuse me," Saraph interrupted. "Forgive my barging in here, but you became a creator when you were made in the image of *your* Creator."

"There's really nothing ruder than interrupting someone for something unimportant," Zoltan scolded.

They stared at one another.

"This is where I first became intoxicated with the wonder of media. My first attempts at manipulating imagery took place right in here. Very successful baby steps, I might add. My mom still has some of the results. The thrill of craft and illusion ... this was my sanctuary from the time my mom had it built for me until I graduated high school. Right in there ...."
He stopped as he pointed and looked toward the door. "Right

here in this little darkroom, I built the portfolio that sent me to USC to take it to the next level."

He looked around. Leaning back against a sink, he patted the top of it with both hands. "This was my refuge during the years leading up to my parents divorce. I think my mom really got it for me for that reason. It was her way of protecting me from the tension of his silence and the viciousness of her verbal attacks. The only thing missing is my music, important for drowning out the sounds of the world outside. Heavy metal...well, not by today's standards. I usually had it so loud in here that it eclipsed my hearing and I felt it in my marrow."

"Your father had nothing to do with you having this?"

"That's what I can't quite comprehend here. He complained about it from the start. It was a waste of money. Said my mom was encouraging fanciful ideas that would never amount to anything in the real world. He acted like he resented it even being in our house, keeping me from higher academic pursuits."

Head bowed slightly, chin in hand, a frown continually moved upon Zoltan's face.

"Strange...I often felt something was a little different from the way I'd left it. Once in a while I found...pictures. Test strips had fallen beneath the sink and such." He paused, then shook his head. "I never even suspected him. Never suspected my mom or my little sister either, of course. I did get into some big-time arguments with my brother, though, whenever I accused him of messing around in my darkroom. I didn't like the idea of him being in here, but him denying it really made me mad. Wow...to think it wasn't even him.

"So what," Zoltan said abruptly, adjusting his thought process. "It's not like I thought he was a saint!"

"No, of course not," Saraph responded.

"He once took me on a business trip with him, completely out of the blue...Las Vegas. I was thirteen, maybe fourteen. Stayed in some young woman's apartment instead of a hotel.

285

She looked more my age than his. Probably college age, actually. After he'd retired to the bedroom with her, I sat on the couch in the living room and watched TV all night, just for the distraction of it."

It was quiet again. Every ten seconds, or so, a drop of water landed in the drain in the other room. Saraph popped several Gummy Bears into his mouth and the juicy noise of his chewing compelled Zoltan to reach out and pop him on the chest. The action was supported by a scowl that conveyed the expectation that the chewing stop.

The observations at Universal Syndicate had stirred the feelings of impotence Zoltan had experienced during recent months. A sense of confusing thoughts filling the void created by his diminishing vitality was palpable.

Among those thoughts, he was recalling the story of the original owner of the clothes that Saraph wore. The stench of alcohol and urine had not completely laundered out of them. And even with the strong smell of developer in the air, it was impossible to ignore in that confined space. He remembered Saraph's report: *"Strange, the fellow folded them neatly and set them on the bridge before jumping."*

"Dear Magician …." Saraph whispered. He waited for an objection but heard only Zoltan's deep, shaky breaths.

"What you hear that is driving you mad is a sound you have created. It is the accumulation of every kind of noise … mind clutter you have indulged since the days you retreated to this dark place years ago. Every element of it the enemy of your soul converts into one note, one constant drone, the exact pitch of your personal destruction. Beneath it is the sound of your first terror, the sound of *alone*. Listen to its frightful groans. Sanity may be closer than you could otherwise have hoped."

"What bridge do you have in mind for me?"

"Bridge?" Saraph asked, slightly startled by the nearness of Zoltan's unexpected voice.

"Like the man who wore those rank and wretched clothes you are wearing."

Saraph had to summon all his strength to resist laughing out loud and further upsetting his pained accuser. Finally composed enough to speak, he answered: "I never met the man. A homeless friend of his had picked up the clothes and taken them to the shelter. He asked that they be cleaned for him, and then he never returned. That is the story I received when I stayed there. I had only asked for some inconspicuous clothing sufficiently comfortable for a humble shepherd on an excellent journey."

Zoltan seethed, ignoring the explanation. "You disrupted and destroyed my career, my life in the world. You seduced me into joining you here in this strange world where, by the conspiracy of your 'gift,' you have stripped me of power, destroyed the one true hero that inspired my dreams, shown me my ruin, and now… now you corner me in this dark place to torment me more. To answer the question you asked earlier: Your gift drove me here, a default to this refuge from hostility."

Conspiracy, Saraph thought. *No wonder the gift is a terror to him, it is too close to the way he thinks, to the technologies he wields and those he fears. He perceives it as in concert with all of the calamities of his own imagination.*

"How many hours have passed?" Zoltan asked. "No… how many remain to this gift?" He was doubtful that he could hold out much longer this way, but hopeful of a report that would encourage his resistance.

"We are ten minutes shy of twenty hours."

"Four hours remaining!" Zoltan protested with horror in his voice.

Calculating a risk, Saraph said, "I am aware of the incident." He waited. As he did, a peace came over him and he began to relax, letting go of the anxiousness he had been feeling about salvaging the value of the gift for Zoltan. He saw all hope of grand adventures slipping away. Accepting that, he realized that the purpose of the gift may be quite different than what he had presumed from the start.

He cleared his throat. "You are not obligated to trust me with the things you are feeling or tell me the things you are thinking, but don't withhold them from yourself. Calculate them to the finest detail so that you do not forget them when this day is through. It may be that such a memory is gift enough. It may be that we could stay right here, go nowhere else, see nothing else, but that this severe poverty will warn you against even greater desolation."

Another ten minutes passed in silence.

Beginnings, Saraph thought. Moved by the circumstances, he silently recited from John's Gospel. '*In the beginning was the Word, and the Word was with God and the Word was God. He was with God in the beginning. By Him all things were made; without Him nothing was made that has been made.*'

He shook his head slowly, thoughtfully. *And so it continues as it has always been*, he thought. *Through Him all things are restored; without Him nothing is renewed that has been destroyed. Creation and restoration, all in Him.* Saraph turned and looked up at the light behind him, mindful especially of its color. '*Safelight*,' he thought, *interesting*. He closed his eyes. '*In Him was life, and that life was the light of men. The light shines in the darkness, but the darkness has not understood it.*'

He began to sing.

Zoltan was still as he listened to the sound of Saraph singing. It so transfixed him that all noise from his own mind was silenced and a great relief from his fears brought calm. He listened long, peacefully. He did not recognize the language in which Saraph sang, but it was a sound he related pleasurably to that of falling waters. The singing stopped.

"You may be interested to know something," Saraph said, speaking barely above a whisper. "Until now I had never experienced darkness. I am a child of that Light that gives life to all.

I was created in the midst of the fullness of His light. I now see that *the gift* is, at least in part, for me. I love Him more, something I didn't think possible. His light and His glory are dearer to me every minute we remain in this wretched darkness. I, like you, am now eager for this day to be completed."

"Take me somewhere, please!" Zoltan answered.

"Only you ... ."

"Please do not make me ... do not ... never mind." Zoltan pressed his palms against his ears. "Forget it! I don't want anything! I don't want to see anything or go anywhere. I want to stay right here until the time is up. There, that's my wish."

"I am not a genie," Saraph answered. "I am not here for the granting of wishes. This is not a fairy tale, or your real thoughts would not be your horror. The problem we seem to be having is that you are stuck on you. So, we idle in the dark, hostages of your fear of more you-centered destinations. We are grounded by your fear of being known, exposure of disgraceful things you believe to be hidden. The incident, for example."

"One little mistake," Zoltan said.

"An act of your will is not a mistake."

"Right, right, you told me that before. Why do you insist on bringing up ... ." Zoltan pressed harder and squeezed his eyes shut.

"Perhaps I can offer a relief to you that will salvage something of your grand opportunity, an adjustment. From here on, your will alone shall not be cause for transportation, but only your spoken will. That should free you ... us."

Zoltan immediately opened his eyes. Were he a dog, his ears would have been raised and his tail pointing.

"Perhaps now we can move on to something a little more adventurous than a dark room," Saraph said. "You no longer have to be afraid to think or to allow a desire to be loaded in that overactive firing chamber of your mind."

He listened for a response and for a moment it was silent.

"You can do that?" Zoltan asked.

"The gift continues to be controlled by your will," Saraph answered. "But this way you don't have to be afraid of your random wants and where they might take us that would expose more than you are prepared to face. It is essentially the same, except for a technical adjustment."

"I wish you would have done that hours ago," Zoltan said, sounding almost back to normal.

"Well, I didn't anticipate you being so . . . ."

"I hate for you to see me like this, even in the dark," Zoltan interrupted, as he began to pull himself together.

"Of course you do."

"You must know from your observations that this is a very unusual . . . a very strange behavior for me. I am usually a very strong person."

"Appearances requiring constant attendance do not speak of strength," Saraph responded.

"I really don't understand this. I don't know what has come over me."

"Magician, you should know by now that pretense is not useful to you on this day."

"It's you that pretends. You know as well as I do that I am normally a very strong person."

They faced one another in the red lighting. Saraph reached up and pulled the string again. It was completely dark.

"Tell me where you would like to go," he said. He was amused by the immediate impact of his provision upon his travel partner's transformed psyche.

As Zoltan began to think of his options and the magnitude of the power of his spoken will, many desired destinations flooded his mind. Then, one thought outweighed all of the others.

"Could you do it?" he asked.

Saraph just waited, wondering about the question.

"I don't really understand what caused me to bring us to this place," Zoltan said thoughtfully. "Marion's ... that hallway either. My office ... now, that was just a very bad, but irresistible idea that the others just helped me fight off initially. And things that are coming to my mind even now ... mostly bad habits as you have identified. The places that strike me as exciting and exotic only cause me to realize that you can think of better ones, places I would not even know about."

"I assure you," Saraph asserted, "you wanted to come here. There is a reason. What you desired I can't say, but it appears now that this was a valuable and necessary visit. We accomplished some important things here. One thing remains, I think. One thing worthy of some closure, or you may fail to revisit it properly."

"'The incident,' as you call it?"

Saraph nodded, forgetting that such an answer was meaningless in the dark.

"Scariest moment of my life," Zoltan began. "I never even went in. Placed two thousand dollars cash in a man's hand. A second later the raid was upon me. Shouting, flashing lights ... I looked back to retrieve my money before running. The man was gone. I was grabbed from behind as cops rushed by me into the back room. As they passed through the curtains beyond the door, I could see people inside through the opening." He paused to decide if he wanted to continue. "Some of them minors, mid-teens maybe," he finally revealed.

"Two thousand dollars and I never even went in. That as much as anything has tempted my return. That kind of thing gnaws at me."

"That's your regret ... the money?"

"Well, the two thousand was the tip of the iceberg, as they say. By the time I'd finished paying for silence and to keep myself out of the papers – from being associated with the incident – it was closer to two million. One bad decision, one wrong move, two million dollars. Hardly painful, but not exactly pocket change either."

"So what was painful, anything?"

"Seeing the minors in there ... that was disturbing."

"You didn't know?"

Zoltan stared. "It is called the Serapeum," he said, obscuring his answer. "Named after the ancient temple we visited, of course. I had frequented the main rooms of the club. But, I ... for six months I'd resisted the invitation – the prodding, the intrigue. It was Trevor," Zoltan said distantly. "He had introduced me to the place shortly after he came to work for me. And he was the one who told me about the private club in the back. I could never be certain, but I have always been suspicious that he set me up."

"One bad decision?" Saraph asked.

Zoltan immediately understood his meaning. "No, of course not. The face of the man and his white-gloved hands haunt me, but not as much as his voice. Daily I hear him: 'Your first time ... unforgettable, but just the beginning ....' Unforgettable all right. But, the beginning? The first bad decision? I no longer know when the beginning was. It was long before I stepped through that door, I am sure of that. It's the end that I want to know about. So far it's nowhere in sight."

"Perhaps it is near. Are you ready to leave this dark place?"

Zoltan stared into the darkness. "There's something else," he said.

"I'm in no hurry," Saraph answered.

"I was being held off to one side of the entry, handcuffed. Other police officers started coming from the back room dragging those they'd apprehended. I turned and faced the wall and lowered my head, not wanting to be seen. I listened as the feet shuffled by and the voices ... some pleading, all swearing. They passed through the door and into the night. Then I heard some shuffling feet that did not pass. They came to a stop immediately behind me. I stood there trembling, waiting for them to move along, afraid to look but wanting to know."

Zoltan stood in silence reliving those terrifying moments. He tried, as he had countless times before, to gain a clue.

"Did you turn around?"

"No. It seemed like an eternity, but they finally moved on." Zoltan again stopped and thought for a moment. "I had always had a good relationship with my son," he continued. "It may be my imagination, but it has never been the same since that day. In fact, from that day forward it seems to me he has despised me. It haunts me, but how do you bring something like that up?"

"How would he have known about the place?" Saraph asked.

"The Serapeum or the back room?"

Saraph shrugged, and for several seconds they stared at one another in the dark.

"I introduced him," Zoltan finally answered.

"How old?"

"His fourteenth birthday. A whim about passage," Zoltan said with a tone of regret.

"Back to the incident: He's had a lot of struggles since that time. I've always wanted to help, but . . . ." He paused. "I really have no reason to believe it was him. Still, I feel compromised by my own indignity. It was not long afterward that he started calling me Zoltan instead of Dad, then by a nickname, Zolt. It seems to me that as a father I became impotent on that day."

"On that day, or from the beginning that you don't remember?" Saraph reached out and patted the nearest wall of the darkroom. "When was this created for you?"

There was a long silence.

"Eighth grade, I think, maybe seventh," Zoltan finally answered. "So, I was thirteen or fourteen."

"Interesting coincidence."

"I've spent a lot of money trying to help him," Zoltan said.

"It's all I know to do at this point. But for that, we rarely even talk anymore."

"Maybe helping *you* would be more effective."

They again stared at one another through the darkness.

"Two million and counting?"

"Yeah, something like that. But you know what was the most expensive?"

"No, tell me."

"The implied 'incident' in that script you put on my desk months ago. You have no idea how much that messed with me, or cost me in distraction."

Zoltan waited in the silence, thinking that an apology might be in order. None came.

"I just remembered a question you asked in Alexandria," he said. "Chuck … ?"

"Oh yes, I remember."

"Chuck is my therapist."

"Hmm, thanks for clearing that up."

Zoltan noticed a movement of the note. Though the relief of tension caused it to recede to the background, still it remained constant. He felt mocked, as if it was the tone of laughter and he was the joke.

"What if I tell you that my will is to go where you would like to take me?" he blurted.

Chapter 28
INFINITY

Zoltan's arms were stretched out wide, and they began making gathering gestures, as he expressed his craving to draw into himself all that he saw before him. He felt as if all that he normally contained within his skin was uncontrollably leaving to move about freely outside of him. Flashes slashed through the air. Some appeared to explode as from the collision of flaming swords. Zoltan thought that he could be cut to pieces. Yet all he truly felt was the encompassing shower of pleasure upon this, his first journey into pure awe.

Completely enveloped in a sensual fervor, it claimed all of his consciousness. His mouth hung open gapingly. Saliva filled it so quickly that he nearly began to choke before he was able to swallow hard to push it down past all of the emotions that were rushing in the opposite direction up the back of his throat.

Zoltan gasped for breath between swallows as he walked aimlessly, slowly turning in circles. His eyes were wide. Had anyone been watching, he would have appeared to be seized by convulsions because of the constant competition between his breathing and his compulsion to swallow.

His heart was racing with such eagerness and longing that he felt it could explode right through his chest at any second. Tears were streaming down his face, his ears felt hot, and the sounds coming from his voice were like those of a mad man. He had never felt such a calamity of excitement. All of his senses were peaked all at once, far beyond any capacity to which they had previously been aroused.

He began to stumble around, like a prizefighter lingering too long after a lengthy pummeling that left him with only the blind, futile ambition to linger on. But the fury of the blows did not let up. He feared he might drown in this pugilism of pleasure.

Suddenly, a pain began to swell in his head. It quickly became extreme, and all other feelings vanished before its severe wrath. Zoltan stumbled forward beginning to wretch, his head drew backward and he fell to his knees and collapsed.

When he began a slow, hazy return to consciousness, the frenzy of excitement was gone, as was the pain. A soft feeling of euphoria had replaced them. He lifted his head with what little strength he could gather and opened his eyes just enough to try and identify the surface he was laying on. Inability to feel anything beneath him stirred his curiosity.

As he peeked cautiously at the area immediately before him, he was awakened again to such beauty, warmth, and sensual delight that he quickly shut his eyes and squeezed them tight as if fending off disaster. But he could not keep them out. Though somewhat quieter with his eyes closed, the beauty around him was undeniable. Zoltan began to erupt from within and shake with laughter.

It was laughter without effort, without editorial motive, without guile, without obligation, without proclamation of hilarity, and most of all, without inhibition. The waters of a spring-fed brook flowing and splashing on its way down a mountain were painted in his mind's eye.

For the moment, he had completely forgotten about Saraph. And not a single question about this place of extravagant beauty or the cause of the extraordinary sensations had crossed his mind. He took no notice of his laughter. He was, in fact, for the first time in his life, unself-conscious.

He lay on his back and laughed moving his arms and legs like a child making an angel in the snow. He rolled over onto his left side and laughed, and then back to his right. He rolled onto his stomach and laughed. He got to his hands and knees and crawled until he collapsed again in laughter, and he lay there reveling in the pure pleasure of it all.

"Oh, my god ... Oh, my god ... Oh, my god!" he emoted. He could not think. He could only repeat these words as he got up and again crawled around on his hands and knees. Squinting, he tried not to take in more than he could handle, daring not to tempt the overwhelming pleasures for fear of the earlier pain. The feeling of his heart rising again to the back of his throat and throbbing suddenly surprised and frightened him. He swallowed hard as his mouth went dry, and he again collapsed and lay still. Face down, Zoltan squeezed his eyes shut.

Instinctively, he wrapped his arms around his abdomen though he had no feeling of sickness. He lay there moaning as he rolled slowly, rhythmically from side to side. "Oh my god," he began again. "Oh, my god, oh, my god ... oh, god." He spoke thoughtlessly to no one. "No more. Too ... oh, my god ... glorious! Too beautiful, too wonderful." Moaning and mumbling, he lay there helplessly absorbed in the sensations that washed over him like a silent tide upon a moonlit shore.

Overwhelmed with exhaustion, he fell fast asleep. When he awoke he opened his eyes to a world of blues and violets that was quite subdued from the vibrant brilliance his senses could not handle before. But it was no less beautiful. He lay still, staring into the dazzling and bewildering depths of flowing forms and blending colors.

Something in the lower left part of Zoltan's field of vision caught his attention. But he could not react. Everything in his mind was happening at an extremely relaxed pace. He was interested in what it was, but he did not feel obligated to his interest enough to respond. Moving only his eyes, he continued to look around even as he intended to eventually identify the source of intrigue.

The object was moving closer as Zoltan continued to stare into the space that stretched out above him. From directly in front of him to the furthest reach of his peripheral vision to the left, his view became blocked. Hazily, he desired the interference to be removed.

"Hey, down there, you do not look so good."

The voice seemed to break a spell, and Zoltan realized that Saraph was standing at his left side and looking down at him. He slowly focused in on Saraph's face, which reflected the calm yet brilliant violet and blue hues around them.

"Listen." Saraph turned and looked high over his shoulder into the distant expanse of space. "Do you hear that?"

"It is the most beautiful thing I have ever heard," Zoltan said.

Saraph looked back at Zoltan with a puzzled expression. "Only because you do not recognize it or perceive its significance."

"At first I thought...." Zoltan paused to catch his breath. "... I thought... it was what I was seeing that was so glorious. I closed my eyes and tried to shut it out. It overwhelmed me." He rested for a moment. "Then the sound, so pure, so sweet," he said, placid as he stared straight ahead. He turned slowly to look at Saraph. "What is it?"

"That is the sound of liquid communication. A new generation is at the door."

"What kind of generation?"

"What kind?"

"What are we speaking of, men, technology, media?"

"Ages... epochs," Saraph stated flatly. "Anchors are drawn, no longer to keep this generation mired in this stagnant cove of sewage and death. All that blind, deceive, castrate, destroy, usurp... all that clutter the minds of men with denunciations of glory's origin... all that impregnate with illegitimate offspring... they are soon no more.

"What was it that the fellow said the other night on your broadcast? What was the name of that show? *Origins!* Yes, that was it. He said, 'We now know how the universe was started and that there was no need for any designer, creator or guiding hand.' The narration reported that the facilities and research cost behind that conclusion was in the billions. Apparently it is more complex and expensive to observe a universe than to create one. The Holy One simply spoke the Creation into being. He is speaking now."

Saraph stared out into the deep beauty. "'Nothing is hidden that shall not become evident, nor anything secret that shall not be known and come to light.'" He recited distantly in a whisper. "The Master spoke but none perceived." He stood and turned slowly, looking, following the horizon as if studying its revelation. Stopping, he looked down at Zoltan who he found to be staring at him intently.

"'There is nothing covered up that will not be revealed, and hidden that will not be known. Accordingly, whatever you have said in the dark shall be heard in the light, and what you have whispered in the inner rooms shall be proclaimed from the housetops.'"

"Send me back. I have power to change things. I can help," Zoltan requested, frightened.

"Help what? Rearrange some priorities? I do not speak of a disaster to be avoided but of the fullness of time. Preparations are complete. Soon... soon our long watch will see its vindication. Our thoroughly obedient preparations will see the worthy celebration of the Lamb's feast."

For a moment Zoltan tried to make sense of a "lamb" in Saraph's statement. Feeling blank, he let it go.

"I can be a part of this new movement," he said, rebounding. I have prepared. I am your man. I am in a position to . . . ."

Zoltan was interrupted by Saraph's playful laughter, as his companion plopped down beside him and looked him in the eyes.

"Position to do what? My dear, dear Magician, you are not listening, not hearing. Concentrate! There is nothing to be done. All is accomplished."

There was a lengthy pause. When Saraph spoke again his tone was grave. "I know your offer is sincere, dear one. But you are in a position to weep and wail. Your great poverty is utterly exposed. So listen, and hope for a revelation of mercy. Wake, O sleeper, while hope remains."

"I am sorry," Zoltan said.

"Sorry?"

"I can see that . . . ." Zoltan's thought was intercepted by a purely sensual distraction. "O-o-oh," he groaned as he closed his eyes and squeezed large tears from their corners that nearly leaped over the sides of his face before rushing into his hair. "That sound," he murmured. "It is like listening at the wellspring of tonality."

"It is precisely," Saraph replied. Reaching over his head with both hands and waving them in a broad, sweeping motion he said, "All that is born out there as pitch and hue is conceived here. Great wonders you summon with the strike of a hammer upon a string and the forcing of wind through a reed."

Zoltan looked out into the expanse of space attempting to comprehend Saraph's meaning.

"Have you ever been in a place where music was happening?" Saraph asked.

Music . . . happening . . . Zoltan's groggy mind was trying to keep pace.

"Well, here sound is happening," Saraph announced.

"Symphony," Zoltan said distantly. "Orchestra seats, season tickets. Music happens there in front of me. My friend is renowned ... conductor. More than ninety musicians." He took a breath and was still for a moment. "He is at the center of all that activity. A wonder, he has told me ... when distance between his movements and sound from the instruments vanishes. An indication, a subtle response multiplies ... exponentially, yet ... incalculably ... fluidly. He says it is like moving sound around in a space."

Saraph listened as Zoltan seemed to fade in and out of focus on his thoughts. He had seen many an arrogant man, many a lost soul confess the error of their ways under compulsion due to profound encounters with impressive revelation. But he knew also to defer optimism until the normal settings were reestablished. The backlash of such episodes was often an embarrassment over weakness, brokenness and vulnerability.

It is likely, he thought, *that pride's vengeance will be fierce to reclaim lost territories, and more, to erase any memory of softhearted admissions.* But, for now he would listen and hope to aid an effective and lasting impression of some value while he had the opportunity.

"Failed," Zoltan said, before squeezing his eyes so tightly shut that his brows nearly met. He clenched his teeth. Taking a deep breath, he exhaled slowly. "My heart aches here. The weight ... so many we have ... ." He paused. "It is too much for me."

Zoltan turned his head toward Saraph, their faces inches apart. His eyes remained tightly shut. "Please take me ... I am not worthy to know this beauty. Something terrible is happening. I don't know exactly ... but I can feel it. I feel I am being crushed."

"It is your call," Saraph answered. "Speak as you will. But I do not advise cowering before truth to which your own soul is a witness lest you should fail to make the acquaintance of either again."

Saraph's tone conveyed great concern, as the nearness of a

flight from the battle for hope was evident. The gravity in his voice was persuasive; and Zoltan felt a strong agreement. He resisted the urge to request the destination that had come to his mind.

"Is this heaven?" Zoltan asked.

"Oh, child," Saraph answered, nearly breathless in reaction to the question. His head fell upon Zoltan's left arm and rolled back and forth. "No, no, no. This is not heaven." Raising his head, they were again nearly nose to nose. "We would not be chatting so soon were this . . . ." Saraph was interrupted by his own chuckle. He rolled over onto his back and gazed up at the colorful expanse.

"I thought maybe some small corner of it," Zoltan offered, feeling a little embarrassed by Saraph's response.

Zoltan recalled the initial introduction to the gift, the transition in his room. *The room?* he thought, with a sense of profound distance. He had a faint recollection of its increasing brightness, then it's fading from view as he had walked away. He remembered a similar feeling of helplessness, of exposed thoughts and unedited communication. It seemed very long ago, and somehow, very present. *Light,* he thought vaguely. He closed his eyes and enjoyed the wonder of his own breathing.

Saraph rolled over and got to his knees. Leaning down, he gently shook Zoltan's shoulder.

"Forgive my intrusion. But I am eager to show you . . . ." Saraph stopped short as he recognized the terrible sadness in Zoltan's eyes.

"Gods we were," Zoltan stated. "In the Roman fashion, gods who would create at will, destroy at whim, make useful whatever opportunity required. Oaks was right. 'Worse than whores!'" he continued, without any change to his slow speech or expressionless stupor.

"I judged many to be that low . . . prided myself on that advantage of judgment. Disdain distanced me from the vermin of the world." He paused. "I must have believed that... I remember believing that," Zoltan mused aloud. "Politicians, preachers, law peddlers, debt hawkers... of course, the whores and pimps themselves. I condemned them all, tried and condemned each in their turn... the kangaroo courts of script and screen.

"But, we were the worst of all. We would sell anything for money and power, raise more money, and buy more power. Our own children... I was quite conscious of...." Zoltan looked up at Saraph's blurry image through tear-filled eyes. "I didn't care. The world ate from my hand. I fed it what it would come back for... the intrigues and titillations of every inclination of hateful and psychopathic minds... our minds." His eyelids closed, weighted.

"Power to ravage the world as a mistress laid bare, craving our next manipulation. To rule the universe if we could, to remake it as we wished. To control it with our ...." Zoltan opened his eyes and hesitated until he again found Saraph in his gaze. "Magic," he said, understanding. "Your title for me is true."

Saraph turned to look out into the distant space before them.

"Planets?" Zoltan wondered aloud.

Beautiful, soft shapes, glowing of colored light and varying in size and distance from Zoltan and Saraph's observation point. Some seemed so close to one another that they appeared as connected. *Others,* Zoltan thought, *are great distances from each other.* Several appeared to him as much larger, and much closer than the sun had appeared from earth, though their light did not discourage his staring. The space between these appeared to be filled with other lights of varying sizes, but more nebulous. And beyond them all, billions of tiny lights.

They were all changing, though Zoltan could not identify one in particular that changed in any way. *They are definitely changing,* he thought. *Maybe some are going out and others are becoming brighter. They are moving like soft waves of color and light.*

The colors before him had softened from brilliant, dazzling flashes of light to the cool violets, and now to warm, rich glows, like scattered fires upon the layered hills of a fading dusk. The starry skies that he had once loved to walk beneath served as his only point of reference, yet this was dramatically different from their beauty. Different enough that he could not be certain that what he was observing was in the heavens.

"They must be planets," he muttered aloud, "a different solar system, a different galaxy, maybe."

"No, not planets. Not these," Saraph softly whispered. He was looking straight up and feeling very pleased that his visits to this place never disappointed the anticipations of memory. He, too, was filled with awe.

"Then, what?"

"Particles," Saraph answered. "You are looking out into the depths of the infinitesimal. What you might call micro-expansive ... the infinite small."

"But it looks like heavens, like billions of stars far, far away."

"And were you able to visit the tiniest one at the *smallest* reach of your vision you would find that it would continue to be so. And indeed it is, just, in a different direction."

Zoltan lay stunned, trying to consider what Saraph had just said. He was finding it impossible to reconcile it with his perception. Beyond ability to marvel, he was disturbed by a sense of limitation.

"I ... I'm sorry," he finally said, "but I cannot comprehend your meaning."

"Only because your eyes are seeing what they otherwise could not without powerful aid ... the assumed limit increasing without bound. There is a wealth of discovery to be made in the vast beyond of the infinitesimal," Saraph said as he marveled. "You think the libraries of man in a handheld storage system is impressive?" He shook his head. "Where are the probes, why no satellites?"

"This powerful aid you speak of...a lens of some kind? A sophisticated tele...." Zoltan thought for a moment. "Microscope?"

"Neither. What I was actually referring to was the gift. The gift of seeing as you otherwise could not, being where you otherwise could not." Saraph looked around. "Infinitized. Immortal passage is the aid I was speaking of. Your other experience produced an assumed limit, which you now can see to be error. What you see before you is without bound. The wonders within the least of these before you are great."

"But how am I seeing this? What is the vehicle, the window that we are seeing through that creates the phenomenon of this vision?"

"You seem to be stuck, Magician. I think you refer again to a lens. Your gadget-mindedness is bent on a trivialization. There is no gizmo, no trick, no device. You look directly upon this scene with your own eyes, as I do with mine."

Zoltan again attempted to process the information. "Then, where are we?" he asked after several minutes. "That is what I need to know. What is our vantage point for this viewing?"

"We are amid an expanse of light particles. The opportunities for such viewings in the universe are as infinite as these particles. But the one we have chosen is within a special little box called a mass spectrometer. It is one of the most elegant machines in your world, and one of my favorite playgrounds. It uses energy charges to blast apart molecules. The ionized particles are spun over a magnetic field in order to measure them in atomic mass units by the difference in their trajectories. Its invention was for unequivocal identification of molecular materials. When it has finished its task, the scientist overseeing its activities will possess an exact measure of atomic mass, a numerical identification of atomic materials belonging to only one molecular composition."

"Such a profound capability, and I didn't even know about

it," Zoltan said.

"Actually, the first developments in this area go back to the nineteenth century."

"The planets, or ...." Zoltan thought for a moment. "The particles are in a machine?"

"Hmm-m-m. A simplistic interpretation, but one that I must affirm," Saraph answered with reservation.

"I thought you said there were no gizmos ... no devices."

"The phenomenon we view is in a machine, true enough. But our viewing is unaided, but by the gift, of course."

Zoltan looked simultaneously puzzled and alerted. "You are saying *we* are in a machine?"

"Again, Magician, this is quite ...." Saraph paused and thought for a moment. "I can see that I should not have mentioned the machine. To reference it in this context would be like traveling one billion light years from earth, landing on another planet and restricting your understanding of the experience to the context of earth's origin. A reality yes, yet, somehow irrelevant. Do you see my meaning?"

"You are saying *we* are in a machine?"

Saraph stared back into Zoltan's eyes for a moment. "Yes," he conceded.

"We are inside of a machine," Zoltan repeated to himself, attempting to appreciate the gravity of his own words. "A machine in a building on earth?"

"One occupying a space on a counter top in a laboratory, if you must."

"What is this we are on, this surface I am lying on that seems like an earth of its own?"

"It is the surface of a single subatomic particle, traveling through space at better than 22,000 miles per second ... albeit, space ... within a machine," Saraph said adding a smile. "We arrived here at an especially beautiful time ... hmm, another word I use regrettably, and to your misleading. The photon pulse had just hit its mark, the flash point of ionization occurring immediately prior to our arrival. The measurements are being recorded as we speak."

"My body is resting upon the surface of a particle?"

Zoltan rolled over on his side and raised up to prop himself on his left elbow as he ran his right hand over the surface beside him. He was disappointed that he could not grasp anything, even as he realized that there was nothing to be grasped. He lifted his hand toward his face and slowly made a fist. He examined it closely.

"This fist… is it not a physical reality?" he asked, looking up at Saraph. Looking back at his fist he contemplated aloud, "How many times have I looked at this fist? How many objects has it held? And now it is a trillion times smaller than any object that has ever been wrapped within it?" He opened his hand and stared at it, trying to fathom the possibility of infinite reducibility.

Zoltan looked again at Saraph. "Tendons, vessels, cells, are those not real?"

Saraph reached into his pocket and pulled out a few Gummy Bears. He opened his hand and held them out to Zoltan. "What size would you like them to be?" he asked.

Zoltan stared blankly at Saraph. He then took a piece of the candy and put it into his mouth. "How odd," he mumbled, as the taste filled his mouth and he contemplated the reality of the dissolving candy. "Still, it seems there must be a point at which it reduces to nothing. Is there not a point of nothing?"

"No, there is no 'point of nothing,' as you call it," Saraph answered.

Zoltan looked around, put his hand to his chest, and closed his eyes. "My lungs were created for earth's atmosphere. How is it that I can breathe in a place where oxygen molecules are like planets to me… galaxies?"

"My dear Magician, God is bigger than the air you breathe.

Be thankful that the breath He gives you is sustained by more than your ability to inhale and exhale oxygen.

"Consider your observation of this event. Your eyes were created to function in accordance with visible light, which is produced by photons, fundamental particles that are also bigger than you presently. Your other senses, too, were created to respond to stimuli that effect neurological responses, all of which are dependent upon fundamental particles that are all much larger than you are at the moment, yet you perceive all that is before you. The extreme heat produced during ionization as electrons are being stripped away from nuclei is not survivable. Why are you not vaporized? And sound," Saraph chuckled, "were you not protected concerning sound, you would quickly be scattered among the particles making up this beautiful array. So, how are we even here talking about this at all?

"In other words, you are not asking any good questions. Your questions are conceived within the limits of your former perspective. Why do you cling to it? The gift is not an exotic travelogue. It is profound. It intends what is truly different. It is an observatory, if you will, of perspectives, a great light. Yet, you are as a boy, bringing with you a flashlight for a hike under the noonday sun, determined to cast little shadows with it, being so proud of its powers. Can you not see that the sun boldly casts the great shadows, and even the shadows speak of its light?

"Like creation, the gift is essentially of a nature that offends you. It is what you might call the miraculous or the supernatural, but what I will identify as God's will, the natural origin and constant sustenance of all that is. Observing that, you object. And by what motivation? If you were just honest, not even wise, you would test your questions as well as their answers by this: 'Based on what?' Then you might at least enjoy the benefit of some good questions."

"So, it ... the gift that is, alters nature?" Zoltan asked, sincerely attempting to understand.

Saraph stood up and walked several steps away. He folded his arms and thought for a moment. When he returned he said, "You are not a religious man. Yet, surely you have prayed."

Zoltan paused and then nodded. "Several times," he replied, recalling his most recent prayers, desperate prayers for his son.

"Why?"

"Why did I pray?"

"What were you hoping for?"

"An answer, I suppose," he said, still uncertain of Saraph's meaning.

"Not help?"

"Yes, help."

"Out loud?"

"No … never have," he responded immediately.

"Really? You spoke silently to an unidentified being somewhere beyond yourself in the universe, to whom you had made no personal acquaintance, and expected that he … it … be so powerful and so fine-tuned to your consciousness and your concerns as to be ready and willing to respond to your silent communication? Further, you expected this being to be capable of transcending all natural laws and humanly accountable means to perform the desired intervention?

"I tell you, the partings of seas, the fulfillment of the prophetic utterance, and the raising of the dead require no greater reach for the hand of God than His answer of a single prayer. It is certainly odd that, in contrast to such bold faith, you presently think it is a big challenge for Him to make the necessary provisions for an initiative He advanced on your behalf.

"Breathing, proportions, physical boundaries and natural laws … these are not very big problems if you do not start with the predetermination that there is no Creator, or that the miraculous is non-reality. They are rather simple providential provisions for the comfort of an invited guest, really. After all, the reality inherent in this experience is quite outside of the scope of laws as you understand them. If the suspension of mortal boundaries is made possible by the sovereign authority of the Giver of this gift, a material adjustment that accommodates our visit is really not impressive, relatively speaking."

Zoltan laid back and stared into the darkening molten space above him. "I know that the gift is real because I am participating in it. Beyond that...." He paused. "It is all I know."

"Your pride prohibits your seeing. In one direction you declare the universe huge and boast of its exploration. In the other you search constantly for the one piece, the answer, the beginning of material construction. Both are trivializations created upon preoccupations with conquest."

"Who are you speaking of? I have rarely looked through either microscope or telescope."

"Yet your productions recklessly, blindly endorse the opinions of some who have. And you methodically censor others whose profound accomplishments and conclusions challenge what you have willfully advanced to the deceptive status of conventional wisdom. And what is your purpose but the conspiracy of your superman complex, the rebellion begun in the Garden."

"It is true," Zoltan whispered after a long silence. "I know someone who ...." He stopped. "What holds ... everything?"

"The glue?" Saraph looked at Zoltan. Then he looked out into the glorious expanse of dazzling color. "It is as you have been told: the will of the Almighty alone."

They sat quietly, watching the changes taking place before them.

"Infinite order and complexity," Zoltan mused aloud, breaking the silence. "I have a brother. I'm sure you are aware of that," he said, staring out into the deep beyond and completing his earlier reference.

"He is the one you just referred to."

Zoltan nodded. "We do not see each other much. It is as if we are from two completely different stories. Same home, same street, many of the same names and faces, same town, same country, same planet, many shared experiences... different stories.

"Yes, they are quite different." Saraph said thoughtfully. "As I told you before, there are two kinds of stories and everyone lives out of one of them. There are those who live within a speculative story based upon chance and guesses. Guesses like... perfect, life-producing order emerging from random material activity, guided by a mysterious force some would call nature. Others give it a god-name derived from an elemental part of the nature they worship. By whatever name, it is the story of nothing and so what.

"And there is the story of God, the true Creator of the universe, and His offspring who live before Him and see their lives in the context of his revelation, His blessing. It is the story of purpose and hope–hope not as in the crossing of fingers regarding a want, but hope as in confidence based upon faith initiated and encouraged by the revelations of God throughout His universe. It would be a folly to think that both are valid. Do not think that because *two kinds of stories* exist within the fragile framework of the consciousness of men that *two stories* exist. No, there is one... one truth, one reality. All are in it, seeing or not."

Zoltan recognized the implication of Saraph's familiarity with his brother. But he was not sure enough to articulate a question.

"Right now," he said "I have this strange feeling, like I am in a chapter of his story. He would so love this. He has told me... tried to tell me about.... Maybe we should move on," he said, interrupting his own thoughts. He paused, distracted. "How long have we been here?"

The soft planetary forms were no longer visible, replaced by a dull, dark violet veil that had been darkening noticeably as he spoke. He looked at Saraph, barely able to make out his image.

"We have not used any of the gift in this place, if that is your concern. The things that have taken place here have happened within a millisecond of time... there. Still, it will be completely dark here soon, and we have spent more than enough time in dark places. I am eager to accompany you to other glimpses of glory."

"I don't think of my brother as a glimpse of glory, but he is on my mind. I would like to see him at his work."

Chapter 29
STEPHEN

The shock of arrival in his brother's laboratory was nearly as great to Zoltan's emotions as the particle universe was to his senses. Suddenly there he was, his brother, Stephen, seated right before him in his lab coat and glasses. That signature vexed look was upon his face.

The compulsion for flight hit Zoltan with the force of a door flung open by a hostile intruder. Saraph looked at him and, immediately recognizing the tension, raised his hand to indicate encouragement for Zoltan to calm himself and give the moment a chance to mature. Zoltan closed his eyes, turned away and bent over, hands on his knees as if battling vertigo or the nearing of a vomit reflex. Wordless, Saraph put his hand on Zoltan's back and stood beside him, waiting.

Hearing his brother mumbling, Zoltan was amazed by the rhythmic tapping of keys. "How does he do that? My secretary does not type that fast, and she's a six-figure professional."

"Your secretary is a six-figure showpiece of your success. As I recall, you have an entire department doing your typing for you."

Zoltan looked toward Saraph and frowned. "Still…," he said, looking back at his brother, "that entire department would have difficulty keeping up with this."

"He will do this for five or ten minutes and then write on

the pad some more, work out some rough thoughts, then rattle those keys awhile. He's as active a thinker as I have observed in your world," Saraph reported with enjoyment and admiration.

"This is how he thinks," Zoltan concurred. "I have watched him since we were kids. How he thinks that fast is beyond me."

"He works with a remarkable confidence of faith. Questions and answers are as fluids being poured together, instantly mixing and flowing to their destination unhindered by doubt or fear of error." Saraph spoke as a proud schoolmaster. "At this stage, I should qualify. Later on he will go back and pick out what is error. But here he is fearless, unconcerned and uninhibited. He is quite comfortable with being wrong."

"Maybe that has been the problem with our communication over the years. We get into discussions and he lets loose this unfiltered thinking. Wacky stuff he has tried to fill my head with."

"Unlikely," Saraph replied. "His spoken words are few, as you know, and nearly always based on the result of the latter part of the process. You have heard more of them than anyone else because he cares for you so greatly. His passion for communicating with you is fueled by love and hope."

"Please! Spare me your reports of his brotherly pity."

From the moment Zoltan had arrived in the lab and his brother had appeared before him, the backlash of resentment toward Saraph had begun to stir. The impression of the particle universe had been great and Zoltan resented the thought of it. Now, back in his element amid the familiar trappings of technology and human craft, he was feeling more himself. The sight of Stephen especially had reminded him of his former life and identity. These arousals felt natural, a relief from those that had inspired awe; and the professional environment tempted his passion for the control and prowess he perceived as he observed his brother at work.

Humility, even a millisecond of its impression, was regrettable in the context of Zoltan's renewed scent of prowess. And his suspicions about Saraph's ill motivation had returned with the increased weight of that regret.

Saraph opened his hands and spread out his arms. "Amazing playground, huh?"

As he turned and looked around, Zoltan was softened by captivation.

"Makes me almost giddy," Saraph said.

"I can appreciate that," Zoltan responded. Completing a full circle, he stood looking at his brother.

"Do you respect Stephen?" Saraph asked, as they watched the scientist take a handful of papers and walk out of the room.

Zoltan was taken back by the question. "It is difficult to respect someone who calls himself a scientist and is always talking about truth," he stated cryptically.

"It is the fundamental nature of science to pursue the truth." Saraph replied. "A *true* scientist would never concoct data, for example, or carelessly put forth a hypothesis, except at the risk of all professional credibility."

"So, give me what is rational, relevant, practical," Zoltan retorted, rejecting Saraph's point. "Not some indiscernible, unverifiable notion about an overarching truth and its origin. Let a scientist tell me what he has observed and by observation established as a particular and useful fact. Matters of ultimate truth? Those are for theologians and their impressionable pew warmers. And *they* are verifiably irrational."

"You know that the truth cannot be known?"

"Do you or Stephen know that it can? That's the point. A dialogue of questions at best, no answers. No rational answers anyway." Zoltan shook his head. "What a pretender. And such a great mind given to the irrational. What a disappointment. What a pretender."

With the distraction of his brother gone for the moment, Zoltan began examining an arrangement of computers and printers along one of the countertops. Saraph walked over and stood before a computer monitor near the place that Stephen had been seated and studied the contents on the screen. Then he went and stood beside Zoltan and studied the long graphs being produced by the printers.

"Hmm, it seems so simple, but he keeps missing it," he mused aloud. "But he's very close now...very close."

"Right, I'm falling for that." Zoltan looked at Saraph and rolled his eyes. "Two pretenders."

Walking around the room, Zoltan was intrigued by the integration of unfamiliar technological systems. "Look at all this..." he said. "We owe a great debt to previous generations of human ingenuity."

"Incalculable," Saraph agreed. "Inherited treasures, legacy."

"Modern technology provides an awesome advantage to the progress of rational vision," Zoltan gushed, like a boy in a hobby shop.

"A major player for sure," Saraph said, arms folded, right hand holding his bearded chin, the index finger pressed into his cheek. "Of course, technology has an equally profound influence in the accelerated advancement of the irrational."

Zoltan stopped and stared at Saraph. A look of chagrin transformed his face as his personal soap-box came to mind. Shaking his head, he conceded, "It is true. The development of instruments of death and destruction does receive disproportionate aid from our applied technologies." He shrugged. "On the other hand, look at the medical industry, just shocking advancements everywhere."

A door opened, and they both turned and watched Stephen as he reentered the room and took his place beside the computer.

"Your brother, by the way, makes great use of some of the most elegant technologies."

"How do you know so much about him?"

"Would you attempt to complete an assignment, especially

one of unprecedented proportions, without careful research?" Saraph answered.

"I am … *was* the assigner in my world," Zoltan proudly retorted, ignoring Saraph's meaning. He was pretending to have no interest in his brother and his work as he continued to investigate the equipment in the room.

"I am not. I am a laborer," Saraph stated with greater pride, though not in himself. "And my assignment brought me here for research."

"What kind of research?"

Zoltan finally came to a stop where his brother was working. He hovered over Stephen, acting interested in the content on the screen while being demonstratively discourteous. These actions were intended for Saraph's observation. Zoltan wanted to amend whatever victory or encouragement Saraph may have gained in the particle universe.

Suddenly the typing stopped and Zoltan pulled back, momentarily startled and instinctively thinking that his brother had stopped because of his rudeness. But the scientist just leaned back in his chair and pushed his glasses up to rest in the thick hair that encroached onto his forehead. He rubbed his eyes. Then, closing them behind deep furrowed brows, he clasped his hands behind his head.

"Stephanos Antoniadis, Ph.D.," Zoltan read aloud from the security badge attached to his brother's lab coat. He stared at him, wondering.

"Stephen is a brother to be proud of. He is a man of great skill, knowledge and accomplishment, and even greater character," Saraph reported.

Zoltan bent lower and watched the business of Stephen's eyes behind their lids. "And I wonder, little bro, am I a brother to be proud of?"

"He is quite proud of you."

Zoltan did not respond. He just stared at Stephen. The

sounds of the printer beside him announced the product of his brother's most recent thoughts and calculations.

Stephen was a handsome man with deep-set eyes and a broad smile. The two brothers shared the strong genetic heritage of thick, dark hair and dark eyes passed to them by their Grecian ancestors. They also shared what their mother called 'the great Nordic jaw line' of their great grandfather, the father of their father's mother. As far as Zoltan knew, he represented their only non-Greek relatives. This assessment, he had been informed, included all current relatives and all known ancestors, however distant. He apparently also supplied the genetic influence responsible for their father's quiet demeanor.

The report Zoltan had received from his dad was that he never heard his Nordic grandpa speak two consecutive words, let alone an entire sentence. Zoltan had always thought it must have been because he went into shock when he found he had joined himself to such a verbal strain of Greeks. And perhaps a similar phenomenon scared the blond out of his DNA when it hit the deep Greek gene pool. Not a trace remained.

Zoltan, favoring his father and the Nordic influence stood tall and broad shouldered. Stephen was naturally barrel-chested, of the stockier sort from their mother's side of the family. And, at 5'8", he was a full eight inches shorter than Zoltan. But the quiet gene of the Norseman went to Stephen, while Zoltan was right at home among the talkers from both the Antoniadis and the Karayiannis side of the family tree.

While both men's faces bore deep lines around their mouths and beside their eyes, they seemed to tell different stories. The language of the lines in Zoltan's face was hard and severe. They made him look fierce at times and pained at others. They had aided his bullying style over the years, even as that style reciprocally chiseled them deeper. Preferring the rugged, etched look that they gave his face and the apparent appreciation of his female friends, Zoltan was compulsive about keeping his face clean. He shaved at least twice a day and often three times.

Stephen's face was a portrait of quiet. Pleasant and warm was the universal assessment of those who met him. Appearing to start from beneath his full bottom lip and wrapping around his face, was a beard as thick as the hair on his head. He kept it trimmed, but full. The attractive contours it covered were a sacrifice to his genuine disregard for vanity.

Zoltan was suddenly impressed with how long the printer had been working. He stepped over to examine the pages it was producing. At first glance it was the thickness of the stack of pages that amazed him. "Look at this! There must be forty or fifty pages here!" he proclaimed. "How is that possible?" Then he bent to look more closely at the sheets emerging from the printer. "What?" he emoted thoughtfully as he turned and made eye contact with Saraph for the first time since arriving in the lab. "It's all math."

Turning back and studying the pages, Zoltan gushed, "There's not a single word of English anywhere that I can see." Then he looked at the Monitor that he had pretended to be interested in earlier. "What is this?" he asked rhetorically, peering back into the paper bin. "Pages upon pages of solid math." Leaning toward Stephen, he stared at his brother closely as if looking at an animal in a zoo that he had never seen before.

"Dear brother," he whispered intimately, "what is in that brain of yours."

Saraph was moved as he observed what he knew was a true sign of thaw. He had been wise not to be taken in by the repentant strains under the influence of the particle universe. But this, here in Zoltan's world, was cause for hope. The man he had encountered in the posh office months earlier would never have acknowledged such revelation. Neither would he have displayed this intimacy and admiration toward anyone, his brother least of all.

Zoltan was staring at Stephen from only inches away when

the printer stopped. Stephen's eyes opened and he simultaneously sprung forward. It gave Zoltan such a fright that he let out a yell and jumped backward, stumbling and nearly falling down. He looked over at Saraph and could not help but join his laughter.

"That, I think, is the first unkind thing he has ever done to me," he said, clutching his chest and catching his breath.

They watched as Stephen picked up the pages and looked them over, spending only seconds on each. Then he set them down and picked up his note pad. As he looked over the pages of notes, he marked through all but a few lines on each. Then he went back to the computer sheets and began doing the same. He laid these side by side and walked to the other side of the counter and pulled a long narrow strand of paper from another printer.

He came back to his chair and sat down and began studying the printed peaks and valleys. He then began circling certain bits of information and making notations throughout the long sheet of paper.

"What is he doing," Zoltan asked.

"He is identifying atomic materials based on measurements. It's like a descriptive sketch or a materials list, if you will. He is going over it and identifying and naming everything in the test he just conducted."

After tearing the sheet into several pieces, Stephen set it down and then picked up his writing tablet again and made several more notations. He then copied all of the original writings he had not marked through onto one page. He leaned forward in his chair and studied the information on the three paper formats. Saraph was pleased to again see Zoltan's near reverent observation of his brother. Finally, Stephen gathered all of the papers together and set them in one pile. He leaned back in his chair, raised his glasses, rubbed his eyes and resumed his earlier position, hands clasped behind his head.

Zoltan stared thoughtfully for several minutes, then folded

his arms, leaned against the counter across from Stephen and looked down at the floor. Deep contemplation was etched in his face. Ten minutes passed. Saraph sat still, periodically looking at each of the men.

The door at the far end of the lab again opened and an attractive woman in a lab coat entered. She appeared to be quite pleased and was humming as she walked. As she came around the end of the counter behind Stephen, she recognized that he was in his customary thinking pose. Stephen's left hand released from behind his head and rose until standing straight, fixed like a stop sign. The woman came to a halt and stopped humming. "OK," she whispered in mock reverence.

As she began to turn and retrace her steps she asked, "How long?" Stephen's hand blinked open and shut five times. "Twenty-five minutes," she interpreted aloud. "I'll be back with these very impressive," she paused for effect, "rather unprecedented findings in twenty-five."

Stephen's left eye was lifted open by the raising of his brow as his right brow simultaneously dipped. "Unfair," he said with a groan.

"No, no, don't mind me. I wouldn't want to break your concentration. I'll be back. Probably not in twenty-five minutes, though. I stopped in the middle of a couple of things to come up here. Maybe a few hours. Nah … probably not then either. I've got a lot to do." She left the room as Stephen's hand went back to its place behind his head, which shook in agreement with the look of chagrin on his face.

"What a lovely assistant," Zoltan commented.

"She is not an assistant. She too is a scientist. They have worked together for six years."

"Really?"

"He has many colleagues and some assistants. She is the only one who recently became his wife."

Zoltan's eyes betrayed his surprise. "Well, that rascal," he said, looking over at his brother and meaning it. "She must be twenty years younger than him."

"I think you are projecting something from your story onto his," Saraph said. "He is but eight years her senior."

Zoltan was quiet for a moment as he remembered with some shame that he had snubbed his brother's wedding. He looked at Saraph and said, "I was out of the country."

"Business, of course. It's important," Saraph replied.

Zoltan looked back at Stephen. "You are a brother to be proud of after all, or to be envied," he jested.

Turning again to Saraph he said, "I never have been quite sure what my brother does for a living. Just what is this place? I mean, I know it's a pharmaceutical company, but what is this place we are in?"

"Do you want to know what he does or where we are?"

"Let's begin with where we are,"

"Well, I have two answers. First, the one we have a start on: we are in a research laboratory. This facility serves the department of Pharmacokinetics and Drug Metabolism for Latco Unitrends."

"Yes, I remember him telling me he was with Latco. Big outfit. And the second answer?"

"The more important answer I will say. This is the meeting place of the three great American geniuses."

Zoltan stared at Saraph for a moment, attempting thinly to conceal the fact that he was taken aback by the suggestion that his brother was held in such lofty esteem by this cosmic observer. This was served with a double portion of humility due to the fact that, against Zoltan's determined resistance, Saraph had gained a similar status in his mind. The resentment and contempt he had developed toward Stephen in recent years were not so far removed that this was not hard to take.

Chapter 30
THREE GENIUSES

Stephen's face reflected the movements of his thoughts as his brother stared at him. Zoltan turned and looked at Saraph.

"You are saying that Stephen . . . ." he finally attempted with resignation.

"Oh, no, no." Saraph chuckled, immediately understanding Zoltan's meaning. "I am not speaking of any persons. I am referring to the three geniuses of American culture: Capitalism, Pragmatism and Logistics."

"Capitalism, Pragmatism and Logistics?" Zoltan repeated, relieved. He laughed.

"Capitalism called the meeting, of course. It is the patriarch, the well-traveled sage, overseer of the American social interface and initiator of its cultural movement. With eyes like an eagle's he spotted this opportunity from great heights."

"What opportunity?"

"Originally, a vast, open land of resources ripe for discovery," Saraph answered. "Then he watched the development of an interconnected system of regional resources ideally suited for economic and technological revolutions. And finally, there came the fertile soils of a consumption-driven society populated by worshipers of craving and stimulation. In his circling gaze since . . . oh, at least the turn of the twentieth century, were the trillions to be made on a smorgasbord of molecular inventions.

"Enhancements, anesthetics, alterations, additives, stabilizers and counterbalances – commerce and currency in a chemically-controlled generation of desperately discontented consumers. Industry evolution demanded that an army of engineers fill laboratories like this one. Yes, capitalism called the meeting and made sure the attendees were prepared."

"So there is sarcasm in your use of the word 'genius' for these three."

"Not at all. Genius is a fragile animal and not inherently good or bad."

"You certainly are not speaking well of capitalism even if its brilliance is evident in your rendering."

"And brilliance, too, implies no judgment. It is as it is applied."

"Pragmatism?" Zoltan asked, eager for the appraisal.

"Yes, the practitioner," Saraph mused. "'Does it work?' is the question written upon the cultural consciousness of your nation. Earlier, you spoke of it quite highly. Weigh it, test it, and put it into practice and judge by experience. The very foundations of government in your land are an infrastructure of adaptations of demonstrably effective articles found in many previously established systems. From this core of cultural soul is supplied the impetus for your velocity of ingenuity and your resistance to stagnancy."

"It must be our cultural soul, because it resonates in my own to hear you articulate it. It makes me proud to be an American," Zoltan said with evident sincerity.

"And well it ought."

"So, being a practical man, give me the flip side."

"It ought to be obvious. You think you can fix everything, master everything by test, experience, revision. And here we are among a plethora of experimental pursuits aimed primarily at correcting a calamity of experiential maladies and disasters. This company alone holds more than three million unique molecules in its compound library.

"You will need more than that. In fact, you will need more than the collective libraries of Latco and all of its global rivals to attend the bleeding of the next generation. But, hey, you're getting prepared. Go over to that door and look through the glass. On the other side of the door immediately across the hall is a quarantine area where drugs are waiting to be tested by quality control.

Now, down a ways, across that big hallway is a door that opens to another hall. At the end of it is the largest DEA secure vault in the country. One hundred and twenty-two thousand square feet of C2 long term storage. Latco built the warehouse and co-ops the storage with other large pharmaceutical companies."

"C2?" Zoltan inquired.

"Narcotics... controlled substance–level two. Liquid morphine, oxycodone and the like. You see, your confidence in a question–'Does it work?'–has blinded you from the simplicity of a most tried and true acknowledgment for those in your condition: 'We were wrong.' It is not a new drug, but humility and contrition that direct reparations and healing. It is these that lead to wellness."

"Hold on a minute," Zoltan protested. "Life expectancy in our country is the highest it's ever been and it's going up. I know of no one that would go back to the days of the dark plagues sweeping through the land. Are you saying that these efforts are of no value to us? Stephen and his colleagues are just irresponsible engineers creating new problems... there is no good in what they are doing here?" Zoltan punctuated his question with an encompassing wave of his hand to reference the activities of the laboratory.

"Certainly not. These scientists are some of the most conscientious and thorough professionals ever assembled. Everything they create is motivated and scrutinized by the question, 'Does it work, does the drug do exactly what it is intended to do?' Anything that does not satisfy that standard they do not consider a drug, but an experiment, or worse, a toxin. The institutional system of checks and balances is nothing short of major league – toxicology, pharmaceutical sciences, animal biology, structural biology, computational chemistry, synthetic chemistry, analytical chemistry, and on and on.

But each discovery must be judged for its own merits. Many are of great, immediate and lasting benefit. Many others will bring profoundly harmful results, not because they don't work, but because they do. They work to cover up the symptoms of distress and pain and anguish and outrage, all of which are perfectly healthy responses to a society experiencing the loss of its moral compass. Yet, you will respond with new experimental initiatives, ever attempting to preserve the silly notion that you are in control. It is the collective mentality that I address. Open your eyes. You are *in* the days of the sweeping dark plague.

"And were you able to observe its aggressive malignancy you would find it most regrettable. As the Band-Aids cover the symptoms and provide for your denial of mortal calamity, the liabilities are growing exponentially. Been to a pharmacy lately? Worker bees behind a counter filling little plastic bottles and putting them into bags just as fast as their little fingers can move."

Zoltan was noticeably upset as he stood leaning on a countertop upon hands that were spread out, his head hung down between his shoulders. As he contemplated the gravity of their dialogue, he could not help but do so in the context of his personal grief due to a decade of ineffective attempts to throw money and a myriad of chemical adjustment at the troubles of his own offspring.

"Have you forgotten your contrition already?" Saraph asked. "Truth is, Magician, the astounding … alarming growth in your brother's industry is necessitated by the unnatural appetites driven by yours. And, need I remind you of the new 'candy' products your protégé, Trevor Langdon, plans to soon introduce?"

"Logistics?" Zoltan asked soberly, trying to distract the tension of his thoughts.

"What chemical balm have you found to be an effective healer applied to the wounds of divorce?" Saraph continued, ignoring the prompt. "How many new drugs are being introduced to address the fallout from previous attempts? Do you have any idea how many new molecular patents are being applied for at this moment, targeted at new tags placed upon the heads of your youth for their deficiencies of attention and character?

In *many* cases, such labels deny the reality of the true attention deficiencies—parental attention. No scientist in this building wants to carry the burden of 'savior' for a people who truly need one."

"Logistics?" Zoltan asked again, eager to move on.

"Delivery, of course: packaging, shipping and distribution. America has been the undisputed logistical champion of the world for many generations. But the metabolism side of this industry takes logistics to a whole different level, the molecular level. Little packages carry valuable, time-sensitive contents through a blood-borne delivery system to precise neurological and biochemical destinations. Thus, the name of this department where your brother works, Pharmacokinetics. Pharmaco means drugs. Kinetics has to do with time: molecular aids metabolized and delivered in a time-sensitive fashion."

Zoltan turned and looked around the lab. What he saw was not the traditional laboratory environment of his early memories, cluttered with glass beakers, Bunsen burners and microscopes. It was a highly technical environment equipped with quantum mechanical measuring systems, fluorescence readers, molecular storage devices, and the most advanced computer technologies capable of supporting the most sophisticated experiments and scientific activities.

"So, Stephen invents drugs," Zoltan mused aloud.

"Actually, no. Stephen has been working on a special project for a number of years. He is attempting to invent a particle satellite capable of gathering and processing data about materials and interactions that some still believe to be 'fundamental.' Officially, he calls it Voyager Jr. But off the record, and more affectionately, he refers to it as his 'Little Cosmic Dung Beetle.' Its focus is decay ... or, I should say, what is thought of as decay.

Hubble explores the universe and sends back pictures. Jr., should Stephen ever perfect it, will explore the microverse and send back interpretations in sound... vibrations. Hubble captures images that convey external appearance. Jr. will answer such questions as, 'what is it?', 'Is there an inside of it?' and 'How does it behave?' It is an elegant machine. He has modeled it after the inner ear. Three parts of its structure - we'll call them fluids - will interpret every nuance of subatomic sound, what you might call activity.

"The project is propelled by Stephen's conviction that many problems and their solutions are beneath the molecular radar. He is also motivated by the belief that God's universe is huge in every direction; that the Creator is ever inviting you to explore the wondrous depths of all He has created and participate as co-creators. The practical focus of Stephen's work is elemental sound, an understanding toward tuning, you might say."

As Zoltan thoughtfully glanced around the room, something caught his eye peripherally; he looked over at a square machine on the counter next to one of the computers. At the upper left hand of the front of the machine, embossed into the plastic casing, were red letters trimmed in silver: Mass Spectrometer. His eyes widened as he unfolded his arms and walked toward the machine. Placing his left hand on top of the casing above the name, he stared.

"This?" he asked, looking back at Saraph.

Saraph nodded.

Zoltan looked pained. "We were in here?"

Chapter 31
LISTENING

Seeing Zoltan's distress, Saraph had walked across the room to stand beside him.

"We were in here?" Zoltan again asked, breaking the long silence.

"We were actually . . . ." Saraph paused. He closed his hands loosely and placed the left one on top of the machine and the right on top of the left. He bent over and looked into the hole formed by his fingers as one looking into a microscope. Standing up again, he looked at Zoltan. "As I told you on the particle, that is a crude perception. But, in keeping with the crudeness of your question I must answer yes."

Zoltan leaned on the top of the machine with his arms folded and his head buried in them. The thoughts that bombarded his mind were so fragmented and chaotic that he tried to just shut them out. Yet, there was one that he could not quiet.

"So, this man to my right . . . ." The muffled sound of his voice from beneath his arms abruptly stopped. At that moment Zoltan could not bear any acknowledgment of Stephen as his brother. His head rolled back and forth in his arms. "He was looking down on us like some kind of a . . . ."

"God?" Saraph finished for him, knowing Zoltan's inclinations. Then he began to laugh the kind of laugh of an adult amused and charmed by the absurdity of a child's attempt to articulate something he clearly misunderstood.

"Oh, no, my friend, nothing like that at all. No, your brother is not a god holding a universe in a machine. He is a man, a scientist, exactly as he appears. You went to a place by my escort according to – and it might help if you used your idea of supernatural here – according to the specific authority given by our Creator, the one and only true God.

"No such transcendence would otherwise be possible. His laws are sure. Your brother and other scientists like him depend on that fact every day for every observation and every calculation. The universe is indeed held in perfect order by the perfect assignments of its Designer and Maker."

Zoltan stood up and placed his hands upon the machine and stared blankly down at it. "I can't get it out of my mind, this image of him standing here looking down."

Saraph leaned over the top of the machine, his head just a few inches from Zoltan's, and he joined his disturbed companion in staring down at the box.

"And do you think he could see you in there?"

"Pretty goofy, I know."

"Maybe it's your ego you're having trouble fitting inside of that box."

Zoltan looked past Saraph toward where his brother was sitting. His eyes caught a glimpse of the long, narrow graph papers Stephen had been working on. He walked over to the papers and pointed down at them.

"These notations are of the things we were looking at in there?" A certain fear of astonishment was in his voice. "Am I on there? Was he up here giving me a name and a material quantification?"

"You are looking at it all wrong," Saraph answered. "You went where he dreams of going, imagines … He is imagining himself there right now, listening, wondering what he might hear, what clues he might find. I know this from watching him, from looking over his shoulder and reading his notes."

"Listening?" Zoltan questioned.

"Yes, listening. Surely among your ideas about memory and the profound proportions of your senses you invested an appreciation for the workings of the ear. So, in the explanation I gave you about the function of the Mass Spectrometer, some striking similarities ought to be evident."

Zoltan put his hands in his pockets and looked down at the floor. He was recalling many hours of research he worked on with Chris Troutman and his team of audio effects engineers.

"The ear converts signals at a molecular level," Zoltan said, thinking aloud. He glanced over at the Mass Spectrometer. "Movements of electrically charged particles – ions." Zoltan looked at Saraph. "Hair cells in the organ of corti in the inner ear, if I recall correctly."

Saraph nodded.

"Those movements generate electrical signals," Zoltan continued. "The brain interprets these with atomic exactness."

"The ear does not enjoy the status of the eye among men because it does not have the eye's sex-appeal. Mirror value, *we* call it. But to us . . . ." Saraph tilted his head and a distant look transformed his face. "It is special," he finally finished, looking up at Zoltan.

Zoltan stood beside Stephen. He looked at the handwritten notes, the torn graphs and the edited typed pages on the counter beside him. He stared at the scientist.

"So, you understand this stuff?" he asked Saraph.

"Forgive me, but it is rather elementary."

"How do you . . . ?" Zoltan stopped, unable to find the words to finish his question.

"Do you think that I have been idle?" Saraph asked.

"Well, earlier you were so critical of productivity and accomplishment and all."

"No . . . vain, self-centered ambition, and reckless opportunism are what I denounced."

The two stared at one another in silence for a moment. Then both looked at Stephen as he changed his position to leaning forward with his elbows on his knees, chin resting in his palms.

"If you were to have a discussion with him about this and were able to convince him of the reality of our journey, you would find him not lording over you, but, rather jealous. While you were there, he was here listening, making observations and recording measurements through the remarkable but unaesthetic capabilities of a machine. You heard clearly what he strains to comprehend through equations and measurements.

"In a very real sense, he gave up his ticket to the particle universe for you. That is, he gave up his right to the gift for you."

"What are you saying?" Zoltan demanded.

"I mentioned my research earlier."

"Wait," Zoltan interrupted. "You also never answered my question."

"How do I know so much about him?"

The anticipation in Zoltan's unflinching glare affirmed the mark.

"It is the same answer. I approached my research as an ambassador, a servant representative, knowing that the inclination of my Lord is toward the humble. Yet, I could not carry out his assignment as any other than myself. So, my love of the exploration of His glories naturally biased me toward the explorers. Your brother is the most humble I could presently find among the great thinkers."

"You had chosen him for the gift?"

Saraph nodded. "My time here instructed me concerning Stephen's heart as well as his mind and his work. I requested each of the opportunities to go ...." He paused and nodded toward the mass spectrometer. "Just doing a little scouting for our travels, being certain he would choose this among several exotic locations. You can imagine my frustration with some of your, uh, choices."

"Yes, you digress," Zoltan quipped.

"Every day before he begins his work, he bows and prays and commits his all to his Lord, the King of Glory, Jesus Christ." Saraph paused. "Glory to the name that by grace passes through the lips of this mild servant. Amen."

Zoltan was uncomfortable with the sudden solemnity in Saraph's tone. He felt a compulsory obligation to bow his head, close his eyes, fold his hands, cross himself, and all other things he related to those who say such things. But, unable to choose spontaneously, he just continued to stand motionless staring at Saraph.

"Of course," Saraph continued, "such submission is the custom of all of his servants. But Stephen has one special benediction he never fails to include in his morning devotions: 'Dear Father, consider my love for my brother, Zoltan, and show him mercy this day. And upon his soul extend Your *charis*, and grant him repentance I plead.' That prayer has not failed to reach the throne of the Almighty one single day since my acquaintance with Stephen began. As I, too, have delivered it personally. But, for Stephen, I am sure it began with his conversion those many years ago."

As Saraph was speaking, Zoltan had turned again to look at his brother. He felt a warm renewal of their former intimacy asserting itself in his heart. But a strong backlash of caution recalled his skepticism. His inclination toward any softening at the report of his brother's prayerful goodwill toward him was checked by his bristling at the inherent suggestion that he should need such a thing.

Who is my brother to judge me, or to show me any of this pity? he wondered.

Turning back to Saraph he nodded toward Stephen and asked, "So, you believe like him?"

"'Believe' is not the word that would apply to one with my advantages."

Chapter 32
JANICE

Stephen looked at Zoltan with the intensity in his eyes that his brother had always called "disturbing."

"This is not story, Zoltan. It is reality. You must deal with that first, and trust God to answer what He chooses."

"What an arrogant idea," Zoltan retorted.

"It is not idea, it is . . . ."

"Yeah, Yeah," Zoltan scoffed, "You told me already. 'It is reality.' Well, I told *you* already that your idea of reality is too far off the map for me."

"Listen for yourself to history, archeology, science, and your heart, whatever you will, but listen carefully. Revelation is that for which we are universally obligated to an account. So, listen, you have to listen. It's important!"

"Stop telling me to listen," Zoltan snapped, irritated.

"No, you must listen! There is nothing more important."

"Fine, but I don't need you to tell me to listen. Just because I don't agree with you doesn't mean that I am not listening. I am your older brother, not some child. A modicum of respect, thank you."

"See, you don't understand because you don't listen. It is precisely as a child listens that you must listen . . . with wonder."

"If you tell me to listen one more time . . . ."

"If I didn't tell you to listen I wouldn't be a brother, I wouldn't be caring," Stephen insisted.

"Great, then just stop caring."

"You see, right there. Any amount of listening and you would know that this suggestion is not a possibility. You're not listening. You're not hearing me. We are on two different subjects. You think I'm talking about you listening to me."

Zoltan got down from his bar stool and walked over to Stephen. He pointed so that his finger nearly touched Stephen's nose. "Now you listen to me!" He stopped and shook his head as if disgusted with himself. "You see what you've done. Now you've got me saying it. Just stop it. You understand?"

"Of course I understand, because I listen. That's what I've been telling you. That's why it is so important. Understanding is the whole point of listening."

"Ok, that's it, I've had it." Zoltan was pointing again. "Don't tell me that one more time."

"I can't help it. How 'bout three?" Stephen leaned toward Zoltan. "Listen, listen, always listen!"

Zoltan's open hand collided with Stephen's face so quickly and so loudly that the two brothers stood as if frozen, staring at one another, uncertain about what had just taken place. It was the first time in all their years together that either had raised a hand to the other. Zoltan was mortified and shaken. It was evident that Stephen was thinking. His brows were bent. He rolled his eyes away from Zoltan to stare out from their left corners. His lower jaw was cocked to his right and his lips were slightly puckered.

"OK," he finally said. "That's great. I think that will do." He leaned toward Zoltan again, stuck out his chin and turned his other cheek toward his brother. "Now this time, when it makes that sound, really listen carefully."

Zoltan looked at his brother with scared eyes and fled the room.

❧

"That was the day I decided my brother was crazy. I thought that anyone who can run me out of my own house must be avoided. I haven't seen him since, until now. Talked to him on the phone briefly a few times, but that's it."

Leaning with his elbows on the counter, Zoltan's long legs were angled toward the other side of the lab where Saraph relaxed against the opposite counter. As his head rested on folded hands, Zoltan found that even now the recollection was disquieting. He shifted and looked over his shoulder at Saraph.

"He was right. I didn't understand and I wasn't listening. I didn't know how, or I didn't know what he meant. I can see that now. Looking back, I know that he tried to tell me. But I was stuck thinking that he was trying to make me listen *to him*."

He looked at his brother.

"Listening, huh?" He shook his head. "I thought it was odd that he spoke about listening with such urgency." Quiet for a moment, he watched Stephen. "I really had no idea what he was talking about. It's a much bigger idea than I ever realized."

His head dropped down and he bounced his forehead upon his hands as he chuckled, then again looked up at Stephen. "How I wish I could hear it from you now: 'It's not idea Zoltan. It's reality.'"

Zoltan again rested his head upon his cupped hands. "It all started over our sister, Janice," he said with difficulty. "She introduced him to . . . ." He looked up and pointed over to a Bible that he had noticed earlier. It sat on a shelf next to Stephen's lunchbox. "She ruined our relationship and I hated her for it. She was so much younger than us . . . I never really got to know her." He paused, thoughtful. "But up to that point I had always enjoyed her."

Several minutes passed before Zoltan spoke again.

"What it did to Dad is nearly unforgivable. Broke his heart. His own children ... It went against everything he'd ever valued and tried to convey to us. Especially the business about sin and fallenness – vulgar to a man who only thought in terms of man's ascent." He looked over his shoulder at Saraph. "Us Greeks leading the way, of course."

Zoltan turned back shaking his head. "Stephen and I were very close before that. In spite of it all, I had expected that one day I would forgive her ... them, and persuade Stephen toward an agreeable compromise. Then, without regard for my plans, she was gone."

He put his forehead in his hands. It was quiet for a moment. There was no sound of printers, no typing, no movement, just the soft, background hum of computers thinking, as was he.

"I have always thought that this 'gospel' that Stephen loves is all wrong. The forgiveness issue is all in the wrong direction. A powerful story, the whole Jesus thing, but why should I be forgiven? A better, more appreciable story from my point of view would be built upon some vehicle for our forgiveness of God. Now that's something I could buy into."

Leaning back against the counter, Zoltan turned and faced Saraph. "Isn't he responsible for this chaos, this pain, if he is there at all? A wonderful girl, our sister, but what about her dreams of family and children. Clearly nobody she was putting her faith in thought much of them."

"The unknown is your agony," Saraph answered. "Why do you speak as a child, as if you expect you should have command over it? Is there a breeze of humility nearby that you could borrow long enough for the admission that there are things you do not know? God, in His wisdom, has not offered any easy resolve to the reality of pain and loss in this world. In fact, He did not even spare Himself of these when He took on flesh and came to save you from their eternal attachment.

"It is man who attempts their rectification in this broken world with every form of noise and distraction he can create." Saraph looked around the room. Then, gesturing with his hands he said, "And every enhancer, anesthetic and elixir he can concoct."

"Anyway, I came to see Stephen as a strange little caricature of a man," Zoltan said, trying to brush aside the entire subject.

"Along with others who believe as he does," Saraph added.

Zoltan gave a mock chuckle. "They deserve it. Hell wielders! Now, how is that rational? They ... ." Zoltan paused to stare at Saraph, disgust emanating from his face like fumes. "*You* would set our culture back among the primitives if you had your way."

The articulation of resentment toward his brother and sister had stirred old defenses. And the thought that he had received *the gift* by default, or by some charity of his brother, had not set well with him. As hardness was reforming in Zoltan's heart, Saraph saw the returning signs of contempt in his eyes. He prepared to battle for the ground hard won and now in jeopardy.

"So, help me make sure that I'm hearing you correctly," Saraph said. "You miss your sister? Her loss broke your heart?"

Zoltan stared at Saraph unable to answer.

"Then I'll assume you're speaking only of anger ... anger perhaps because your expectations are not power and your perception is not control?"

Zoltan turned away. For several minutes he thought about his anger. He wondered about sadness, like a child might wonder about something of an adult nature. He tried to comprehend sorrow.

"He is right, you know," Saraph said. "Things of greatest importance should not be at the mercy of those of lesser importance."

"Important to whom?" Zoltan responded.

"Lesser things are merely of personal importance. Those of greatest importance are universally important, whether you acknowledge the fact or not. You accept gravity as a hard reality of nature. If a loved one dies because of a blow to the head from falling, it would not occur to you to demand a revision of reality concerning gravity to serve your questions about your personal loss. You would not denounce natural law, nor would you begin to practice denial of its authority in the wake of the tragedy."

"I'm sure you must have enjoyed hanging out with him here," Zoltan said. You sound just like him. Your belief in God is the obvious implication."

Saraph indicated disagreement with the slow, rhythmic movement of his head back and forth. "Not my belief, but God *Himself* is the reality behind all other realities, just as gravity is a reality holding many others in its balance. Yet, you think He should accommodate your offended sensibilities with explanations, apologies, and due adjustments to His nature. When He remains as He is and has been, you are angered that your sensibilities do not rule Him. You decide He is not there, or if there, He is irrelevant.

"Your self-righteousness has assured you that He and all those who acknowledge Him are merely by-products of an antiquated mythology. *That*, of all things is irrational. But how would you know? Magician, listen to yourself and gain understanding. Your demand for what is rational is driven by your sensibilities, ignorant of a true regard for reasoning."

Zoltan put his hands in his pockets and began walking to the opposite end of the lab. He stopped at the door and bent to peer through a narrow rectangular window. "Looks like someone is getting her retina scanned at the door across the big hall. Several others are lined up behind her for theirs. Oh … wait a second, a fingerprinting too. They're really serious about security around here."

"Biometric fingerprint scanning," Saraph corrected. "Both

scans are required for access to the vault. Maybe representatives from one of the other pharmaceutical companies. Could be the Drug Enforcement Agency, they make regular visits here. All C2 storage and protection is DEA mandated and regulated."

"Stephen once told me that death is a reality rooted in sin," Zoltan muttered, his breath clouding the glass.

"Yes, death is a part of this fallen world, the first offspring of sin. It was not this way in the beginning. It was introduced with sin. But, given the present condition, sin's consequence is not always the direct answer to questions of pain and loss. There are others, deeper than sin, which you find equally objectionable."

"Like what?"

"God's sovereignty, His holiness, His will, His wrath, His wisdom . . . and dare I mention His glory. The Scripture teaches you that 'for the joy set before Him' Jesus endured the cross and sat down at the right hand of the throne of God. Sin required atonement. But the cross was more directly the result of God's character, His love, His holiness, His glory. Sin held no power, no claim or authority over Him. It was His will to lay down His life for those He loves . . . for you."

Saraph walked over to stand beside Stephen, watching as his closed eyes moved and his face twitched with changing expressions. He looked over at Zoltan. "Sovereignty, holiness, glory . . . am I not correct, Magician, in assuming that you find all of these anathema to your philosophical position?"

"I cannot disagree," Zoltan stated, still looking through the window. He was trying to appear more interested in what was on the other side than in the conversation. "No, I cannot deny that I dislike the sound of those quite intensely," he said, turning to walk beside a counter full of gadgets and machinery that he had never seen before.

"If those are realities in the universe, intrinsic to your Creator's character," Saraph continued, "you may satisfy your sensibilities for the moment by denouncing them as irrational. But you are deluding yourself to believe it is rational to do so."

Suddenly, Stephen sat up in his chair and wrote furiously on his note pad. Running his index finger beneath each of the six lines of the equation, his hand began to shake as he went over it again and again. He tore off the page, shot off of the chair and walked briskly past Saraph, then Zoltan. He opened the door and left the room. Zoltan and Saraph looked at each other and exchanged shrugs.

Zoltan walked back to the place where he had been standing earlier, hands in his pockets. Saraph did the same. They leaned against their respective counters and looked at one another.

"Perhaps it was my expectation that she live a long full life that collided with the reality of something far less," Zoltan said.

"Or far more," Saraph suggested. "God's will perhaps. Big story versus small, infinite purpose versus finite human scripting. One hundred years is only marginally different from ten where life is but a moment's wisp. Have you ever considered that her days had been determined according to God's good pleasure? Perhaps you were given a great and bountiful gift in full measure, her life connected to yours. Can you think of any natural right that supposes more?"

Zoltan removed his hands from his pockets, walked over to Saraph and stood directly before him. "The hourglass empties," he said flatly, displaying an urgency concerning the value of the gift.

"If you don't mind, I would like to revisit an earlier question," Saraph requested.

Zoltan nodded.

"Do you respect him?"

Zoltan smiled. "Greatly... he's one of the strongest men I have ever known. I know of no one with deeper character or more integrity. At times I have wished to see the same in others I have encountered who claim to believe as he does."

"If you did, would you not just discount them as you have Stephen?"

Zoltan stared at Saraph for a moment, considering his point. "Suffice to say, I have seen precious few. Your own 'research' bears out my point. Did he have many rivals for your … this 'gift'?"

Saraph was thoughtful before responding. "By the nature of my assignment, those I considered were but a select few, all servants worthy of the name. Stephen was not the best among them, either for his genius or the devoutness of his faith. But the preservation of wonder in him delighted me. It is the brightest mark of the most humble."

Zoltan put his hands on Saraph's shoulders. "So, your attention came to me because of his prayers?"

Saraph nodded.

"You are telling me that you chose me in spite of me, rather than because of my profound accomplishments and abilities? You were not at all impressed with me?"

As Saraph considered how he might answer, Zoltan began to chuckle, which quickly became a full outburst of laughter that relieved the awkward moment. Saraph joined the laughter.

"Ah-h-h-h, I like it!" Zoltan said. "A classic irony. The ego-maniacal king of self-promotion gains favor…." He stopped, tilted his head and looked at Saraph out of the corner of his eye. "… charis … solely on account of his humble and un-known brother. I am struggling with its believability, but my goodness … very amusing."

Saraph stood up straight.

"I have to tell you something," Zoltan said, letting go of his shoulders.

"What's that?"

"The thing about memory – the charis analogy that I said Trevor stole from me … I actually got it from one of Stephen's speeches about listening and modified it to make the point about sound and memory."

"I figured as much," Saraph responded. "But that's OK, because it wasn't original with Stephen either."

Zoltan frowned, again he tilted his head and looked at Saraph out of the corners of his eyes.

"By the way," Saraph added. "Your brother may not be unknown for long. I have never seen him bolt from the room like that before."

Zoltan looked back at the door through which Stephen had exited the lab. "I hope you are right," he said, meaning it.

"The hourglass empties," Saraph reminded Zoltan with sudden sobriety.

After a moment of preparation Zoltan said, "I am worried about my son."

Chapter 33
SINGERS

*Z*oltan's left hand was clutching Saraph's right arm. Confusion had dictated the attachment upon their arrival. Side by side they stood, motionless. Saraph's face betrayed no reaction. Zoltan's reported grave concern.

Wild beauty, Zoltan thought. He watched, perplexed by the busy layers of flowing movement before them. *People ...* dancers, he thought, catching glimpses of what he perceived as human forms flashing through the movements. He listened. The impression of a lilting dirge was strong, beautiful yet taunting. *That note again. Why do I keep hearing it? I never noticed it before, but today it seems to be everwhere,* He thought. *Almost everywhere. Strange ... I don't remember hearing it in Stephen's lab.*

Zoltan closed his eyes to concentrate. He wanted to identify the sound. Immediately he felt sickened. He opened his eyes. Perspiration covered his face, which had lost its color. His shirt clung to his back. His right hand covered his stomach. The word *"pyre"* came to his mind and lingered like a one word lyric accompanying the mysterious musical impression of the one note.

The note seems to come from out of these movements. It's spun from them somehow. "No," he said aloud, unknowingly. "They come from it."

The thought grew. Zoltan surmised that the entire auditory

and visual impression was driven by the note.

No, that can't be right. He attempted to focus and follow identifiable forms, but was only frustrated by these efforts. "Like colorful silk and light flowing down together from three blades of a spinning fan," he mused aloud. *No, no, no, the note must be coming from them,* he thought, going back to his original interpretation. *They must be creating it.* Zoltan stared.

"They must be singing it," he muttered. "But who are they?" he asked, turning to look at Saraph.

The sight of Saraph's clear and stationary form standing so near disoriented Zoltan. Saraph's lips were moving. But whatever was coming from them was indiscernible. As dizziness distorted Zoltan's thoughts, the note, too, broke apart into many tones. A symphony of sounds played loudly. All were distinct from one another. Yet, all formed a constant—just one note.

My consciousness is made of sound, he thought, reacting to the overwhelming experience. *The world is sound.*

Tears collected in trembling lashes. Spilling over, many began to fall upon cheeks that were gaining back their color.

"I am sound."

Zoltan reached up and pinched his nose, then gave it a wipe with his sleeve. Biting his upper lip, he waited, staring.

"I am song."

As the vertigo subsided the sounds collected and the many returned to their master; the one note reformed. Signals poured into Zoltan's left ear in perfect synchronization with those entering his right, ushered by a constant third tone. Whether a signal was 132 cycles per second or 741, the exact mathematical difference between the signals as they blended with the constant third was a continuous, pulsating frequency of 123 cycles per second. This was the signature tone of the note.

The nature of this activity was imperceptible. Yet, Zoltan sensed an order to the cumulative reemergence of the note. Shaking back and forth, his head was full of ideas. But one stood out from them all.

"A spiritual malevolence is at work here, a manipulation of sound . . . ." He paused. "Of space and perception."

The sound of his own voice seemed to be absorbed into the density of the note, and Zoltan felt as though he'd entered a tunnel. Saraph stared back at him, as if from the other end of the tunnel. Zoltan acknowledged the scent of marijuana, which had been strong since they'd arrived in this place. He knew exactly where they were.

Looking over Saraph's left shoulder, Zoltan spotted a distant table, where a black bong in the shape of a skull rested amid other drug paraphernalia and an empty bottle. Beads of perspiration covered his face as he looked back into Saraph's eyes. Many of the droplets connected to form steady streams on his brow and face as the note continued to gain volume.

"I couldn't hear you earlier. What did you say?" Zoltan asked, needing to hear Saraph's voice.

"That was awhile back." Saraph thought for a second. "I said that your discernment of three was quite intuitive. I suggested that it's more like the three mirrors of a rotating kaleidoscope displaying layers of colored materials with light. Still, there are only three, and of course, many reflections. I explained that spatial lenses alter the convergence of patterns of light rays. Important only if you are having difficulty seeing."

Zoltan was relieved to hear the clear sound of Saraph's voice. But he had no memory or comprehension of the context of his words.

"What is this?" he asked.

"What did you ask for?"

They stared at one another.

"I am speaking to you, Magician . . . to your heart. Can you hear me?"

Hearing many things, most of which confused him, Zoltan continued to stare at Saraph without understanding.

"What was your heart's desire? What did you ask for?"

For a moment Zoltan took his eyes off of Saraph and looked around, compelled to locate something. He looked blankly into the moving figures with his eyes, but he was mesmerized by what he was hearing. A fear of wandering too far gripped him, though he remained standing still. He turned back to look at Saraph, but a dizzying mosaic of information impaired his vision. He could not locate his companion.

"Saraph?" Zoltan requested childishly.

He heard Saraph shouting. "Prince Antoniadis, son of favor!" Immediately he saw that they remained side by side.

"Concentrate on me. Concentrate on my voice with all your strength!" Saraph instructed in a commanding tone.

Zoltan was trembling. He heard a tone coming from Saraph's mouth and he focused on it with all of his mental strength. As *it* became clearer, the *note* receded and all other sounds found their normal balance. Zoltan was breathing hard as he reached up and took hold of Saraph's shoulders. The compassionate face of his escort again became blurred, but this time because of tears that flooded Zoltan's eyes. Scared, he closed them and pulled Saraph to himself.

"Please don't leave me."

Cheek to cheek, Zoltan felt the vibration from Saraph's voice. He felt safe as it continued. Then he noticed behind the vibration of the tone that Saraph was trembling. Alarmed, Zoltan took a step back, still grasping Saraphs shoulders. He took comfort in the look on Saraph's face, not realizing that his own eyes were still closed.

"Why are you trembling?" he asked.

"Open your eyes," Saraph ordered, interrupting the tone.

Still catching his breath, Zoltan obeyed the command.

"What was that … that … losing sight of you standing right here. I've never been so terrified. What was that?"

"That is not what terrifies you," Saraph responded. He contemplated Zoltan's condition. "What did you ask for? Why did you come here?"

Not daring to look away, Zoltan just stared into Saraph's eyes. He sensed a distraction in those eyes, and realized that Saraph was concentrating on something else.

"What did you ask for?" Saraph asked. "Listen to your heart."

"I asked to see my son." Zoltan paused. "Understanding. My desire was to really see my son, to understand his battle."

"Then look!"

Eyes again filling with tears, Zoltan shook his head.

"Do not be afraid," Saraph consoled. "I am close by. Listen for me."

As if speaking for his entire trembling body, Zoltan's chin quivered. "Everything was vibrating," he said. "Everything… the whole universe…." He paused. "I could feel it. It was so strong, so loud that…."

"Keep talking with me and you will know that I am near."

"So much movement. I couldn't see."

"So, listen!"

Zoltan stared. He resented Saraph for these simple instructions.

"Magician, it is your request, your true will. It is the one desire that all others have led us to. Listen while you have the opportunity."

Zoltan made a round motion with his head, trying to indicate the space that was all around them. "What is it?" he asked, wanting to know about the note.

Understanding, Saraph returned a question. "What does it sound like to you?"

"I don't know. I heard it earlier, almost everywhere, especially in Alexandria and at the studio… and in the dark. But it was in the background, not this strong."

"Help me to understand your experience," Saraph suggested,

"because mine may not be the same. If you could see it, what would it look like?"

Zoltan thought for a moment. "A question mark," he finally answered. "At first it feels flattering. Then it is like pure concentrated doubt."

"Indeed, it is the only note he has to work with," Saraph said matter-of-factly.

"Who?"

"Your enemy, Satan. His music led him to be impressed with himself and to doubt the goodness of God's sovereign authority. He has tempted others to serve that same doubt ever since that day. It is all he knows and all he has to work with. He dresses it up with the dynamics of varied tempos and volumes. And, of course, he uses saturation to create the illusion of universal preeminence, the very thing he has convinced himself of."

Saraph was speaking conversationally in a calming tone, attempting to settle Zoltan's thoughts for the focus ahead. Yet, he himself was fearful of the nearness of disaster.

"'The entire Garden, or the liberating power of this precious question mark.' Do you recall your history … the temptation? So he continues. And, like your friend, Trevor, one finds that he is walking away from far more than he is walking toward when he falls for that deception. The choice is quite clear after all: responsibility to self, based on feelings, or responsibility to God, based on the wisdom of His Word and His Creation mandates. Casting off the greater responsibility as if removing shackles leaves one stripped of responsibility, as well as dignity, a baby confined to a little playpen of slavery."

Even as Saraph tried to remain steady in his tone, he realized that his voice was elevating with the volume of the note. The intensity he conveyed was reflected in Zoltan's eyes.

"Your own example may be most instructive," he said, almost shouting. "Consider the size of the universe. Then consider the local obsessions that inhibited you from embracing the gift and spending this day exploring it." Saraph raised his left arm and pointed. "Go now! Look and listen with all your heart. I will be right here."

As Zoltan turned and looked to his right, the dancing forms again filled his view. He remembered Saraph's instruction to stay connected by continuing to talk with him.

"I feel like I'm at the back of a crowd that prevents me from seeing." He took a step, then another. Still seeing only the layers of light in the beautiful, busy movements, he spoke thoughtlessly. "I wish I could get closer."

Chapter 34
CLOSER

The density of the flowing forms in front of Zoltan was noticeably reduced. But now they were all around him. The two travelers found themselves near the middle of the dance. A seductive beauty drew Zoltan's attention more toward the center. It captivated him. Barely breathing, he did not notice the steps he slowly took to his left, away from Saraph.

The note was active all around him, but he was not bothered by it as before. A vague idea was aroused, encouraged by a feeling of power and importance. The soothing one note symphony was in a crescendo passage, of which Zoltan took no notice. He sensed only invitation, an opportunity to acquire exotic trophies of beauty and return home with new powers of craft and technology. A dull awareness of his son remained. He had completely forgotten Saraph.

The increasing force and volume of the note gained his attention. Uncomfortable, he mumbled dreamily to himself. "I probably should leave this place."

"You would leave your son like this?" Saraph questioned.

The voice seemed to come from far away, but it grabbed Zoltan's attention.

"I haven't seen him, have you?"

"You have not looked. Stop thinking of yourself and you will see."

Looking to his right and to his left, Zoltan tried to see beyond the circle of movement that enveloped him. Glimpses of guitars, laughing skulls, a fire-breathing dragon and a bloody, tormented face appeared to him through the activities of the dancers. Shaken by a haunting awareness that his son's possessions were all around him, Zoltan's mouth became like wax.

He no longer cared to see. *The note*, he frowned, and shuddered. Recalling Saraph's voice, he thought, *Of course, this all belongs to him. It's part of his magic and he doesn't want me to find out about it or get my hands on any of it.* His eyes began to burn and blink rapidly. His lips tightened. Fear and contempt consumed him.

What is this? This isn't even about my son. This is all about Trevor and his scheme to destroy me and get me out of his way. The old man and his gift is all a clever cover, but I see this for what it is.

"No one will even care! No one!"

Startled, Zoltan turned toward the sound of his son's voice and plainly saw him standing no more than seven or eight feet away. "Martin!" he yelled, as he saw the gun and lunged. Repelled by an invisible force, Zoltan found himself sitting on the floor with his back to an orange door, looking up at his son. Saraph stood near by. The dancing forms were barely visible, though they did not otherwise appear to be impacted by these actions. The symphony of the note was also unaffected, except for a reduction in volume.

Zoltan was conflicted, as thoughts about his importance battled with those about Martin's. *This moment is mine. He's my son! I must do something. No, this is not about me. This is about Martin. What can I do? How can I help him? What can be done to save him?*

"Do something!" Zoltan shouted at Saraph while getting back to his feet.

"Not one!" Martin shouted. "Not . . . ."

Standing directly to the right of Martin, amazement and

torment were etched upon Zoltan's face.

"Will anyone even notice?"

"Notice? You'll kill *me*, Marty. Please, son … I beg you. Saraph!" he yelled, pleading with his eyes and shaking as he turned toward his escort.

Tears fell from Saraph's eyes as he observed Zoltan's agony. Noticing a movement, Zoltan looked back at Martin. The gun was no longer pointing directly between his eyes, but was pressed against the side of his face. The barrel was flat against his temple.

"Our Father …." Saraph paused, his voice raspy. "In the great name of Jesus, on behalf of this favored one from among the rebels, the slanderers, the captive and oppressed, I cry out. Extend the great reach of your mercy to him and his son. Show Martin that he is precious. Consider this request from the heart of your humble servant, I pray."

"A prayer? Are you kidding?" Zoltan's eyes were fierce with contempt as he looked at Saraph. "We are right here. You can do something yourself, and you default to praying? I tried to do something and you prevented it because of some silly rule. My son's life is … I was beginning to respect you!"

"I have defended and strengthened Martin from the moment we arrived," Saraph said calmly. "He is presently protected by a greater hand and from a greater reach than mine. And had the veil not prevented your action, your son would be dead. The tension applied to the trigger at that moment could not afford even the slightest touch. He is beyond your heroics. This moment is beyond delicate, and beyond anything that I had anticipated. Trust God alone, Magician."

They heard a distant commotion outside the apartment.

"Morons!" Martin hollered.

Zoltan stared at his son, clueless about the outburst. Martin's eyes were opened and he was staring up at the wall in front of him where two guitars were mounted. Zoltan glanced over at

Saraph, and as he did his eyes caught glimpses of the dancers. He quickly returned his focus to Martin just as his son shut his eyes tightly.

The note ascended another crescendo movement. Its plucking was as thunder in their minds. Its dissonance stuck to Zoltan's consciousness like a dense humidity. Nothing that Saraph had explained meant anything to him now. His head was as cluttered as his son's apartment. Full of suspicions about Saraph and a calamity of ideas about how he might save his son, he was oblivious to the influence of the note. And under that influence, Zoltan did not question a single thought. If it came into his head, he was certain it was right.

It occurred to him that from his current position he was absolutely powerless. *Saraph is holding me here like a prisoner while he does nothing as well. We are both useless to Martin. Why? Why would he prevent my action for my son? It is up to me to save Martin. That is clear. I am his father. I must do whatever it takes!*

Zoltan thought about the dancers. *They don't react to anything we do. So, they don't know that we are here. We must be on a different plain or dimension. That's it. 'The gift' is a dimension of its own, like a layer of digital media. We can see both Martin and these spirit creatures. But neither can detect us. I have to get to where the dancers are and distract them to break their influence over Martin.*

Saraph was concerned about the dancers as well. He was uncertain that he could continue to protect Martin, even as he anticipated an answer to his prayer. His eyes were heavy with sorrow and concern as he studied father and son.

Zoltan under the influence of the note, that is hard to predict. How do I get him safely back home before he creates an irreversible disaster? The note … that sinister craft!

Saraph determined the exact amount of time remaining, certain that he could better care for Martin if giving him full attention. He began to devise a plan. *There's no way we could stay here that long without Zoltan doing something....*

There was a sound from the back hall just outside the door. As a fowl stench came in through the cracked-open door, Zoltan looked around, trying to comprehend what it was and where it came from. Simultaneously, the note accelerated in tempo and ascended to an oppressive volume in his head. Zoltan felt mocked as inadequate and impotent, an unworthy father. He was reminded of the man with the white gloves. His former self-focus and thoughts about his importance had turned rancid. *Who am I kidding to think that I can help my son?* he thought.

Zoltan pressed his palms against his ears as he tried to concentrate on Martin. He sensed it all had something to do with the note, but he could not identify what or how. *Now*, he decided, overwhelmed by the chaos of sensory bombardment. *I have to do something now.*

Saraph sensed a desperation in the dancers as he witnessed the impact of their doubled efforts. He took several steps forward and planted his feet. Yet he hesitated, uncertain. He looked at Zoltan and saw the panic in his eyes.

"Clear your mind," Saraph said. "Do not hope for a mercy among their lyrical teachings. And do not devise a plan that might leave you in their possession. All could be lost!"

Zoltan *was* lost. He was lost in his desperation and did not hear Saraph.

"Pigs! I live among a bunch of stinkin' pigs!" Martin yelled viciously. Then he opened his eyes and rolled them in the direction of Zoltan. He closed them again.

"Why am I alive at all?" he hollered.

Seeing his son's tear-filled eyes for that brief instant and then hearing these words, Zoltan was broken. He heard a voice, a murmur outside the door, but paid no attention to it. The volume of the note was deafening as he opened his mouth and shouted, "I want to be where those wretched spirits are!"

Shock was in Zoltan's wide eyes as he completed the last words and saw Martin's right arm whirling toward him, gun in hand. There was an explosion of light and sound as the gun went off. A force picked Zoltan off of his feet and threw him backwards, slamming him against the wall.

"You think that's funny?" he heard Martin yell.

Zoltan looked down at his shirt to locate a hole. He looked toward Martin and for a few seconds just stared. Then, looking up at Saraph, his eyes were wide and his mouth hung open. He fell forward, face to the floor.

Chapter 35
PARTING

"Enough silly business from you, little one."

Zoltan felt two hands grab him by the shoulders and lift him like a child, setting him up, propped against the wall.

"I am a child of our Creator as you are. That is all. Save your worship for the one who is worthy."

Still shaking, Zoltan could not bring himself to look at Saraph. His knees were up at his chest and his elbows rested upon them. His forearms were folded back covering his head, which was tucked between his flexed biceps. From this position he had watched Martin. Presently, he was listening to the sound that was no more, but for his memory. It was the sound that had come from Saraph's voice. The force of that sound had lifted and thrown him from harm's way. It had unmasked the dancers and sent them on a flight of terror and rescued him and his son from the spell of their sorcery. It was a warrior's shout and a trumpeter's blast.

Finishing his prayers of praise and thankfulness, Saraph lowered his hands and rose from his knees. He sat down between the father and son on the corner of Martin's bed, near where

Zoltan sat on the floor. Martin was kneeling, his upper body collapsed upon the bed, exhausted from his sobbing.

"The battle is not over," Saraph said. "Your son is far from safe and even further from well."

Zoltan kept his head buried in his arms as he recalled the brilliant light. He remembered looking up at Saraph and seeing the flames dancing in the terrible warrior's eyes and upon the golden armor of outstretched arms, the force of liberation coming from his open mouth. He raised his head slightly to look over at the floor where the charred remains of clothing from a homeless shelter were scattered.

He looked between his arms at the splintery hole in the door jam just behind where he had been standing. A thought of the sight of Martin staring down at the smoking gun in his hand brought tears to Zoltan's eyes. He recalled three beautiful creatures in long, flowing robes looking at Saraph, terror on their faces. Their illusions broken, crushed by the sound of his voice and illuminated by his brightness, they had looked at one another in confusion and then were gone. He again saw Martin's arm swinging around and the gun pointing at him.

"Why did he shoot at me?" he asked dreamily.

"He was shooting at a voice outside the door." Saraph answered, "one that he felt was mocking him. You just happened to be standing directly between him and the voice."

"He didn't see me?"

"Of course not."

It was quiet for a moment before Zoltan began rolling his head back and forth in his arms, mostly groaning and partly chuckling.

"What's that?" Saraph asked

"Oh, just the look on the faces of those … ."

"Yes, and now, the reality of your little maneuver. They will return soon with many more, and return with a vengeance."

"That sound," Zoltan said, "what … ?"

"I proclaimed the Name of 'The LORD' in my native tongue," Saraph answered.

"I only heard a sound … a tone!" Zoltan concentrated on his recollection for a moment. He shuddered. "An entire city could be crushed … ."

Saraph laughed. "Ever heard of Jericho?" he asked.

Strange, Zoltan thought. *It didn't have any effect on the world. Martin didn't even appear to notice it. But, what was that strange behavior afterward, looking at the floor behind him and around the room. Maybe he did notice.* "Martin sure looked confused by something," he said aloud.

"That was the answer to my prayer," Saraph stated. "It was unrelated to my proclamation, except that The LORD waited until after the dancers had fled to send it so that Martin would not be distracted."

"What a … ." Zoltan put his face in his hands. "I can still hear it."

Saraph looked down at Zoltan and smiled. "I am glad you are impressed, child." He laughed. "Wait 'til you hear the sound of the trumpets when the Master returns. Now that will shake your world."

Still absorbed in his recollections, Zoltan was only partially listening.

"Forgive me, but, why didn't you just do that to begin with?" he asked.

"What?"

"That proclamation that obliterated the note and the dance. And your … ." Zoltan thought for a few seconds. "Your revelation, your power."

"Because I wanted to avoid the very problem that we now face."

Zoltan did not want to know what the problem was. So, this answer was quickly erased from his mind by the distraction of another troubling question.

"Please forgive me again. Who am I to expect you to explain anything. But if you would … why wasn't there someone like you here before, someone protecting my son?"

"That is the second really stupid thing I have heard you say," Saraph scolded. "Your son, by your encouragement, rejects the free gifts of the Kingdom of God, and with your blessing welcomes the influences of darkness to populate his life. And you want to know why we're not just hanging out here with them battling over him. Light and dark, heaven and hell just holding hands … yin and yang. What a quaint idea!

"We do not trivialize evil as you do. That is the answer to your question. Now, back to the problem I mentioned."

"What is it?"

"I must stay with Martin. And you, Magician, must complete our journey unattended."

"What?" Zoltan protested, lifting his head and looking up at Saraph. Stopping with a jolt, he stared. The brightness of Saraph's robe was not an earthly brightness. And in the fearsome, unbearded face of the great warrior he saw a remnant of the escort with whom he had spent his day of immortal passage. Tears spontaneously filled Zoltan's eyes and spilled onto his face. He dropped his gaze and shook his head.

"Forgive me, please …." Forcing himself to look back up at Saraph, he continued. "Forgive my mistrust, my unbelief, my arrogance." He looked away, emotional, then back to the warrior's eyes. "Forgive my calloused heart, and my wicked accusations of ill will. And … that foolish complaint I just made.

"I'm sorry for accusing you of ruining my life. I knew it wasn't true. I knew it was getting away from me well before you showed up. And Universal Syndicate … it was all but over. I saw it coming."

"I forgive you, my friend."

Zoltan looked down and hid his face again.

"Do you know that before today I had assumed that I was

broke in the whole area of crying? I just never did it … ever. Now look at me." He rubbed his eyes and pinched his nose. "See what you've done to me, Saraph? The mighty Zoltan, a sniveling mess, a broken man."

"It's one day. You'll recover your composure."

"I hope not completely."

They sat in silence for several minutes.

"I was just thinking," Zoltan said, daring to look again into Saraph's eyes. "How did we arrive here at such a precise moment?" He looked away. Several more minutes passed before he looked back up at Saraph. "You actually saved my life with your invitation – mine and my son's. How did you know? I mean, when you first showed up, how did you know … that script you gave me in the beginning, all that was going on with Martin?"

"I didn't."

"None of it?"

Saraph shook his head. "I only knew Martin's name, which I learned through Stephen's prayers. The script? I came up with the idea and some details were provided."

"Well, your timing is uncanny."

"It was not my timing," Saraph responded. "In fact, I was pondering this as I kept one eye on you and one eye on Martin when we first arrived here. I was wondering about the extraordinary unlikelihood of our coming to this moment in this place by the measures that we have: the day on which *the gift* was commended to me, our first meetings and my concern that you might not accept the invitation, the earlier visitations and their impact upon both of us.

"I was thinking about my original anticipation of exploring the universe together. I was considering the possibilities before you, and that among them you chose this at this moment. And I was amazed, because your son was living his life, and unknown to either of us, was coming to a tragic decision.

"It is evident that the hand of the LORD has reached out, even by the gift, and He has spared this son of yours. This perhaps...." Saraph paused to consider the proportions of his thought. "Perhaps *this is* the gift and all else its unwrapping," he said distantly. "I am trying to fathom the size of God's love, that He would care for such intimate details in the life of one so invested in hating Him, so actively despising Him.

"Long I have contemplated God's loving government of infinite complexities, of movements and relationships, His wooing of hearts, and His merciful use of even the manifestations of chaos and sin. Such brokenness led me from the prayers of Stephen to you, and then you and me here... to a hope.

"I was thinking of the four living creatures before the throne of God. They see all, and are continually moved to worship for His wondrous deeds, great mercies, perfect judgments, and the glorious revelations of His love. I was recalling the sounds of heavenly throngs joining in the privilege of His praise and adoration."

Saraph rose to his feet. "Look," he said, "I am but a servant, no less a delight to my Lord whether dressed in rags or the armor of His Majesty's hosts. We are His creation, His children, you and I."

Zoltan stood also and the two travel companions gazed at one another.

"The thing you did was terribly foolish," Saraph said. "Yet, you did it in the face of great personal risk, likely the first you have ever taken for your son. I gave you clear warnings that you could lose all—and all forever. Yet, you could not keep yourself from the wild attempt. The note played its part, but there was far more at work in you than that madness.

"For those moments you forgot all of your plans, all about yourself, and thought only of him... how you could help him. I witnessed the evidence of a great turn in a war. A profound transformation in your character is within reach. That was a sacrificial leap worthy of the great and lofty title of 'Father' – that high calling of the sons of earth."

Saraph turned and walked several steps away and stood with his back to Zoltan. There was a long silence.

"A deeper understanding entered my mind in the midst of that chaos. An understanding about another Father and His Son. You turned from long invested estrangement to risk all to save your son. This Father, for a terrible moment in time, turned from eternal union, turned from His one and only be-gotten Son in order to redeem forever many children born of His love."

Saraph stood there in silence for several more minutes. Abruptly he turned and walked back to face Zoltan.

"We have drawn a great deal of attention by our exploits here. *They* will return with greater numbers and greater author-ities once they have held council regarding these reports. You destroyed the veil. It is no more. The boundaries of the gift will now only hinder me in defending both you and your son. And you both are in great danger.

"I have been too casual about getting you to safety. The mo-ment is urgent. I will give my attention to Martin's protection, or they will make quick work of his thin resistance upon their return. But you cannot be near here."

Zoltan thought hard before asking, "Is there any other way?"

Saraph reached out and placed a hand upon Zoltan's shoul-der. "I am not ubiquitous, nor omnipotent. For you to be here will be a great danger to you, a danger beyond the scope of my protection. You have seen how the treachery of their craft works upon your mind even when not directed at you. And you have seen how quickly things can change. You are my chief concern, but I now have two to protect. This is the only way I can do both.

"Two hours and ten minutes remain. But the danger that

I warned you of, the danger of losing all is great, greater than ever. Without a doubt, they recognized you. It is they who created you … the mighty Zoltan, that is. Certainly you understand now that it was they who deceived you, encouraging your self indulgence, keeping you from seeing Salmone's generosity. And it was they who prepared to dispatch you once you were no longer of any use to them. They know your tendencies. They fashioned them. They know you. Anywhere you would choose, they would likely be searching for you there.

"There is a place. You must make this one more request, and remain in that place until your return."

Zoltan's teeth were clenched and the muscles of his jaws pulsated from his nervous flexing. As he struggled with the suddenness of their parting, he looked over at Martin sleeping upon the bed, then back at Saraph. "Whatever happens to me … thank you."

Saraph's eyes were wet and his breathing labored. "I am only staying with him until his help arrives."

"You called someone?"

Saraph laughed and shook his head. "I was referring to his father. You can only be of help to him on the other side of the gift, back in your usual life. But that is not the primary reason you must successfully make it back."

Staring down at the floor, Zoltan recalled the laws. He looked up into Saraph's eyes. "A day of seeing only. Nothing can be changed on this day."

"Including your heart," Saraph said. "You can alter nothing, including decisions relating to the condition of your soul. Child, you are not ready to face eternity. If they were to find you and destroy you … you would be lost. That is the danger I warned you of. That is why you must not linger here."

"But if I return?"

"A new day, and change will be possible. It will be up to you."

"The place?" Zoltan asked.

"It is a place I would not have thought of prior to ... ." Saraph hesitated. "I only think of it now because I can't attend you further, and it is a place that I would not go." He paused again, thoughtful. "It is also a place that you would never choose. Therefore, it is the one place they would not suspect and would not search. By the Lord's grace it will give you enough time."

"Why will they look for me? Why would they care?"

Saraph smiled. "That's a question you would not have asked twenty-two hours ago. Your importance was assumed as I recall. But, to answer your question: You crashed their party ... and they saw you. They know you. Your fame is of their doing. And they saw you with me. I told you, this gift is unprecedented. Nothing like this has happened in their domain. You are marked. You represent a threat to them that is beyond their comprehension. They will be hellbent on destroying you."

"What about when I get back? Won't they be searching? What about when they find me then? Look at what they were doing to him. And I'm his father. I won't be hard to find then."

The look in Saraph's eyes was grave. "You can be sure of that. But you were already in their hands, a mere puppet. You will have a hope of change then, the power of new decisions. I pray you'll use it quickly and soundly. I pray you have listened. Should you make such a change, remember this: He that is in one who believes is greater than the powers in the world that seek to destroy."

"Now, about the place of safety." Listen to me carefully. "It will not *feel* safe. You will encounter them, but those you encounter will not know you and will not know of you." Saraph thought for a moment. "Well, those you encounter initially will not know of you. You are fortunate that there is little time left. To live, you must only suffer their interrogations to the end.

"Zoltan," Saraph said, taking him by both shoulders. He had saved the use of the name for one opportunity to gain a trust.

"I have two selfish motives here."

Zoltan stared, anticipation in his eyes.

"I love you," Saraph said. "Your loss would be bitter for me. Yet, my love is not to be compared with the love of God for you. And He entrusted *me* with your care."

Zoltan nodded his head. "I'm listening."

"Do not let them deceive you into revealing anything of the gift. Do not boast in the nearness of your flight. Do not speak of your previous visitations. And above all, do not use *the gift* to take flight of them. Measure your words to support the mystery of your appearance. They love their deliberations. Their assumptions of ownership and of your lengthy stay are your safety."

"They will bark like dogs, laugh like hyenas. But mockers and barking dogs are not so bad if you endure them. Trust me … stay, no matter the temptation to flee. Will you trust me and choose this place?"

Zoltan looked at the mighty friend before him, his use of the name 'Zoltan' still weighty in his mind.

"Exactly two hours remain," Saraph said.

Zoltan wiped tears from his eyes before placing his right hand upon Saraph's, which was still resting on his shoulder. "Yes I will go."

Chapter 36

VOICES

"Pity, yes! Pity of all pities! But do not pretend some special pity, or grope clinging to an idea."

Zoltan heard the muttering voice, as he had several others. But his attention was on his own eyes, as if they were watching from within the dense black. He desired even a hint of a shadow. Like two glowing orbs in an infinite sea of impenetrable blindness, they were all he sensed of himself. He was aware of them burning with a wide-open madness of expectancy. They craved even the remotest rumor of light from somewhere. He feared them. He feared being discovered by them. Yet, they were his, and they occupied his entire consciousness.

"Surprise!" a voice pealed in mock cheer. "Shocked? Hmm, you expected candles, maybe some cake and confetti? And really, just who do you think you are?"

The voice ought to have startled him, but he was so consumed by the watching of his own eyes and their fevered search that he hardly even noticed it. This seemed to disarm the one to whom the voice belonged. Evidently taken back by Zoltan's indifference, another voice joined in:

"Really! Is this the game? You're going to pretend that you don't hear us. So how long do you think you can pull that one off? You're here for a long time. Next you'll be trying to get us to believe that you don't belong here."

"Oh, yeah!" the first voice mocked, "That has worked every time."

Zoltan stared. He saw nothing. But he just stared into the void. He wanted to look around, but he had no sense of direction or placement. The very idea of looking was devoured by the blackness. He was stunned by the stark, cold reality of complete darkness, as his mind began to catch up with the shock of aloneness.

"Sorry little worm in a black wormhole. Pathetic, is it not? What is more the cause for pity is that you thought otherwise. Your eyes are probably wide, your mouth hanging open. You are actually surprised!"

"Idiot! You pretended to contest His existence, while you lived like He was right there personally overseeing your safe passage to Never Never Land. Reckless fool! Humans!

"The libraries of the ancients, the museums of the affluent, east to west, north to south, they all testify to the vulgarity of your inherent flaw. It is that curse beyond the histories and generations of your wretched race from the beginning of time until this very present and undeniable reality in the vacuum of meaning."

"That silly notion that you are special!" A third voice punctuated.

"Hey! I was getting there. I was building up to it."

"Sorry, I couldn't wait."

"Yes, and dearly significant, true?" came the more serious tone of the first voice. "Isn't that what you thought?"

"Special, 'ey? Yeah, look around you, you're special all right. We tried to tell you. We did everything we could to convince you to reject the myth of your importance, to face the fact that you are not precious at all, but merely an insignificant particle of dust on the face of a great ball of stone destined for destruction. We could have saved you this horrible shock."

"But you insisted on believing you were Boy Destiny, some-one who mattered."

"Please! You think you matter now? Does this darkness know your name? Do you think He is missing you?"

"Who?" Zoltan asked weakly.

He had been so stunned by the sudden introduction of sheer darkness that he had missed most of what the voices were say-ing, and what he did hear he only dimly discerned to be directed at him. But this unchecked response had broken through his lips before he even sensed its compulsion. The empty sound of his own voice in that dense blackness startled him. It seemed to have no penetration beyond his own ears. Yet, he was heard.

"'Who?' Did he say, 'who?'"

"At least he's not pretending not to know we're here any-more. Hey, you, what do you mean, 'who'?"

Still dull and shaken, Zoltan answered, "Do I think *who* is missing me?"

Silence prevailed for several seconds before a voice again spoke. "I won't say it, not here, not in the one place it is not spoken."

"Well, how about this," another voice broke in. "Does the word 'Creator' mean anything to you?"

It was long before anyone spoke again. This time it was Zoltan who broke the silence. "Who is he?"

"Ah! He's determined, isn't he?"

"Keep pretending."

"Why should I expect the one you speak of to miss me or to be thinking of me?"

"You always have. Why change now?"

Zoltan sensed a strange desire to believe that what the voice was saying was true. But he could only weakly respond, "If that is so, I am not aware of it."

"Oh, really? So, all of these years that you kept trying to change the world with your special plans and ideas, while we kept demonstrating for you the emptiness of them all and the futility of your efforts, you were motivated by... what, your daddy's encouraging words?"

Howls and snickers broke out from the other voices. "Oh, that was really bad. I mean, *mean* that was!"

"I'm thinking that qualifies as cruel. Yeah, that was low, low."

"I liked it. That was a good one. That's putting your finger right on the old shame button!"

"I was motivated by myself," Zoltan said.

"Yourself! And it is yourself that told you that you have special significance? It was yourself that concocted that it was important to advance your ideas and philosophies, like doing so would actually have some meaningful result? We could have saved you the trouble of wrapping your self-indulgences in all of that pretentious rubbish."

"You could have had a lot more fun, could have spent a lot less time obsessing over your personal value and accomplishments."

"Value!" someone scoffed. "You just presumed that on your own?"

"Yes, of course," Zoltan said, finding it a strange thing to question.

"Wait! Wait! Back to this 'myself' business: Just where did your finite brain come up with that? You just stepped onto planet earth with some notion from yourself ... a consciousness that just naturally presumes you to be its royal subject?"

"No, even you, our deluded elitist, even you are not capable of such uninfluenced presumption."

It's not common for people to have a sense of importance and destiny? Zoltan wondered. *They talk like I'm the only one who thought this way....* He ignored the voices for a moment. *I thought Saraph said they wouldn't know me here. Maybe the news already reached here ahead of me.* The thought made him tremble. *Keep them deliberating,* he recalled. *That was Saraph's instruction.*

"That attitude is downright common," he said out loud.

Gasps and moans filled the dark, dank air. "He doesn't get it at all," one voice said.

"He really is missing the entire point, isn't he?" said another, sounding exasperated.

"Common!" barked another. "Common, yes! That is the idea! Not only common, but petty and pithy. You all think that way! Are you such a simpleton? That is the very thing we are talking to you about. Every one of you believes that he himself is important and that his life is deeply precious. Yet each, remarkably, believes his own notion of preciousness and importance to be unique."

"Even a vulgar hermit dies alone, lamenting the loss of his precious opportunity as his life slips away, never questioning the validity of the assumption that there was actually an opportunity at all."

"Mine is different from that. I am...a dreamer!" Zoltan replied.

An explosion of uproarious laughter followed, and Zoltan realized that a crowd had gathered around him in the dark.

It took several minutes for the voices to settle down. "Oh, really, *you* are a dreamer? I wouldn't have imagined that!" said a new voice.

"You are *that* special among men that you are one of those, those... na-a-aw... not a real dreamer!" The voice paused for effect before blasting, "You're all dreamers, you idiot!" A chorus of vicious laughter sent chills down Zoltan's spine.

But he was intrigued by the banter. More, he welcomed the distraction from his consciousness of the dark. The more the voices multiplied, the more constant their chatter, and the more relieved he felt.

"I know," chimed in another voice, "you thought you were an especially important dreamer, a mover of men, a visionary of culture craft, trend-setting and thought-expansion. You were *really* important."

"Yeah, we've never seen that before, have we?"

"No, never," several voices chided at once.

"Your insults are hollow. I *am* important," Zoltan said.

"Uh, and where is the insult?"

"Wait, wait. We never did get his name."

"Oh, how rude of us. Our hospitality is slipping."

"And what is it?"

"Zoltan."

The voices erupted in jeers and laughter, the likes of which Zoltan had never heard.

"Is that a joke? You're kidding right?

"Mr. Human Being himself. No wonder he thinks he really was important!"

"No, no … you guys missed it. He said, 'AM important!'"

"Oh, you're right. He thinks it's not over. Wow, this one's got it really bad."

"Going back are you? Must have been something sudden. He definitely wasn't expecting … well, us!"

Zoltan wanted to answer with a bold "Yes!" so badly that another shiver went up and down his spine. Remembering Saraphs instructions, he decided to keep that to himself.

"By the way, of what importance *ar-r-re* you – doctor, lawyer, politician?"

Zoltan thought for a moment, then gave the answer that seemed most efficient: "A Magician."

"Oo-oo-oo, magician! We don't hear that one much."

"That almost strikes me as insightful."

"Yeah, honest, even. Unless he's talking about an actual performing magician."

"Are you?"

Zoltan did not answer, but waited.

"Well, no matter. Tell us: Do you think that the young school teacher is a lesser visionary of cultural and generational impact, or the nurse the carrier of a smaller dream than yours because she receives fewer public lauds than a magician? And both have bigger dreams stored up, other visions that keep them always wondering if there isn't something more that they could or should be doing."

"And you're all fools as far as we are concerned!" cried a distant voice that Zoltan did not recall hearing before. A silence fell over the gathering that had been filled with chatter and delight.

"Why?" asked Zoltan, puzzled by the stark change in the tone of the debate.

"Because you are so gullible, blind and dull. You all actually believe all that rubbish. You cling to your shallow hopes, like a flame hugs the wick until paraffin's end. And there is not one of you who possess even a modicum of originality. Where did you get the notion from? From Him of course. It's not even your own. You couldn't come up with an actual will or a true dream any more than you could make up your own identity."

"And who are you? What makes you the experts and the judges of me, of us?" Zoltan asked. He directed his question at the voice that compelled the submission of all the others.

"A just question. And forgive us if our answer betrays our vexation. 'Watchers!' Observers toiling in exile. Outcasts. We have measured your breadth and width, counted your steps and surveyed your winding and stumbling paths for long generations. We have stirred your hearts against your neighbors, educated your scholars in the pathos of despair, and with surprisingly little resistance, advanced our cause through eager little egos such as your own. Yes, we have cause to know you, and to do all we can to sift, spoil and ruin. For what are you that you should be invited? Who are you that you should be favored as if possessors of treasures?

"Did we not bear beauty enough? Did we not sing sweetly, dance lightly and move gracefully in the fair light of our practiced splendors? And for what do we owe our banishment, but for a slight hope of a modest assent to our own pleasures and designs. Are these such grand schemes that they should threaten the house of a great King?

"Yet, have you been warned by our demise, or counseled by our exile beyond Graceland? Quite to the contrary! Your gullible minds continue to embrace some myth about your rights of will. I'll tell you about the power of the grand liberty that you hold so dear: Here in my left hand, behold an offering... a gift. And in my right, a great treasure, the thing that I myself do prefer. You may choose whichever your heart desires. Oh, but I must inform you that should you happen to desire that which is in the left and choose it over the right, you will be a villain and a curse forever. There now, indulge in your liberty!"

Zoltan began to feel clouded in his thoughts. Those hours he had spent with Saraph were becoming a dusty volume on a crowded shelf of a dark room. Much of his former bias was returning, and his heart was hardening. Yet, he noticed the fact and was saddened by it. In tempering the lively banter of the other voices, the one had also recalled the thick gloom of the deep darkness.

The owner of the voice sensed Zoltan's suffering and leaped upon the moment as a lion upon the lame deer. "And what of this business about you being so precious? Have you forgotten those Sunday school lessons of your youth? You know... the story of Abraham and the promise he received that he would become the father of many."

"I never went."

"Oh, one of those. Then listen and you might learn something."

"What was it the Creator likened his offspring to? Let's see... grains of sand on the seashore, wasn't that it? Yes, I believe that was it. A lofty calling that is, wouldn't you say? A grain of sand!

"Better yet, one among trillions of grains of sand. There is the revelation of your significance, my friend. A true description of the whole bunch of you. And right from your Creator's mouth. One of ol' Abe's kids, as dull, as unexceptional, as lifeless as a bit of sand. But, hey, you put enough of them together and it makes a nice postcard for someone really important to look at."

"Yeah, like us!" a voice blurted out.

"Tha-a-a-t wasn't the point I was getting at you dim-witted imbecile!

"An accurate vision of your sorry race it turned out to be," the speaker continued. "Why He values you I have no idea. His own odd postcard to Himself, I guess. But it is we who measure you, we who influence the entire flow of human activity by our divisions of realms and dominions, what you so blandly call disorder and disfunction. Give us some credit. It's really much more amusing than that if you were to see it from our vantage point."

"It's not called *man*ipulation for nothing!" cried another voice, which was followed by laughter and responsive mockery from the others.

"Would you stop using that one? I told you last time, it's old and unbearably corny."

"We are the lords of trend and fashion, the masters of myth and song, old and restated, repackaged, redressed. We are the whisperers speaking through the smoke of smoldering fires fanned and kindled anew. Who are we to judge? We are your masters. We are your teachers. We are the ones who … ."

"Who are you talking to?" interrupted Zoltan. A lengthy pause followed. "It seems to me that you are either speaking to impress something upon yourself or to deliver a speech you've rehearsed for an audience that is not here. I no longer care who you are. You cured me of that curiosity with all your yacking. In fact, I regret having asked now that your desperate eagerness to answer has been exposed."

A restless silence followed Zoltan's words. "Hullo!" he called in playful mockery. He felt restored in part to his wit by a recollection of Saraph's instructions. "Measure your words," he recalled, and, "They love their deliberations." He was nervous about slipping and revealing something costly. But he was comforted by the memory of the words, "Their assumption of ownership and of your lengthy stay are your safety."

"OK, how about this: Who ever you are trying to convince, me or you, why bother? What does it matter to you?"

"Hmm, a smug one, clever too," the lead voice added soberly. "It is the last remaining pleasure," he answered. "We don't mind admitting it. Or, at least, we're beyond denying it. Yes, far beyond that.

"Our one consolation is robbing Him of you, since He so delights in you. Reminding you of your own participation in our victory... well, that is an added bonus. It assures us that you will be thinking about the details of our success for a very long time."

"Look here, you are wasting your words on a corpse," Zoltan said. "I do not claim or cling to any of the warmth of sentiment for inherency or destiny that you have lobbied to denounce. A bit of tarnished silver spinning on the lathe of evolution, if you want my impression of our race. And me, personally? I fondle only the enjoyment of my own honing being a turn or two beyond that of my contemporaries. There is no flame here for you to extinguish. If you had watched as well as you boast of watching, this would have been evident to you. The importance I spoke of was purely immediate, nothing beyond that."

Zoltan was not certain that he believed this, but he was sure he once did. He was pleased that his retorts were apparently aimed accurately enough to cause some disturbance among his antagonists. But the muzzled background chatter was a result he regretted. He began to feel some discomfort as the silence spread and all murmuring and whispering ceased. Feeling proud, he began to guess that he had offended his hosts by delivering a blow they could not answer. But even his pride could not quiet the terror he felt standing in the darkness unable to see an offended adversary.

"I think he means it," a shy voice finally offered, breaking the silence.

"Yeah, I agree," spoke another. "He really thinks this way, I tell you."

"Our craft has been spun, his thoughts are as ours. You can see that, listen to him," ventured a nervous voice, daring to participate.

"Yeah, I kinda like 'm myself," said another weakly.

"Nonsense!" the lead voice hollered angrily. "I have listened and his words betray him. Personhood is not the industry of evolution. I know! We invented it before any of you rats joined the party. Don't tell *me* what he thinks and how effective we've been. His heart is revealed and hope is yet in it."

"What if...?"

"What if? I have the reek of this foul hope in my very presence, filling my nostrils, choking my breath, and you ask me to wonder 'what if'!"

"I agree."

Zoltan turned toward the direction of another voice that he had not heard before as if expecting to see someone walking toward him from a distance. The voice was coming from further away than any that had yet spoken. He knew with certainty that the name of the being belonging to this voice was Sedition, though he did not know how. The voice was the tender voice of a young child.

Her tone was thoughtful and its effect was total command of all others present. Zoltan could hear in it a profound deliberation. It was the voice of one who had patiently observed from a distance, and who was now bringing forward an evaluation with the full force of unquestioned authority.

"Have you found anything unusual here?" she asked.

"No I haven't. But I must say, I am … we are grateful for the privilege of your unexpected visit," the previous leader said.

Sedition's voice bore down on Zoltan, yet it spoke past him as though he were not listening. Zoltan suddenly felt that he was the focus of an examination of grave consequence. His momentary flash of boldness seemed silly and foolish to him now.

The voice passed by him closely as it spoke to the others and then moved a short distance away. It approached again and circled him as it drew nearer, slowly as if he were being studied from every direction.

Facing the invisible examination, he was compelled to turn and follow the direction from which the voice came at him. He turned in circles in the dark, desperately trying to see someone before him to whom he could direct a question or make a defense. Feeling it, he followed even as it was silent.

"So, you've learned nothing special. That's good. I was sent to see if we have come across an oddity. There has been word of a disturbing, unnatural breach of the never-before variety. It included an encounter with one of the great, evil warriors. So far, his involvement in an otherwise small incident is a mystery. There was a notorious man and his son. And, get this … separate dimensions. The warrior protects the son, who was rightfully ours. Many were sent and a battle has ensued. Typically, the father appears to have disappeared. They figured this was a long shot, but sending me here shows how serious they are about this matter. Keep your eyes open … so to speak."

Several minutes passed without a sound.

"Interesting." The voice whispered directly into Zoltan's left ear, giving him a shock that would have made him holler had terror not gripped his throat. "Interesting that your heart rate has more than doubled with the aid of my report."

"Let him have a little of himself."

The voice faded into the distance. "Before long he'll be begging for our company. Then we will discover if there is anything unusual that we should report."

Zoltan listened but the voice did not speak again, nor was there any other to follow it. He wanted to ask if anyone was there, but he was frozen with dread of the silent answer he knew he would receive. He trembled. There in the shocking reality of absolute darkness, a horror had lain in wait to ambush him the instant he was left to himself.

The darkness was so dense, so utterly still and unnervingly silent that he could feel it pressing in around him, and all of his senses felt as though they were being compressed. Yet, the darkness did not prevent his sight. Rather, he could see everything. It was as if he stood before a surrounding cosmic mirror and nothing of himself could escape its revelation. His ears strained against the pitch of perfect silence. His nostrils flared with longing for the scent of grass, rain or even air to cover the calamity of nothing.

His skin felt like that of a drum, stretched so taut that each beat of his heart startled him and threatened to burst right through the thin covering. Yet, he sensed most loudly a mortal need for contact. Like an extreme fear of heights applied to every direction, terrible was the trepidation stirred by this intuitive calculation of distance. This most basic sense, which he had never identified before, was announcing its alarming report: Cut off from all!

He sensed complete separation from the presence of God and all He had created. It was this very presence that he had taken for granted, choosing not to notice. It was this, too, that was the very basis and motivation of his quest for meaning, his assumption of purpose, and his desire for the significant life. The presence of God. He had lived in it and had not noticed, not until now, at the alarm of its loss.

All he could see, all he could think of, all he could feel was exclusively and absolutely himself. All he had previously desired to have and to clutch – his life, his self-centeredness, his opinions and philosophies—was now his, all his in imperial proportions. He, the very subject of his indulgences and occupations throughout his life, the keen focus of his every moment, the common theme of his fondest desires and disciplines was now overwhelmingly awarded to him.

The immeasurable reality of infinite separation from every other person in the universe immersed his soul in sorrow. Zoltan frantically tried to look into the darkness, begging it to reveal some distraction, some direction that he could rush toward, finding only that it was not madness but sanity that was inescapable. He wanted to hide, but could not evade his own view. Hoping to just hear one of the voices again, Sedition's words had proven true. Zoltan longed for the return of the voices. But they were gone.

Gone, he thought. With clarity he saw a vast and constant termination that a simple mind preferring its enormous role in a very small story had never considered possible. *Lost*, the word seemed to impose itself upon his mind. A word that once inspired his boast, now distinguished his personal insignificance in an infinite sea of lifeless but undying souls.

Raw emotion forced its way through Zoltan's clenched teeth. He stood in the dark and screamed his unrestrained reactions to complete separation. Wave after wave of unleashed torrents swept over his soul, bringing no relief by their expulsion into the black abyss. His lament was inexhaustible. Licking dry the saliva his throat craved for swallowing, the flames of anguish compelled his soul to protest, and the darkness consumed his voice.

Many minutes passed with screaming and blind perseverance before Zoltan was stopped by a thought. "He tricked me," he said, barely able to whisper. "He was one of them after all. He deceived me into agreeing to come here. 'The one place they'll never expect.' How could I be such a fool?" He paused. "How could I be such a fool?!" he hollered. "Saraph is the destroyer he pretended to be saving me from, and I left my son there with him!"

The thought silenced Zoltan. He stared in the dark at the shock of his undoing.

"No," he whispered, remembering the tone that disarmed the dancers and Sedition's report of the warrior defending his son. "I know he is good."

Hearing a breath near his right ear, Zoltan jumped with a fright and jerked his head around in the dark, looking.

"I thought that might be more effective than endless chatter."

Zoltan sensed that he and Sedition were face to face and nearly touching.

"I'll see what my superiors think of these revelations and I'll be right back."

Two hours, Zoltan recalled. *I just have to hang on for two hours. Not even that much now.*

He tried to calculate how long he'd been there. He went over every word he could remember, every scream, to quantify each in terms of time. But when he attempted to apply this toward a total, he discovered a frustration. The dark repelled a consciousness of time. And without a time context, Zoltan was unable to mark his progress.

He decided to just focus on the idea of two hours. Desiring a consolation, he randomly picked thirty minutes as his current state of progress. He had been there an hour and twenty minutes. When ten more minutes had actually passed, he claimed an hour as his new mark. Seconds later he determined that he was in the final moment of the two hours. And even as he tried to persevere for a few more minutes, he despaired that these decisions had been meaningless. Certain that two hours had long passed, the idea of two hours also became meaningless. The flame of Zoltan's hope in time was extinguished. Fighting to breathe, his anticipation of Sedition's return erupted from his mouth in curses hollered into the darkness.

Chapter 37
MORE VOICES

"Zoltan, surely you don't think that the fact that you have never been late to anything, and that you have never missed a day of work in your entire life affords you this occasion to check out in the middle of this mutiny. I think we've got to fight this thing with all we've got, man."

The voice seemed small and distant, like that of Sedition just before she was gone the first time. He had been yelling curses at the top of his lungs. But he heard the small voice and silenced himself immediately, so great was his longing for the sound of any other person.

"You're not still upset about our cancellation of the Jupiter series are you? Come on, it's the broadcast biz. Ratings man, that's all."

"Hey, give a call, let me know what's going on. Really, this is not like you. Whatever it is, we'll work it out, OK? Talk to ya."

Zoltan's eyes were squeezed as tightly as he was able to squeeze to keep the darkness out. But what was this new harassment? What dark humor brought this round of strange mockery in a familiar voice? He was still out of breath from screaming and his face retained the deformity of his severe anguish.

He heard a loud click and a buzzer, and a distorted voice began assaulting his scrambled mind. "Zoltan! This is your mother." Sedition's voice had last come from somewhere directly in front of him. The last voice was from in front also, but from further away and to the right. This one came from above him even further to his right, and from a greater distance. Though a bit muffled, it did indeed sound like his mother.

His face tightened even more, but no amount of tension could squeeze out his anxiety. *Now a hovering being that brings my mother's torment as well?* he thought. *How do they know me so well? How have they mastered every detail of my misery, my fears and my weaknesses?* He tried to resist any thought that these torments might be endless. "I know you are there. I can see your fancy little red sports car in front of your door. Please open this ridiculous iron gate. My goodness, son, who do you think you are, the president? When you told me you had moved I had no idea .... Oh, never mind all that. I've finally found this castle of yours. I had been meaning to come see you sooner, but it just wasn't possible. Your cousin called, and, well, a lot of people are worried about you," click.

There was a long pause. Then, buuzz bu-u-u-u-u-z-z-z.

The noise was so offensive that Zoltan pulled back. When he did, he realized that he was unable to move his head freely. It was firmly pressed against something soft and wet on his left side. The thought occurred to him that he was not standing but was in a horizontal position. He did not know why, but he was aware of gravity. And with that realization, shock forced his eyes open. Wet against his face was his own bedding, and before his eyes was his bedroom. He stared straight ahead, barely able to grasp any of the information that his eyes were revealing to him.

Bu-u-u-u-u-u-z-z-z – Bu-u-u-z-z-z! Click.

"Zoltan ... please!" came his mother's voice through the speaker on the wall across the room. "He is not answering," he heard her say more distantly, indicating that someone else was with her. But Zoltan did not take much notice of this.

His body was rigid. His eyes were wide-open. They alone began to move. He surveyed the familiar details of his room. A light caught a rounded contour of a golden statue, and his eyes focused on it, though his mind did not recall its significance. Nearby an engraved crystal sculpture translated the many languages of light from throughout the room. The startling beauty and the mystery of close memories captivated him.

Recognizing the lingering sound of trumpets and chimes, he directed his attention to a shelf on the adjacent wall. The intricately carved courtiers stood side by side on a wooden platform before an ornate carriage and two black horses behind a golden gate. Tiny maidens and their silver hammers were all in their places, having struck their silver chimes.

Zoltan rose up onto one elbow, turned his head to face the clock and stared. His mind so rushed with thoughts that not one was discernable among them. Slowly, in response to their combined influence, he slid out of his bed onto his hands and knees and began to crawl toward the middle of the room. He reached the spot where he had been standing when he said, "Yes, I accept," and collapsed to the floor. Pressing the side of his face onto the rug, he stroked its soft, white surface with both hands.

He jumped to his feet and made quick steps of the distance to his desk. Looking down at the magazine on its surface, he saw a small green Bible. It rested directly over a photograph of him and P. Salmone II. On top of the Bible was a red Gummy Bear and a note that read: Last one! Tears filled his eyes as he picked them up. After putting the Gummy in his mouth, he tossed the magazine into the trash can beneath his desk.

"Yes!" he attempted to yell. His hoarse voice only produced a squeaky crackle. Bending down, he snatched the magazine from the trash, then tore out some pages and threw them into the air. "Yes, I'm back! Ha ha-a-a-a-ah!" He held up the little Bible. "Thank you Saraph! Thank you, thank you. I love you,

you raggedy little weird … mighty, amazing whoever you are!"

Bu-u-u-z-z-z-z bu-u-u-z-z click … "Mr. Zoltan, this is Officer Stanley with the Orange County Police Department."

Zoltan's celebration was brought to an abrupt halt as his mouth went dry and he lost his breath. He stared at the speaker on the wall.

"Mr. Zoltan, this is Officer Stanley. I am here with your mother who is obviously very concerned about you. We also received a call from one of your business partners a little while ago, just concerned, sir. Sir, if you are there, please let us know. We are not asking for any information other than confirmation of your safety. Just an indication of your well-being, sir, and we'll leave you alone."

The phone on the desk rang twice. After a brief silence Zoltan heard the voice of his secretary, Marion. "Hey Babe, give me a call when you have a minute. I know you don't want to deal with this place anymore, but there are some crazy things going on around here. Trevor's up to something crazy, like you tried to tell me. I haven't gotten all the details yet, but … something … all kinds of shuffling going on. There's other stuff too, but I just thought I'd pass that along. Call me."

Zoltan felt a little disoriented by the sudden flood of activity. He was sure he didn't want to answer the intercom, but more sure that he must.

Buuuuuzzz. "Zoltan, if you are there, answer me, will you!"

Zoltan walked to the speaker and reached out and pushed the button. "Mom, what are you doing here, you on vacation?"

He leaned his head against the wall, exhausted by the thought of this untimely encounter. "Dear god, not now," he said, before realizing he had not released the intercom button. He jerked his hand back.

"Dear God? No, son, I told you, this is your mother. And what do you mean, 'not now'? No, I'm not on vacation! I *was* on vacation! I flew in from Nova Scotia to see you. I got off of the plane exactly one hour ago and came right here. I don't even know why. I just felt I had to. So, what kind of treatment is this? Plus, you … ." Her voice cracked and the sounds of crying came through the speaker. "You sound terrible!" There was a lengthy pause. "You're scaring me here. You OK in there?"

Zoltan pushed the button. "I'm fine, mom. Please forgive me. I'll be right down."

His mind was flooded with questions about his return and vivid images confirming his recent travels. Memories poured in as he slid against the wall, melting down until stopped by the floor.

"Marty!" he said with a jolt. "I've got to get to Marty? How could I have forgotten?"

He jumped to his feet, ran through the doorway and down the hall to the stairs.

Chapter 38
RECOVERING

"He's kind of in the way where he is. Do you think I should say something? It's kinda awkward."

"Is he *kind of* in the way, or is he *in* the way? Is he keeping you from taking care of your patient?"

"No, I guess not. I can keep working around him."

"Then I wouldn't say anything."

Zoltan heard the low, muffled voices of nurses just outside the door but he did not hear a conversation. The spoken words merely blended with many background noises – other activities from out in the hall, beeps and hums of the blood pressure machine and the heart and oxygen monitors, and an occasional request over the first-floor intercom.

His eyes were closed but he was not sleeping. He was stunned; but not the kind of mouth-open stunned of a fan watching the humbling of his favorite team by an inferior opponent; and not the kind of heart-stopping stunned of a person receiving news of a great, personal loss. No, Zoltan was stunned like a boy on the front lines of war, a child overexposed. His thoughts were like a mass of insects caught in trap. Hundreds deep, they were connected, yet not one conscious of another amid the tumbling, stirring movement of a dual constant: each one clinging to existence, each one wanting out.

He heard Martin move in the bed before him and all of

those thoughts were freed. Zoltan stared up at his son, who stared back beneath lids not half open.

"Zol…"

Martin's eyes closed as if the effort to speak so exhausted him that sleep was spontaneous. A few minutes later his eyelids twitched several times, then again cracked open. The general anesthesia was weakening but not yet weak.

"Wha-a-ya… doing? 'Mbarr-r rssing. Please…." He paused and licked his dry lips. "Please… get up."

Eyelids again sealed, Martin slept.

Zoltan stared.

The door to the small recovery room swung open.

"Zoltan, please forgive me. I would normally never leave you hanging like this. I was called to an emergency surgery just as we were finishing up with Martin."

Dr. Norman Kreeger's tall frame was bent over and his hand was upon Zoltan's shoulder. The nurse had come in behind him. She was standing before a computer screen beside the bed. Having gained entry into Martin's file with her thumb-print, she was using her index finger to navigate within the file.

"I hope one of the nurses explained…."

Seeing the vacant look in Zoltan's swollen, blood-shot eyes, Dr. Kreeger stopped himself. He looked at the nurse, who had turned from the computer screen. She stared back, blank, intimidated by the intensity in the doctor's gaze and the unexpected silent questions: *What's going on? Is everything ok?*

The morbid qualities of the moment transformed Dr. Kreeger's usually calm demeanor. He looked at Martin lying in the bed. Stepping around Zoltan, he quickly moved to the head of the bed and checked the reports on the digital displays of the three machines. Then he studied the information on the computer screen. He leaned over and looked closely at Martin's left arm. A deep sigh and the shake of his head indicated his relief. Thus satisfied that all was proceeding normally, he looked at the nurse and nodded. She left the room.

The doctor looked down at Zoltan, who had remained kneeling beside the bed. Zoltan raised his head and the two men stared at one another. Dr. Kreeger wondered about the depth of pain he saw in his friends eyes. He walked across the room, grabbed a chair and dragged it over to the bedside. Sitting down on the edge of the chair, he leaned forward and propped his elbows upon his knees. His folded hands hung down, relaxed.

"Look…" he began, as they again gazed into one another's eyes. "For a man with only one kid, you have needed my skills far too often. But you've never looked like this. You've been through… well, *we've* been through a lot together with this young man. And, if not for him, I doubt that we would be such friends. He will make it again, Zoltan.

"He is stabilized. I'd say his recovery appears to be normal at this early stage. And the surgery… well, it is too early to say much. Success so far, we'll call it. As to seriousness…." Dr. Kreeger looked at his hands and then back at Zoltan. "Not as bad as the motorcycle accident or the head injuries from the climbing incident." He flicked his brows. "But worse than the two stabbings and all three of the car wrecks.

"The nitty gritty: He's out of the woods as far as reaction to the drugs and alcohol. I wouldn't classify this officially as an overdose. Though, I'm no expert on that. He simply passed out. It's the combinations of chemicals in his system that worries me, not the amounts this time. Very dangerous!"

Zoltan lowered his head and transferred his stare to the floor.

"Physically, his arm is the most serious concern we're looking at right now. I'm estimating that the lower part of his arm was without circulation for three hours or more before you found him. I'd like to tell you we saved it."

Dr. Kreeger shook his head as a frown moved upon his face.

"I don't want to mislead you. It is too soon to say."

He stopped and thought for a moment.

"I know the three open incisions are grotesque. I hope that wasn't too much of a shock to see. The procedure is called a fasciotomy. When we attempt to restore arterial supply like this, there is a great deal of swelling in the muscles, a natural reaction. The inherent danger is something called compartment syndrome. The pressure from the swelling will become greater than the renewed pressure of the blood circulation. There are three muscular compartments in the arm. We open their facial envelopes in order to relieve the pressure by making room for the muscular swelling in an attempt to avoid arterial strangulation."

He stood and walked to the head of the bed where Martin slept soundly. Zoltan looked up and watched as the doctor reexamined the three open incisions traveling the length of Martin's left forearm. He felt frustrated and guilty for his inability to care more about these explanations concerning the severity of his son's condition. But his friend's words were being absorbed into a cloudy accumulation of memories, questions and disturbing thoughts.

Dr. Kreeger walked back to the chair and took his seat beside Zoltan, resuming his original relaxed position. Zoltan again stared down at the floor.

"So, we're not out of the woods yet. The next twenty-four to forty-eight hours will tell us a lot. Worst case is the possibility that the arm will reject the bypass, the arterial restoration. That would require its removal. Even if the bypass is a complete success, the possibility remains that there has been permanent muscular or neurological damage that will limit the arm's functional restoration. At the moment we can only wait."

Of everything he'd just heard, "twenty-four to forty-eight hours" and the word wait took command of Zoltan's attention. The activities of his recent twenty-four hour journey and a sense of urgency about a response seemed to crash head on with the idea of waiting for anything. An agony made him lift his head and turn his eyes to meet those of his friend.

"I want to say something," Zoltan said in a scratchy whisper.

"Anything... please. We've always been frank with one another," the doctor answered.

"No, not to you."

"My goodness, where's your voice?"

Zoltan turned away. For several minutes he stared, his memory locked on recent screams in the dark. He shivered and looked back at the doctor.

"You're a Christian?"

The communication was as words shaped by air alone; and Dr. Kreeger's concern for Zoltan exceeded his concern for Martin. He reached out and put his right hand on his friend's shoulder.

"What's on your mind?"

"I've been kneeling here since they brought him into this room several hours ago. I keep trying to pray, but...." Zoltan paused and shuddered. "I wish I could tell you."

"Tell me what? You know you can tell me anything."

"No. No, it's too crazy. I've been... I've seen things that...."

Tears filled Zoltan's eyes, and as he lowered his head and looked at the floor they fell onto his folded hands. He shook his head continuously for several minutes as Dr. Kreeger sat beside him and waited, his hand remaining on Zoltan's shoulder. When the doctor left his chair to kneel beside his burdened friend, Zoltan did not notice. Nor did he notice when the door opened and a nurse appeared briefly before turning around and clumsily running into the doorframe on her way out.

"I keep trying to pray for Martin. But...." He stopped, and again defaulted to shaking his head. Then looking over into the kind eyes of his kneeling friend, Zoltan felt for an instant that he was looking into Saraph's gaze. He stared, arrested by the familiar intimacy.

"Something is missing," he finally said.

"A relationship?" Kreeger asked suggestively.

Zoltan continued to stare, unable to respond, though his eyes confirmed that the suggestion hit the mark.

"What is in the way?" Kreeger asked discerningly.

"My father," Zoltan answered, surprising himself with the immediate response.

"Why?"

Zoltan thought for a moment. "The God I know to be speaking to me ... the God I want to speak to .... " He paused again. "I'm sure He is the one you know and worship. I just can't accept it. I can't embrace a belief that Dad rejected – a faith that ... where hope for some ... for me .... " He paused. "And certain condemnation for the unbeliever – for him."

"Certain?"

"Trust me on this one."

"I'm sorry, but I can't do that," Kreeger responded. "Only God himself can be trusted with such understanding."

They again stared at one another. Then, Dr. Kreeger looked up and nodded toward Martin. Zoltan turned and looked at his sleeping son.

"What would he say?" the doctor asked. "If circumstances were different and it was he and I having this conversation and you lying there. Based on his knowledge of you, would he not be certain of your condemnation as well? Yet here you are on your knees, longing for the words to express your faith in the living God."

Zoltan turned back to look at the man kneeling beside him.

"It would be a shame," Dr. Kreeger continued, "to reject the truth and so great a gift as eternal life based on an errant allegiance, and worse, a wrong assumption that he did too. If you are willing to acknowledge that there are things you don't know, to leave room for God to be God, I think you will find your barrier removed."

"How do I ... what do I ...."

Dr. Kreeger bowed his head. "Heavenly Father, I approach Your throne in the Name of Your beloved Son, Jesus Christ, on behalf of my friend, Zoltan. We share a concern for Martin and ask for Your mercy. You are his Physician. We depend on You. As Your servant I ask for wisdom for myself and all who care for him to administer Your healing touch. Lord, we desire his complete recovery and restoration. But we desire Your will above all, believing that You have his true and complete healing at heart.

"Now, Father, for Zoltan I request clarity in recognizing the words he longs to speak to You and the boldness to speak them."

He looked at Zoltan, whom he found to be still looking back at him. "You know the Gospel, my friend. You know everything you need to know. I can't help you from here. It must be from your heart."

He turned and lowered his head, and for several silent minutes Dr. Kreeger waited. Just as he began moving to again look over at Zoltan, he heard him begin to speak.

"Dear God, I am afraid to change. You have shown me my condition. You have shown me Your love."

There was a long pause. Zoltan heard the voice of Saraph in his mind: '*An act of your will is not a mistake.*' He thought about *the gift* and its activation, and wondered about the power of his will. He remembered standing in his room, scared, just before he accepted the "invitation." He stared, distracted by the memory of that moment, shaken by its nearness and similarity to this one.

"No," he said, "I am unwilling to change. That's the truth of it. God, I am wrong and You are right. And I am unwilling to change."

The room was again silent, except for the sounds coming from machines attached to Martin. It was not the prayer that either man was expecting. Dr. Kreeger wrestled with the idea of adding helpful, repeat-after-me type prompts. *Maybe I should do more*, he thought. *Maybe I should offer some help. Lord, should I give him some more guidance?*

In the absence of any affirming thought or answer, the doctor remained silent. Then, from the intercom in the hall beyond the door he heard his name and a request for his response.

Zoltan did not hear it. He was busy with distractions of his own. He remembered Saraph telling him that a single answered prayer was as great as any miracle ever performed. He recalled Solomon's book on a table in ancient Alexandria. His eyes were open and he stared as if he were looking out toward the Pharos and the Mediterranean Sea. Then he placed his hand over his shirt pocket and felt the little green Bible that it held.

Dr. Kreeger's pager began vibrating on his hip. He grabbed it and looked to see who was calling. He frowned and looked over at Zoltan, whose eyes had closed, having heard in his heart the words he wanted to speak:

"Dear God," he said aloud, "I'm willing for You to make the change in me, whatever it takes. I ask You to make the change ... please, with all my heart."

The door opened and a nurse poked her head into the small recovery room.

"Dr. Kreeger, I apologize, but Dr. Mansfield is on the phone. He says it's urgent."

The doctor looked at Zoltan and, for a moment, wondered what was of greater urgency, matters of the flesh or those of soul and eternity. Realizing that the subject of the call might pertain to both, he placed a hand on his friend's shoulder. "I've got to go. I'll be back in awhile to check on Martin." He drew up one leg and planted his foot, preparing to stand. Hesitating, his eyes were still fixed on Zoltan's.

"You are a different man than the one I knew in the past. That was a dangerous man's prayer." He stood up and walked to the door. Before leaving the room, he turned and looked back at Martin sleeping in the bed and then at his kneeling friend. He nodded. "There's power in that prayer. Everything is about to change."

ISBN 1425142796

9 781425 142797